the
ENCHANTED
GREENHOUSE

the ENCHANTED GREENHOUSE

SARAH BETH DURST

BRAMBLE

TOR PUBLISHING GROUP
NEW YORK

THE ENCHANTED GREENHOUSE

Copyright © 2025 by Sarah Beth Durst

A Bramble Book
Published by Tom Doherty Associates / Tor Publishing Group
120 Broadway
New York, NY 10271

www.torpublishinggroup.com

Bramble™ is a trademark of Macmillan Publishing Group, LLC.

The Library of Congress Cataloging-in-Publication Data is available upon request.

ISBN 978-1-250-33398-8 (hardcover)
ISBN 978-1-250-32463-4 (ebook)

Our books may be purchased in bulk for promotional, educational, or business use. Please contact your local bookseller or the Macmillan Corporate and Premium Sales Department at 1-800-221-7945, extension 5442, or by email at MacmillanSpecialMarkets@macmillan.com.

First Edition: 2025

Printed in the United States of America

0 9 8 7 6 5 4 3 2 1

For my mom,
Mary Lee Bartlett,
who taught me to love stories
and has a much greener thumb than I do.

I love you.

the
ENCHANTED
GREENHOUSE

CHAPTER ONE

The plant was innocent.

Everyone agreed on that. Still, when the judge declared it in his reedy voice for the official record, Terlu nearly cried with relief—after she'd been arrested, her primary worry was that they'd blame the plant. He wasn't to blame. It was all her. She'd tried to make that clear.

She shifted in her chair to watch while the court bailiffs escorted the spider plant away. He raised a tendril toward her, and Terlu lifted her fingers to her lips and then toward the newly sentient plant.

I won't cry. She refused to cry when she hadn't done anything wrong. Very illegal, yes, but not *wrong.* So far, she hadn't shed a single tear, at least not in public, but right now, all that prevented her from sobbing out loud was the scowl on the prosecutor's face as he glared at her, as well as the head librarian's hand on her arm, which was the only touch of kindness in the courtroom, both literally and figuratively.

Leaning closer, the head librarian, Rijes Velk, whispered to her, "I will see that he is safe and cared for. He'll always have a home with us."

Terlu swallowed hard.

Not going to cry.

Stiffly, gratefully, she nodded at Rijes Velk and then faced the judge.

The judge was swaddled in embroidered robes that transformed him from a skeletal man with spidery limbs into a wide mushroom of ruffled silks. He reminded Terlu of a hermit crab, the kind that used to swarm the beaches of her home island—his gnarled body tucked inside his ornate outer shell, with only his claws exposed. She had to look up to see him, seated on the dais, raised high above the accused. *Above me,* she thought miserably.

He was framed by stained glass windows that showed a stylized map of the Crescent Islands Empire, each jeweled bit of land caught within panes of sapphire blue. Instead of warm amber daylight, it cast the whole courtroom in a bluish tinge, which made all the painted faces glaring down at her from the balconies on either side of the dais look even more cold and unfriendly. It was all designed to intimidate and overwhelm, and it was, Terlu thought, rather effective.

If the judge was a hermit crab, then she was an oyster, extracted from her shell, splayed open and exposed to the elements. She fidgeted with the sleeves of the tunic they'd given her. It was a gray cotton, soft from use and vastly oversize, and she wondered how many other (much taller) criminals had worn it before her. She knew how she looked in it: like a child playing dress-up, rather than a woman in her twenties. *Or more accurately, I look like a chipmunk.* She was short and pleasantly plump, with wide eyes that made her always look slightly surprised, round cheeks, and smile creases around her mouth. She was certain she looked more like a chipmunk than a criminal, if chipmunks were lavender and gray. Her mother had purple skin, while her father was tinted more pink, and Terlu had ended up an agreeable shade of lavender, which matched nicely with the gray cotton. But however nice and innocuous she looked, it didn't seem to be making a bit of difference in the way the case was going. She'd even tried to tame her curls for the court appearance, as if tamed hair would make her appear any less guilty.

The problem was she *was* guilty: she'd cast a spell. She'd gathered the ingredients, researched the words, deliberated on whether it was wise, decided it wasn't at all wise, and did it anyway. She'd created Caz, a sentient spider plant, to keep her company in the empty stacks of the Great Library of Alyssium. She'd made herself a friend because she could not handle one more day of being friendless, of being so far from her family, of living sequestered in her silent and empty corner of the library where the only choice was find a way to bear the isolation or admit that she'd failed to find a place for herself, that she'd made a mistake in leaving home, and that her family and friends were right to say she'd never flourish out in the world on her own.

Terlu honestly hadn't thought anyone would mind.

She'd harmed no one. She hadn't even inconvenienced anyone. And Caz himself was delighted to be alive and thrilled to be her companion. The patron who'd noticed Caz, though, had been neither delighted nor thrilled.

Only the most elite sorcerers were allowed to use magic. The spellbooks that filled the Great Library were for their use alone, by imperial decree. The imperial investigator who took the case was not about to let one low-level librarian be the exception to the rule. As the prosecutor, he'd argued eloquently for her guilt.

Frankly, she didn't think he'd needed to argue so hard. She'd obviously broken the law—a talking, walking spider plant was kind of unignorable proof.

And so, Terlu wasn't the least bit surprised when the judge pronounced, "Terlu Perna, Fourth Librarian of the Second Floor, East Wing, of the Great Library of Alyssium, you have been found guilty of illegal magic use. Sentencing will commence immediately."

Beside her, Rijes Velk rose. "I plead for leniency."

Like the judge, the head librarian was also encased in embroidered silk, but unlike the judge, she looked as if she belonged in such finery. She was an elegant woman with silvery-gray hair, which had been braided to echo the latticework on the great door to Kinney Hall.

Her onyx cheeks were painted in gold with symbols that indicated the oaths she'd taken, to honor the history, wisdom, and knowledge of the Crescent Islands. If Terlu hadn't known that Rijes was old enough to be her grandmother, she would have assumed she was simply ageless.

Terlu was both honored and amazed that such an important and elegant person had chosen to speak on her behalf at her trial, especially given the whole *obviously guilty* situation.

"Librarian Terlu Perna intended no harm," Rijes Velk said, her voice ringing through the vast courtroom, up to the spiral dome above. "Furthermore, she caused no harm. Not a single citizen was hurt. No property was damaged. Nothing was broken, stolen, or lost. There were no ill effects whatsoever from her lapse in judgment. I therefore ask—*plead*—for mercy from this court. This is her first offense, and she has learned from her mistake. She will not work magic again. I personally guarantee it."

Terlu let out a little gasp in surprise. That was a tremendous statement, to have *the* head librarian promising her good behavior. She heard the sorcerers in the balcony who had come to watch the show whisper to one another and shuffle in their viewing boxes—clearly also surprised at this endorsement.

The prosecutor rose, his scarlet robes rippling as he moved. "It doesn't matter what you promise. It doesn't matter what the convicted intended, or what she intends after this point. What matters is what others do in reaction to this case. If her punishment is light, then *I* guarantee that the empire will see more illegal magic use, and it will not all be without consequence. I implore you to send a message to all who contemplate using magic without the proper license that the law is the law, and the emperor's will is not weak."

"Mercy is not weakness," Rijes Velk countered.

"Your Honor, my counterpart would have you feed the growing unrest—"

Rijes cut in. "Terlu Perna's case has nothing to do with any—"

They argued back and forth until the judge raised one of his crablike hands. "I have made my decision. Terlu Perna will be made an example of, for the health and safety of the empire."

Terlu felt her mouth go dry. She clenched her hands together on her lap, bunching up the fabric of her tunic. *An example? What does that mean? What are they going to do to me?*

"She will be transformed into a statue and placed in the Great Library, to serve as a warning to all librarians, scholars, and patrons who might be tempted to defy the law."

There was a stunned silence.

It was a harsher punishment than any she'd imagined—far, far harsher. She began to shake. Her heart beat as frantically as a hummingbird's wings.

The drums began to sound, the signal that a verdict had been reached, deep and low and echoing. She felt them in her bones, each beat reverberating through her entire body.

Around her, the courtroom erupted into shouting. Rijes Velk stormed toward the dais, while Terlu sank deeper into her chair and hugged her arms around herself. It was only when the judge demanded silence that she realized she was screaming like a dying rabbit.

It all happened quickly after that.

Terlu was shuffled out of the courtroom by two court bailiffs. She stumbled as she walked, unable to remember how to place her feet one in front of the other. All the shouting had faded as if she'd been shoved underwater, smothered by the swirl of her thoughts.

A statue.

Her, transformed into a statue.

Will it hurt?

Will I live?

Will they ever transform me back? The judge had made no statement about the length of her sentence. *Is it forever?* No, it couldn't be, could it? That would be too cruel. But if it wasn't, wouldn't the judge have set a duration? She'd never heard of such a punishment, but then she also hadn't heard of any librarian breaking the ban on magic use by non-sorcerers. With all the spellbooks in the Great Library, she couldn't imagine another librarian hadn't been tempted, but perhaps she was the first to be caught.

She wished she'd been more careful. More clever.

She didn't wish she hadn't done it. If she hadn't cast the spell, then Caz would have never existed, and he'd been so happy to be alive. She'd never wish to undo that. She hoped that Rijes Velk would keep her promise—that she'd keep Terlu's spider-plant friend safe and happy.

The bailiffs delivered her to a black stone room shaped like an octagon. It had no windows and no light except for a single candelabra in the center of the room that was lit with a dozen white candles, and it smelled of tallow and burnt herbs. A bearded man with sunken cheeks waited beside the candelabra. He held a bowl in his pale hands.

She recognized what he was instantly: a sorcerer with the ingredients to a spell.

And just as quickly she realized what this meant: there would be no reprieve. No last-minute mercy. Her punishment had been decided long before the judge had delivered his verdict.

She stared at the sorcerer.

She felt too empty to scream or cry now. She wished she'd had a moment to thank Rijes Velk for trying. Terlu truly did appreciate her kindness.

"Change," he told her.

She noticed a folded tunic, a library uniform, on a chair. She hesitated for only a second before stripping off the gray clothes and pulling on the familiar blue of a Fourth Librarian. At least she wouldn't face her fate dressed like a criminal. She wondered if this was Rijes Velk's kindness as well, or if they simply wanted their example to be uniformed as a librarian. The sorcerer watched her dispassionately, and she wondered what he'd do if she tried to flee. She knew she wouldn't get far—undoubtedly, there were guards on the other side of the door—and she didn't want him to cast the spell while she was fleeing. If she was going to be transformed into a statue, she didn't want her face to be frozen in fear. She wanted to at least try to be brave.

"Will I live?" Terlu asked.

The sorcerer hesitated. "Yes." And then he began the spell.

As her blood slowed and hardened, as her breath caught in her throat, as her eyes froze in place, as her flesh turned to polished wood, it occurred to her that perhaps that wasn't the right question to ask. But she couldn't think of a better one.

If I live, I can hope.

Darkness.

Silence.

She didn't know which was worse—the darkness or the silence—but she was suffocating in both. She couldn't open her eyes. No, she couldn't close her eyes.

Where am I?

She listened. There was nothing. No breath. No heartbeat.

A creak, then a sliver of light, and she could see shapes and shadows: shelves, a crate, and a cart. There were voices behind her, muffled, arguing about where to put a stack of chairs.

She was in a storage closet.

She wanted to call out to the unseen voices, ask them to talk to her—no, beg them. She wanted them to move to where she could see them. She needed to see a face, to look into someone else's eyes, to see a smile. She wanted to tell them she was awake, alive, aware.

I am here!

The door shut.

She dreamed sometimes, or almost dreamed, since it was never true sleep. Statues can't sleep. In her favorite dream, she was standing in sunlight, listening to music. Ahh, music! And she was tasting a pastry. Or tasting a kiss. And there were people all around her, voices and laughter that were the most beautiful music. All around her, it smelled like roses.

But the dream never lasted, and then once again there was nothing, nothing, nothing.

She wasn't afraid anymore.

Or angry.

Or sad.

But she wished . . . Oh, she wished. For sunlight. For breath. For a kind voice. And so she dreamed and remembered and drifted through the days, losing her grasp on time and on herself.

In the silence and the dark, the statue endured.

When, at last, they came to place her on the pedestal they'd installed in the North Reading Room of the Great Library of Alyssium, she wanted to thank them.

At least now, she wouldn't be alone.

CHAPTER TWO

Snow fell gently on the statue, which was, the statue thought, lovely but unexpected. Flakes dusted her nose and fell onto her unblinkable eyes, and she wondered why she wasn't in the alcove in the North Reading Room on her usual pedestal.

Clearly, I missed something important, she thought.

She used to have a view of floor-to-vaulted-ceiling bookshelves filled with priceless (and dusty) books and scrolls. Now she was facing a grove of pine trees, wreathed in snow and laden with pine cones.

She knew she'd been drifting ever since her transformation, but this time, she must have drifted for quite a while and slept very deeply to miss being moved from the Great Library to . . . wherever this was. *How long?* she wondered. *How much did I miss? Where am I?* Between two pines, she spotted a glint of reflected sunlight, but she couldn't identify what—

Suddenly, she shivered, and a ripple spread down her wooden limbs.

Given that she was an inanimate object, she shouldn't be able to shiver, so why did— It intensified into a shudder, and she heard a creak that sounded like a tree bending. *Oh no, was that* inside *me?*

And then: *crackle, crackle, crackle.* She felt bubbles rising from her toes up to her knees, through her thighs and into her torso, where they swirled faster and faster.

For so very long, she'd felt nothing. And now suddenly, she felt everything.

She burned. She froze. She hurt. She felt as if she were being ripped apart, and then she felt as if she were soaring through the clouds, her head spinning with a thousand colors. She was an exploding star, bursting with indescribable pain and incandescent joy.

And then Terlu Perna, formerly the Fourth Librarian of the Second Floor, East Wing, of the Great Library of Alyssium (jewel of the Crescent Islands Empire), and much more recently a statue made of wood on display in the North Reading Room, condemned for the breaking of imperial law regarding unauthorized spellwork . . . collapsed into a heap on the snowy forest floor.

She was flesh again.

Terlu felt the wet snow seep through the thin fabric of her librarian tunic. It prickled her left thigh and her hip at the same time as the breeze chilled her bare arms. She sucked in air and felt the cold burn her throat, and she expelled it in a laugh.

Oh, she could feel! She could breathe! She could move! She could talk! At the top of her lungs, she sang, "La-la-la!" Her voice cracked, her throat dry from disuse. A bird startled from the top of a nearby pine tree. "Sorry!" she called to it as it flew away, red wings bright against the white sky.

She breathed again as deeply as she could and inhaled the scent of pine and the crisp taste of winter, so sharp and clean that it hurt all the way down to her lungs. In fact, now that she noticed it, all of her hurt: every joint and every muscle ached so badly they shook, but she couldn't stop smiling. She was alive again!

For a moment, it overwhelmed her. She had very nearly given up hope. She'd had, after all, no rational reason to hope, except for the simple fact that she'd remained alive.

Terlu pushed against the ground to stand up.

And promptly fell down.

"Ow."

More snow soaked through her tunic. Pushing with both hands, she rocked forward into a squat. "Steady," she said. "You can do this, Terlu." Her voice was stronger now, only wavering a little. Slowly, she stood. Her knees wobbled, and she grabbed on to the branch of the nearest tree. Its bark bit into her palm, but she didn't fall.

She shivered as the cold seeped into her skin. Wouldn't it be terrible if she finally was restored to human and she froze to death immediately? Yes, it would. *Whoever restored me can't have intended me to freeze.*

Whoever restored . . .

Of course! There had to be a sorcerer nearby who'd cast the spell to free her. Probably they just didn't know that their spell had taken effect already. As soon as they realized it had, they'd show up with blankets, coats, hot chocolate, and a really excellent explanation for where she was and why she was here, and she could thank them from the bottom of her soul.

"Hello!" Terlu called. "I'm . . ." What was the word? Awake? Alive? Fleshy? She didn't want to shout that she was fleshy. "I'm here! Over here! Hello?"

She waited for someone to answer, but no one did. The snow fell as soft as a whisper, and the wind brushed against the branches, making a *shush, shush* sound. It felt as if she were the only living soul in the forest, but that couldn't be. Someone had to have been responsible for the spell that revived her, so where was that someone?

"You did it!" she called. "You saved me! Yay! Can you come out so I can thank you? Really, I'm very grateful! And also cold!"

Still, no one answered.

Terlu wrapped her arms around herself, but it didn't help much. She tried a hesitant step forward. Her legs shook like a baby deer's, but she kept herself upright. She took another step and then another. Ahead was the glint she'd seen between the pine trees. She aimed for that, since every other direction was just trees and snow.

Why would anyone cast a spell to restore her and *not* stick around to see if it worked? It was irresponsible spellwork, that's what it was. At the very least, the sorcerer could have pinned a note to her that said, "Just have to duck out for a quick bite to eat. Be back soon." Or they could have left a sign telling her which way to go. Or an arrow. It wouldn't have been so hard to make an arrow out of rocks or stray pine cones: *This way to warmth and food!*

Unless whoever it was didn't want her to find shelter?

What if this was a strange part of her punishment that she'd somehow not known about? She *had* been in shock at the verdict—well, no, not at the verdict. She had been one hundred percent guilty. She hadn't expected, though, for the punishment to be so severe. No one had. Terlu thought of Rijes Velk arguing for leniency . . . but they'd wanted to make an example of her, and that was that. She'd been wood-ified. Or should that be solidified? En-statued? There wasn't a proper verb for it, which bothered Terlu—if you were going to do a thing to someone, there should be a verb for it, and if there wasn't, you should reconsider doing it at all.

Snow fell harder. It swirled around her, and she held her arm in front of her face to keep it from flying into her eyes. It was ankle-deep between the trees, and she had to march her feet, lifting her knees up high, to make progress. The pine trees were clumped together with branches that poked her skin every time she brushed against one.

Ducking under a thicker branch, she knocked into it with her back, and an armful of snow fell onto her neck. She yelped and scooted forward. So soon after her reawakening, she wasn't ready to react to anything that fast—she fell forward onto her knees. All the air rushed out of her with the jolt, and pain shot through her knees.

Tears pricked her eyes. "Hello? Anyone? Please! I need help!"

Refusing to care, the snow continued to fall.

Gritting her teeth, Terlu picked herself up and stumbled onward. Pushing another branch aside, more carefully this time so the snow didn't dump on her again, she stepped out of the forest into a clearing.

Ahead of her was a window. Many windows. A wall of windows, framed in black iron that curled delicately around the panes in branch-like patterns. The structure was massive—at least three stories high and so wide that she couldn't see its corners. Tilting her head back, Terlu looked up and up to a glass cupola on the top. Snow fell on it.

Stumbling forward, she reached the glass wall and pressed her hands against it as she looked inside. It was cool but not icy, and she noticed there was no frost on the panes. Instead the glass was cloudy, as if hot air inside had fogged it up. *It's warm inside,* she realized. Gloriously warm! All she could see through the foggy glass was a tangle of shadows. And . . . green? It was filled with green.

It's a greenhouse, she realized. *An enormous greenhouse in the middle of the woods.* It had to belong to someone, even if it was dark inside. If she could find the owner, perhaps she'd find her rescuer?

Not that they were a very good rescuer, leaving her out here in the cold. She'd forgive them, though, if they let her inside. *I'll forgive them instantly.* They'd made her flesh again. Knocking on the glass, she called out again, "Hello! I'm out here! Please let me in!"

She walked along the glass wall, knocking as she went. It had to have a door, didn't it? Or a window that opened? *I suppose I could break the glass.* But that would let the cold inside, as well as her, and what would the owner think of that?

If they hadn't left her alone in the cold, she wouldn't need to break a window.

Still, she'd rather not. It wouldn't be the best introduction. Besides which, she wasn't certain she could. It was thick glass, and her arms were shaking so badly that she wasn't certain she had any strength in them.

Only as a last resort.

The wall seemed to go on and on, as the snow thickened at her feet. Her toes were beginning to feel numb, as well as her fingertips. She wondered if she had frostbite. She'd never been this cold before. She'd grown up on a sun-drenched island called Eano, where you were in far more danger of sunburn than frostbite. She used to walk barefoot through the sand and feel it tickle her toes on her way to her cousins' house, and she'd swim every sunset in the sun-warmed water before her parents called her in for dinner. At the height of summer, you could cook mussels and clams by leaving them out on the rocks, and you had to drink fruit juice to stay hydrated or you'd risk the wrath of the cluster of grandfathers who'd hand out pitchers of guava and watery sweet-berry juice at every street corner. Remembering, Terlu could almost taste the hint of sweet-berry. It was the flavor of the summer solstice, when the whole island would be decked out in flowers and smell like chocolate and cinnamon and citrus as every baker and aspiring baker would compete to create the most delectable pastries for the Summer Feast . . .

At last she reached the corner of the greenhouse and turned—to see more glass.

I have to break it. If I stay outside any longer, I'll be an ice statue instead of wood. She didn't know if that would be ironic or just pathetic. She laughed, slightly hysterically.

Terlu scouted the ground for a rock or a sturdy branch. Everything was coated in snow, but she spotted a medium-size branch that had fallen off one of the pine trees. She picked it up, and sap stuck to her palms. Carrying it back to the wall of windows, she eyed the glass. If she hit it in the center, it should be the weakest there.

"Sorry," she said to her unknown host. "Very, very sorry. I'll clean it up, I promise."

She swung the branch at the glass.

It hit solidly. She felt the impact shake through her arms, but the glass didn't break. Dipping the branch down to rest for a second, she caught her breath. It felt like her muscles hadn't been used in months, which was accurate. Hefting up the branch, Terlu tried again.

Not a dent. Not a scratch.

She whacked it again and again. After the fifth try, she stopped, panting. Either she wasn't strong enough or the glass wasn't really glass. Or it could be spelled to be unbreakable. She knew the windows in the palace had such spells on them. When the emperor visited the lower canals in the poorer parts of the city, he was said to travel in a carriage made entirely of glass enchanted to be unbreakable. It was possible this greenhouse bore the same spell. In which case . . . *This will never work.*

She dropped the branch and sagged against the glass wall. Her only option was to find a door. For that, she had to keep moving. Maybe after a brief rest . . .

No. Keep moving.

She didn't feel quite as cold anymore. Perhaps because so much of her felt numb. Forcing herself forward, she trudged along the glass. She leaned her hand against it for support . . . which was the only reason she noticed the door.

It was halfway down the wall of windows. Her fingers brushed against the latch before her eyes recognized it. She stopped and stared.

At last her brain caught up with her fingers and eyes.

A door!

An actual door!

"Please don't be locked," she pleaded with it as she twisted the handle.

It pushed open easily, and Terlu stumbled inside. All she saw was green as she was hit with a whoosh of warmth. She closed the door behind her and leaned against it. Suddenly warm, her fingers and toes began to tingle and then burn. She sank down onto the warm gravel as the winter wind swirled behind her outside, and she blew on her fingers and rubbed them until the pain subsided. As she nursed her fingertips, she gawked at the summery green before her.

"Wow," she breathed.

The greenhouse smelled of fresh dirt and a thousand flowers, the perfume of the perfect summer night when the cicadas sing tenor to the bullfrog's bass and the moon is heavy with the promise of a fall harvest. Except there was no moon out, and the only sound was the *swoosh, swoosh* of snow on the glass ceiling high above, so that made it a somewhat inaccurate analogy. She thought it smelled wonderful regardless.

Terlu peeled herself off the floor. Bits of gravel clung to her wet hem and stuck to her wet skin. She brushed them off and then examined her hands again. Her lavender flesh had pinkened from the cold, but there were no splotches of white. The pain had nearly completely subsided. She wiggled her toes experimentally, and they felt much better. *I didn't freeze. Yay!*

"Hello? Is anyone here?" she called.

Her voice was swallowed by the greenery.

She walked forward on a gravel path between the plants. She'd never seen such an overabundance of vegetation before: Vines climbed the pillars up to the roof of the greenhouse, thick bushes with enormous elephant-ear-size leaves lined the path, and trees with spindly trunks and a crown of fernlike leaves stretched high above them. In between, she caught glimpses of flowers: shiny red cups with brilliant yellow stamens, clusters of tiny white petals, and yellow-and-orange striped lilies. It was all crowded so tightly together that Terlu quickly lost sight of the walls of windows. The only view of the outside world was directly above her, through the windows of the cupola, where it looked merely white, either from the snow or the sky—she couldn't tell which.

The only sound was the crunch of her shoes on the gravel and the squish of the melted snow between her toes. She was still shivering where her wet tunic touched her skin, but it was vastly warmer inside. She expected her clothes would dry quick enough.

As she drew closer to the heart of the greenhouse, it became even hotter, and she soon saw why: a white porcelain stove in the shape of a spiral shell. It radiated heat, causing the air to waver near it. A bench with blue tile encircled it, and she dusted off a few stray leaves that had fallen on it and sat. Sighing in joy, Terlu cozied up to the stove.

She couldn't see any hatch for inserting wood, and she didn't smell smoke. A magical stove. Unusual, but not impossible. Well, clearly not impossible, since here it was.

Oh, wow, she could curl up and sleep here. Granted, the bench could use a few pillows, and it needed to be cleaned. She doubted anyone had sat here in ages, given the thickness of the dust and the number of stray leaves on and around it. As she looked at the plants that filled the vast room, she wondered if anyone had been in this greenhouse in years.

She began to feel a bit uneasy.

She couldn't be alone in this vast place, could she?

Terlu was no expert, but even she could see that the plants had been allowed to grow wild. They wound around each other in tight braids and tangles, filling every bit of available space. *What if there's no one here? What if I'm alone?*

She felt panic bubble in her throat. Her heart began to race, and she gulped in air. After so much time unable to speak, unable to have a simple conversation, unable to touch anyone or be touched . . . *I can't be alone here.* Maybe this greenhouse was abandoned, but someone nearby had cast—

"*Rrr-eow?*"

A winged cat walked around the stove on the blue-tile bench. He had gray fur, amber eyes, and brilliant emerald wings that lay crossed on his back. When he reached Terlu, he paused and looked at her.

"Hello!" Terlu said. "Aren't you a beauty."

Almost certainly agreeing with her, the winged cat proceeded toward her and climbed onto her lap. He kneaded her thighs through her tunic with his claws, turned around once, and then settled onto her. His emerald-green feathers ruffled as he shrugged his shoulders into a more comfortable position.

"Um, okay, welcome," Terlu said, enchanted by such unexpected feline friendliness. Gently, she stroked between his ears. The fluttery fear in her throat receded as she petted the winged cat. Slowly, her heart calmed, and she could breathe without feeling like she was about to shatter. His fur was as soft as velvet. She smiled as he tilted his head so she'd pet his cheeks and neck. "So happy to meet you. I was beginning to think I was all alone here."

He purred.

CHAPTER THREE

"Do you have a name?" Terlu asked the winged cat.

He didn't answer, of course. She wasn't surprised. She'd never heard of a talking winged cat. She'd read a travelogue once about a distant island that was rumored to have a breed of talking lizards. The explorer had claimed they were prophetic, but he'd also devoted an entire chapter to the glories of a type of hallucinogenic mushroom so his other claims were considered suspect.

"Is there someone around here who feeds you?" she asked. "You don't seem feral."

The cat was contorting himself so that she could pet beneath his wings. In her experience, strays were never this friendly . . . unless he'd been raised with humans and then abandoned? If so, that would explain why he was so desperate for cuddles.

"I know how you feel," she told him. "That's me too."

That was the whole reason she'd cast the spell that destroyed her life in the first place: she'd been lonely. It was that simple. *And that pathetic,* she thought. She had believed that a position at the library would mean helping researchers find obscure bits of knowledge, educating curious patrons, and sharing her favorite books with like-minded colleagues. She'd specifically requested and interviewed for a public-facing position only. By the time she'd finished her training, though, the imperial laws regarding magic had tightened even more, restricting the vast majority of the volumes in the Great Library. Only the most elite sorcerers were to be granted access to the spell-books and related materials, and Terlu wasn't senior enough to be assigned to those luminaries. With apologies from the beleaguered librarian in charge of the second floor, Terlu had been reassigned to the stacks, where she was lucky if she saw another soul once a week, and then only briefly. The library, as a rule, did not attract social beings.

Terlu was good at many things: she'd excelled at all her classes and proven herself to be a very organized and efficient researcher— her professors had universally recommended her for the librarian position when she'd asked for references. She spoke nine living languages and could read six extinct ones, including the complex and highly nuanced First Language, plus she was fluent in several dialects used by the exclusively seafaring clans of the outer sea. She could also bake an excellent blueberry pie (thanks to a cookbook she'd found in the library), play an eight-string guitar (at least a few primary chords), and sketch a reasonable facsimile of whatever she was looking at.

But she was *not* good at being alone.

She liked to talk, she liked to listen, and she wasn't interested in listening to herself talk. She was the kind of person who could walk into a shop and know everyone's stories, from the customers to the stockers to their cousins twice-removed, by the time she walked out with a tub of butter and a half-dozen eggs. This was not a useful skill, however, in the empty and quiet library stacks, and it wasn't useful inside an abandoned greenhouse either.

I'm not alone here. There's the cat.

"How about we look around and see if we can find anyone?" Terlu asked the cat. "And maybe see if they have something to eat?"

Now that she was warm and mostly dry, she noticed she was hungry. In fact, "hungry" felt like a massive understatement. Her stomach was writhing as if it wanted to punch all her other organs. Scooping the cat in her arms, Terlu stood.

The cat promptly squirmed out of her arms, fluffed his wings, and then climbed up onto her shoulder. She tensed, hunching her back, unsure of what he was doing and how he could possibly balance there. He flopped around her neck so that his front paws draped over her left shoulder and his hind paws draped over her right.

She laughed as she straightened, her new furry scarf snug around her neck. "Aren't cats supposed to be aloof?" She loved that he wasn't.

He yawned in her ear.

"Any suggestions for which way to go?" Several paths split from the white spiral stove and its toasty blue bench, disappearing into the greenery as they curved out of sight. One led back to the door she'd come through, but any of the others could lead to help and (hopefully) an explanation. Perhaps there was a grand house associated with this greenhouse. Or even a village. She wouldn't know until she looked, and she had zero interest in sitting around, waiting for someone to come looking for her, especially after her experience with nearly freezing outside in the snowy woods. "How about left?"

As if in answer, he swatted her face with his tail. She decided that was a yes.

She started down the gravel path between wide-leaf plants. Orange-and-blue flowers grew on either side of her, their petals shaped like bird wings. Other plants leaned above the path as it curved and wound between their stalks. After a few twists, though, the walkway ended in a circle with an empty bird cage in the center, its door wide open. Ornate with jeweled flourishes, it looked large enough to hold a peacock. "Your former lunch?" she asked the cat.

Terlu heard a flutter above her, and she looked up. Perched in the rafters was a bird with flowers growing out of its feathers. Roses cascaded from its tail, a lilac sprig sprouted from its head, and bluebells coated its wings.

"Not lunch," Terlu said, "for either of us."

The flower bird opened its mouth and sang a trill like a soprano's aria. Even more remarkable, with the song came the delicate scent of a just-bloomed flower.

"Beautiful," she said.

The winged cat swatted her cheek with his tail, as if offended she was admiring another creature. She grinned and reached up to pet his chin.

Returning to the white stove, Terlu tried another direction, and her second-choice path meandered for longer through the thick greenery before ending in a glass door rimmed with fancy ironwork. "See, I knew it had to lead somewhere."

She opened the latch and went inside . . . into another equally large greenhouse.

This second greenhouse was so thick with humidity that the glass walls dripped with moisture. Sweat pooled in Terlu's armpits, and she was grateful her tunic was thin. The air felt heavy, and it was an effort to fill her lungs.

She looked up and squinted at the top of the greenhouse. Cradled beneath its glass peak was an orb that looked to be made of molten gold. An imitation sun, it swam with every shade of yellow, from pale lemon to deep amber. Circling it were dragonflies with sparkling diamond-like bodies and golden wings. They danced together in pairs and trios in a musicless promenade.

Beneath the false sun and its insect dancers, the plants in this room smelled like stew, in particular one with cabbages that had been allowed to simmer for too many hours. She wrinkled her nose, and the cat sneezed. He shifted, tickling her neck with his feathers, as he sat upright on her left shoulder.

"Yeah, I think it stinks too," she said to him.

The flowers, though, were extraordinary: six-foot scarlet blooms shaped like trumpets, sprays of yellow heart-shaped blossoms, and deep purple flowers with thorns as long as her arm. Most grew directly in beds of soil, but a few cascaded from pots. Oblivious to the heat, more diamond dragonflies flitted between them, each exquisite, twinkling as they flew, drawn to the lurid blossoms.

Holding her sleeve over her nose, Terlu hurried through the swampy greenhouse. Moss and vines choked every inch of the plant beds, and she heard water dripping and trickling all around her. The gravel was soggy beneath her feet, and frequently she had to hop over puddles. But the path was straight and soon she and the cat reached the door on the opposite side, framed by two more scarlet trumpet flowers. She opened it and plunged through.

Greenhouse number three was full of ferns. It smelled like a summer forest and was far cooler than the prior room, with fans that rotated overhead instead of a miniature sun. Even the colors were more restful: soft, almost furry green in every direction. "Much better," Terlu said, and the no-longer-overheated winged cat flopped bonelessly around her neck as if in full agreement.

She walked farther in along a path made of gray and blue slate of various shades. Like in the prior rooms, it split into multiple branches that were swallowed by greenery. On the side of every path were more and more ferns. She'd never imagined the world held this many different varieties of ferns: fluffy fronds and pointy fronds and red ones and yellow-spotted ones and . . . Goodness, it was an excessive number of ferns.

Terlu tried calling out again, just in case. "Hello? Is anyone here?"

She didn't expect an answer, and she didn't get one.

The silence pressed in on her, and she felt herself gulping for air. *You're okay,* she told herself. *You'll find someone.* Reaching up, Terlu stroked the cat's neck. There had to be someone here, at least to feed the cat.

She kept to the widest route, hoping it would lead to the exit. Above her, two fans whooshed softly, drowning out the soft patter of the falling snow.

Sure enough, Terlu found the next door, framed in the same delicate ironwork as the others. "How many greenhouses are there?" she asked as she opened it. She was proud that her voice only shook a little, even if it didn't fill the cavernous room. She spoke louder. "And do these count as multiple greenhouses, or is it a single greenhouse with multiple rooms? If so, are they greenrooms? No, that doesn't sound right. Greenhouses within a greenhouse." She'd studied linguistics extensively, but none of the texts she'd read had answered this specific question. Language was rife with oddities. It was one of the things she loved about the discipline.

A single smaller room, the next greenhouse was filled with shelf after shelf of pots. Inside, it was the perfect temperature. It reminded her of the first day of spring in Alyssium, when people filled their window boxes with seedlings and aired their freshly washed sheets out on their balconies. She walked farther in while the winged cat purred on her neck. The vast majority of pots only held soil, but a few had a green shoot punching through like a tiny fist raised in victory. Next to one was a trowel.

Stopping, Terlu stared at the trowel. Her knees felt watery, and her lips curved into a smile. "There *is* someone here."

A gardener.

Someone had been tending to these pots, planting new seedlings or bulbs or whatever was in the soil. These plants weren't overgrown and neglected; they were new growth, clear of weeds and debris. "Hello? Hello!" She rushed through the rows of pots into the next greenhouse—and walked directly into the most beautiful sight she'd ever seen.

It was a room full of roses.

Everywhere she looked, roses climbed out of pots and over trellises, up the windows and into the cupola, every shade imaginable: pink, yellow, white, champagne, sky blue, purple, fuchsia, coral, dusty pink, salmon pink, deep red, an even deeper red so dark it was almost black . . . And the scent! It was intoxicating. Terlu breathed it in. It was such a rich, luscious scent that it made her feel as if she were floating on clouds at sunset.

The cat sneezed.

"Don't be like that," she said. "It's nice."

He stretched his wings and flew up toward the rose-coated rafters. Her shoulders felt instantly colder without him, and she wished he'd come back. Eyes up toward the ceiling, Terlu followed the cat as he soared, emerald feathers extended, across the greenhouse. She was so intent on watching the cat that she nearly missed seeing the man.

On his knees next to a rosebush with an overabundance of pale pink buds, a gardener was pruning dead sprigs. His back was to her, and he had one basket next to him filled with twigs and a bag that was filled with clippers, trowels, and other tools.

"Oh!" she cried. "Hello, hello!"

Startled, he dropped his clippers as he jumped to his feet. The clippers clattered onto the slate as he swiftly turned to face her.

Without thinking about whether she should or not, whether it was appropriate or not, whether it was welcome or not, Terlu threw herself forward and hugged him. She wrapped her arms around him, pinning his arms to his sides, and she squeezed, her cheek pressed to his chest. It had been so very long since she'd touched anyone. Clinging to him, connecting with him, made her feel like she was really, truly here and whole again. "I'm alive, and you're real!"

A second later, she realized she was hugging someone she'd never met and who might not want to be hugged, and she sprang backward—and the moment of connection was over. "Oh, I'm sorry. I shouldn't have— I'm so terribly sorry. I won't do that again."

He looked shocked, as if she'd dumped a bucket of water on his head.

He also looked very handsome, even though there was a smear of dirt on his gold-hued cheek that she very much wanted to wipe off. She resisted the urge, though, since he was looking at her with so much confusion and alarm in his face that she thought he might flee if she tried.

She knew what he was seeing when he looked at her: a short, plump, pastel-colored woman who was pretty in the same kind of harmless way that bunnies are pretty. She had a wide smile, big purple eyes, and round cheeks, plus chipmunk-brown curls that bounced around her face. She did *not* look like the kind of person who ever popped up somewhere uninvited or did anything unexpected, which always seemed to mean people were extra shocked when she did exactly that.

"I'm sorry," Terlu repeated. "It's just—I thought this place was abandoned, and I didn't know if I was going to find anyone ever. And I didn't know what I was going to do if I couldn't find anyone. Except for the cat. Who is very nice. And soft." She was babbling, she realized. She closed her mouth and attempted a friendly smile.

"Who are you?" he asked.

I really shouldn't have hugged him. That was not okay behavior. Should she apologize more? She desperately wanted to touch him again, to reassure herself that this wasn't a dream. "I'm Terlu Perna, Fourth Librarian of the Second—" *Formerly Fourth Librarian . . .*

"How did you get here?"

She pointed the way she'd come. "Through a door, which I was very lucky to find. It's cold outside, and I wasn't prepared for—"

His expression lightened. "Oh! It's *you*! It worked!"

She blinked at him. *It's you,* he said. But Terlu had never met him before and had no idea who he was or how he'd know who she was. "I'm sorry?"

He was smiling at her, and it was dizzying to be smiled at after everything that had happened and all the shouting and accusations from before she'd been changed—the last sorcerers she'd met had been less than friendly. There had been a *lot* of scowling from the balconies in the courtroom. But *this* sorcerer looked happy to see her. He also looked remarkably handsome, even more handsome the longer she looked at him. He had gorgeous gold-and-black hair— jet-black streaked with gold that matched the golden sheen of his skin—and eyes that were as green as the cat's wings. He hadn't shaved recently, and his speckled-gold almost-beard looked soft enough to pet.

"Do I know you?" she asked. "Do you know me?"

Still smiling, he pointed his finger at her. "You're the statue." He had short fingernails with soil stuck under them. She'd never seen a sorcerer with dirt under his nails, but he had to be one if he'd cast the spell that restored her. Unless he wasn't the one who had cast it? She hadn't found anyone else. It had to be him. "You woke up."

"Yes, I did," Terlu said. Was she not supposed to? Maybe it had been a mistake and that's why she'd woken alone and in the cold.

He marveled at her. "I didn't think it was going to work."

Terlu felt herself begin to blush, knowing her lavender cheeks were deepening to a vivid magenta, which made her blush harder. She'd never been looked at like this before. He was staring at her as if she were a wish he'd been granted—gazing at her with his deep-as-the-sea, beautiful green eyes. "You were the one who restored me? Thank you so much. I . . . Thank you. Really, I am so very grateful." She'd feel even more grateful if he'd point her toward a snack. Or better yet, a very large meal with at least half a loaf of bread. Would it be rude to ask for food so soon after he'd restored her life? She wasn't certain about the etiquette of these kinds of situations. Some sorcerers were known to be fussy. "I thought the transformation was going to be permanent. I didn't expect to ever be human again. To breathe, to smell, to talk—you have no idea how great it feels to be able to fill my lungs again after so long!" She cut herself off before she waxed on too long about the joy of having lungs and a heart and a nose. Just having skin again was glorious.

He walked in a circle around her, as if checking to see if any of her was still wood.

"How. . . ." Terlu swallowed hard. She needed to ask how long it had been, what today's date was, but she couldn't make the question come out of her throat. She wasn't ready to hear the answer. She knew, deep in her bones, that she wasn't going to like it. Instead, she asked, "Why did you save me?"

"Because you're a sorcerer."

"I'm not a sorcerer," she said. "You are."

His smile faded. "I'm not a sorcerer."

"But you restored me. That requires a spell. You have to be a sorcerer." It was illegal for anyone else to work magic. If her trial and punishment had made anything clear, it was that. It didn't matter the kind of spell, the intent of the caster, or the results; the emperor refused to allow anyone who didn't have the proper training to attempt any spellwork whatsoever.

"I was sent the spell, along with the statue. You, I mean. You *were* the statue, weren't you? You aren't trying to trick me?" He was scowling now, his eyebrows low and his forehead crinkled. His eyes were still beautifully green despite the scowl, and she told herself firmly that she shouldn't be noticing that, especially while he was accusing her of trickery.

What sort of trick could she possibly—never mind. It didn't matter. She had far too many more questions to ask. "Yes, I was the statue," Terlu said, "but who sent me to you? Who are you? And where is this? It's not Alyssium. I would've heard if there were such an extensive greenhouse anywhere in the capital. Which island is this, and why am I here?" He wasn't looking at her as if she were the sun and moon anymore, and she missed that. Actually, he looked a bit like a wild bear when he scowled. A handsome golden bear still, but not a happy one. She added, "If you don't mind me asking."

"You're supposed to be a sorcerer," the gardener said.

"I'm sorry, but I'm not."

"Then what are you?"

"I'm a librarian."

"Oh."

He stared at her, and she stared at him. *I'm usually much better at this sort of thing,* she thought. She'd mangled this conversation from the beginning. *I shouldn't have hugged him.* Taking a breath, she marshaled her thoughts to begin again. She'd start over, introduce herself, ask her questions one at a time, and then—

With a *humph*-like grunt, the handsome golden bearlike gardener picked up his basket and his bag of tools. "You should rest. Whoever you are and whyever you're here, you went through a lot. Rest and eat."

That *did* sound like a good idea, and she had been through a lot, but—

"My cottage is just outside the greenhouse. You can stay there until you, um, leave." As if that resolved everything, he began to walk away.

"Wait, where are you going?" Terlu asked. *I'm supposed to leave? Leave and go where?* Why was he walking away from her?

"I . . . ahh . . . I have to think . . ." He picked up his pace. "I just . . . I have to go. I have work to do?"

If she weren't fully aware that she was the least intimidating person ever to exist in the Crescent Islands Empire, she would have thought he was fleeing her. *That's not possible.* He was dismissing her because she wasn't a sorcerer and therefore not worth his time. Once again, like home, like the library, she was somewhere she wasn't wanted and didn't belong. Except this was worse, because she didn't know how she'd gotten here.

"Please," she called after him. "I still don't understand why I'm here or who sent me here or where *here* is or anything."

"Neither do I," the gardener said over his shoulder. He then turned a corner, leaving her staring at only roses.

CHAPTER FOUR

The cat meowed from the ceiling and jolted Terlu out of her shock. She hurried after the gardener. "Wait, please! I don't understand—" She rounded the corner and saw the path split five ways, each vanishing beneath a canopy of roses.

Had he really just . . . left? Who did that?

Sure, he'd said she could rest in his cottage, which was lovely of him, but she didn't know where it was. Or who *he* was.

"Come back, please! I don't even know your name." She picked a path at random and started down it. A few yards in, she decided he couldn't have gone this way—there were too many roses that crisscrossed the walkway for him to have used it. She pivoted and hurried back to the junction. "You can work while we talk. Or I can help you work. I know how to make myself useful. Favorite family story: Once, there was a storm coming, and no one had given me a job to do, so I decided to move every single chicken into the house. I was three years old, determined to help, and the chickens were feisty, but I got them all in before the wind hit. My parents retold that every time it stormed—they said it was the funniest sight: three-year-old me waddling determinedly with my arms full of fussy poultry. Hey, you can't just bring someone back to life and then walk away!"

Except that was exactly what he'd done. He'd fled, as if he were the criminal and she an imperial investigator. She hurried down the second path, which ended in an arbor overflowing with copious amounts of roses. A cascade of snowy white roses spilled over dark green leaves, stunningly beautiful but unhelpful.

I lost him. She wanted to weep, which wasn't like her at all. She was more of a put-a-smile-on-and-blunder-ahead kind of person than a weeper, at least under usual circumstances. But she hadn't been under "usual circumstances" for a while, and right now she was hungry, achy, and bone-deep tired. She wished she were back in the library, even as quiet and empty as it was, by one of the great fireplaces with a mug of hot chocolate in her hands. "Get it together, Terlu," she said out loud. "At least you know there's someone here."

It wasn't much consolation since he'd practically run from her, but she was still better off than she'd been before she knew there was someone else on this island, wasn't she?

The silence was beginning to sound loud. She thought of the storage room, and she hugged her arms, reassured to touch flesh and not polished wood. *I'm not there anymore. I'm alive again. And I'm not alone.*

Returning to the heart of the rose room, Terlu looked up at the rafters. "Kitty? Want to come with me?" She spotted a bit of gray fur and a flash of green feathers, but he didn't fly down. Of course she didn't expect the winged cat to come when she called—as friendly as he was, he was still a cat. It was nice that he hadn't abandoned her entirely. "What do you think I should do?"

He didn't answer, but it didn't matter because she'd already decided to walk down a third path. If it failed, she'd try the fourth and then the fifth. Rest and food could wait. *I'm not giving up. I'll find him, and he* will *answer my questions.*

Hopefully.

In addition to the roses on the trellis above her, this path also had miniature rosebushes tucked along both sides that boasted blossoms with tiny overlapping petals in pale pink. Fallen petals were strewn over the slate stones as if the garden were a bridal bower.

Thankfully, this path ended in a door. As she opened it, the cat swooped low over her head to fly through above her. Following him, she stepped into an array of flowers more varied than she could have imagined. While the first and second greenhouses had been saturated in green and the rose room had been filled with delicate and elegant pastels and jewel tones, this one looked as if it had been drenched by a rainbow.

"Wow," she said, gawking at all of it.

Lilies bloomed in a thousand different shades of yellow, red, orange, and white, with stripes and polka dots. Bell-like flowers in pink and blue clustered on bushes. Fat firework-like clumps of brilliant white flowers exploded on another.

Between them flew butterflies like no butterfly she'd ever seen—their wings changed color with each flap: red to blue to yellow to black to silver to purple. She marveled at the ripple of rainbow as they floated from blossom to blossom.

"Hello?" she called, more out of politeness than any belief the gardener would answer.

She walked through and wondered: What was this place? Where did all these plants come from? And the flower bird, the dancing dragonflies, and the color-changing butterflies? Why were these extraordinary greenhouses here? Leaning over, Terlu inhaled the scent of a cluster of purple flowers on a bush. Lilac? She'd never seen a lilac with such large blooms, but it smelled like lilac, heady and sweet.

"Rrr-eow."

The cat flew past her, his feathers brushing her cheek.

"Oh? Do you know where he went?" Terlu asked.

Whether he did or not, following the winged cat seemed like a much better idea than wandering aimlessly, hoping to stumble across a man who'd made it very clear he was done talking with her. She kept the cat in sight as she wound through the glorious flower beds.

She noticed there were no weeds in any of the beds, despite the riot of colorful growth. The ones with lilies had only lilies, and the lilac bushes were rooted in weed-free soil. A wheelbarrow by the side of the path was piled high with plant debris. These were clearly not abandoned greenhouses, as she'd first thought. A butterfly landed on a lily and closed its wings. Colors shimmered over it in waves, red to purple, chased by blue then green, green then gold. *There could be more than one gardener.* She'd already walked through more enormous greenhouses in this complex than could possibly be cared for by a single person, and there seemed to be no end in sight. She liked the idea of finding a different, friendlier gardener.

Walking faster, Terlu followed the winged cat to another door and opened it—to be greeted with a whoosh of winter wind and a swirl of snow. She shut the door. "Not that way."

Landing on the ground, the cat pawed at the door. *"Rrr-eow."*

"You don't want to go outside. It's cold."

There wasn't anything out there but snow and trees . . . was there? The gardener had said his cottage was outside the greenhouse, nearby. Could that be what the cat wanted? Or did he just want to chase birds?

The cat rubbed against her ankles and then headbutted the door. Terlu noticed there was a hook near the door with a heavy beige coat hanging on it, as well as a thick red scarf.

"What's outside?" Terlu asked the cat.

He meowed again.

She took the coat off the hook and wrapped herself in it, then added the scarf for good measure. It was soft wool, and it smelled faintly of pine and cloves and nutmeg. The far-too-large coat swallowed her, which she didn't mind since it would keep her warm. "All right, but if you just want to chase sparrows, then I'm coming right back in."

Ready this time, she opened the door and stepped out into the snow. It had piled up as high as her ankles and drifted even higher against the side of the greenhouse, and it was still falling, now in fat flakes that clumped together, dotting the sleeves of the coat and the ends of the scarf. Flapping his wings, the cat flew out of the greenhouse toward the forest.

"Wait for me," she told him.

Testing the handle to make sure the door wouldn't lock behind her, Terlu closed it and then waded into the snow. After all the flowers, the wintery air tasted like fresh mint, clean and sharp on her tongue.

Ahead were the pine trees, their branches painted with snow, and between them—was that a cottage? It was! With the winged cat flying beside her, she headed for it. She saw a curl of smoke rising up from the chimney and smelled woodsmoke, tangy in the air. Snow coated the cottage's roof, and icicles had dripped down in front of the windows. It looked like it was laced with sugar.

Closer, she saw it had gray shingles, green shutters, and a green door, the same colors as the winged cat. Snow-filled window boxes were in front of the two windows on either side of the door, and the walkway had been cleared at some point—the snow was half the depth as elsewhere. Someone must have swept it aside before the latest batch of snow. The gardener? Was this his cottage? He'd said it was just outside the greenhouse, but how could she be certain she'd chosen the correct door to exit the vast structure? Surely there were other inhabitants in other cottages on the island as well.

Well, I did say I wanted to find a different gardener.

The cat glided to the front door and landed on the stoop. He pawed at the door, and Terlu joined him, knocking with her chilled fist. She shoved her hands back into the coat pockets as soon as she'd knocked, waiting for whoever lived in the cottage to answer the door.

When no one came, she knocked again and then peered through the window. She could only see a bit of inside, given the position of a cabinet, but she saw the corner of a wood table and a fireplace beyond it. Within the hearth, amber flames danced merrily.

He *had* said she could rest in his cottage, so she wouldn't really be breaking and entering if she went inside, right? Unless, again, it wasn't his cottage.

Terlu tried the doorknob, and it twisted easily. Pushing the door open a few inches, she called out, "Hello? Anyone home? May I come in, please?"

Propelling himself with his wings, the cat darted past her ankles inside the cracked-open door. She supposed this must be where her new furry friend lived. *Not a stray.* She was a little disappointed. She'd started to, privately of course, think of the gray-furred, green-winged cat as her cat.

She stepped in and closed the door behind her. Inside, it was toasty warm. And tiny. And perfect. Dripping snow on the front mat, she looked around and loved every inch of it. Beneath a window on her right was a bed piled invitingly high with pillows and blankets. A narrow desk with neatly stacked papers and envelopes sat beside it. On her left was the kitchen with a sink and cabinets, all very neat and clean with plates and bowls stacked beside cups. Opposite the front door was the fireplace, with a hefty cushioned chair that looked perfect for curling up with a book, and in the center of the room was a table with a bouquet of lilacs in a pitcher. A little wooden door near the sink most likely led to the washroom. Dried herbs and flowers hung from the rafters, and it all smelled like—

"Soup." She breathed the word like a benediction.

It wasn't just the dried herbs she was smelling; it was the rich, heavy aroma of cooked . . . whatever was cooking over the fire. She didn't care what kind it was. It was glorious, beautiful soup! She started toward it before it occurred to her that it was rude to help herself when she didn't even know if this was in fact the gardener's home.

The judge who had condemned her wouldn't look kindly on her if her very first act after being restored was to trespass and steal.

On the other hand, the judge wasn't here, and the soup was.

It *had* to belong to the gardener, she told herself, didn't it?

She dithered by the door for another moment, while the winged cat curled up on the comfy chair and spread his feathers out to dry in the heat of the warm fire.

Hunger won, as well as the amazing smell of the soup.

I'll only have a little.

After taking off the borrowed coat and scarf and hanging them on a hook by the door, she retrieved a bowl from the kitchen cabinet, crossed to the fire, and ladled herself two scoops of cut-up vegetables and broth. She didn't hesitate when she sat at the table—she immediately put a spoonful in her mouth.

At the Great Library of Alyssium, all the librarians' meals were prepared by unseen cooks in a kitchen on a level devoid of books. Several of their cooks were high-caliber chefs, with a pedigree that included many noble houses and often even the imperial palace. They were expected to provide meals for the sorcerers who consulted the library, and so for that reason, they often turned out perfectly roasted meats, delicately spiced pastries, and mouthwatering desserts with custards that looked like they were made of molten gold. Terlu had often ordered just desserts for her meals, especially near the end, when she felt she needed more and more comfort food. Once, she'd gotten an exquisite puff pastry swan, a leftover from an imperial party that had been held in one of the grander rooms of the library. Her fondness for sweets was part of why a lover had once described her as "pleasantly huggable," a description she was perfectly fine with if it meant she'd gotten to eat pastry swans. She'd also had some amazing meals on her home island of Eano: a coconut curry made by one of her aunts that had been known to reduce grown men and women to tears, a duck roasted over a fire pit after marinating in a special secret sauce, and dragonfruit jelly on a hot, buttery donut . . .

But Terlu thought she had never tasted anything as good as this soup.

Did he make this?

It had herbs she had no name for, but they made her feel as if she were being hugged. It was warm and nutty, and the vegetables— which she also couldn't identify—were sometimes sweet and sometimes tart and always perfect. The broth warmed her throat, straight down to her stomach, and she felt its warmth spread to the rest of her.

It was impossible to think about anything else while she ate, and so she just ate and tasted the sweet and the spicy and the nutty and the warm, while the winged cat purred louder and louder by the crackling fire.

After making sure there was plenty still in the pot for the gardener, she had a second bowl, and then finally, for the first time since becoming human again, felt like herself. She smiled at the cat, at the cottage, and at the empty soup bowl. And she began to think again.

Clearly, this was the gardener's cottage, and just as clearly, he planned to return soon—he'd left his soup to cook, so even if he hadn't been expecting to be feeding her, at the very least he intended to come back for his dinner once he was done with his work. If she just waited here, then he'd come home, and she'd be able to have the conversation that she'd wanted to have in the greenhouse. He'd answer her questions, and she'd figure out why she was here, whether it was intended as a gift or a punishment, and what she was supposed to do next.

While she waited, she cleaned and dried her bowl and spoon, as well as the little puddles of water she'd left when she'd tramped in snow from the outside. That took only a few minutes. After that, she looked out the window at the snow, which was now falling lightly, and the greenhouse. She hadn't noticed earlier, but during her meal, the sun had set, and the outside was settling into soft shadows. *He'll be home soon.*

When "soon" didn't come soon enough, she picked up a book that was on his desk, *The Care of Orchids* by Evena Therro, and sat on the foot of his bed to read. The winged cat had claimed the only chair that wasn't wood, and the pillows were so downy—they felt the way fresh-fallen snow looked like it should feel.

Opening the book, she began to read.

She didn't intend to fall asleep, but with the falling light outside, the gentle whisper of snow on the window, the warmth of the fire, and the softness of the pillows . . . she was lost by the end of the third chapter.

CHAPTER FIVE

Terlu woke to sunshine and honey cake.

Daylight streamed through the windows, brightening the snow outside so it gleamed and sparkled with a thousand flashes of color. Sitting up, she stared out the window at the pine trees and the freshly fallen snow and the greenhouse while her brain caught up to her body, and she remembered where she was and that she was flesh again.

She looked around and saw that the cottage was not precisely as she'd left it: the soup pot no longer hung over the fire, the dishes she'd used and cleaned had been put away, and a plate with a thick slice of honey cake was sitting on the table next to a fork and a neatly folded napkin.

How nice!

Oh wait, this isn't good.

The gardener had come home. And Terlu hadn't woken. In fact, the entire night had passed and a slice of the morning, and she'd slept through it all. She glanced at the chair, and the winged cat was gone as well. What must the gardener have thought when he found her asleep in his bed? He'd said to rest, but all night? In his own bed? Yet he hadn't woken her up. Where had he slept? Had he slept? He'd done plenty of chores. *Including making me breakfast.*

At least she assumed it was for her; she had no actual way to know that, unless he'd left a note, which it didn't look like he had. She imagined what such a note would say: *Dear stranger in my bed.* Or *Dear intruder.* Or *I liked you better as a statue.* She got out of bed and ran her tongue over her teeth. Her mouth felt gummy, and she wished she had her brush and paste. Also, a privy.

"Um, hello? I'm awake now? Are you still home?" Of course he wasn't.

She checked the narrow door by the kitchen sink and, happily, found the washroom, complete with a sink, toilet (with a pull-chain to flush!), and all the amenities. Fresh water was in a deep bowl next to a sponge and a towel that smelled like rosemary. Had he left this for her, as well as the honey cake? She wished he'd stayed for her to ask.

Guilt swirled inside her, also hunger. She loved honey cake, but she'd eaten his soup and slept in his bed the entire night, and to assume he was fine with her taking more . . . *I am the worst houseguest ever.* She could bake him a blueberry pie as thanks. Everyone liked pie. Of course he'd have to loan her the ingredients, which wouldn't make it much of a thank you. She picked up the towel and noticed there were clothes beneath it—pants of the softest wool she'd ever felt and a knit top, as well as clean socks and undergarments, all of which looked her size—and that decided her. He'd left these for her to use, and he'd thought of everything. There was a wedge of soap, as well as jar of toothpaste.

Terlu washed, changed, and emerged, half expecting him to be in the cottage waiting for her, but he wasn't. It was empty. She felt a little shiver. *Just a cottage. Not a storage closet.* And she wasn't on a pedestal; she could walk outside whenever she wanted.

She glanced at the chair, wishing the cat had stayed.

It was quiet, except for the soft crackle of the fire in the hearth. It burned low, and she wondered if she should add another piece of firewood or if he preferred it low. She left it as it was and sat at the table to eat the honey cake in silence.

He'd left a syrup for the cake, which she poured on top, and the moist cake soaked it in. She took a bite—it was perfection: vanilla and honey and lightness. It tasted like sunrise, and all of a sudden she didn't mind that she was alone. She didn't *feel* alone anymore. She poured water from a pitcher by the sink, and she discovered it tasted like strawberries and mint, which was amazing in winter. She marveled at it. Perhaps there was another greenhouse room full of herbs and strawberries, miraculously ripe in the heart of winter.

Terlu cleaned after she finished and tried to think of how she could leave a thank-you, but she had nothing and didn't want to use any of his paper without asking—she'd already eaten his food, slept in his bed, and used his toothpaste. *I'll simply have to find him,* she resolved.

The coat and scarf were where she'd left them, and she put them on. She was pleased to discover that her night's sleep had cured her of the aches she'd felt when she'd transformed back into flesh. She hoped there wouldn't be any lasting effects from her time as a statue. That would be nice. She wondered if there had ever been any studies done on the long-term effects of transformation spells. If she had access to the Great Library, she could check, but she had the sense that she was a very long way from the stacks she knew. She wondered how far. How had she come here? Had she been loaded onto a boat like a piece of lumber? Had she been shipped with supplies? Or had she been treated like a person as she traveled? Did whoever transported her know she'd once been a person? Why had she been sent anywhere? She'd been positioned on her pedestal for a purpose. Every new librarian received their training in the North Reading Room, and so they'd all been told her story, in whispers or as a lesson. They'd read the plaque beneath her and wonder: Why had she done it? Why had she risked so much? Sacrificed so much? It hadn't been for the good of the empire, and it hadn't been for her own wealth or personal gain—why would anyone want to cast a spell to create a sentient houseplant? She wondered if anyone knew the ignoble truth: it was because she didn't think she could take one more hour in the stacks without anyone to talk to. She didn't want to quit, and she didn't want to leave—she loved the library, and she believed that she could be good at her job, if she could just solve this one little problem. Even more, she didn't want to slink home and admit that she'd failed to make it in the capital city. Her family hadn't wanted her to leave, and they hadn't understood why she'd been so desperate to find a place where she felt she had purpose. Maybe it had been pride or some other personality flaw that had led her to casting the spell that created a self-aware spider plant named Caz, but she had truly thought that since she wasn't doing any harm, as Rijes Velk herself had pointed out, no one would mind or even notice.

She'd been very, very wrong about that.

In retrospect, she supposed the sudden appearance of a talking plant had been rather difficult to ignore.

Anyway, that was the past, and now she had an unexpected present to face. It was clear what she had to do: find the gardener, thank him, and apologize. And then bombard him with as many questions as he'd answer before he ran away again, including how much time had passed since her trial. She couldn't keep avoiding that question just because she was afraid she wouldn't like the answer.

Outside, the day was crisp but beautiful. She inhaled deeply. Overhead, birds were singing to one another, cascading trills from high in the branches. She caught a glimpse of a red cardinal, bright scarlet against the white snow, green pine, and blue sky, as it flew over the top of the greenhouses.

The snow crunched under her feet as she let herself inside and then hung up the coat and scarf. "Gardener? Kitty? Good morning!"

Silence greeted her.

"Good morning, flowers," she said to the plants.

None of them answered her either.

She walked between the lilies and lilacs, inhaling their heady perfume and listening for any hint of sound from any direction that would tell her where to go. She thought she heard a hum to her left. She followed that path.

Opening the door to the next greenhouse, she was greeted with music.

Smaller than the prior rooms, this greenhouse was an octagon filled with flowers both in pots and planted directly into the soil, all in full blossom: tulips, daffodils, lilies, roses, and orchids, as well as tulip trees, magnolia trees, and dogwood trees. Every flower on every plant and tree was singing wordlessly in perfect harmony.

No one had written this music. It flowed and evolved, notes tumbling over one another and then joining in chords more by happy accident than design. The harmonies melded and split and flowed around her, washing over her as gently as a stream over stones, and Terlu stood on the path and felt the tears flow down her cheeks. She wasn't certain why she was crying—*I'm alive. I slept, I washed, I ate.* She had no reason to cry. *Stop it,* she told herself, but that had no effect.

If she hadn't just been thinking about Caz, then it might not have hit her so hard, but she *was* thinking about him, the friend she'd made and lost, when she walked into the greenhouse of singing flowers.

She cried for the life she'd lost along with her new friend. Even if she hadn't particularly liked that life, it had been hers. She'd earned that library position, though it hadn't been what she'd dreamed it would be. She cried, too, for Caz himself. Was he happy? She hoped so. Was he safe? She wondered if she'd ever know. Did he know what had happened to her? Did he mourn when she was turned into a statue? Did he know she'd been saved? Did anyone? She thought of her family on Eano, her parents and her sister and her aunts, uncles, and cousins, and she wished they were here or she was there. If she could find a way to write to them . . . but what would she say? How would she explain? She didn't even know if they knew what had happened to her, how badly she'd messed up. It was better if they didn't know.

They could mourn the woman they'd hoped she'd be, rather than worry about the criminal she was.

The floral music flowed around her, soothing her and comforting her, and at last her tears stopped. She took a shaky breath and wasn't sure if she felt better or just more damp. "You sound beautiful," she said out loud. She wondered if any of them could hear her, and if they did, could they understand her? Were any of them like Caz was, fully awake and aware? "Hello? My name's Terlu. Can any of you speak?"

The flowers didn't stop singing.

Not like Caz then.

Terlu walked through the greenhouse, counting the singing plants and trees. Sixty-three—no, wait, there was a little bluebell in a bright pink pot that was singing high soprano, beneath a dogwood tree that crooned in baritone. Sixty-four, an extraordinary number. She knelt next to the bluebell and admired how its petals widened with each crystal-clear note.

This was a chorus that an emperor would envy.

Who had enchanted them all to sing like this? This required a *lot* of spellwork, very advanced spellwork too. Could the gardener have done it? He'd woken her, but he'd claimed he wasn't a sorcerer. Had he lied? Why would he lie? It wasn't illegal for sorcerers to cast spells. If he was a sorcerer, it would be safer for him to tell the truth. So she supposed it wasn't him? But if he wasn't responsible for this chorus, then who was? Who else was here?

She left the singing greenhouse through a door painted with musical notes.

One of the other miraculous things about this place, in addition to the wealth of plants and the harmony of the flowers, was the way the doorways truly separated each room. Heat, moisture, cold— none of it leaked into the next greenhouse, even when the door itself was open. *It has to be a spell, a very complex and advanced one.* Like with the singing flowers, but more practical. Terlu stepped across the threshold and noted that, once again, this climate was entirely different from the prior one. It was hot and dry and far quieter, with paths and garden beds that were filled with sand. Cacti grew here:

tall ones with arms that reached toward the ceiling, as well as short, spiky nobs that poked through the ground. A few had starlike yellow flowers clustered between their leaves and one had a cascade of trumpetlike pink flowers. She spotted a rabbit-size gryphon on top of one of the larger cacti. It let out a little leonine roar before it flew up to the rafters. She wondered if it was friends with the winged cat.

She found the next greenhouse quickly and walked into a pleasantly warm room full of potted trees. Fruit trees? Ooh, were any of them orange trees? Imagine a fresh orange only a few weeks from the winter solstice! Her home island boasted fantastic groves of orange trees, but they were never ripe in winter. Her favorite Winter Feast treat had been candied orange covered in chocolate. Her first Winter Solstice in Alyssium she'd scoured the city for a confectioner who'd sell candied chocolate orange. She'd found one that sold an orange-liqueur chocolate, but it hadn't been the same.

Terlu opened the next door, wondering what wonders she'd find. But instead of a display of glorious green or a false sun or an unexpected chorus or a random gryphon, she walked into a plant graveyard. It was such a shocking contrast that she gasped out loud. Her breath hung in the air, a cloud of mist, and she hugged her arms as she walked farther in.

Above her, the glass was splintered, with a few panes that were fully shattered. Snow had drifted inside and was sprinkled across the beds of brittle and withered plants and broken glass. The brown skeletons of shriveled vines clung to the pillars, and the remnants of sprouts sat curled in pots of dry dirt.

What in the world had happened here?

All the other rooms she'd seen had been brimming with life, but this greenhouse was silent and cold. Her footsteps crunched as she walked to the door on the opposite side. She hurried through into another just-shy-of-freezing room full of desiccated plants.

Why had this happened? How had the gardener allowed it?

She continued through dead greenhouse after dead greenhouse, shivering, until at last she'd had enough and reversed directions. If she'd known how many had been abandoned, she would have borrowed that coat again.

Her shoes crunched on the gravel, the only sound as she walked back through the silent greenhouses. They were shrouded in their silence. She'd seen a total of five abandoned rooms, but who knew how many more there were? She walked quickly, not merely because of the cold—it felt like she'd infiltrated a graveyard. As a living being, she didn't belong. She felt her heart beat faster, her breath shorten.

She was halfway across the first dead greenhouse, almost back to the living, when she saw the gardener hurrying toward her.

Smiling in relief, Terlu opened her mouth to greet him.

"You shouldn't be here," he snapped.

Friendly as always. She'd hoped that the honey cake and the clothes had been a peace offering, an apology for waking her in the cold and then dismissing her yesterday, but she supposed not. "Sorry. I didn't know—"

"Come where it's safe." He herded her through the door back into the desert room with the cacti and the air that felt as warm as a sweater. She felt the heat soak into her skin as the winged cat wound around her ankles.

She knelt to pet him.

"He yowled at the door until I came," the gardener said.

"You did?" Terlu asked the cat. "Thank you for worrying about me. You didn't need to, though. I was on my way back." Spreading his wings for balance, the winged cat clambered up her skirt. She cradled him as she stood up.

"You shouldn't have gone in there," the gardener said. "Those rooms are not structurally sound. In a few of the lost greenhouses, the ceilings have collapsed." He scowled at the door as if it were at fault for letting her in.

Terlu shivered at the thought of the glass ceiling collapsing on top of her. Squirming out of her arms, the winged cat climbed onto her shoulders and flopped around her neck. "You should put up a sign. Or keep it locked."

"I'm the only one here," he said, with an unspoken *And I know better*. He added, "Well, the only one aside from Emeral, but he can't open doors."

"Emeral?" She *knew* there had to be someone else here. How else could those flowers be singing? She hoped this Emeral would be able to explain what had happened and why she was here and what she was supposed to do. "Is Emeral the sorcerer?"

"Emeral is the cat." He pointed to the winged cat, who purred in her ear.

Okay, fine, not an unknown helpful sorcerer. "Hello, Emeral. I'm Terlu Perna." Looking up at the gardener, she waited for him to introduce himself. When he didn't, she asked, "What's your name?"

He looked surprised she wanted to know. "Yarrow. Yarrow Verdane."

That felt like progress, at least a little. "Nice to meet you, Yarrow. Thank you for saving my life. Also for the soup, the honey cake, the clothes, and use of your bed last night."

Yarrow shrugged. He picked up a tote bag with gardening tools—he was going to walk away again, but this time he wasn't going to catch her by surprise. She kept pace with him.

"What happened to those greenhouses?" she asked.

"The magic failed."

"Why?"

"It just failed."

"What has been done to try to fix it?"

He stopped walking. "You. You were supposed to fix it."

She halted too. "Me?" That made no sense. She knew nothing about fixing greenhouses. She didn't think she'd ever even been in one before, unless a florist shop counted, but she didn't think it did, or at least it wasn't the same scale. "Why me?"

Yarrow shrugged again. "I appealed to the capital—asked them to send a sorcerer to help restore the spells that enchant the greenhouses. For nearly a year, I got no answer. And then . . . they sent you. But there appears to have been a mistake because you say you're not a sorcerer."

A mistake. The word hurt. Once again, she wasn't wanted. She thought of the day she'd decided to leave home, how she'd felt when she'd realized she had no place there anymore, no future that she wanted and no future that wanted her . . . This wasn't the same, of course, and she knew it was silly to feel that way—he wasn't saying anything about her personally, just that he needed a sorcerer to fix whatever spell kept the greenhouses intact and warm and hospitable.

She supposed it was appropriate. Her whole life had been a series of mistakes, one after another: a mistake to leave Eano for a hazy dream of a future with purpose, a mistake to think she could make it at the Great Library, a mistake to create Caz.

The magic wasn't a mistake. Getting caught was the mistake.

She took a breath and asked the question she should have asked the moment she woke, the one she knew would have an answer she wouldn't like: "Could you tell me . . . That is, I need to know . . . What year is it?"

Yarrow gave her a curious look. "Imperial year 857."

She'd half expected it. All that time on the pedestal . . . All the days that drifted into more days, the darkness that melted into the next night . . . She knew it had been more than a year. She'd guessed three, four at most.

Six, though. Six was a blow.

Terlu felt herself start to shake. *Six years.* She supposed she hadn't aged while she'd been made of wood. But her family . . . Everyone she knew . . . A lot could happen in six years. Was Rijes Velk still the head librarian? Were any of the librarians she knew still there? What had changed in the world since she'd been absent from it? Was her family well? What had she missed?

"Are you all right?" Yarrow asked, his voice gentle for the first time.

Keep it together. Squeezing her hands into fists until she felt her fingernails digging into her palms, Terlu forced herself to smile. "Yes, of course."

He studied her as if he didn't believe her.

She changed the subject as dramatically as she could. "What happened to the sorcerer who created all this?" Terlu swept her arms open to encompass the entirety of the greenhouse complex, and Emeral squawked in objection. She scratched his cheek, and he leaned into her fingers and settled down again. His feathers tickled her neck.

"He died," Yarrow said.

"I'm sorry for your loss."

He shrugged in response.

Kneeling by one of the cacti beds, he stuck his finger into the sand. He pulled it out and then poked another area. Belatedly realizing she was staring at him, he explained, "Checking moisture levels. It's fine."

"Ahh. All the plants in the dead greenhouses . . ."

"It happened too fast, too widespread. It froze so quickly . . ." She heard the pain in his voice. "I saved as many as I could. It wasn't enough. Not nearly enough."

Terlu knew what that felt like, failure. She tried to think of something to ask or say and all she could think of was to repeat, "I'm sorry for your loss." She hoped it came through in her voice how much she truly meant it.

This time, he looked up at her. "Thank you."

She was also sorry she didn't know how to help. She wished she were a sorcerer or at least knew something about gardening beyond the basics. "How many—"

"Half. More. Out of three hundred sixty-five greenhouses, one hundred ninety-one have failed. With some, when they failed, I was able to save the plants. But too many others . . . I need a sorcerer to recast the spells that keep the greenhouses whole and protected. I can't do that myself."

Terlu could hear how much he wished he could, and she wanted to reach out to him and take his hands—she didn't know him well enough for that, though. She only knew his name. And she didn't know if it would help him to be touched. Some people needed it; some people fell apart if you did. "If there's anything I—"

"You were my hope," he said.

She felt pierced through the heart. "I—"

Yarrow held up his hand. "It's not your fault."

Pressing closer to her cheek, Emeral purred harder, as if he sensed she was upset. She took a deep breath. She knew it wasn't her fault—she hadn't caused the greenhouses to fail, nor did she ever claim to be a sorcerer—but still . . .

"There's no regular boat that comes to Belde," Yarrow said, "but if I put up a flag, there's a sailor who runs a regular supply ship that will stop by. I'll pay her fee, enough to transport you home or wherever you want to go."

Terlu didn't know what to say to that. If someone had given her that offer on the day she'd been sentenced, she would have taken it. She would have happily gone anywhere to escape her fate, especially if she could've taken Caz with her. But now that she was free . . . *Six years,* she thought.

In a small voice, she said, "I don't have anywhere to go."

CHAPTER SIX

With the winged cat acting as her scarf, Terlu followed Yarrow through the greenhouses. He didn't speak as he led. Just a gruff "Follow me" and then a few "hmms" and grunts as he paused to examine plants and flowers along the way. He took a different route than she had before, choosing a left fork in the rose room instead of going straight, and Terlu craned her neck to see the new greenhouses.

There was one devoted to miniature trees. Beneath the branches, she glimpsed tiny woodland creatures living beneath them: three-inch-tall deer, tiny rabbits, minuscule chipmunks.

Another greenhouse was dedicated entirely to moss and filled with iridescent butterflies.

A third was full of vegetables: tomatoes that had been coaxed to grow like trees, cucumbers and squashes that were suspended from a latticework near the ceiling, beds of carrots and lettuces in neat rows. It had the same kind of neatness and precision that she'd seen in Yarrow's cottage, and she was certain he'd designed and planted everything in here. She wanted to ask him about it, as well as the tiny woodland animals, but he was already in the next room.

He waited for her by a door to the outside. It wasn't the same door as the one closest to his cottage, of course, but it looked similar and also had a row of coat hooks beside it. He handed her a red coat. He was wearing a beige one, and she couldn't help noticing again how handsome he was, in an utterly-unaware-of-his-own-handsomeness way. It wasn't a classic nobleman kind of beauty, with everything as chiseled and combed and coiffed as a resplendent peacock; it was the kind of beauty of a perfectly symmetrical tree. Terlu imagined telling him he was as handsome as a tree—a tree with golden bark, black-and-gold leaves, and emerald-green flowers?—and decided she should never become a poet. She accepted the coat, and Emeral flew from her shoulders as she pulled it on. She was pleased that it fit her better than the other coat, and she wondered if he'd chosen it for her or if it was just chance. *It must be chance.* Why would he spend any time thinking about her coat size? Still, this wasn't a coat that would ever fit over his broad shoulders. She found herself studying his shoulders, blushed, and looked up toward Emeral instead.

Settling on one of the rafters, the winged cat began licking his hind leg.

"You're staying here?" she asked the cat.

"He comes and goes as he pleases," Yarrow said.

Of course he did—feathery wings or not, he was a cat—but she still wished he'd come with her. She let him be, though, and followed Yarrow.

Outside, the sun had crossed to touch the tips of the pine trees. Her breath instantly fogged in front of her, and the snow crunched under her feet. It smelled sweet, a mix of sea salt and pine, chilled. Yarrow led her between two pine trees onto what could have been a road, if it weren't buried in snow and completely impassable to anyone not on foot or sled or skis. Wide and winding, it cut through the woods. Their footprints were the first to break the smooth white.

"Mine is the last cottage to the east, but there are more along the road to the west, toward the dock." He pointed as he spoke. "Choose whichever one you want, and it's yours, but you'll have to fix it up yourself. I can't spare the time from the plants."

"But—"

"You're welcome to whatever supplies you need."

She looked between the trees toward the first cottage. From here she could see its roof had caved in. "My sister Cerri can fix anything. Once, the sink pump in my family's kitchen stopped working, and she took apart all the plumbing. By the time she was done, we not only had a functional sink, but she'd built a shower, complete with a contraption that you'd fill with embers from the fire that warmed the water before you cleaned yourself. Unfortunately I don't have the same kind of skill."

He shrugged. "Then pick a cottage that already has working plumbing."

She also didn't know how to fix roofs, windows, or chimneys. "But I don't—"

"Tools are in the shed behind my cottage. Return them when you're done."

Without waiting for her to reply, he tromped away through the snow, back toward the greenhouse. He kept leaving her speechless, and not in a good way. She ran through the conversation in her head, wondering if she'd said the wrong thing or just said too many things.

At least he didn't tell me I had to leave right now. She could stay until she . . . Terlu didn't know how to finish that thought. Until she was ready? Until she had a plan for her life? Until she'd outstayed her welcome? Instead of dwelling on it, she turned her attention to the practical.

Any cottage she wanted? Well, not the one with the caved-in roof. She could look for one that hadn't yet collapsed. She envisioned herself huddling in a fallen-down hut with a hibernating bear, then told herself to try to think more positively. One of the cottages could be perfectly fine.

Hugging her coat around her, Terlu stomped through the snow along the road, toward the west. The sun filtered through the pine trees and spread over the snow, making it twinkle. Blue sky was overhead, so blue that it looked like a painting.

The next cottage had a bulbous roof that overhung wide windows. Everything was round from the door to the windows to the chimney, which made it resemble a toadstool, especially with the red paint and white trim. It looked charming, but more importantly, it looked structurally intact.

I could live here. Couldn't I?

By myself?

Just me?

Terlu shuddered and then told herself firmly not to be ridiculous. Lots of people lived on their own and were fine. She waded through the snow to the front door. Hoping it was unlocked, she squeezed the handle and pushed. It swung open with a creak, and she poked her head inside—and the bright eyes of many, many formerly sleeping gryphons blinked at her. Each was about the size of a large raccoon, with the head and wings of an eagle and the body of a mountain lion. From the state of the cottage and the pile of rodent bones scattered over the floor, it was clear that this flock was feral. She wondered if they were related to the gryphon she'd seen in the cacti room.

One of the gryphons hissed.

Terlu shut the door and backed away, quickly.

Or not just me.

Next cottage then.

She hurried down the snowy road. The next cottage was tucked between two pine trees with branches that shielded the roof from much of the snow. Between the clumps of snow, she could see pink coral tile peeking out. Short and squat, this cottage had been painted in sunrise colors: yellows and pinks and roses. The paint was chipped and peeling, but it still looked cheerful. One window was broken in the front, but it looked otherwise intact. *All right, attempt number two.* She opened the lemon-yellow door more slowly this time and peered inside.

No family of gryphons peered out, nor did she see any hibernating bears. Terlu dared to venture in. Sunlight spilled through the windows so there were no dark corners, only layers of gray. By one corner was a bed, collapsed in the center where the netting had worn away. Another corner had a table that was coated in dust. She ran a sleeve over a corner to reveal painted flowers. The chimney was full of debris, leaves and twigs. It would have to be cleaned out before a fire could be attempted, and that was no small task. It looked very clogged.

She wondered if the kitchen sink pump still worked. Crossing to it, she tried it. It was stiff, but she managed to lift it up. No water came out, though.

The chimney she could fix, presumably—at least it was obvious *how* to fix it; just clean it out—but a water pump? As she'd told Yarrow, she didn't have her sister's skill with plumbing. Or anything, really, as her sister used to delight in pointing out. Still . . . *I wish Cerri were here now.* She'd be able to fix up one of these cottages in an afternoon. By day two, she'd have transformed it into a palace. Terlu, however, had no such skills.

She wished she'd written home when things had gotten difficult at the library. But Terlu hadn't wanted her family to guess she was miserable. It wasn't as if they could have done anything anyway, and all it would have done was make everyone feel bad—and she'd feel like even more of a failure. Still . . . she wished she'd reached out. Things might have turned out differently if she had.

Terlu tried the next cottage, which looked like a cake with frills carved out of wood instead of icing, but all its windows were cracked or outright broken and snow was strewn across the floor. As she trudged to the next cottage, she wondered who they'd all belonged to. It was clear that each home had once been loved very much. In the next one, Terlu found a child's toys, a rocker carved like a bear and a doll that was missing an eye. Another had a framed sketch of a couple, their arms around each another, both of them smiling at the artist.

Why had the owners left? Where were they now? And why had Yarrow stayed behind? There was a peaceful kind of sadness to the row of abandoned cottages, but no answers.

After the cottage with the artwork, she found one that seemed like it could be livable, with a more reasonable amount of work: a blue cottage, its walls painted a pale noonday blue and its door and shutters a deep twilight blue. Cobwebs clung to the rafters, but she saw no inhabitants other than spiders. It had a hammock-like bed strung from the ceiling, though she wasn't sure she'd trust it—she didn't know how long it had been there—but she could pull in a proper cot from one of the other cottages. In fact, she could take her favorite pieces from each of them and assemble them here.

It could be nice.

Lovely, even. She imagined it clean and neat and full of flowers. She hoped Yarrow would let her pick blossoms to fill her cottage. *My cottage.* That had a nice sound to it, didn't it?

Well, didn't it?

I'm not a child anymore. I can handle living on my own. She'd had her own space in the library, and she'd been fine. She'd hated it, but she'd managed. Sort of. For a while. Until she'd been statue-ified.

Okay, she hadn't been fine.

"You can make this work," Terlu told herself out loud.

She could try to convince Emeral to stay with her, so she wouldn't have to bear the silence and solitude. His purr was capable of curing any kind of sadness.

Crossing her arms, she tried to look at the cottage objectively. It wasn't as nice and cute and sweet as Yarrow's cottage. And the amount of work to make it as lovely . . . It was daunting enough that she wanted to pivot and race back to the comfort of his home. She'd have to clean the chimney and, well, everything. Plus there were a few holes here and there that could do with patching so the wind wouldn't whip through on stormy days. She wondered if the roof leaked. She supposed she'd discover that the next time it rained. Craning her neck, she examined the ceiling—she didn't see much water damage on the roof above the rafters, though there were stains on the wall beneath the windows.

Terlu tested the pump at the sink, and after a few hearty pumps, brown water spurted out. She kept pumping until it ran clean. *That's a plus,* she thought.

Seeing the fresh, clean water, her heart felt lighter. She could see a little bit of a glimpse of a future here, if she worked at it, at least an immediate future if not a long-term, life-full-of-purpose kind of plan. She wasn't afraid of work, which was a good thing since there was a lot to do before the cottage would be livable.

But what to do first?

Heat, definitely. She had to clean the chimney. She'd need . . . She wasn't quite certain what she'd need. A brush? With a long handle and stiff bristles. And a broom to sweep all the soot out once she'd knocked it down. Perhaps a ladder so she could climb up onto the roof.

Oh dear. She'd never climbed up onto a roof in her life. She wondered how slippery it would be with all the snow and ice. She wondered if Yarrow expected her to fix any broken bones herself with the tools from the shed behind his cottage. And what if she couldn't make it livable enough before nightfall? Would he let her return to his cottage? She wouldn't take his bed again, of course, but she could curl up like Emeral by the hearth. Surely, he'd lend her a blanket. At least by his fire, she wouldn't freeze to death.

Making to-do lists in her head, Terlu left the blue cottage. For thoroughness, she continued down the road, though she thought the blue cottage was likely the best she was going to find. She also loved that it was blue, which she knew was superficial of her, but it made her think of the sky on a summer day on Eano when the waves played at your feet and the dolphins swam just offshore. It felt like a good-luck color. Maybe she *could* make a home here, at least for as long as she was allowed to stay. Or for as long as she wanted to stay, whichever came first.

Terlu followed the road to where it ended, on the western edge of—what had Yarrow called this place? The island of Belde. Stopping, she wrapped her coat tighter and looked out at the sea. On Alyssium, you rarely had an uninterrupted view of water—there were other islands and tons of ships, both sailing and cargo ships, going to and fro. On her home island of Eano, you'd see fisherfolk out in their canoes, sometimes a dolphin or two frolicking in the waves. But here, there was only the blue sea. There was no sandy beach, only rocks, and the waves crashed against them, white froth billowing up with each crash. In the distance, she saw the shadows of what could be other islands, smudges of a grayer blue, but they could also have been clouds.

A dock led out into the water, but no boats were tied to it. Just a dock with an empty flagpole at the end, with a box beside it, secured to the deck. She thought of Yarrow's offer to summon a ship to take her away. *I could do it right now.* Walk out to the end of the dock, raise a flag, and summon a stranger to come and take her wherever she wanted to go, but where would that be?

Home? In disgrace? She couldn't do that to her family. It wasn't just that they'd be disappointed in her or that she'd be embarrassed to admit she'd failed to thrive, though that was all true—it was the fact that reaching out to them could endanger them. She was still a convicted criminal. Her parents, her sister . . . She wished she could tell them she was alive, but without knowing whether or not she'd been pardoned, how could she risk it?

She still had no clear idea why she was here. Why had someone sent *her* here in response to Yarrow's request for a sorcerer? The plaque on her pedestal had been very clear she'd been a librarian. Sending her had to have been a mistake. And if so, the second that soon-to-be-in-trouble official discovered the truth, she'd be shipped back to the Great Library and reinstalled in the North Reading Room. No, she couldn't ask her family to harbor a convicted criminal.

It was better if no one knew she was here, and it was smarter to stay until she knew who had made this mistake and why—and what she wanted to do about it.

She'd never had any real vision for what she wanted to do with her life. Becoming a librarian had been a suggestion of one of her professors, and it fit her skills, but it had never been her passion, the way sailing was for her cousin Mer or carving for her aunt Siva or fixing things for her sister Cerri. She'd wanted, when she left her family and her home, to find some kind of life goal. That's what she'd be missing on Eano: a passion and a purpose. That's why she'd felt she had to leave. She knew she had no future there, and she was tired of being the one in the family who hadn't yet found her path.

She just wasn't sure where she *did* have a future or what her destiny was supposed to be.

Staying here for a bit might be good for me. Terlu could think about what she wanted and what her life should be, now that she had a second chance.

Yes, that's what this is: a second chance. And maybe the solitude will be nice for figuring all of it out. It could even be essential.

Or she'd miss the sound of voices so much that she'd start talking to the trees.

She turned back from the sea and noticed one more building that she hadn't explored. Set back from the shoreline, it was more of a squat tower than a cottage. Made of stone, it was two stories tall with a conical roof that was blanketed in snow. A lighthouse? Except it didn't have a light on top. A grain silo? She trudged across the snow toward the tower.

A key was dangling from a hook beside the door. She plucked it off and tried it in the lock. It opened easily, and she poked her head inside. "Hello?"

She was getting a bit tired of saying that, especially given how infrequently her greeting was returned, but still, she wasn't going to barge into a previously locked whatever-this-was.

What *was* this place?

Sunlight filtered in through murky windows and lit dust that floated in the air. It sparkled like flecks of gold above the sturdy worktable that stretched the length of the room. She walked inside. Every wall was filled with shelves that were overloaded by books, journals, and papers in haphazard stacks, to the dismay of her librarian heart. Gardening gloves and pots of various sizes were heaped in one corner. A desk piled precariously high with papers sat beside one of the filthy windows, facing the dock and the sea beyond.

It was very much the opposite of Yarrow's warm and tidy cottage. It looked more like a laboratory. Or a workroom of some kind? Not a living space. In one corner, she spotted a narrow set of stairs—perhaps they led to the owner's living quarters? She doubted that anyone lived here now. It was draped in the kind of undisturbed dust that only can accumulate in the absence of anyone. A cold stove sat in one corner of the room. Cobwebs clung to it, and Terlu shivered. It was clear that this place hadn't been used in years.

She touched one of the papers on the nearest shelf. It was stiff but not brittle to the point of dissolving into dust. *Definitely a workroom,* she decided. All the notes, the random garden supplies that looked more like unfinished experiments, and the overflowing desk . . . Terlu examined the desk. In the center of all the papers was a pot with a dried-up ball of leaves. The leaves had curled in on themselves as if hugging their core of desiccated soil.

She picked up the pot. "Oh, you poor thing."

Tucking it under her arm, Terlu prowled through the rest of the workroom, examining everything like a detective searching for clues. A pile of mostly burnt papers lay next to the stove. She knelt to look at them.

Why would any scholar burn their own work?

Studying the few words that were still legible, she realized she recognized them: this was written in the First Language, the extinct tongue of sorcerers—the language of spells.

Ah, it's a sorcerer's workroom.

This could have been the workroom of the sorcerer who'd made the greenhouse. It seemed likely. She wondered if there was a clue in this tower as to who the sorcerer was and why they'd done all of this. "Or I could be just jumping to conclusions," she said to the dead plant in the pot.

She wished that Yarrow wouldn't keep wandering off so quickly. She still had a hundred questions bubbling inside of her, and each minute she spent on this island seemed to generate more.

What had happened to the sorcerer? Why was this place abandoned? Why had the people left, abandoning their homes? Why had Yarrow stayed? Why had no one else come to fix the greenhouses? And why was she the one who'd been sent, when at last Yarrow's request had been answered?

Clearing a space, Terlu set the pot on the worktable and studied it. There had to be something special about this shriveled bit of plant to be the only one on the sorcerer's desk. His last experiment? His legacy? She wondered if she could determine what kind of plant it had been. Perhaps that would give her some insight into this place and its sorcerer. She reached into the pot and touched one of the brown curled-up leaves. Crisp, it felt like an autumn leaf. It looked fernlike, with a brittle, lacelike quality to the leaves, but it was difficult to tell, as shriveled as it was. If she added some water, would that plump it up more? If so, it could make it easier to see the shape of it. "What are you?" she whispered to it. "Tell me your secrets."

She went to the sink and pumped the pump a few times until water flooded out of the spout. Finding a glass, she rinsed it and then filled it with water. She supposed this was a silly idea. Even if the water did loosen up the leaves enough to examine the plant, the odds of her being able to identify it were low. She wasn't a plant expert. Still, though . . . it could be another question she could ask the gardener, the next time he popped up. He'd probably respond better to a plant question than an existential why-am-I-here-and-what's-the-purpose-of-my-life query.

Terlu poured the water over the knob of plant matter. She waited a minute for the moisture to sink into the leaves, and then she poked it to see if it had softened enough to unfurl.

The plant yawned, stretching out its leaves to reveal a deep purple bud.

"Ooh," Terlu said.

The bud unfolded to reveal purple petals. It looked a bit like a rose. She studied it before reaching in to touch one of the petals.

And then it spoke. "Just what do you think you're doing?"

Terlu felt her jaw drop open as she, wordless, stared at the impossible rose.

CHAPTER SEVEN

As a librarian who had once brought a spider plant to life, Terlu knew she should be uniquely suited to react in a sensible way to a talking rose. Still, when the moment came, she was completely flustered. "You're alive!"

"Ugh," the rose said, "you're one of *those*." It waved its lacelike leaves and pitched its voice high. "Ooh, a talking flower! How's it possible? She doesn't have a throat or lungs or lips. How can she be talking?"

"If you're really asking, the talking is due to a complex spell that involves seventeen ingredients and precise pronunciation of five lines of First Language text," Terlu said, "but what I should have said was: How are you alive after who knows how long without water, soil, or sunlight?"

The plant lowered its leaves sheepishly—*her leaves,* Terlu amended; the rose had referred to herself as "she." "Oh. Sorry," the rose said. "I thought you meant— Well, I can exist dormant for a number of years. I'm what's known as a resurrection rose. My name's Lotti."

"Nice to meet you, Lotti. I'm Terlu." She tried very hard not to gawk at the rose. She hadn't expected to find a sentient plant here, so soon after what happened with her spider plant. As far as she knew, they were rare. Was this fate? Or did the universe have a twisted sense of humor?

"You said 'who knows how long.' How long was I asleep? Years? How many years?"

It was a very good question—and one that Terlu sympathized with. *Six years,* echoed in her head. Judging by the state of the workroom and the layers of dust, it could have been far longer for Lotti. Terlu wished the gardener was willing to talk. She had even more questions now. "I don't know. I just got here myself. In fact, I'm not quite sure where *here* is." She wondered how much of her own story to tell the plant and decided it wasn't a secret. "You see, I was recently resurrected myself."

"I don't know what that means since you're a human and not, well, *me,* but I don't care enough to ask," Lotti said. "Let's find Laiken. I'm sure he can clear all of this up."

"Laiken?" Wait, was that the name of the gardener? No, he said his name was Yarrow. Did he know about Lotti? If so, why had he left her to shrivel in an abandoned workroom?

"You know Laiken. Bushy beard. Never combs his hair. Very powerful sorcerer who created the wonderous Enchanted Greenhouse of Belde."

Not the gardener then, and he didn't sound like anyone Terlu knew and certainly no one she'd seen here, but if the rose was talking about the sorcerer who had created all of this . . . the one who Yarrow had said died . . . *You don't know they're one and the same,* she told herself. She couldn't say he died when she wasn't certain they were talking about the same person.

Lotti began to vibrate and then, using her leaves as if they were legs, jumped several inches straight up to the rim of the pot before plopping back down. "Oof. One more try." She crouched, squishing her petals tight together, and then she leaped up with petals and leaves extended. On her second try, she nearly cleared the top of the pot.

"Do you want help?" Terlu offered.

"No, I got this." Third try, Lotti wound her leaves in a circle as if she were trying to build momentum. She only reached halfway up.

Fourth attempt, she tried to climb, using her leaves like arms.

"Really, I could just lift you—"

"Nope," Lotti puffed. "If you could not watch, please . . ."

Terlu turned aside politely and tried not to worry. She was glad that the water had helped Lotti—no one should be forced into that kind of not-life. Still, though . . .

I wish I hadn't been the one to wake her.

Given that she'd been convicted for bringing a plant to life, any judge who saw Lotti would be very, very suspicious. This time, Terlu hadn't cast a single spell, but would anyone really believe her? It felt like a terribly suspicious coincidence. To the outside, it would look like she'd been revived merely to make the same mistake again. She'd be popped right back into the North Reading Room if anyone knew. "It was an accident!" didn't sound plausible when it was a crime she'd already committed. *Even I would judge me guilty.*

If the first punishment was eternity as a statue, she couldn't even imagine what the fate for repeat offenders would be. The thought of being transformed again, of losing this precious second chance before it had even begun . . .

I can't let anyone find out.

Luckily there was no one here to—

The door banged open, and Yarrow filled the doorframe. In an exasperated voice, he said, "Are you *always* where you're not supposed to be?"

Terlu yelped. And panicked. Her mind started whirring like a pinwheel in a windstorm: *I can't go back—I can't go back—I can't—I can't.* She started feeling the squeeze in her throat that she'd felt when the spell was cast on her, and she remembered how her limbs had stiffened, how her eyes and her mouth had dried, how her heart had slowed while her mind panicked. She heard a plop and a tiny cheer as the rose successfully jumped out onto the table.

Quickly, Terlu scooped the rose back into her pot. "Shh, please. I'll be back. Promise," she whispered, and then she spun around to face Yarrow, who stood in the doorway. Words tumbled out of her mouth, high-pitched and silly-sounding, "Yes, of course, you're right, so sorry, I shouldn't be here. Silly me." She hurried across the work-room, grabbed Yarrow's arm, and propelled him out of the sorcerer's tower, back into the sunlight.

I can't lose this. I can't. I can't.

What could she say to distract him?

I could kiss him.

That would certainly distract him. But no, that was absurd. She barely knew him. Just because his golden lips looked kissable . . . No. What else? What was it she was supposed to be doing? Looking at cottages! "Of course this wasn't one of the cottages. I don't know what I was thinking. Clearly not for me. I did find one cottage that I think would do nicely."

"Good." He stared at her hand on his arm.

She stared at her hand too. It occurred to her that, until Yarrow, it had been six years since she'd touched anyone. Beneath his coat, his arm felt solid. Muscly. He probably spent a lot of time shoveling. Or hauling soil? She wasn't certain what gardeners did. Had she really had the idea to kiss him? What in all the islands was she thinking? *It's been even longer since I've kissed anyone.*

A moment passed.

Neither of them spoke.

Terlu removed her hand. "I'll show you." Backing away, she hoped he couldn't tell that her voice was shaky. She charged toward the road.

Behind her, he didn't move.

She thought for an instant that she'd messed it all up—he was going to go back into the workroom and see the sentient plant, and then she absolutely would look guilty after rushing out of there without explaining. *He'll never believe any explanation now.*

She shouldn't have tried to hide the rose.

And what was Lotti going to think of her? Terlu had essentially done what Yarrow had done to her, rushing off without any expla-nation. *I've mishandled all of this.*

But she didn't know how to fix it. Not immediately, at any rate.

As soon as Yarrow left her (which, based on their prior interactions, should be in less than three minutes), she could scurry back to Lotti and apologize profusely and explain. She'd tell the little rose everything: what she'd done and what had been done to her. Maybe the rose would understand.

Not many had understood. At the trial, she'd seen it in their eyes: disapproval, disappointment, pity. Especially pity from the other librarians. She wondered if anyone had told her family about her fate and what they had thought. She'd written to them every week up until her arrest, sometimes only a few lines—a description of a citrus tea that reminded her of home, a note about a shop with tools that Cerri might like, a request for a recipe, an anecdote about a street performer who'd danced with silk scarves.

She wondered what they'd thought of her silence after that. Had anyone told them about her fate? She half hoped they hadn't and that they'd thought their daughter died of natural causes, an illness or an accident, rather than that she'd caused her own downfall.

Yarrow didn't reenter the sorcerer's tower. Instead he merely locked it with the key and replaced it on the hook, which did make her wonder why he locked it at all—perhaps the door didn't latch firmly enough without the lock? *Or it's to discourage people like me from letting themselves inside.* He trotted down the path toward her, away from the resurrection rose, and she felt like she could breathe again. She flashed him a smile that she didn't feel and began to chatter about the various cottages: which ones she liked, which one had a flock of feral gryphons, and what work she'd need to do to make one livable.

"I have a chimney brush," he said, "and a ladder."

"Great!" She hurried toward the little blue cottage. "This is the one. What do you think?" She looked back at him in time to see his face fall. He recovered quickly, reverting to his unreadable stoic face that he wore so often. "You don't like it?"

"It's fine," he said. "It's perfect."

"I can choose another one."

"It's yours." He turned and began to stomp off, and she was going to let him this time. She had to return to Lotti, as well as work on the cottage.

Terlu glanced up at the sky. The sun had dipped behind the tips of the pine trees, and the snow was layered with shadows. She was never going to get the chimney cleaned out and the hearth prepared for a fire before it was fully dark. She should ask Yarrow for a lantern. "Yarrow . . ."

"Aren't you coming?"

"I . . . What? Where?" He wasn't just walking away again?

"You can't stay there tonight," Yarrow said over his shoulder. "It'll take a few days of work before the place is livable. Maybe weeks, if there are any leaks in the roof, unless you're good with roofs?"

She'd never fixed a roof in her life. Catching up to him, she said, "I can try."

He grunted.

Terlu realized after a few minutes of walking in silence that they were headed back to his cottage. She ran through the questions in her head and settled on the most recent: "Whose cottage was that, the blue one?"

"My sister's," Yarrow said.

"Oh. Is she . . ."

"Gone."

"I'm sorry."

He shook his head. "She's not . . . I mean, she left, with the others. She used to send letters . . . She's fine." Reaching his own cottage, he opened the door and held it for Terlu as she went inside.

She halted just inside the doorway and gawked. It was immediately obvious what was different. He'd moved in a second bed, wedged it in between the first bed and his desk, and piled it high with blankets and pillows. Curled in the center of the new bed was the winged cat, his emerald-green wings tucked around him. He opened one eye as they entered and then tucked his head closer, his nose under his paw.

Behind her, Yarrow closed the door and was hanging his coat on the hook. "I know it isn't luxurious, but the bedding is clean. Or it was, before Emeral shed fur and feathers all over it."

He sounded embarrassed, but she was amazed. Despite brushing her off before, he'd taken the time to haul in a new bed and made it so inviting that Emeral had already settled in. She'd thought Yarrow only wanted her off this island and out of his (gloriously streaked-with-gold) hair, or at least as far from him as possible, but this . . . This was kindness. She swallowed hard. It had been a while since someone was kind to her, she realized, even before the whole statue debacle. She'd tried so hard for so long to be friendly, to make friends, to be useful, to please, and she'd been told so often: *Stop trying so hard. You try too hard. Just . . . relax. Be yourself.* It was advice that she could never seem to take. Most recently, or recently six years ago, there'd been a librarian, a woman about her age on the third floor, who had agreed to meet her for tea once. Eilia. She'd had white-and-purple hair and a fondness for ginger cookies. But Terlu had pushed too hard to be friends and had ended up pushing her away. *You're a lot,* Eilia had told her, after she'd asked to meet up for the third time in the same week and baked her a tray of ginger cookies with orange zest. *It's nothing personal,* Eilia had said, *but at this point in my life, I don't have the time and energy for a lot.* It had felt quite personal. Shortly after, Terlu had stumbled across the spell to create an alive and aware plant . . . Anyway, this was nice. "Thank you."

He shrugged and looked away. "If you aren't comfortable, I can also stay in the greenhouse. I've done that before. It wouldn't be a problem."

"Oh no! I'd never kick you out of your cottage."

"I know I'm a stranger."

Cheerfully, she said, "A stranger is just a friend you haven't yet met." And then she winced. Had those words actually come out of her mouth? That was the kind of saying you said to four-year-olds, not to grown men who you'd be sleeping next to.

Wait. Sleeping next to?

With this configuration, she really would be sleeping inches away from him. She felt heat rising into her cheeks. "In winter when I was a kid, all the children in my home village used to sleep in a big pile in the same room around the stove. I thought it was so we could be together, but in retrospect, I think it was so the adults only had to feed a few fires instead of heating lots of separate houses. Those nights are some of my best memories."

"Hmm." It was a noncommittal noise, but better than silence.

Encouraged, Terlu asked, "You mentioned you have a sister?" He could try thinking of her like a sister, unless he didn't like her. Did he have fond memories of her?

"Mmm." He crossed to the kitchen. "Do you like zucchini?"

"What?"

"Zucchini." He glanced over his shoulder at her hopefully. "Also called courgette or baby marrow. It's a kind of summer squash that's edible if you harvest them when the seeds are immature. I like them roasted with black pepper."

She'd never had zucchini before. She'd also never encountered such an abrupt subject change. But if he didn't want to talk about his sister, that was fine. She wasn't going to push. "Sounds delicious. Can you grow vegetables year-round here?"

He brightened at the question. "There are four greenhouses devoted to edible plants, and they're each kept in a different season so that there is always one ready to harvest." He talked as he sliced zucchini, which looked like matte-green cucumbers to her. "There's also one greenhouse devoted exclusively to tomatoes, which are technically classified as fruit, despite their treatment in recipes."

"A whole greenhouse of only tomatoes?" It wasn't what she wanted to talk about, but she was happy that he was talking. He grew twice as animated when he was talking about his garden, his normally deep and gruff voice growing more excited. It was, frankly, adorable.

"Yes! They're sorted by shape: globe, beefsteak, cherry, grape, plum, and oxheart, as well as whether they're bush tomatoes or vining. We have every variety in the Crescent Islands Empire, which is three thousand seven hundred six. One of my cousins used to be able to identify the exact type of tomato by taste alone."

He had the most soothing voice she'd ever heard. Combined with the soft crackle of the fire and the warmth seeping into her, she felt all the muscles that had knotted up begin to unwind. She had to remind herself there was still a plethora of questions she needed him to answer. Otherwise, Terlu could have listened to him talk about tomatoes for hours. "Did that cousin live in one of the cottages too?"

"The round toadstool-like one, with his parents." He fell silent. He continued to slice zucchini, then laid out the medallions in a dish with a dollop of oil. Over on the bed, Emeral stretched, pushing at the pillows with his paws and arching his back.

Terlu waited to see if Yarrow would say more.

He didn't.

She pushed a little more. "When did they leave? Your family?"

"I was a kid when the sorcerer dismissed my cousin's family," Yarrow said.

Okay. So, a while ago. "And where did they go, after they left?"

"I heard they settled in Alyssium eventually, and Aunt Rin opened a florist shop that caters to nobles—my aunt wrote to my father a few times." He didn't look at her while he spoke. He focused only on the food, slicing tomatoes to lay on top of the zucchini.

"A florist shop sounds lovely."

He grunted and glanced at her. His eyes, she noticed, were as green as the zucchini. And he'd shaved, which made his cheeks look soft. His black-and-gold hair was tied back with a gold ribbon, and it occurred to her to wonder if he'd made an effort for her. *No,* she thought, *he's just a neat and orderly person.*

"What about the others?" she asked. "From the other cottages?"

He returned to his tomatoes before he answered. "A season later, Laiken dismissed Uncle Rorick, Finnel, and Percik, and they joined Aunt Rin's family in Alyssium."

Laiken—that was the name of the sorcerer who the rose was

looking for. *I shouldn't have left her.* "Why did he do it?" Terlu asked. "The sorcerer, I mean. Why did he send your family away?" She kept her voice soft and gentle, so as not to startle him back into silence again. It felt like trying to lure a feral cat to her hand. She was grateful for every tidbit of himself he shared with her.

He slid the dish of zucchini into the brick oven. "Said we didn't need so many gardeners running around the place. By the time he died, it was just my father and me."

She hadn't seen his father or any hint he was still here. Had he died too? How did she ask that? How long ago? "Your father . . ."

"He left too." Returning to the kitchen counter, he began to make a salad, chopping a fresh head of lettuce and dumping the leaves into a bowl.

At least his father hadn't died. She breathed easier. Still, though . . . "He left you? When? Why?" She knew she was being too nosy. Any second now, he was going to clam up and quit answering. But she wanted to know more about him, her rescuer.

"He was sick." Yarrow shrugged. He added a handful of red berries to the salad, followed by a handful of shelled sunflower seeds. "No doctors here."

That must have been incredibly hard, both for Yarrow and his father. She tried to imagine what it was like, to send your sick father away not knowing if he'd recover and to stay behind on an abandoned island not knowing if you'd survive. How long had Yarrow been alone? "When was that?"

He was quiet for a moment, and she wasn't sure he was going to answer. While the silence stretched, he mixed herbs with oil before pouring the freshly made dressing onto the salad. "About two years ago."

That was too long to live alone. Even with the company of a winged cat. Her heart went out to him, and she wished she dared reach out and hug him. "None of them came back to check on you? Or just to visit?"

He shrugged and set the salad on the table. He did it all with such smoothness that until it was on the table in front of her, she didn't realize it was the fanciest and freshest salad she'd ever been served.

"But you can't care for this many greenhouses on your own." She didn't have to know about gardening to know it was too much work for one person, especially if the magic that kept the greenhouses intact was failing. "Have you told them—"

"Can we . . ." He ducked his head so he wouldn't meet her eyes. ". . . not talk?"

Terlu felt her face flush. She shouldn't have pushed. It wasn't any of her business, and she barely knew him. She began to apologize. "I'm—"

A *thwack* sounded against the door.

The cat's ears twitched forward, but otherwise he didn't move.

"What was that?" Terlu asked.

He shrugged. *He does that a lot,* she thought. Shrugs and grunts seemed to be his favorite form of communication. It was a minor miracle she'd gotten so many words out of him. *Not a miracle. A mistake.* She should have waited until he was ready to open up to her. Her curiosity wasn't more important than his comfort. She needed to be more patient and not—

Another *thwack.*

"Snow falling off the roof," Yarrow said.

From outside, a voice screeched, "Let me in!"

Who was— *Oh.*

"I can explain," Terlu began as Yarrow opened the door.

On the step, in the snow, the resurrection rose shivered. *"Finally."*

CHAPTER EIGHT

The rose hopped inside the cottage, using her leaves to propel her forward. Once she was on the mat, she shook like a dog, spattering bits of snow that melted into tiny puddles.

"Ahh . . ." Yarrow said, staring at her.

"You. Left. Me." Lotti had a very piercing voice for a plant no larger than a fist.

Terlu wished she could sink into the floor. "I'm sorry. I panicked. I was going to come back." Every word felt pathetic in her ears. She hung her head. Out of the corner of her eye, she saw the winged cat was eyeing the little rose with interest. His tail flicked back and forth. Stepping in front of the cat to block his view, she murmured, "Emeral, don't you dare."

Yarrow's mouth opened and closed and opened again. "How did— Who are—"

The little plant drew herself up taller, all three inches of her. She opened her purple petals wide. "I'm Lotti the Resurrection Rose, and I demand to see Laiken, Master Sorcerer and the Creator of the Glorious and Magnificent Greenhouse of Belde."

The cat spread his wings and began to shift back and forth on his hind paws.

Yarrow shook his head and tried again. "What did you mean she left you? Where did you come from? How did you—"

Terlu jumped in quickly. "I didn't create her. I know you aren't going to believe me, but all I did was—" Before she could finish explaining to either Lotti or Yarrow, Emeral launched himself out of the bed, wings spread. Terlu tried to grab him, but he soared over her head, and her fingers merely brushed the tips of his feathers. On the floor, Lotti shrieked. Spinning around, Terlu dove for her, hoping to reach her before—

Miscalculating, Terlu bumped into the side of the table. The pitcher of lilacs fell over, and water spilled across the table and onto the floor. Landing in the water, the cat skidded, his paws splaying out. He flapped his wings frantically, crashing into the desk and knocking the stack of papers over, while Lotti tried to scramble away from all of it.

After catching her balance, Terlu scooped Lotti into her hands. The little plant was sopping wet and also prickly. And *not* happy.

"You wake me, abandon me, and then let me be attacked by a monster? What kind of person are you?" Lotti was so furious that she was vibrating. She also seemed to be expanding—her leaves were plumper than they had been. The extra water was good for her, Terlu noted.

"He's not a monster," Terlu said. "He's a cat."

Yarrow was staring at her, the resurrection rose, the winged cat (who was licking his feathers on the hearth), the puddle on the table and floor, and the mess of papers on his desk.

Terlu felt panic rising up in her throat. She shouldn't have left Lotti. She should have tried to explain to Yarrow right away. Maybe he would have believed her if she had just taken a risk and trusted him. "I can explain."

"I demand to be taken to Laiken right now," Lotti said. "You obviously don't know how to care for a plant." She squirmed out of Terlu's hands and landed on the table.

Flinching, Terlu felt as if she'd been slapped. She thought of Caz, her spider plant. She hadn't been able to protect him either—he'd been taken from her as soon as what she'd done had been discovered. She'd seen him once at the trial, when he'd been presented as evidence, but she hadn't even been allowed to speak with him, not even to say goodbye. *I would've liked to have said goodbye.* She'd begged the head librarian to make sure he was okay and that he had people who would make sure he wasn't lonely and that he had the right kind of soil and that he watered himself often enough but not too often—Rijes Velk had promised she would, but had she? Was Caz safe? Was he happy? Did he miss her? *I miss him.* "You're right," Terlu said quietly.

Ignoring the puddle, Yarrow knelt by the table, eye level with Lotti. "You're . . . By the sea," he swore. "You're one of Sorcerer Laiken's creations. I thought that all of them—" He cut himself off. "Is there anything you need? Fresh soil? More nutrients?"

Using a kitchen towel, Terlu started to mop up the puddle around the pitcher. She then intercepted Emeral as he began to stalk toward the table. Scooping him in her arms, she cradled him and petted his cheek. Liking that, he folded his wings and purred.

"I'm quite well as is," Lotti said, sounding mollified. "I'm not a high-maintenance plant. I can take care of myself, now that I'm awake. If I have access to water. And if I'm not torn apart by a vicious feline."

Lifting his eyes, Yarrow looked at Terlu. "I knew you had to be a sorcerer!"

There was so much hope in his face that she wanted to say she was, just so he wouldn't stop looking at her as if she were the first star in the sky, but it wasn't the kind of thing you lied about. It was one thing to tell a library patron that their hair looked nice when it didn't; it was quite another to claim you were a different kind of person entirely. "I'm not," Terlu said. "And I didn't break any laws. I didn't cast any spells. All I did was give her some water. She came to life on her own. She must have just been dormant."

His face fell, and she felt as if she'd disappointed a puppy.

Emeral squirmed in her arms.

"Can you *please* control your monster?" Lotti asked.

Yarrow opened one of his kitchen drawers and took out a roll of red ribbon. Unrolling it, he dangled it in the air. Eyeing it, Emeral launched himself out of Terlu's arms at the ribbon. Yarrow released it, and the cat flew up into the rafters with his prize.

"Clever," Terlu said.

Lotti slapped one of her leaves against the table. "Can we get back to talking about me? What were you about to say about Laiken's creations? You thought all of them were what? You need to finish that sentence. No, never mind. Just take me to Laiken. He'll explain it all."

Terlu met Yarrow's eyes. He'd said that name earlier. Laiken was the sorcerer who'd made these greenhouses, the one who had dismissed Yarrow's family, the one who'd died and left his creation to decay and fail.

"I can't . . . He isn't . . ." Yarrow ran his hand through his hair.

He's not going to find the words. She gave him a moment more, but he continued to look as if he wanted to disappear out the door and vanish into the snow. Gently, Terlu said to Lotti, "He passed away."

"He . . . When? How?" she squeaked. "No, it can't be true. Of course, it's true. His workroom . . . It's full of dust and cobwebs. I should have known as soon as I saw it. Oh, my Laiken!" The rose's petals tightened, closing her into a bud again.

Yarrow glanced at Terlu as if he expected her to know what to say.

Tentatively, Terlu asked, "Do you want to talk about it?"

Lotti widened her blossom and shouted, "No! I do not want to talk about it! I want to meet the sorcerer in charge, whoever inherited the greenhouse from Laiken. Take me to them!"

Clearing his throat, Yarrow said, "There hasn't been a sorcerer since Laiken. He never took an apprentice or a partner or named a successor. He wouldn't allow anyone new on the island. He didn't trust anyone else not to destroy what he'd built."

Lotti's petals drooped. "He got worse then."

Terlu sat on a chair beside her. "What do you mean?"

She sighed heavily, her leaves shaking. "I wish I'd been there, at the end. He might have listened to me. Oh, you should have seen him when he was young! He was like sunshine just to be near. He built this place as a gift to the world."

"I didn't know him when he was young," Yarrow said. "He was already over one hundred when I was born. In the time I knew him, he didn't listen to anyone."

"He only wanted to protect us," Lotti said. "All of us and all of this."

Terlu knew some sorcerers were long-lived, but even if Laiken had expected to never die, it was still unforgivable that he'd left Yarrow here with a massive, sprawling greenhouse to care for all by himself. He could have trained an apprentice or left arrangements for another sorcerer to care for the island's enchantments or even simply hired more gardeners. It was too vast for one person, with or without magic, and no one should be asked to shoulder such an enormous burden on their own. It was far too much responsibility. Endless work with no reprieve.

"I must have been asleep for a long time," Lotti said softly, sadly. "I don't know you, either of you, which means he must have let me stay dormant . . . a very long time."

Yarrow nodded.

"I just arrived," Terlu volunteered. "You wouldn't have known me."

Lotti wiggled her roots around to face her blossom toward Terlu. "And your first act was to wake and abandon me? Don't think I have forgiven you for that, because I haven't."

"I . . ." How did she explain she'd been afraid? That wasn't an excuse. She'd been cruel to leave Lotti like that, especially since she knew better—she knew how she'd felt waking alone and confused and cold in the forest. "I'm sorry." The words felt insufficient.

"Humph," Lotti said.

Yarrow pulled on his coat. "There's something I should show you."

"Me?" Terlu asked. She was surprised he still wanted to talk with her. He had to think the worst of her now. She was fully aware of how badly she'd messed up.

"Her," Yarrow said with a nod toward the resurrection rose.

She felt herself blush. *Of course he didn't mean me.* She thought of all the times when she'd waved at someone waving at her, only to realize they were waving at a person behind her—this felt the same, except magnified. *He never wanted me here.* She was a mistake.

Belatedly, he added, "You can come too. If Lotti is all right with that."

The rose lifted her petals into the air. "You may come if you carry me. Gently."

Feeling as small as a worm, Terlu scooped up the little plant and tucked her within her coat. She followed Yarrow out the door, back into the snow. It was closer to sunset now, with the low light causing the trees' shadows to stretch out long on the white snow.

He led them into the greenhouse.

Lotti let out a little gasp. "It's grown so much! Oh, Laiken, I wish you were here!" Her voice hitched in a sob.

Yarrow didn't speak as he led them through the path. That seemed to be the way he was—not someone who was used to much chitchat. She wondered if that meant he was the kind of person who liked silence or who just liked other people to fill the silence.

Either way, she got the distinct sense that he didn't like her very much.

Lotti was not overly fond of her either.

I've messed everything up.

How could she fix this? There was always a solution, unless one got oneself stuck as a statue, but even that wasn't finite, as it turned out. *I'll find a way to make it up to them. Somehow.*

Terlu was still trying to figure out what to do or say when Yarrow led them through a side door to yet another greenhouse that she hadn't seen before. She wondered if there was a map to all the rooms somewhere, or maybe she could make one.

This greenhouse was smaller, with only a few plants. Just a handful of pots were on the shelves—a few were flowers, such as an orchid and a daisy. One was a small bush with clumps of thin leaves. Another was an ivy that swept from the top shelf to the floor.

"Oh!" Lotti said.

"What?" Terlu asked.

"I know this room. Yes. I know these shelves, these pots, this air." She then screeched at the top of her lungs—if she'd had lungs, "WAKE UP!"

There was silence. Only the hum of the stove in the center of the greenhouse, and the sound of gravel under Yarrow's feet as he walked down the row, surveying the pots. Like the other rooms, it smelled of fresh dirt and clean air, but with so few plants, it only smelled very faintly of green growth and flowers. It reminded Terlu a bit of a near-empty hospital: clean, silent, waiting.

"Water them," Lotti commanded.

"I have watered them," Yarrow said. "It doesn't make a difference."

"Try again."

Crossing the greenhouse to a pump, he filled a watering can and returned to the pots. He added water to each of them, checking the soil to make sure the water was the appropriate level of moisture for the type of plant. Some he only gave a few drops; others he filled until their pots dripped. When he finished, he set the can down and stood beside Terlu and Lotti.

"Why aren't they already awake?" Lotti asked. "Are they . . . They're not dead. I can see they aren't." Her voice was shaking more and more with each word. She jumped out of Terlu's hands and landed beside one of the pots. "Come on, please wake up! Don't leave me alone! Laiken is gone. I can't lose you too!"

Terlu looked around the room as she slowly realized what these plants had in common, or more accurately, what Lotti and Yarrow both thought they did: They were supposed to be like Lotti. Like Caz.

But for some reason, they weren't.

A thought hit her like a thunderclap:

It's not a coincidence that I'm here.

Yarrow was talking. "I must have been . . . around eight or nine? . . . when they went silent. It was the first indication we got that there could be something wrong with the magic, though it was years before any of the greenhouses themselves failed. *That* only began after Laiken's death."

"You have to wake up," Lotti pleaded.

As Lotti continued to beg the plants to talk to her, Terlu turned the words over in her head: *It's not a coincidence. I'm meant to be here.* They felt right. True. Yarrow had appealed to the capital for a sorcerer to help his plants, which included a greenhouse of enchanted plants who were supposed to be awake and aware but weren't, and in response, they'd sent Terlu Perna.

While Lotti pleaded with the silent plants, Terlu asked Yarrow, "Who sent me here?"

His eyes were glued to the little rose.

"Please," Terlu begged, "I need to know."

Glancing at her, he withdrew a letter from the inner pocket of his jacket and handed it to her. "My request was passed around awhile before it was answered. A long while." He then shifted his focus back to Lotti, who was pleading with a silent philodendron.

Terlu opened the envelope and unfolded the letter. It was on very familiar stationery, emblazoned with the seal of the Great Library of Alyssium. She felt the silken softness of the paper, and she smelled the rich, dusty scent of the stacks held within the fibers. There was a humming in her head, and she made herself sit down cross-legged on the gravel path while she read the words. It was written in an elegant hand and very brief. Addressed to the Head Gardener of Belde, Yarrow Verdane, it said that the writer hoped to provide a solution to multiple problems at once, and it directed Yarrow in how to perform the spell that would release Terlu, with the spell written out phonetically and a clear list of ingredients.

It said nothing of who Terlu was or why she was a statue or why she was sent here, nor did it mention any pardon or any official end of her sentence.

But there was a signature at the bottom, in clear swooping letters: Rijes Velk, the head librarian of the Great Library of Alyssium.

She'd sworn in court that Terlu wouldn't work magic again, staked her reputation on it. Yet she'd sent Terlu here, with a spell to be cast illegally—why?

A solution to multiple problems, she'd written.

Terlu's heart beat faster as she turned those words over in her head.

In front of her, Lotti was screaming at the philodendron to wake and crying for Laiken to come back, to not be dead, to not leave them like this. Yarrow was trying (and failing) to console her. He had a panicked look on his face, as if he were seconds from fleeing.

I know why I was sent here.

"I'm supposed to wake them," Terlu said out loud.

CHAPTER NINE

It was the only explanation that made sense.

Yarrow stared at her. "What do you mean?"

Using her leaves, Lotti shook a pot as she shouted, "Wake up, wake up, wake up!"

Terlu wrapped her arms around herself, but it didn't make her feel any safer or less exposed. She didn't know how Rijes Velk had gotten her statue out of the Great Library and all the way to the island of Belde, but she very much doubted it was with anyone's permission. If she were here, Terlu would've asked her how she'd done it. You didn't just remove a full-size human statue from the library without anyone noticing, especially from as prominent and well-guarded a site as the North Reading Room. She couldn't imagine how the head librarian had managed it. She hoped Rijes hadn't endangered herself in the process. But regardless of how . . .

It seemed clear to her that regardless of *how,* these plants were *why.* It was far too much of a coincidence otherwise. She was guilty of plant magic; suddenly, here she was in an enchanted greenhouse that needed magical help.

"Rijes Velk thinks I can help," Terlu said.

"Can you?" Yarrow asked.

Her throat felt closed. Unable to form the words, she shook her head. She couldn't use magic again. *I don't want to go back.*

If Yarrow knew what she'd done, if he knew she was a convicted criminal, he'd . . .

He was looking at her, his green eyes wide, unreadable.

He wouldn't do anything, she realized with a start. *Because they'd arrest him too.*

He wasn't a sorcerer, yet he'd cast a spell to restore her. If he turned her in, he'd have to admit where she came from and what he'd done—he'd be in as much danger as her. He wasn't going to turn her in.

I can trust him.

She trusted the head librarian, and Rijes Velk had sent her to him.

"Then why did you say . . ." Yarrow began.

"Because I did it before. Or I did something closely related. I . . . cast a spell." Terlu had to look away, afraid of what she'd see in his eyes: disapproval, disappointment, pity. "I hadn't planned to. I discovered the spell while I was cataloging journals from the collection of a late sorcerer . . ." It was only when she stumbled on one of the rare ingredients in a shop that sold gently used accessories, she started to daydream about it. "It was like a game at first, seeing if I could find the ingredients. No, not a game. An intellectual exercise. I told myself that perhaps I'd write a paper about the difficulty in casting a complex spell. Not that anyone would publish it. I'm not a sorcerer or a professor. But it was a fascinating challenge—the spell itself is linguistically convoluted, with unfamiliar words that you do *not* want to mispronounce." She'd heard plenty of cautionary tales of sorcery gone wrong—they were presented as proof of why the stricter laws against spellcasting were necessary. Once, a sorcerer was trying to start a fire and instead he set himself aflame. Another time, a young sorcerer tried to summon a water horse to carry her across the waves, but instead she drew a herd and destroyed her village. And another time, a young girl had experimented with a spell and lost ten years before she was discovered—she'd transformed herself into a rock. Moss had grown on her by the time her family finally found her. "But I became more convinced that I could do it.

I researched the history of the words in the spell, studying their etymology, until I was certain of each one. Over the course of multiple months, I located every ingredient."

Lotti had stopped shaking the pots and was now listening to Terlu. She hopped closer to Yarrow, who hadn't said a word. Terlu felt the weight of their silence, thick and heavy as a blanket of snow. She hugged her arms over her chest, the letter from Rijes Velk clutched tight.

This wasn't a story she'd wanted to tell to an audience. She'd done it once already, and she was never going to forget the condemnation in the judge's eyes or the vicious victory in the imperial investigator's. But she'd started, and now she had to finish. "His name was Caz, and he was a spider plant. He was kind, he was smart, and he was funny, and they took him from me as soon as they found him." She risked a glance at Yarrow.

He was holding himself very still, watching her as if she were a bird that might startle and fly away. She couldn't read what he was thinking, but she didn't see disapproval or pity. If anything, she would name the look in his eyes *hope*.

"They wanted to make an example of me," Terlu said, "and so they sentenced me to be transformed into a statue. There was to be no reprieve." In the spaces between words, she could still hear the drums that sounded after her sentence had been announced. She imagined she'd be hearing those drums echoing inside her for the rest of her life.

"But I was sent the spell to revive you," Yarrow said.

"Luckily for me, not everyone agreed with my sentence." Holding up the letter, she showed him the seal and the signature. Lotti hopped closer to see too. "It's signed by the head librarian at the Great Library of Alyssium, the woman who defended me at my trial. I don't know how, but somehow she got your letter and thought I . . ."

"*'I hope to provide a solution to multiple problems at once,'*" Yarrow read.

Lotti gave a high-pitched shriek. "You know the spell to wake them!"

Terlu shook her head. "I don't." She'd cast a spell to create a sentient plant, not wake one. "And even if I did, I can't cast it. I can't . . . I can't face that again. You don't know what it was like. The silence. The helplessness. The loneliness." *Please don't ask me to.* Except that she had already been asked, indirectly at least, by the one woman who had shown her kindness during the nightmare of her trial—the woman who had saved her.

"We wouldn't ask you to do something you don't want to do," Yarrow said.

"*You* wouldn't," Lotti said in a growl. "*I* would."

The mere act of telling them what she'd done and what she could do was almost akin to volunteering, but still . . . She felt as if she had a lump the size of a fist in her throat. It was hard to swallow, hard to breathe. The drums in her head were as loud as they'd ever been.

"You could cast it," the rose said, "but you won't. Coward. These plants are innocent."

Terlu flinched. It wasn't that she didn't want to help, but . . . "If I'm caught . . ." She closed her eyes. It was far too easy to remember how it felt, without a breath, without a heartbeat, without a voice. *A solution to multiple problems at once.* The words echoed in her head.

"You won't be caught," Yarrow said.

"You don't know that." Terlu opened her eyes again. He had moved, stopping inches in front of her. She had to tilt her head up to look at his face—his eyes earnest, his lips soft. She read sympathy, understanding, maybe resolve, but not pity. *He has a kind face,* she thought.

"I do," Yarrow said. His hands twitched as if he wanted to touch her, but he didn't. He kept his arms by his side. "There's no one here. Just me. And Lotti. There's no one but us on all of Belde. You're safe."

"We'd never, ever betray you if you do this!" Lotti cried. "They'd have to pry it out of me with a hand trowel! No, with *pruning shears.*

Please, Terlu Perna. Without Laiken . . ." Her voice broke. "Please, these plants are all the family I have left. Please, wake them."

"I . . ." She looked at Lotti, at Yarrow, and then at the letter from Rijes Velk, the woman she most trusted and admired in all the Crescent Islands Empire. It was clear what they wanted her to do. The words of the letter were louder than the remembered drumbeats.

"Please, Terlu," Lotti said. "Without them, I'm alone."

Terlu raised her eyes to gaze at the plants—asleep, silent, and drifting in and out of nothingness, like she had been. She knew what that was like, to be held in a prison within your own body, alive but unable to live. "I don't know the exact spell—waking a sentient plant is a different task than creating one—but I would recognize it if I saw it, for example in a sorcerer's workroom."

"And once you saw it?" Yarrow asked.

She met his green, hope-filled eyes. "Once I have the words . . . I can cast it."

It was past sunset when they reached the late sorcerer's tower. Inside, it was shrouded in shadows until Yarrow lit the lanterns that hung from hooks on the wall. He placed a few on the worktable as well. Soon a warm amber light spread across the table, desk, and shelves. It was still chilly but not as shadowy.

"Where do you want to begin?" Yarrow asked.

Just inside the workroom, Terlu froze for an instant—it was a simple question, but he said it with such trust that, for a heartbeat, she forgot to breathe. *He trusts me.*

Cradled in Terlu's hands, Lotti piped up. "How about we begin by putting me down?"

"Right. Of course." Terlu set Lotti down on the worktable.

The little rose waddled over to one of the jars, examining herself in the reflection. "Ooh, I'm looking nice and prickly." She twisted to view her leaves from another angle.

"You look great," Terlu told her.

Lotti sniffed. "Obviously."

The workroom, on the other hand, did not look great.

Terlu unbuttoned her coat, then shivered as she scanned the room with her hands on her hips. It wasn't as cold as the outside, but it was close. Now . . . where to begin? The desk? The shelves? Maybe she should start with the worktable, since it held the sorcerer's in-progress experiments? Or maybe she should start upstairs in the sorcerer's living quarters?

Or maybe I shouldn't be doing this at all. What if this is all a truly terrible idea? "Just . . . once more, before we really begin . . . you don't think this is a mistake?"

Lotti flapped her petals. "Ugh! How can it be a mistake to save lives?"

"You won't be . . ." Yarrow stopped. ". . . statued? Statue-ified?"

I was right, there's no word for it. "I didn't think I would be before. I wasn't harming anyone. I didn't think anyone would mind. What makes it different this time?"

"This time," he said simply, "you aren't doing it alone."

There were no more perfect words he could have said.

Still . . . "I'm going to look upstairs first. He might have kept his most important notes closest to him." She managed to walk across the workroom without looking as if she wanted to flee.

Lotti hopped across the table toward the cold fireplace. "How's the chimney? Can we light a fire? And by 'we,' I mean 'you,' garden boy, because that's obviously not my thing." She waved her leaves. "I don't want to be tinder."

Yarrow stuck his head beneath the chimney. "A few abandoned nests. Some cobwebs. But it'll be fine for handling the exhaust from the stove." Opening up the wood-burning stove, he added, "Might smell a bit."

Leaving them to figure it out themselves, Terlu climbed the stairs. She held on to the walls as the steps creaked and groaned. Halfway up, she halted—the drums were loud again in her memory, or maybe that was just her heartbeat.

This time, she told herself, *it'll be different.*

This time, she wasn't doing it for herself—Lotti needed this, so did Yarrow. And the sleeping plants. Firmly, she took all of her doubts and fears, wadded them into a ball, and shoved them down. She climbed the rest of the way up. *I have to help them.*

Resolved, she took a deep breath of the dusty air . . . and coughed.

Upstairs was sad, drab, and mostly bare. A bed with dusty sheets and blankets was in the center of the room. A grimy mirror hung on one wall. Curtains were pulled over the windows, keeping it all dark and shadowed. No desk. No bookshelves. Only a bedside table with a solitary notebook on it.

Terlu picked up the notebook—her fingers felt instantly grimy— and blew the dust off its green leather cover. Flipping through, she saw it was handwritten, and the notes quit halfway through. The rest was blank. Perhaps it was his most recent notebook? If so, it wasn't going to be of much use. She needed spells from his early work, from when he established the Greenhouse of Belde and first created the sentient plants. Closing it, she wondered what this sorcerer would think of her searching for his spell. Would he support her or condemn her? These were his plants, after all. *Perhaps he'd approve.*

Out of the corner of her eye, she saw a dusty mirror with a hint of herself: brown untamed curls, round lavender face, slightly frightened purple eyes. And then a shadow flitted across the mirror.

Terlu glanced behind her—no one was there.

Still, she shivered. There was something unsettling about the abandoned bedroom. Even though the sorcerer was long gone, she couldn't help feeling as if the shadows were watching her. It felt like the kind of place that held ghosts.

"Sorry for intruding," she said out loud.

No one answered.

There's no one here. Just my imagination.

She'd never encountered a ghost herself, but she'd heard plenty of stories. On the sixth floor of the Great Library, it was said that the ghost of a librarian lingered in the stacks, unwilling to rest until she'd read every book in her section. The current librarian would leave a new book open each week, flipping the pages every so often.

Terlu wouldn't have minded the company of such a ghost, but she hadn't had the seniority to be allowed up on the sixth floor.

Regardless, there was nothing useful in the late sorcerer's bedroom.

Taking the green-leather-bound notebook with her, she returned downstairs. "Looks like he kept all his work downstairs." She dropped the notebook onto the table and then shed her coat and scarf. The workroom was already warmer now that the fire was lit. "This was the only item up there, and it's too recent to be useful."

"Not surprised to hear it," Lotti said. "He worked here. Slept there. But it was still a good idea to check."

"Only thing upstairs is the remnant of his memory," Yarrow said. "Unless the bats came back. I had to clear out an infestation of bats the first winter after Laiken died. Relocated them to the island caves. You didn't see bats, did you?"

"No bats. Just dust and a lot of creepy shadows."

Defensively, Yarrow said, "Cleaning abandoned buildings hasn't been my priority."

"It wasn't a criticism," she said quickly. "You've done amazing, especially on your own, with all the greenhouses and your own cottage and no one else to—"

Lotti slapped the table with her leaves impatiently. "Yes, yes, he's great, but my friends are comatose. Can we get back to that? You know, before you lose your nerve and I have to face the fact that the man who was like a father to me is gone—long gone—and my siblings and friends are, like, one step up from inanimate objects."

"Sorry. Yes, of course." *I won't lose my nerve. I'm doing this.* Terlu began to riffle through the brittle papers. Hundreds of loose papers were strewn over the table, coated with a layer of dust. "The first step is to figure out the organizing principle behind all his notes."

Hopping up onto the top of a thick dust-laden book, Lotti gave a flowery snort. "Laiken was a brilliant man. A revolutionary mind, bursting with creativity. He was capable of leaps that other sorcerers could only dream of. But he was not organized. He was constantly losing his socks . . ." Trailing off, she let out a little sob. "Ah, Laiken."

"How do you constantly lose socks?" Terlu asked, her voice light, wishing she could hug the little rose. "Don't you just keep them on your feet?"

"He had itchy toes," Lotti said.

By the stove, Yarrow grunted. "That's more than I wanted to know."

"It was probably a fungus," Lotti said.

"Much more than I wanted to know."

Lifting a paper up to the lantern light, Terlu frowned at the words. "This isn't . . ." She turned the paper sideways and then upside down. "Huh. That's . . . odd."

Concerned, Yarrow asked, "What's wrong?"

"I can't read it," she admitted.

"Let me see," the rose said. "Ah, it's in the First Language. You found a spell!"

Terlu took the paper back and scowled at it again. "It's not. I can read the First Language, and this . . ." It was extremely unusual for her to encounter a language she couldn't read even slightly. Fascinating, really. She should at least be able to sort out the root of the words, if not their precise meaning, but the etymology of these phrases eluded her, as if they weren't even . . .

"You can read First Language?" Lotti asked, awed.

"Yes, fluently. And this isn't it. How old was Laiken?" Terlu asked. Perhaps he'd written in an extinct language? One that shared some of its linguistic markers with the First Language? She didn't know every extinct language, though she'd encountered many of them in her studies. When the Crescent Islands united under its first emperor, there had been a concerted effort to standardize the language of the islands—a practical convenience that, in its often brutal enforcement, had led to the terrible loss of many beautiful languages and dialects. She mourned the lost languages.

"He never said," Yarrow replied, joining them at the worktable. "He was ancient, though. Lived well beyond an ordinary lifespan. How can I help?"

"Are you good with languages?" Terlu asked.

"Not at all. But I can clean the table." He began neatening the worktable, starting by carrying anything made of glass or ceramic—beakers, tubes, jars, pots, cups, mugs, plates, saucers, bowls—over to the wide sink on the side. He filled the sink with soapy water and dunked them in. She watched him for an instant, then returned to studying the sorcerer's texts.

Lotti scooted herself forward so that she was directly in front of Terlu. "I want to help! I demand you let me help!" Her petals were rolled up like little fists.

"Sure," Terlu said absently. She continued to stare at the vaguely familiar yet not-quite-right words. Putting it down, she picked up another sheet of paper, and this one was written in standard island speech. Same handwriting. It was a list of supplies for the greenhouse. "We need to identify which papers are important and which are day-to-day minutiae. I am thinking that the less important texts are going to be in standard Crescent Island speech and the spells will be in the First Language. We can make a third pile for the unknown language and figure out its significance later." She skimmed the next page. A recipe for potato soup, using twelve varieties of potatoes and fistfuls of roasted garlic. "Lotti, how about you do the first sort, and then pass the interesting ones to me?" She picked up the paper in the unknown language again. It bothered her that she didn't recognize it as any of the languages she'd studied. The pattern of words was familiar, but the letters . . . They shouldn't be combined in that way. Belatedly, she realized that Lotti hadn't budged. "Sorry. You don't have to, if you don't want to. Would you rather do something else?" She hadn't meant to boss the plant around.

"You . . . you want me to . . ."

Terlu glanced at Yarrow. She didn't know what she'd said to upset the little rose.

"You trust me to . . ." Lotti sniffled. "I didn't think you'd say yes. He never let me help, no matter how badly I wanted to. Said I was too little, that I was to look pretty and not . . ." The rose appeared to be crying, even though she had no eyes and no tear ducts. Water pooled on the tips of her purple petals. "I'd always ask, and he'd always say no."

Yarrow dabbed her petals with a towel.

"Thank you," she sniffed.

"When I was little," Yarrow said, "I wanted to help one of my uncles cut firewood. That was his job every winter, and I know it was an important one—we needed cut wood to survive. But my father told me I was too little. I wouldn't be able to lift the axe. I'd hurt myself. I hated hearing that."

"What did you do?" Lotti asked. "Did you do it anyway?"

He shrugged. "My uncle taught me how to properly stack wood, so it wouldn't rot, and I did that instead." Without adding anything more, he resumed washing the beakers and bowls.

"That was a terribly unsatisfying story," Lotti complained. She turned to Terlu. "Was he trying to make a point? I think he was." Raising her voice, she called to Yarrow, "Hey, garden boy, did that have a moral? Am I supposed to stack wood? Wait, no, never mind. I don't care. *My* point is I was never allowed to help at all. I was decorative."

What a terrible thing to tell someone. "You're more than decorative," Terlu said. Her resolve to help the little rose strengthened. She deserved to have her friends around her, supporting her, especially while she mourned.

"I most certainly am!" The rose vaulted herself over a crumpled-up paper. Using her leaves, she picked up a page and then abandoned it. "Not that one." She moved to the next. "Nope, boring. Ah, here's an unreadable one." She passed it to Terlu.

Terlu started a pile for each type of paper, while Yarrow cleaned around her. Wordlessly, he lifted up the stack and dusted underneath it, and then he cleaned a stool for her to sit on. Perching on it, she continued examining the pages, while Lotti sorted.

Yarrow began to hum to himself as he cleaned, which was more than a little surprising to hear. He didn't seem like the humming type, but she liked it. It made the workroom feel more alive. It also helped that the stove was beginning to pump out heat.

As they continued to work, she began to feel more and more convinced that she was doing the right thing. This wasn't a terrible, horrible mistake that was going to lead to her being re-statue-ified. *It's the right thing to do.*

Outside, the wind picked up, and she heard it whistle through the pine trees. She was grateful for the crackling fire inside the stove and for the light from the lanterns. As she studied the pages that Lotti passed to her, she began to notice a pattern. It wasn't so much that she recognized the language. It was—

"It's a code," she said out loud.

Yarrow looked over from the bookshelf, where he was straightening volumes. Lotti was trying to knock away a smudge of soil she'd left on one of the papers. "A code?" the rose said. "Oh, that makes sense. He *did* worry all the time that people would misuse his spells. I don't know what he thought they'd do, specifically, or who 'they' were, but it was one of his favorite rants."

Now that Terlu knew what she was looking at, the arrangement of letters made much more sense. She still couldn't read it, of course, but she understood *why* she couldn't read it. "He wrote his spells and his notes on spells in code."

She glanced over at the pile of burnt pages. Any spell he hadn't written in code he must have burned. *Wow, that was . . . cautious of him.* But it did match what Lotti had said about him—he hadn't started out like the kind of person who would put his notes into code, but by the end, he'd become one. Something had changed him, and what remained in his workroom was the detritus of his fear.

"Can you crack it?" Yarrow asked.

That was an excellent question. "It depends what kind of code it is. If he did a simple one, such as shifting the alphabet, it will be easy, but I doubt he did anything that straightforward. If I can find a text that I recognize . . ." Perhaps a spell she knew, or even just a common phrase. She could use that to crack the rest. "Or there might be the key to the code somewhere in this room. A codebook." She didn't know if Laiken would've written his secret down or trusted himself to remember it. "Lotti, you knew him. Do you think Laiken would have created a codebook?"

Lotti considered it. "I never saw one. If he had one, wouldn't he have had to consult it?"

Excellent point. "If that's true, then it has to be the kind of code that isn't impossible to remember, which means it won't be impossible to crack." She felt more and more excited. She hadn't had a puzzle like this to unravel in . . . Well, she had no idea how long. Certainly not since the last time she was flesh. "I need to find more examples." With enough texts to compare, it should be possible.

All three of them set to work:

Yarrow piled papers and journals into a stack, combing the workroom to find more, while Lotti scanned through them, dismissing most to the "useless" pile and the rest to the "possibly not hopeless" pile. Perched on her stool, Terlu studied the growing number of examples written in code.

Outside, the night deepened. Moonlight glistened on the snow, making the windows of the workroom almost seem to glow a magical pale blue. The crackle of the fire was louder than the wind outside, and Terlu thought despite being as far from the Great Library as she'd ever been, *this* was what she'd imagined being a librarian would be like: sorting through texts in the companionship of others who cared just as much as she did.

When Lotti began to sing in a voice that sounded as sweet as water in a stream, Terlu thought it was just perfect. Yarrow hummed in harmony with her, his voice as deep as the sea. The fire continued to crackle, and Terlu worked on into the late hours of the night.

CHAPTER TEN

It was Yarrow who called a halt.

"You haven't eaten," he said. "And you need to sleep."

Waddling out of the middle of mountains of papers, Lotti piped up. "I've slept enough for six lifetimes. Get me a cup of water?"

"Terlu and I need to sleep, even if you're fresh as a daisy," he told the rose as he filled a glass and laid it on the table, a safe distance from the papers.

"Hah! Daisies dream of being as fresh as me. Just need a quick drink, and I'll be as good as new." Climbing up the side of the glass, Lotti plunged herself in and sighed.

He's not wrong, Terlu thought. Her eyes felt gummy, and her neck ached like it did when she hadn't moved enough. She hadn't cracked the code yet, but she kept feeling as if she was close. It was elusive— every time she thought she'd figured out the pattern, it slipped away.

"Um, a little help here?" Lotti said, waving her leaves in the air.

Yarrow fished her out of the glass and laid her on a towel. He glanced at the window, which reflected the lanterns as if they were amber stars. "It has to be after midnight. Let's return to my cottage, I'll heat up some soup, and then we can catch some sleep?"

Soup sounded excellent. Her stomach answered for her with a magnificent growl. She patted it consolingly. *Food first, then sleep,* she promised it. "I used to study through the night regularly when I was at university, until once I showed up to an exam so tired that I wrote every answer in a different language, absolutely none of which were the language being tested."

Lotti shuddered. "Okay, yes, humans need to sleep. No spellcasting without sleep. Especially no casting spells on my friends without sleep."

Terlu slid off the stool and stretched her arms across her chest and then over her head. She was nowhere close to being able to cast a spell, but it was a valid point. She'd be useless if she couldn't think clearly.

Waving her leaves, Lotti shooed them toward the door. "I'll soak and sort until you get back."

"You can come with us," Terlu offered. She didn't want to abandon the little rose for a second time. Yarrow grunted his agreement, which from him was an enthusiastic invitation.

"This is my home, or it used to be," Lotti said. "This is where my memories are. Of Laiken. He was . . . I'm not ready to . . . I just want to stay, with whatever echo of him remains." She then added, "But thank you."

Terlu bundled herself up in her coat, while Yarrow put on his and then opened the door. Glancing back, she saw Lotti in the glow of the lanterns, hopping between the stacks of papers. *She'll be okay.* She was, as she said, home. *She needs time to grieve.*

Stepping outside, Terlu felt the crisp cold seep into her throat, lungs, and bones. Overhead, the sky was blue-black, with stars scattered across it, looking like strewn diamonds. The silvery moon shone above the silhouettes of the pine trees. It was a beautiful night. Very late. She'd lost track of how late it was.

The snow crunched under their shoes as they trudged down the road toward Yarrow's cottage. He'd pulled his hood tight so that all she could see was the shadow of his profile. She wondered what he was thinking about. Was he worrying about the risk they were taking? Or perhaps he was thinking about his family? Or the sorcerer? His responsibility to the greenhouses? The wonder of the existence of sentient plants? The mystery of magic, of the night sky, or of three strangers coming together for a single enchanted purpose?

"Got a good crop of garlic this year," Yarrow said. "You like garlic?"

"Um, yes?" She adored garlic, actually. "Especially roasted garlic."

"I'm going to add more to the soup."

He didn't say anything further. Around them, the forest was silent. "I've never seen garlic growing," she ventured. "Only after it's been peeled and cooked."

"It's a bulb," Yarrow said. "Its scape can grow up to four feet tall—'scape' is what you call the green stalk part. It's edible too, but you can cut that back so the plant concentrates its energy on the bulb. Makes for a bigger bulb."

I found his secret. Every time he talked about plants, he lit up. He loved them. Enough so that he'd appealed to faraway strangers in the imperial city for help, when he very clearly was not someone who was fond of people.

"Has to be planted deep in dry, loose soil," he continued. "Sunny is best, so it's in one of the greenhouses with a false sun."

She remembered the glowing orb in the swampy room. It would be nice to see a false sun in a room that wasn't quite as hot. "I assume the false sun is a spell?"

"Yes."

"Will you show me sometime, the garlic greenhouse?" As soon as the words were out of her mouth, she wondered if that was asking too much. He could only be making polite conversation, except he didn't seem the type to be bothered with silences, which was frankly just as nice as someone who was happy to chat all the time.

He turned his head and smiled at her. "I'd love to."

Maybe I don't have to worry so much about what he's thinking, if he's just thinking about plants and not wishing I were someone a lot more useful and a lot less . . . unlawful. That was a nice thought. She hugged it to herself as they walked in silence back to Yarrow's cottage.

Inside, it was lovely and warm and perfect. She'd spent only one night here so far, but walking into Yarrow's cottage still felt like stepping into a familiar embrace. She thought of the run-down blue cottage. As cute as it could potentially be with a *lot* of work, she wasn't certain it would ever feel as perfect and wonderful and cozy as this cottage. She was secretly glad it wasn't habitable yet. He shed his coat and immediately set to tasks: coaxing the low fire higher, positioning a skillet over it to warm, and then peeling cloves of garlic.

"How can I help?" Terlu asked.

Without turning around, he said, "You can pet the cat."

She grinned. That hardly counted as a task, but it was something that she could quite happily do. Emeral was still lounging on the new bed. As she sat on the side, he stretched, splaying out his toes and his feathers. "How was your day, Emeral?" She stroked his back beneath his wings, and he began to purr.

Yarrow tossed the garlic into the skillet, where it sizzled.

"Are there other winged cats on the island?" Terlu asked. "Where did he come from?"

"Got left behind," Yarrow said. "When my sister went to live with our aunt and uncle . . . She'd had a cat who had kittens, and they'd rounded up all but one. Couldn't find the last one. They searched and searched, but the boat couldn't afford to wait anymore. I promised to send him on when I found him."

"But you didn't?" It was more of a statement, but she made it sound like a question anyway so he'd keep talking. Purring, Emeral pushed his head into her hand so she'd pet his neck and his chin. She obliged.

Yarrow shrugged. "He didn't want to leave."

It was, at least, a friendlier kind of shrug. Before, when she'd asked about his family, she'd felt like she was pulling words out of him. Now . . . he wasn't acting as if he wanted to bolt.

"He's good at making it clear what he wants," Yarrow said, amusement in his voice. "You can feed him, if you like. He'll love you forever if you do. There's a direct line from his stomach to his heart."

Terlu hopped off the bed—or not precisely hopped but stood up with enthusiasm. After bending over the worktable, perched on a stool, for hours on end, her body felt too stiff for rapid movements like a hop. She wondered if she'd aged while she was in statue form and decided it didn't matter if she had. It felt good to ache; it meant she could feel. "What does he like to eat?"

"There's a bit of grouse in the chill box." He nodded at a cabinet near the sink. It had, she noticed, a thicker door than the others. She hadn't looked through any of the cabinets to see what was inside them. "Can't grow meat in the greenhouses, so I set a few traps in the forest, mostly for Emeral's dinner."

Crossing the cottage, she opened the "chill box" and felt a breath of cold air. *Hence the name. Makes sense.* "Is this another spell?"

"Just a lot of ice. No shortage of that this time of year."

She supposed not everything here was necessarily enchanted.

"In summer, there's enchanted ice."

Of course there is. Like the rest of the cottage, the icebox was neatly organized, and she found the grouse quickly. It was beside the zucchini he'd sliced earlier, the vegetable soaking in some sort of marinade. She felt a bump against her elbow and looked down to see that the winged cat had followed her.

Closing the icebox, she fed Emeral a bit of grouse with her fingers, and he bit into it delicately. She laid another chunk on one of the saucers and put the remainder back in the box before washing the grease from her fingers.

"In summer, he mostly eats rodents and birds," Yarrow said. "In winter, I help. It would be simpler if he liked fruits and vegetables, but . . . carnivore." He shrugged. Adding the toasted garlic to the soup, he stirred. The smell was beginning to spread through the cottage, and Terlu found herself salivating. She set bowls on the table and filled glasses with water. She also filled a bowl with water for Emeral, which he licked at noisily between nibbles.

"So it's been just you and Emeral? For two years?"

Another shrug.

She wondered if he missed his family. Had he ever thought about asking them to return, or even following them where they went? She didn't ask out loud. She didn't want to push, not when they were finally talking easily. "The soup smells amazing."

He carried the pot to the table and scooped soup into the two bowls. He then set the pot on the bricks of the hearth to cool. "Just me and Emeral since my father left. The plants, the ones like Lotti . . . they went silent long before then, before Laiken died. Never knew why. Always wished they'd wake again."

"Lotti didn't recognize you, but you've lived here your whole life."

"Either Laiken kept her away from his gardeners, which is possible, or she could have gone dormant before I was born. Also possible. Laiken's plants are long-lived, and he himself lived at least twice a normal lifespan."

Terlu sipped the soup. The warm bite of the garlic filled her mouth, her nose, and her sinuses, and she felt as if she were tasting soup from the emperor's own table. He'd added herbs she didn't recognize that made it taste as sweet as a late-summer fruit, while still as earthy as a potato should be. "You are an incredible cook."

He shrugged a third (or fourth or fifth . . .) time. "I have the right ingredients."

"It's more than that. This . . . You could make the imperial family weep."

"My grandfather taught me to cook," Yarrow said. "He could look at a plant and tell you six ways to prepare it. He had a recipe for a peach tart that I've never been able to replicate. Just tasting it would make you dream of summer for a week."

They ate their soup while she tried to imagine what such a tart would taste like. She thought of summer on her home island, her toes in the sand, the sun beating down so hard that it felt like it was soaking into her bones. Summer to her tasted like coconut and pineapple, and it smelled like the lotion that her parents insisted they slather themselves with before they went outside. It tasted like cooked crab and like the sweet candy that stuck to your fingers no matter how hard you sucked them. "Have you ever left the island?"

"Never wanted to," Yarrow said. "All the wonders of the world are already here, within those glass walls." He waved his spoon toward the window, and she looked over her shoulder. Only darkness lay outside. She couldn't see beyond the reflection of the fire in the hearth. "If I can keep them alive."

He was talking easily, much more easily than earlier, and she knew why: they were working together now. *We're practically team-mates.* United to save the sentient plants. It was a nice change, and it kept the memory of the drumbeats away. *He won't betray me.*

After they finished, Terlu helped clean the bowls and put away the uneaten portion of soup. "Do you know why Laiken let the talking plants fall dormant?"

He shook his head as he scrubbed the pot. Suds ringed his wrists like ephemeral jewels. The soap smelled like lavender, and she wondered if he made his own soap like he did everything else on Belde. *Laiken was a fool to discard his gardeners,* she thought. If they were all like Yarrow, they were extraordinary.

"I don't know," he said. "They were his confidants and companions. He loved them."

Forcing dormancy was a cruel thing to do to a friend. Or even a stranger. But especially a being you supposedly loved. She thought of the judge at her trial and the vicious delight of the prosecutor. He'd seen her punishment as his moral victory. She wondered if the plants had known what would happen to them. Did they know they'd be left in a suspended sleep? Did they expect to ever wake?

I have to help them; I can't just leave them like that.

"You can use the washroom before me, if you'd like," Yarrow offered.

Terlu thanked him. Still thinking about the sentient plants, she cleaned up, discovering he'd gifted her a soft sheath for sleeping— another item left behind by a relative who'd left him, she assumed.

She cleaned her teeth, brushed the snarls out of her hair, and then emerged.

He blushed and looked away quickly, mumbled something, and then slipped into the washroom past her. She glanced down at herself to realize that the sheath hugged her body and the neckline dipped down. Whoever had worn it before her had been smaller. No one had ever accused Terlu of being scrawny. She'd been born cuddly, and nothing in her life had changed that, including being turned into a statue. The statue spell had preserved all her curves and bulges, despite not eating for six years, and she was happy for it. She wouldn't have known herself without the full softness of her flesh. Still, though, it did make the sheath cling to her curves.

If it bothers him, he doesn't have to look.

And if it didn't bother him . . . Well, she didn't mind if he looked. Especially when he could cook like that.

Terlu crawled into the bed and felt all her muscles sink into the mattress. While she was eating the soup, she'd momentarily forgotten how tired she was, but the instant she lay in the bed, she felt as if a building had crashed on her—except it was a soft, comfortable building made of pillows.

From across the room, the winged cat flew up to her bed. He settled on top of her legs. She hadn't quite finished getting into position when he arrived. Carefully, she tried to twist onto her side. Emeral fluttered his wings in protest. She held still. It was fine.

She lay beneath the blankets and the winged cat until she heard Yarrow climb into bed beside her. He'd extinguished the lights in the lanterns on his way, leaving the fire burning to cast its dancing amber light around the cottage.

Yarrow spoke. "I think Laiken was afraid of his own mortality. He knew he was going to die someday, though maybe not as soon as he did, but that's why he made them sleep. I think he was afraid that after he was gone, no one would love them the way he did."

If he was right, that was both sad and scary. "Did he ever try asking you to care for them?" She knew the answer to that. He hadn't.

Laiken had written his notes and spells in code, he'd never taken an apprentice, and he'd dismissed all his gardeners but a father and his son. How sad and difficult must that have been—to watch the person you were supposed to trust became more and more paranoid. If Laiken had reached out for help, what might have been different?

"I would have said yes," Yarrow said. "I would have cared for them until my last breath, and I would have ensured they were cared for beyond that."

"I'll wake them," Terlu said. She saw his silhouette beneath his blankets. So close. She wanted to reach out and touch his hand, to show him she meant the words—he was only a few inches away. It would be so easy . . . But she wasn't sure how he'd react—he hadn't liked it when she'd hugged him, and he was still an almost-stranger—so she didn't move. "I promise."

CHAPTER ELEVEN

Terlu didn't know how she was going to keep her promise. After three days of struggling with the coded texts, she wasn't any closer to cracking the cipher. Sighing, she rubbed her neck and stretched her arms.

Across the workroom, Lotti was muttering to herself as she, using a leaf as if it were a thumb and fingers, flipped through one of Laiken's journals. He'd kept many. They dominated three-quarters of his shelves, plus Yarrow had found more in a chest under the stairs.

The problem was Laiken hadn't intended his notes for anyone else's eyes, especially as time went on. The early journals from before he created the greenhouse were written in a slightly archaic version of island standard, but as he aged, his paranoia had increased, and by the later journals, which appeared to hold the majority of his spells, he seemed to be employing not only a code system that she was becoming increasingly convinced relied on a codebook but also the occasional mirror writing or backward writing or, worse, both. And then there were the pages he'd destroyed: ripped out and presumably burned. Yarrow had found more half-burnt scraps beneath the stove. She had no idea what had been lost and whether the spell she needed still existed.

Lotti flopped backward and waved her petals in the air. "Gah! This is hopeless!" She shouted up to the ceiling as if the sorcerer were upstairs and could hear her, "Laiken, you're the worst!"

"When is that journal from?" Terlu asked.

"The era where Laiken decided that he'd torture future readers with his experiments in sketching. Brilliant man. Genius sorcerer. Terrible artist. Look at this!" Scooting around the book, she propped it up so that Terlu could see. "Is that a rabbit? Is it a cat? Is it a fish? Is it a human liver with eyeballs? Who knows?"

Terlu grinned. "I think it's a bird."

Lotti trotted around to the front of the journal. "It would need wings."

"The word next to it is Ginian for 'sparrow.'"

"Ginian?"

"It's a language that was spoken on the island of Ginia before the fourth emperor of the Crescent Islands Empire wiped it out about three centuries ago."

Lotti gasped. "The empire wiped out a whole island?"

"Not the people, but they, like many the empire conquered, lost their language and a lot of their culture. Ginia was one of the islands who fought back against joining the empire, but they didn't do it with ships or armies. Instead they turned their entire island into a labyrinth to trick and trap the imperial soldiers. Every building visible from the ocean was a facade, and you had to solve a puzzle to access the true homes, deep inside the mountains. It took an entire decade before they were conquered, and when they were, the emperor was determined to prevent this from ever happening again. All teachers, all elders, all keepers of wisdom—they were removed and rehoused to other islands, separated from one another, and he sent in imperial teachers to ensure the next generation wouldn't rebel."

"How sad."

"Empires are not . . ." She trailed off before she said anything truly treasonous. Librarians of Alyssium were trained to be impartial, but how could anyone who studied history not have feelings about it? She'd never understood that. History was full of people, all of whom had lives and dreams that were affected by the dry laws and military actions that filled university textbooks. Emperor Mevorin liked to insist every action taken by the empire was for the good of its people, but far too many of its actions throughout history had been for the good of the empire, which was *not*—regardless of what the emperor espoused—the same thing. An empire, unchecked, was a selfish beast of insatiable hunger. Terlu took a deep breath and dredged up a smile. "It wasn't all lost, though. You've heard of hedge labyrinths? Gardens with bushes shaped like mazes? The Ginians invented them, and so their legacy lives on."

"Laiken built the most magnificent maze," Lotti said. "It fills an entire enormous greenhouse. Or it filled. Who knows if it survived."

From across the workroom, Yarrow spoke up. "It did, so far."

"Huh." Terlu scooted closer to Lotti to study the journal with the poorly drawn sparrow.

"According to legends, the Ginians placed their greatest treasures in the hearts of their mazes. Centuries later, treasure-seekers still show up on the island, thinking they're going to find gold and jewels." Considering, she looked at the date on the journal. "Do you know *when* Laiken made this maze?" This journal was from the period when he'd just begun to use codes. She showed the date to Lotti.

"I don't know," the rose said.

"Could it have been around then?"

"Sure. Maybe. I'm a plant. I don't own a calendar. I know it took a few seasons before it was finished to his satisfaction. He never let me help, of course."

She wondered . . .

Hopping back to her papers, Lotti asked, "What did the Ginians keep in the hearts of their mazes if not gold and jewels?"

Terlu, the former Fourth Librarian of the Second Floor, East Wing, smiled at the little rose. "Books, of course, the ultimate treasure. All their stories. And their knowledge."

"Ah, and the emperor destroyed that, I assume."

Terlu shook her head. "Even he couldn't bring himself to do that. He stole it. It was housed in the section of the library that I was assigned to—that's why I know about it, even though the Ginia Rebellion was excised from the official history books, due to how much it embarrassed the emperor." The more she thought about Laiken's labyrinth, the more she wondered . . . She had a very strong hunch about what a sorcerer would consider a treasure.

"Laiken never said what his treasure was that he placed at the heart of his maze," Lotti said. Her petals tapped the notebook that had been frustrating her. "You said before he could have used a codebook, and I said I never saw one, but just because I never saw one doesn't mean he didn't use one. I wasn't with him all the time, and I . . . I know I don't remember everything. Do you think—"

"Yes, that's exactly what I think." Terlu jumped to her feet. A codebook would explain why she was making so little progress. "Or at least I think we should find out. Yarrow?"

He grunted, but it sounded like a yes.

The maze, Yarrow said, was his least favorite greenhouse.

"Why?" Lotti asked, bouncing beside him.

Terlu was carrying the winged cat, draped around her shoulders again.

He ticked off the reasons on his golden fingers. "It has no logic. It has no purpose. The plants aren't unique and don't service the mission of the greenhouse. And I get lost in it." He mumbled the final reason.

"You haven't solved it?" Terlu asked. She had been counting on that.

Yarrow shrugged. "It's never been necessary. Laiken laid his most elaborate spells on that greenhouse—the plants are spelled to grow on specific paths so they never need to be pruned; the enchanted windows, stove, and fans regulate the temperature without the need for intervention; a spelled stream keeps the plants watered; and the dragons keep the flowers pollinated."

Terlu halted and gawked at him. "The— How? Why? What?" She

pictured the dragons of Ilreka, with their jeweled scales, spiked tails, and sixty-foot wingspans. The wind from their wings alone would shatter the glass of a greenhouse. How could—

"Very tiny dragons."

She shook her head. "Those don't exist."

He shrugged again. "Don't let Emeral chase them."

It was a significant walk to the maze, through an apple orchard greenhouse, a citrus grove (with Eanoan oranges!), and a greenhouse filled with vines in motion: as she watched, they braided themselves into elaborate plaits. Half of the greenhouse had woven itself into a living blanket, and the rest was braiding itself into thick ropes. Green mice with leaves instead of fur scampered to the tops of the ropes. The leafy mice squeaked to one another as Terlu and Yarrow passed beneath them. One of them dropped a pink fruit, and it splatted on the walkway.

If there are leaf mice, why not tiny dragons? She had no real idea what kind of wonders were squirreled away in the Greenhouse of Belde, either drawn to the enchantments or created here. Maybe, when the spell was done, she'd have a chance to explore and find out. Maybe, just maybe, Yarrow would want to show her.

"Do you take care of the creatures as well as the plants?" Terlu asked. She thought of the color-changing butterflies and the diamond dragonflies.

"Mostly they take care of themselves," Yarrow said. "Laiken spelled them that way. Even the ones he didn't create are enchanted to live in harmony here."

She watched the leaf mice play and thought of the citrus grove. "Will there be ripe oranges in time for this year's Winter Feast?" Terlu asked.

"You want a Winter Feast?"

"You don't celebrate?" She supposed it wouldn't make sense to, on his own. The solstice celebrations were all about coming together with loved ones, to rejoice in the light together. Also, there was lots and lots of food. "The Great Library closes to outsiders for the Solstice Feasts, both Summer and Winter, but the Winter Feast was always my favorite. For the Winter Feast, all the librarians are invited to the head librarian's office. She resides at the top of the tallest spire. Eighty-six steps from the top level of the stacks to her office, and each step would have a tray with a different delicacy on it. Each recipe was from a different island in the Crescent Islands Empire, selected by the librarian in charge of the food history section of the Great Library. There were crab puffs from Dault, stuffed figs from Tirza, marinated beef skewers with pearl onions from Blaye. You'd gather everything you wanted and, when you reached the head librarian's office, she'd wish you light in the darkness."

"Must have gotten crowded up there," Lotti said.

"Oh no, that was the best part." Terlu smiled, remembering it. "Each librarian would leave the office through the window, lowered in a gondola lit with twinkling lights—magical lights—all the way down to the canals. You could then feast with others by the water, if you wanted." A few stayed, and they'd talked and laughed late into the night until all the solstice lights dimmed and were replaced by stars above. It was her favorite night of the entire year.

"Eighty-six delicacies?" Yarrow said.

"The tricky part was not dropping your plate while you were in the gondola."

"Huh," he grunted. Then: "You should put on your coat."

There were two dead greenhouses to cross before they reached the door to the maze. These were absent of plants, either dead or alive, and Terlu wondered if Yarrow had been able to rescue them before the temperature plummeted. She hoped so.

At the end of the second greenhouse was a door that didn't match any of the other doors she'd seen. It wasn't wreathed in delicate ironwork. Instead it was made of interlocking plates. Halting, Yarrow stared at it and grunted again, a less happy grunt this time.

"Aren't you going to open it?" Lotti asked.

Terlu noticed it didn't have a handle or a knob. "It's a puzzle."

"You don't need me for this," Yarrow said. "I'm of more use tending to the gardens than playing with Laiken's toys."

"You know how to open it, though, don't you?"

"You have to align the pieces."

"How?" Lotti asked.

"Carefully," Yarrow said.

If the rose had eyes to roll, she would have. "You don't know, do you," Lotti accused. "I thought you'd come here before."

"Not in a while," Yarrow said. "Self-sustaining ecosystem. It doesn't need me, while plenty of other rooms do. Give me a minute—I'll remember." He crossed his arms and stared at the door.

Terlu studied the plates, some silver and some bronze, but all of them ovals. It reminded her of the scales of a fish. "Maybe they're all supposed to point the same direction?" She began to rotate them. "Or silver in one direction and bronze in the other? No, that's too simple."

"Ooh, maybe they're petals," the rose said. "Make them into flowers!"

"A chrysanthemum," Yarrow said suddenly. He pointed to the center of the door. "All the petals point out from the heart of the flower. Technically, chrysanthemums are a composite of many flowers—disk florets in the center of the bloom and ray florets on the perimeter—but the effect is one massive bloom with concentric circles of petals. See, I knew I'd remember."

"Because I reminded you," Lotti said. "I am obviously the brains of this operation."

Stifling a laugh, Terlu didn't point out that Yarrow had been about to leave. She rotated the "petals," beginning in the center with a circle that pointed out and continued on. As she worked, the winged cat flew off her shoulders and up to perch in the rafters. He began to groom himself.

"White and yellow chrysanthemums can be brewed into a nice tea," Yarrow said. "It's best if you use closed buds and add honey."

"One of my friends is a chrysanthemum," Lotti said darkly.

"You can harvest the flowers without harming the plant."

Three circles done. She started on the fourth. Some of the petals were easy to twist and others rotated so smoothly that they promptly flopped to point downward. She fixed the ones that had drooped and finished the fourth circle.

"I hope you ask permission first," Lotti said.

"Always," Yarrow said.

Terlu loved that he said that with complete sincerity. He probably did ask. While she squatted to finish the petals at the bottom of the door, he aligned the ones at the top.

As she turned the last petal, she heard a click, then another click, then another. One by one, starting at the center, all of the petals lifted, until it truly resembled a flower.

All three of them (four, including the winged cat) stared at the door, waiting for it to open. It just sat there, looking decorative.

"Huh. That was anticlimactic," Lotti said.

Terlu pushed on the center of the door, and it swung open. Inside was what looked like another world. Above, the sky was amber with ripples of green, like the aurora to the far north, and ahead was a pine forest—or no, a wall of evergreen. There were no gaps between the trees. The needles wove together in a thick mat that allowed no hint of light. She stepped in and marveled at it. It stretched as far as she could see in either direction.

"How is this a maze?" Lotti asked.

Yarrow grunted. "You'll see."

Terlu and the rose walked (or hopped) through the doorway. Yarrow moved to close the door behind them—and the winged cat swooped through. "Catch him!" he shouted.

But Emeral was already soaring up toward the amber-and-green sky.

"Well, that won't be good," Yarrow commented.

Peering to the left, Terlu tried to see any break in the evergreen. It appeared endless, but in the far distance, she thought she saw two figures, a tall one with black-and-gold-streaked hair and a short and plump one with a mess of brown curly hair. She pointed. "Us?"

"Mirrors," Yarrow said. "He replaced the windows with mirrors, and that"—he waved at the ceiling—"is an illusion. We're still inside a greenhouse. Just a very large one."

"But how do we get into the maze? Is it right or left?"

"Neither," he said. "Straight ahead." He scooped up the rose, then marched forward directly toward the needles. Lotti gave a little shriek, and the trees scurried back as Yarrow reached them, lifting their roots out of the ground to retreat.

Reaching out a leaf, Lotti poked at a branch. The evergreen didn't react. Terlu followed the two of them through the gap in the pine trees.

Ahead of them was a maze of sunflowers. Green stalks stood side by side, forming the walls, while the enormous flowers drooped, their brown faces ringed with brilliant yellow petals. It smelled mildly earthy, no strong floral scent, mixed with a hint of pine.

"Hah! This is easy!" Lotti said as she scurried down Yarrow's torso and legs to the ground. "You just needed someone little like me to figure it out." She headed for the space between the stalks.

Quickly, Yarrow caught her, cupped in his hands. "You don't want to do that."

"Hey! Why—"

A tiny dragon, about the size of a teacup, shot between the stalks. It breathed a candle-size spurt of fire at Lotti and then soared upward. It flew in front of Terlu, only inches from her face.

It was exquisite: an exact miniature of the great dragons of Ilreka. Each scale was a tiny jewel, and its wings were as delicate as a butterfly's. It looked as if it were made of blown glass. "Wow," she breathed. "I thought you might be joking." The leafy mice had been fascinating, but this . . . this was extraordinary.

"I never joke about pollinators," Yarrow said.

"Wait, pollinators?" Terlu asked. "They act like bees? Fascinating." She turned in a circle, looking at the array of sunflowers—they stretched as far as she could see. Little dragons flitted from one sunflower to another, landing on the brown hearts of the flowers.

"What do you call a bee that's been put under a spell?" Lotti asked.

Terlu raised her eyebrows at the little rose.

"*Bee*-witched."

"No," Yarrow said.

They walked into the sunflower maze and immediately the path split. "Keep a wall to our left at all times," Terlu suggested. "It won't be quick, but if we keep a wall to our left, it'll eventually lead us through."

"Why do bees hum?" Lotti asked. "Because they can't remember the words."

Terlu let her fingers brush the sunflower leaves to her left as they walked. It was only a few yards in before they hit a dead end, but she didn't slow—she kept her fingers out, brushing the leaves as they walked.

At each junction, she chose left.

"What's a bee's favorite flower?"

"Please don't say bee-gonia," Yarrow growled.

"Ooh, you're good," Lotti said. "How about, what does the bee say to—"

Terlu held up her hand. What was that sound? She looked up and saw a flock—a school? a flight? a herd?—of miniature dragons. Hissing, they spiraled in the air. Their wings glowed in the unearthly amber-and-green light from the false sky.

Yarrow called, "Emeral, no!"

High in the sky, the winged cat dove at them, and they scattered. Flapping his wings, he changed directions and flew after the flock.

"Ooh, a perfect distraction," Lotti said. She darted down Yarrow's leg and between the stalks before either Yarrow or Terlu could stop her. In a few seconds, she was out of sight.

"Come back," Terlu called. "We have to stick together!"

One of the dragons, a ruby-red beauty, wheeled midair and then flew toward the maze. It disappeared behind the heads of the flowers. Terlu shoved aside the stalks to rush after Lotti—

The flock of dragons coalesced above her, ignoring the cat, and dove. Yarrow yanked her away from the sunflowers, as Emeral pounced on the dragons from above. They veered away from his claws. She felt the tiny talons of a golden dragon rake through her hair.

Yarrow held her against his chest, his arms wrapped protectively around her, and Terlu buried her face against him. The flurry of wings stirred up wind around them. A second later, it was gone. She peeked out.

"Lotti?"

The little rose didn't answer.

CHAPTER TWELVE

For an instant, within Yarrow's arms, Terlu felt safer than she ever had, as if all was right with the world and everything would turn out just fine. But then he released her.

"We have to save Lotti," he said.

She liked the "we." It had been a long time since she'd been a part of a "we," perhaps all the way back to Eano with her sister and cousins. In the city and especially in the Great Library, it had felt like everyone was on their own, even before they all figured out their paths and she didn't. But as nice as the "we" was, she still grabbed his sleeve as he turned to charge forward. "Keep the sunflower wall to your left."

Yarrow shook his head. "We don't have time to solve the maze."

"We don't have time to get lost," Terlu said firmly. "If we're thorough, we won't miss her. If we're not, we'll run in circles." She was certain she was right about this, and she braced herself for an argument—but he didn't argue.

A sharp nod. "You lead."

She started forward, and he followed.

"Lotti!" they took turns calling. "Are you okay? Where are you? We're coming!"

Above, the false aurora rippled, and the sunflowers turned their heads to face it. If she wasn't so worried, she would have been fascinated by the light show. She'd never heard of a spell that could create such an effect, but then she hardly knew everything there was to know about magic. In the library, she'd been responsible for whatever tasks the second floor, east wing librarian set for her, which often included rebinding old texts and sorting through donated material from retired sorcerers—some of which was interesting and important and some of which was decidedly not, though she was certain that the sorcerer who had cataloged the various ways to enchant socks to be tear-resistant found his topic of study intriguing. She'd been more interested in *why* the long-gone sorcerer had been drawn to socks as his focus. What led a person to devote their life to enchanted socks? Similarly, what had led Laiken to devote himself to creating this greenhouse? And why had he crafted this maze with its false sky and miniature dragons and sunflowers that—

Ahead, the row of sunflowers lifted their roots out of the soil and tiptoed into a new position before piercing the soil again.

Terlu gasped. "It *moves*."

Yarrow trotted past her at a near jog. "Plants in here can do that."

"Yes, but . . ." She knew the evergreens at the entrance had shifted, but she'd thought the maze itself would be stationary, though she supposed there was no reason it had to be, except for the fact that plants normally didn't uproot themselves and wander about. She kept pace with Yarrow, keeping the flowers to their left, but the effort felt pointless—if the maze was continually shifting, that made it unbeatable. "It's cheating."

"I never solved it, remember? This is why."

"It can't be solved if it rearranges itself." If the walls were constantly moving, it was impossible. The sunflowers could keep presenting them with dead ends until they were too exhausted to continue. "It could take years." They could die of old age before the maze let them through. It could hide Lotti from them for an infinite amount of time. "I'm sorry. This won't work."

Stopping, he eyed the stalks. "We could break through."

"But the dragons . . ." A cramp squeezed her side, and she leaned over her knees to pant.

"If we're quick . . ." He withdrew clippers from within his coat. "I hate to do this. It's not the plants' fault they've been spelled to behave this way." With his free hand, he touched one of the sunflower leaves, as if in apology. "But we can't abandon Lotti."

She saw in his eyes how much he didn't want to do it. "There has to be another way."

"Any ideas?"

"If it's endlessly shifting, Laiken would have had to solve it anew every time he wanted to visit his treasure," Terlu said. "I think it's likely he had his own secret path through the maze." He'd liked both puzzles and secrets.

Above, she heard a yowl and then Emeral streaked by, chased by a flock of dragons. They flew like a swarm of bees, clustered together, their wings making a whooshing sound.

The key isn't the sunflowers; it's the dragons.

Maybe they could be tamed.

"Do you have anything to eat?" Terlu asked.

Yarrow grunted. "I don't think now is the time—"

"Not for me. Do you have anything that a dragon might like?"

His face lit up. "Ahh!" Quickly, he began to unload items from his pocket: an egg with a blue shell, a chunk of cheese wrapped in a handkerchief, a handful of nuts in a little pouch, dried seeds, and nuggets of honeycomb. "This," he said, as he unveiled the honeycomb. "Little dragons are pollinators. Perhaps they'll be drawn to honey?"

Terlu had many questions about how he had all these items—the nuts and seeds made sense, given the variety of plants in the greenhouse, but the cheese? Where had it come from? She had similar questions about the flour he'd used to make the honey cake. Did he trade for all of it? If he did, who facilitated the trades? Was it the sailor who could be summoned with a raised flag? Had that same sailor brought Terlu in statue form, or had it been another supply runner? What had they thought of such a delivery? Had they known that Yarrow intended to revive her? How many knew Terlu was here? Did anyone know besides Rijes Velk and the supply runner? So many questions, but this wasn't the time to ask any of them. Lotti was somewhere in the heart of the maze, likely scared, certain she'd been abandoned again. Terlu wondered if anyone ever recovered from that—did you ever stop being afraid you'd be alone again? "All right, how do we draw their attention so they notice the honeycomb?"

Yarrow moved with purpose toward the sunflowers. He opened the clippers and positioned the blades around one of the stalks, lightly touching the green—and he waited.

Above, the dragons howled.

They broke off pursuit of the winged cat and pivoted midair. In arrow formation, they flew at Yarrow and Terlu. Lowering the clippers, he held up the honeycomb in the palm of his hand. Terlu tensed. She didn't know what she'd do if the dragons attacked him. Pull him to safety? Try to hit them away and hope they didn't shoot flame? Throw egg and cheese at them?

The first dragon, a golden queen, swooped down and delicately broke off a bit of honeycomb with her talons. Another, a green-and-black scaled one, grabbed another chunk. A third. A fourth. Until the honeycomb was all gone.

"Pollinators," Yarrow said.

The other dragons wheeled off toward the sky, searching for the cat, but the half dozen who had secured their treasure began to fly between the sunflowers with purpose.

"Hurry," Terlu said. She ran after them, and Yarrow jogged beside her.

In front of the dragons, the sunflowers shifted out of the way, forming a straight path. Terlu and Yarrow followed the little dragons with the honeycomb to the center of the maze.

On top of a pile of watering cans, gloves, hats, pine cones, and

various glittering rocks—the dragons' treasure—was the little resurrection rose.

"Took you long enough," Lotti complained.

While the dragons munched on the bits of honeycomb, Terlu and
Yarrow sorted through the treasure hoard. It was an unusual as-
sortment: an uncut ruby the size of Terlu's fist, a single left-hand
gardening glove, a stick shaped like a heart, a solid-gold brick . . .

"They didn't hurt me," Lotti explained. "They just scooped me
up and brought me here."

"Every time Laiken came to access the heart of the maze, he
must have brought them a treasure," Yarrow said. "They must have
thought you were one too."

"I *am* a prize," Lotti agreed.

Kneeling by the stack, Terlu tossed aside a diamond. Yarrow
picked it up and whistled. "I don't know much about gems, but this
must be worth the entire island."

Lotti unfurled her leaves. "Ooh, let me see."

He handed it to her, and she placed it in the center of her blossom. "It suits you," he told her. "But I wouldn't get too attached. It's
part of the dragons' hoard."

Sighing, Lotti set the diamond aside.

Terlu continued to sift through the tiny mountain of junk and
jewels. *If I were a sorcerer who wanted to protect my secrets, this is
precisely what I'd do.* Or maybe not precisely. She wasn't sure she'd
think of an ever-changing maze of sunflowers guarded by miniature
dragons—that was rather specific.

A little golden dragon with obsidian-black wings broke away
from the others and trotted toward them. He picked up the diamond with his talons and set it back into the center of the rose. He
chirped wordlessly at her, nodded his head, and then waddled back
to the honeycomb.

"I like that dragon," Lotti said, closing her petals around the diamond.

At the base of the hoard, Terlu found it: a slim book, bound in green leather, with no markings on the cover or the spine. She extracted it from the pile and opened it.

"Yes!" she cheered.

"What is it?" Yarrow asked. "Is it the spell?"

"Better!" Terlu crowed, holding it up for him to see. "It's Laiken's codebook." She plopped onto the ground, cross-legged, and began to read through it. "He *was* writing in First Language, but he mixed it with . . . ooh, that's interesting. I haven't seen that dialect in a while. Knew it had to be connected to Ginian. But it's an older variant."

"Can you break the code?" Yarrow squatted beside her and peered at the book.

She beamed at him. "Oh, yes. Very much yes."

He reached into his pocket and pulled out a chunk of chocolate. He held it out toward the dragons and then pointed toward the codebook. After miming it a couple of times, the dragons seemed to understand: the chocolate for the codebook.

A few minutes later, the three of them and their prizes exited the maze—straight through, with sunflowers opening a path to the door. Above, the aurora danced with the dragons as they cavorted in the sky, shooting tiny flames like they were stray fireworks.

Emeral was pawing at the greenhouse door. He'd clearly had enough of chasing and being chased by tiny dragons. Terlu picked him up, and he snuggled against her, tucking his head beneath his wings, as if he wanted to pretend the dragons didn't exist.

"Thank you," Yarrow said solemnly to the little dragons.

"We'll bring more honeycomb and chocolate next time," Terlu told them.

Yarrow glanced at her, his eyebrows raised.

"They liked it," Terlu said in answer to his eyebrows.

"Yes, they did."

She couldn't tell what he was thinking, and he turned away before she could ask.

They hurried through the greenhouses and outside, down the snowy road, to the sorcerer's tower. While Emeral flew to curl up on the hearth, Terlu shed her coat and immediately headed for the stack of encoded notes that Lotti had separated out from the rest.

"What do you need?" Yarrow asked.

"Paper," she said immediately. She liberated a charcoal pencil from the array of beakers, jars, pots, and gardening gloves, while Yarrow located blank papers in a drawer in Laiken's desk.

"How else can I help?"

She shook her head. She just needed to concentrate. "I don't know how long this will take me . . ." She'd work as fast as she could, but it would take a bit of time to understand how Laiken constructed his code and then learn to use it with ease.

"I'll bake you honey cake."

Terlu grinned. He was a man of few words but an excellent understanding of what was required for a proper research project. "Thank you." She kept reading.

"Thank *you*," he said. "You . . . don't have to do this. You could have raised the flag on the dock and left on the next boat. Not everyone would have stayed."

Placing her finger on her spot in the text, she looked up at him and studied the sadness mixed with hope in his deep green eyes. A lock of black hair with a streak of gold had fallen across his forehead, and she fought the urge to push it away from his eyes. How could she look into those eyes and then walk away? The way he'd gazed at her when she first met him, like she was the answer . . . The way he was looking at her now . . . *It's worth the risk. He is worth it, whether he knows it or not. And so's Lotti.* Softly, she said, "I'm sure your family would have come back if they'd known what it was like here."

He shrugged and then looked away. "I'll return with honey cake," he mumbled. With that, he bolted out of the tower, and she watched him leave, wondering how many thoughts and feelings went un-voiced behind those deep-as-the-sea eyes.

From across the table, Lotti said, "You save his greenhouses and that boy will walk across water for you."

"That's not why I'm doing this," Terlu said. But it was nice that she knew he'd return, unlike when she'd initially arrived, when he'd fled at the sight of her. In the maze, it felt like they were facing the world together. She'd liked their brief time as "we."

"Why *are* you doing this?" Lotti asked, curling her petals around another charcoal pencil. Carrying it, she waddled closer to Terlu. "He's right—you could leave. You don't have to stick around and help us. You have plenty of reasons not to and no real reason to stay. You aren't connected to Laiken or me or any of the plants here."

But I could be. Rijes Velk had thought she could do good here. She'd given Terlu a second chance. *And I'm not going to waste it.* If she could be useful . . . if she could have a place here . . . if she could have a purpose . . . that was worth any amount of effort. It was why she'd left her family and her home island in the first place, and it was what she'd failed to find in the Great Library of Alyssium.

"Because I want to," Terlu told Lotti, taking the spare pencil.

She did not say out loud: *Because I need to.*

She needed her second life to matter.

CHAPTER THIRTEEN

It took Terlu another three days and many honey cakes to unravel the code.

On the morning of the third day, Yarrow joined her and Lotti in the workroom and placed a mug beside Terlu. She inhaled chocolate so rich that all unrelated thoughts flew out the window. "Did you make this?"

He nodded. "The trick is knowing when to harvest the cocoa pods."

She cradled the mug in both hands, and the warmth sank into her palms. She breathed in the chocolaty steam and thought she'd never smelled anything so wonderful. He'd sprinkled bits of hazelnut on top, and ooh, was that a swirl of caramel? Yes, it was.

"You then have to ferment the beans," he said. "I wrap them in banana leaves to ferment, then roast them, shell them—you want just the nibs—and grind them."

She took a sip.

It was like drinking a sunset, where the sun had stained the clouds the deepest, richest rose. Molten sunshine was dripping down her throat.

"The sweetness comes from sugarcane syrup," he offered. "You have to boil it down, strain the fibers out, then boil it some more until it's almost but not quite caramelized. Made a bunch of batches last winter."

"You grow the sugarcane as well?" She took another sip, closed her eyes, and let the warm chocolate spread through her. It felt as if her blood had been replaced by chocolate. "Wow," she said, opening her eyes to see Yarrow watching her reaction.

"Every type of plant in the Crescent Islands grows here." Then his smile faded and his shoulders slumped as he added, "Or used to, before the greenhouses began to fail."

Terlu wished she could say she knew how to fix everything, it would all be fine, and she had just the right magic spell that was guaranteed to work to solve all his problems and make the pain in his voice vanish, but fixing greenhouses that had been drenched in enchantments . . . that was magic so far beyond her it wasn't even in the realm of possible. She had a single goal: waking the sentient plants, and she *had* made progress on that. "So I think I know—"

Lotti jumped in. "You know how to restore my friends?"

"Maybe." Setting aside the hot chocolate reluctantly, she picked up a notebook and showed them the page she'd been studying. "This is one of the entries he made from around the time that Lotti went to sleep. It's not that the spell that created them has to be recast— they're still sentient. They're just asleep, as Lotti said. I worried that she was being euphemistic, but it's the literal truth."

"Knew it!" Lotti said. "They're still them."

"It seems that after he let you fall dormant, Laiken began looking for ways to encourage the other sentient plants to sleep too." She kept her tone light, but her word choice was deliberate. After reconstructing Laiken's journals that held his notes on the sentient plants, Terlu was certain her interpretation was correct: the sorcerer had deliberately let her wither.

"Wait, excuse me, no." Lotti hopped across the table to the journal. "He didn't *let* me fall dormant. It was an *accident* that I fell asleep. He forgot to water me. I don't need much, and he lost track of days. He'd gotten more confused by then."

Not from what his journal said. He'd kept meticulous notes, in code: he'd been stretching how long the little rose could go between waterings. He'd *wanted* her to be dormant. Terlu pushed on. "But you're the only one of the sentient plants who could become dormant naturally. If he just stopped watering the others, they'd die, and that's not what he wanted. So he experimented with them, after he'd reassured himself that you could survive your hibernation unharmed. As near as I can tell, he started his experiments about fifty years ago?" She glanced at Yarrow, who nodded.

The rose shook, and she wrapped her petals tighter together into a quivering bud. "No. You're wrong. Laiken loved me. He loved all of us!"

Perhaps he did love her, in his own way. "I think he wanted to protect you. He thought if you were asleep, you'd be safe. If you were all asleep . . ." It was the kindest explanation for why Laiken had allowed Lotti to shrivel and fall into what was essentially a coma when he could have simply cared for her. Other explanations were much more cruel. Gently, Terlu asked, "What do you remember of that time, before you fell asleep?"

"He was absent a lot," Lotti said, still closed into a bud. "Busy. With the greenhouses."

"He'd already begun to dismiss gardeners by then," Yarrow spoke up. "My father said Belde was on its way to becoming home to a small village about fifty years ago, but Laiken didn't want that. He refused to allow new people to settle here, and he began to require that gardeners leave if they wished to marry, rather than allow their spouses to settle here, which was a change from earlier years, when my father was a child. As time went on, the sorcerer did more and more himself and kept more and more to himself."

"He forgot about me," Lotti insisted. "It wasn't deliberate. I refuse to believe that."

"It could have been an accident with you," Terlu agreed. Who was she to say? She hadn't been there. The only insight she had was what the sorcerer had written down. Let the rose keep idolizing her creator, if she wanted to. She didn't need to face her past or confront the truth or any of that if all it was going to do was hurt her—there was no point in unnecessary pain. None of them could change what happened; all they could do was shape what happened next. Terlu pointed to a spell. "Regardless, this is how he made the others sleep. It took him a number of years to perfect the spell, but eventually he did."

Yarrow bent over her to look at the page. She felt his warm breath on her cheek. His breath smelled like sugary chocolate. "So, you're saying they're in an enchanted sleep?"

"Essentially, yes," Terlu said. "I've identified the spell he used, and, I think, the counterspell, though he never tested it so I don't know if—"

Lotti flapped her leaves in alarm. "You *think*? You don't *know*? And what do you mean 'he never tested it'? Does that mean you'd be trying a new untested spell on my friends? What if you make it worse?"

She'd thought about that. "There isn't much worse than the not-life they're in."

"How do you know what they're—oh." Lotti closed her petals into a bud, this time in embarrassment. "Sorry. I forgot. Your statue phase. It's just . . . What if the spell goes wrong?"

Statue phase. What a way to describe her lost years.

"It's a risk," Terlu said. She looked at Yarrow, into his deep-as-the-sea eyes. He was so close that she felt like she could see every emotion within him: hope, fear, pity, pain, sorrow—but what won was hope. "I could try this, and the plants might die. Or transform. There are a thousand ways a spell can go wrong. It's why the emperor made it illegal for anyone but a trained and approved sorcerer to work magic. But I've been studying this spell. I understand what the words are doing." It was all about the language—the syllables conveyed the intent, and the sentences executed the command. That's what magic was: words that brought thought to life. And Terlu was very, very good with words—or at least with words like this. She couldn't guarantee that the right ones were going to come out of her mouth in a random conversation, but this . . . *this* she felt confident about. Mostly confident. Pretty confident.

"I trust you," Yarrow said.

That was the most beautiful sentence she'd ever heard anyone utter.

Blushing magenta, Terlu turned back to the page. "It requires specific ingredients." She showed him the list she'd made: an apple blossom bud, an acorn that hadn't sprouted, pollen from a daffodil, as well as another half-dozen plant-based items that she was only half-certain she knew what they were, but one hundred percent certain that Yarrow did.

"Got it."

For anyone else, any*where* else, it wouldn't have been possible, especially in winter, but for Yarrow, in this place . . . She wondered if that was why the sorcerer had created the greenhouse in the first place, to have access to anything he'd need for his spells. *I don't think so.* From his notes, he didn't seem to have been amassing power for any other purpose than tending the plants, but if he'd wanted to . . . Perhaps that was what had made him so paranoid, knowledge of what other sorcerers could do with these resources if they had access to them. She wondered if the emperor had known what a jewel was hidden away here. Had Rijes Velk realized how valuable this place was when she decided to answer Yarrow's letter? Or had she just seen a problem that required a solution?

So many wonderful spells could be cast with the plants on this island. Had Laiken ever paused to consider the *good* that he could have done if he'd opened his greenhouses to the world, instead of trying so hard to isolate them?

She supposed that was the question: How much did you trust people to do the right thing?

Yarrow trusts me.

She wasn't going to let him down.

"I'll have all of this within an hour," Yarrow promised, taking the ingredient list. He nodded at the mug. "Drink your chocolate before it chills."

Less than an hour later, the three of them met by the shelves of sleeping plants. *Enchanted sleep,* Terlu thought. *It sounds kinder than statue-ified, but is it?* She doubted it. She wondered if they dreamed and, if so, what plants dreamed about. She only remembered her dreams in fragments—each filled with all that she'd lost.

Yarrow set down a basket, and Lotti leaped into it. She began tossing ingredients over the side onto the walkway. "We'll need enough to fix everyone," she declared.

Sitting cross-legged beside the basket, Terlu sorted through the ingredients. "Yes, but I think we should start with just one. In case it doesn't work."

"It'll work," Yarrow said.

Picking up a branch with berries on it, Terlu examined it. The spell hadn't specified how many white-cloud berries, but this would do. "Thanks for the vote of confidence, but I'm not a sorcerer, and this is an untried spell. For all I know, it could turn plants into ducks."

"Gah!" Lotti said. "No ducks." She shuddered, all her petals vibrating, and added darkly, "Had a bad experience with a mallard once."

"You *are* a sorcerer," Yarrow said to Terlu.

She shook her head. They'd been through this, and she'd thought she'd been very clear: she wasn't the person he'd hoped she was. She tried not to let it hurt that he wished she was someone else.

"A self-taught sorcerer," he amended. "You learned the language. You studied the texts. Yes, you did it without official sorcerous training, but just because it wasn't all formal doesn't mean you didn't learn. Tell me: When you cast the spell that created your spider-plant friend, did it work?"

It did. First try. "Only because I'd prepared . . . All right, point taken, but I still think it's wiser to start with one plant, if only because then we can greet them and acclimate them one by one. It'll be a lot if we wake them all at the same time." She knew how shaken she'd been when she was revived. "I don't want to cause them any distress."

He shrugged. "I just think you shouldn't undervalue yourself."

She opened then closed her mouth. "Thanks." He didn't say much, but when he did, his words hit her right in the heart.

Lotti flapped her leaves at them. "Enough with the mushiness! We've plants to save!"

Terlu felt herself blush.

Ducking his head to avoid her gaze, Yarrow knelt beside her and began to organize the ingredients into piles, dividing them by type.

Lotti climbed out of the basket and scurried up onto the shelves with the potted plants. "Hmm . . . Who first . . ."

"Choose a friend," Terlu suggested.

Lotti waddled past another pot. "Not you then," she said to the fireweed.

Yarrow neatened the piles of ingredients, straightening the stems and branches and lining the berries and nuts into precise rows. It reminded her of the rituals of the Temple of the Stars, whose acolytes believed that if they did not position the sacred stones in precise patterns, the stars would cease to shine and sailors would lose their way. She'd read their myths once, full of stories of lost wanderers and forgotten dreams, saved by the careful precision of those on land. "How did you learn to be a gardener?" Terlu asked him. "Did you study somewhere, or were you self-taught?"

"There wasn't a school, if that's what you mean, but I had plenty of teachers. My father. My grandma and grandpa, before they passed. Uncles and aunts. Lots of cousins. Everyone had their specialty."

He misses them. She could hear it in his voice. She wondered if they ever missed this place, if they were ever tempted to return, if they were just waiting for an invitation. "You should invite them for the Winter Feast."

He raised his eyebrows. "Much too far to travel for a meal."

"It's not just a meal."

He shrugged.

"You're not taking into account the cakes."

Yarrow grinned. "Honey cakes."

"And blueberry cake. Lemon cake. Vanilla swirl cake. Also, candied oranges. Have you ever had candied orange covered in chocolate? It's amazing. My grandfather candied the orange slices himself. Secret recipe. He never told anyone. So far as I know, he never even wrote it in code. You know, it makes no sense that Laiken wouldn't arrange for anyone to refresh his spells on the greenhouses, given how much he cared about protecting his plants."

"He thought he'd always be here," Yarrow said.

Pausing by an orchid, Lotti asked in a forlorn voice, "How did he die?"

"An accident," Yarrow said. "He fell down the stairs. A great sorcerer, perhaps the greatest sorcerer of his generation, but he still broke his neck. My father was the one to find him when he didn't come to care for the orchids. He used to tend them himself daily—he wouldn't let anyone else touch them. After Laiken died, my father said his spirit lingered to lecture him about the care of orchids for three hours, before finally falling silent."

"Orchids are fussy," Lotti said, dismissing the one she'd paused beside. She moved on to the Venus flytrap. "Foolish Laiken. He should have kept me awake. Maybe I couldn't have kept him from falling down the stairs, but at least then he wouldn't have died alone." Her voice wavered on her last words.

Terlu imagined how she must feel, both angry and sad and then angry that she was sad and sad that she was angry. There was a horrible helplessness to knowing your fate was out of your hands. Lotti hadn't been able to save herself, and she hadn't been here to save him.

"I'll keep you watered," Yarrow promised.

"You'll teach me to water myself," Lotti said, and then added wistfully, "Please? I want to know how to work the pump. I don't want to have to depend on anyone ever again." She heard the knot of emotions in Lotti's voice. *She'd relied on Laiken, and he'd let her down.* Terlu's heart ached for the little rose. Their stories weren't similar, but she knew how it felt to be powerless over your own fate, to be set aside and forgotten.

"I don't know if—"

Terlu spoke up. "If you attach a rope to the pump handle, she could use that for leverage. Perhaps even attach a weight to it? She shouldn't have to ever fear that she'll be abandoned again." No one should ever have to fear that.

He considered it and then nodded. "We'll find a way."

"Good," Lotti said. And then added to Terlu, "Thank you." She moved along the shelf, past several of the sleeping plants, including a delphinium and a thistle. "Don't wake the orchid first. How about the philodendron? He was a steady fellow. Quiet and unassuming, despite the size of his leaves."

Yarrow lifted the pot with the philodendron off its stand and set it on the walkway beside Terlu. She took each ingredient and combined them, twisting a stretch of grass around the packet and then knotting it as if it were a ribbon.

"Do you have a trowel?" Terlu asked. "I want to bury the ingredients between the roots. That should focus the spell on its target." Or at least that was the theory as she understood it. She was acutely aware of her lack of formal training. Usually it took years at the university before an imperial sorcerer was allowed to experiment with spells, and even then they were supervised by multiple senior sorcerers, to prevent accidents. This was, at best, foolhardy. But she didn't see much choice. She couldn't leave them stuck in an enchanted sleep, not when there was a chance she could wake them, as Yarrow had done for her.

He pulled a trowel out of one of his many pockets, and he dug a small hole in the dirt, carefully so as not to break the plant's roots. She handed him the packet of spell ingredients, and he tucked it into the hole and covered it up. "Ready," Yarrow said.

She supposed that was it. Everything was ready.

She'd been over the spell again and again, ensured that each syllable conveyed the precise meaning she wished it to. She was confident in the words.

Why then was she so nervous? *Because I'm breaking the law. Again. Willingly.*

The last time she told herself it was worth it and the consequences wouldn't be extreme, she had been very, very wrong.

This is different.

There was no one on the island who would report her. Yarrow and Lotti both wanted—even needed—her to do this. *I'm not in this alone. Not this time.* Furthermore, it was the right thing to do. She couldn't leave these plants in a state of suspended animation. They were supposed to be awake and aware, and if she had the power to restore them, then she had to. She'd already been through all of this, the pros and the cons, the rewards and the risks, and it was far too late to turn back now. She'd promised, and she had no intention of breaking that promise, regardless of the consequences. Terlu took a deep breath and then exhaled slowly. She shook out her hands and tried to calm herself.

I am a self-taught sorcerer.

And:

What the emperor doesn't know won't hurt him.

Terlu positioned herself in front of the philodendron and began: *"Myrd vi se hwathan. Myrd dor a chasacan. Myrd rywy. Allecase-ansara . . ."* She spoke each syllable smoothly, as if this were a language she'd learned at birth. The words echoed in her head, a chorus of thought and speech, and she held the philodendron in her mind as she spoke.

Wake. I want to meet you. It's time to wake.

She finished the final word in the spell.

The philodendron didn't move.

Lotti shifted closer. "Did it work?"

"I don't know." Maybe it took time before the effects were noticeable? She hadn't asked Yarrow how much time had passed between when he cast the spell on her statue and when she became flesh again, but then that had been an entirely different spell. Maybe this one had a delay. Or maybe it hadn't worked. Perhaps she'd missed an ingredient. Or she could have translated a word incorrectly— *Unlikely,* she thought. And all the ingredients were as fresh as they could be.

Perhaps these plants weren't asleep, at least not anymore. Perhaps too much time had passed, and they were ordinary plants now. Maybe their ancestors had been alive and aware, but that didn't pass into their seeds. She had no clear idea how that worked. If a plant dropped a leaf and then grew a new leaf, was it still the same plant? Did the seeds inherit the knowledge and wisdom of their elder? If these weren't actually enchanted plants but were only the children of them, maybe it wasn't possible to wake—

Across the greenhouse, the orchid yawned.

CHAPTER FOURTEEN

All around the greenhouse, plants woke up.

On Terlu's left, a coil of ivy climbed out of its pot and wound its way, snakelike, up a pillar. The orchid rotated its pale pink-and-white blossoms as if viewing the full greenhouse with its stamen. A daisy bloomed and lifted its leaves in a stretch, while the delphinium bent as if it wanted to fold itself in half.

Lotti danced with her petals in the air. "You did it! They're waking!"

"But they shouldn't be—" Terlu began.

On her right, a fireweed burst into flame.

"Fire!" Lotti shrieked.

Yarrow rushed over to it and drenched it with a full watering can. It began to sputter and cough. He knelt beside it while a nearby prickly pear grew a bud that opened into a yellow blossom with a loud, "Eeeeeeee!"

Nearby a chrysanthemum let out a high-pitched yelp.

It worked! It really worked! Except that they were supposed to wake one at a time. Instead, every plant in the greenhouse was stretching and twisting and waking.

The philodendron in front of Terlu was the first to speak. "Sooo." His voice was deep and slow, each vowel stretched like caramel. "Not. Dead. That's niiiice."

Terlu smiled at him. "Hello. Welcome back. I'm Terlu. And that's Yarrow, helping the fireweed. And Lotti. You remember Lotti?"

Lotti bounded over to the philodendron. "Dendy! So great to see you! I saw you before, of course, but you couldn't see me, because you were asleep, yet now, you're awake and so am I and here we both are! You remember me, right? Give it a second. You were just revived. I'm the resurrection rose that visited with Laiken. He's the sorcerer who created us. You remember him, of course, and if you remember him, you must remember me."

The philodendron said nothing for a long moment.

"Ooh, hello, welcome back!" Lotti hopped toward a thistle. Its bulbous flower was nearly twice the size of the tiny rose, and it loomed over her atop a thorn-covered stem.

Quivering, the thistle leaned back. "No! I won't! You can't! Don't let her near me!"

Lotti slowed a few feet from the thistle. "You don't understand. We woke you! You're okay now. You're alive and aware and alert. Isn't it wonderful?"

Nearby, the delphinium whimpered.

She headed for the chrysanthemum. "We were friends. Don't you remember?"

"I rememmmber her," the philodendron, Dendy, said, so softly that Terlu had to bend down closer to hear. His leaves undulated as he spoke. "We all dooo. Sheee was Laiken's first. Sheee . . . forgetsss."

"What do you mean?" Terlu asked.

By Yarrow, the fireweed was babbling. "Wet. This is wet. I am wet. But I am fire. I am wet fire. Oh, this isn't right. None of this is right."

The prickly pear began to cry, loud tearless sobs.

Yarrow awkwardly patted the sobbing prickly pear with one hand while dabbing the wet fireweed with a cloth. His face was a picture of panic. "Why did they all wake at once? And why are they all so upset?"

"It's a shock when you first wake," Terlu said, unsure. All of these plants had been asleep for far longer than she'd been a statue, and she'd found the experience of regaining flesh to be extremely disconcerting. *How are we going to explain how long it's been without further upsetting them?* And what should they say when one of the plants asked about Laiken? Inevitably, one was going to ask. She hoped they could delay that moment. It would be better if they could adjust to being awake and aware again before they learned that bit of news—it was going to be a major blow. She wished the spell had woken them one at a time, as she'd planned. Why hadn't it?

It's the ingredients. She'd buried the packet with the philodendron, but she hadn't put away the other supplies. All of them were out, exposed to the air, and so the spell had drawn from all of them to affect a far wider area than she'd intended. The words hadn't cared which items they activated.

I made this mess.

This was the difference between being a properly trained sorcerer and a self-taught one. She didn't have anyone to tell her what not to do.

The fireweed wailed.

"Yarrow, help them!" Lotti demanded. "You're the gardener. You're supposed to know how to take care of plants." She hopped from plant to plant, welcoming them and gushing that she was so happy to see them, but the plants didn't seem happy to see her.

On another shelf, a myrtle began to sing in a deep mournful voice. Its leaves vibrated as it sang, shaking the entire bush, as well as its pot. *"Oh, how my heart yearns for the sea, longs to be free as the blue, blue sea . . ."*

The prickly pear wailed louder.

"The darkness!" the morning glory screamed. "It came!"

The ivy slithered down from the pillar and wrapped itself around the prickly pear's pot. Reaching with a puffy arm, the cactus hugged a strand of ivy. Cradled by the ivy, the prickly pear began to calm down. Its yellow blossom closed back into a bud.

That's what they need. "Just comfort them," Terlu suggested.

"They're scared." She scooted closer to the calla lily. "Hello, I'm Terlu. I'm so happy you're awake."

The calla lily dipped its bloom toward Terlu. "Thirsty?"

"Yarrow, I think the plants might need water?"

"*That* I can do," he said, relief in his voice. He filled a watering can and moved from plant to plant, offering each one a drink of water. Some plants accepted and some didn't.

Lotti trailed behind him, talking to each plant, explaining where they were and that they'd been woken from an enchanted sleep, yay! And then following her welcome with a barrage of questions: Did they remember anything about before? Did they know their name? How about did they remember that one time when she'd accidentally distracted Laiken while he was casting a water spell and he'd flooded half the greenhouses? No? Good.

"You're Laiken's pet," the Venus flytrap said.

"I am *not* a pet!" Lotti said.

"She waaas the first of usss created," Dendy, the philodendron, said. Using his tendrils, he pushed himself out of his pot and flexed his roots. He gathered up a ball of soil before plopping onto the walkway beside Terlu. Caz, she remembered, had also carried his soil in his root ball. The spell gifted them with mobility, as well as sentience. "He was raaarely without herrr."

"You went with him everywhere," the flytrap said to Lotti. "You were here when he brought us each to life, and you were here when he condemned us to a living death."

"Death and darkness!" the morning glory cried.

Lotti shrieked, "I was not! I did not! I was dormant. It's not my fault."

The ivy slithered closer to the rose and circled her. "You helped him when he came to trick us. You lied to us."

"I never lied," Lotti said. "*You're* lying."

Dendy spoke. "Sheee doesn't remember. It isn't herrr fault."

"See!" Lotti said. "Wait—what do you mean I don't remember? I wasn't here. Tell them, Terlu. You found me dormant in Laiken's workroom. When I went to sleep, all of you were fine. The green-house was fine. Everything was fine."

"Everyyy time she's dormant," Dendy said softly, "she fooorgets."

Breaking off its song, the myrtle wailed, "I can never forget! The blue, blue sea! She has haunted my dreams! Salt on my leaves! Oh, the salt on my leaves!" It shook as if it were sobbing. Scattered leaves fell, and the daisy hopped its pot closer to console the shaking shrub.

Lotti flounced down to the walkway and plopped herself in front of Dendy. "I haven't forgotten a single moment. We were friends! *You* seem to have forgotten that."

The flytrap asked, "Where is he? Our betrayer—where is he?"

"We *were* friends. Family," the ivy hissed. "Until you sided with *him.*"

They did not seem fond of the sorcerer.

Or of the little rose.

Terlu wasn't sure who to comfort: Lotti, the newly awakened plants, or Yarrow, who was watching the drama unfold with a look of growing panic. He hadn't had to handle any emotions but his own in years, and she thought it likely that he ignored most of his.

Lotti shrank into herself, closing her petals into a bud. "I don't understand. Why are you all so angry? I didn't do anything! I was dormant too! I was dormant *first*! You were all awake when I went to sleep! I wasn't here when you were made to sleep!"

"Yesss, yooou were," Dendy said, more kindly than the others. "Yooou've forgotten, but yooou were here when Laiken cast the spell to take our liiives from us. Yooou told us it waaas merely a waaatering spell. It would keeeep our soil moist."

"You lied," the ivy repeated, circling Lotti. "Liar. Betrayer." It slithered tighter around Lotti, looping around her with its vines, while the little rose closed in on herself.

Smoke curled from the top of the fireweed.

"Please," the thistle begged Yarrow. "Don't let him make us sleep again."

Enough. Stepping forward over the ivy, Terlu scooped the little plant up and cradled her against her chest. Trembling, Lotti clung to her shirt. "You're scaring her," Terlu scolded the plants. "She doesn't remember any of this. Do you, Lotti?"

Sniffling, the rose shook her petals. "No! But . . . there are . . . gaps. I thought . . . He wouldn't water me sometimes, and I'd lose days, weeks, months. He'd get angry when he had to repeat himself, when I didn't remember . . . But I wouldn't betray anyone! At least, I don't think I would." She wailed, "I'm sorry!"

From beside the shaking fireweed, Yarrow said, "It sounds like she was his victim too. All of you were." A thread of anger laced through his voice. She felt it too, unfurling inside her, like boiling water in her stomach. If the sorcerer were here . . . You didn't treat living beings this way. He'd brought them to life; that made them his family. You didn't treat family like this.

Muffled, Lotti said into Terlu's shirt, "We weren't *victims*. We were *beloved*. He wouldn't have hurt any of us. He loved us. He just wanted to protect us."

Dendy sighed, curling his tendrils around his pot. "That's what heee said when heee cast the spell, that it was for our own goooood."

"He was a liar," the ivy said. "A filthy liar."

"One by one, we all fell aaasleeeep," Dendy said.

"For our own good, he said." As it spoke, the ivy was winding and unwinding around the nearest pillar, clearly agitated. "He never intended to wake us. Why are we alive again now?"

"Where is he?" the thistle asked, trembling. "Is he coming?"

The prickly pear sobbed louder.

Terlu glanced at Yarrow. He didn't look as if he was about to answer, so she took the lead. "He's not. He died a few years ago. It was Lotti who insisted we wake you all. She assisted with every step of the process. Whatever happened before, Lotti helped you now."

Shifting in Terlu's hands, the little rose peeked out from behind her petals.

"We are graaateful for such help," Dendy said gravely.

"He's dead?" the ivy said, withdrawing into a coil.

"He's not coming back?" the thistle asked. There was hope in its voice.

Yarrow said firmly, "He's not."

Opening all its blossoms at once, the morning glory proclaimed, "The darkness lifts!"

That's what they need to hear, Terlu realized. *That they're safe.* Now she knew what to say, the same thing she would've wanted to hear.

Circling through the greenhouse, Terlu reassured each of them that they were wanted, they were safe, and everything would be okay. Lotti kept silent, only piping up to echo what Terlu said, while Yarrow checked the health of their roots and stems, also echoing her. No one was going to make them sleep again, and no one was going to harm them or take them away.

By the time she'd talked with each of them, the sun had set, and the plants were beginning to curl into their pots—some of them calmer and some merely exhausted.

As near as Terlu could tell from what the plants said of their last day, Laiken had been afraid for them—he'd kept repeating this was for their own good, to keep them safe from anyone who would want to take them and use them. He'd never specified who might want to take them or why, but he was insistent that this was his only choice.

"He's gone. You're safe," she told them over and over, until they calmed, one by one.

She returned again to the philodendron on the walkway. Of all of them, he was the only one who had kept calm throughout the whole ordeal. "Dendy, will you all be okay for the night, or should we stay here?" Terlu asked. She could bring Lotti back to Laiken's tower and then return to spend the night with the other awakened plants.

"Yooou twooo won't fit in a pot," Dendy observed.

"We could bring in bedding," Yarrow said.

"I'll stay with them," Lotti volunteered. "I . . . think I owe them. Even if I don't remember. I'll stay, in case any of them needs anything—and if they do, I'll come get you. And maybe they can help me remember."

Terlu asked Lotti, "Are you sure?" The other plants hadn't been kind to her. "You could come back to the cottage with us for the night. We'll be back in the morning."

Yarrow knelt beside the philodendron and spoke softly to him.

"I'll be fine," Lotti said. She climbed down Terlu's pants and hopped onto the ground near the ivy. "These are my friends." She added with more of her old spirit, "Or they will be."

With reluctance, Terlu and Yarrow left Lotti and the other sentient plants. Caught up in their own thoughts, they didn't speak much as they walked through the other greenhouses and then outside to the cottage. The temperature had plummeted further, and Terlu's breath misted in front of her as they hurried between the pine trees.

Inside, she continued to shiver while Yarrow built up the banked fire.

"Do you think they'll be okay?" she asked.

"I don't know," Yarrow said.

When she was a little warmer, she hung up her coat and crossed to the kitchen cabinets to set bowls on the table while Yarrow heated up the soup. "Do you think Lotti will be okay?"

"She's a survivor."

"Are *you* okay? I know . . . that is, I'd gotten the impression that Laiken was important to you. Finding out that he cast that spell against their will . . ."

"He took their lives from them," Yarrow said. "Because he was afraid."

Filling their glasses with strawberry-mint water, she waited, giving him space and hoping he'd say more. He had to be feeling a lot. This sorcerer . . . While he didn't sound loving, he'd been a father figure, in a way. He'd created everything on this island, including everything that Yarrow cared about. It had to hurt to know he'd intentionally harmed his own creations, that it hadn't been an accident or something that had gone wrong. He'd deliberately taken the plants' ability to think, feel, move, and experience life, with no plan to ever wake them again. It wasn't a punishment for anything they'd done, like it had been with Terlu. They were innocent.

"He was supposed to protect them," Yarrow said. "All my life . . . Everyone on this island was dedicated to protecting every plant, and he . . . He was the one who started it all, who taught us." He shook his head. "He shouldn't have done it."

"It's okay to be angry at him."

"It's pointless," Yarrow said. "He's dead. It doesn't matter how I feel about it."

She set the glasses on the table. "It matters to me."

He looked at her startled and then nodded, but he didn't say anything more about it. Instead he said, "I'll need to secure a few flies for the Venus flytrap. There are spells on the greenhouses to control which insects are allowed in which area, and I don't know if any are allowed in the sentient plant room. In fact, I should talk to each of them tomorrow to determine what kind of environment they'll thrive in. The myrtle seems to miss the sea? I don't know what to do with that. Maybe move his pot to the dock so he at least has a view? One of the greenhouses used to have a spectacular view of the ocean, but it failed early on."

That gave Terlu an idea.

A terrible idea, but still an idea.

"Do you think . . ." She paused. Maybe it was better to not give voice to the idea? No, she couldn't do that. "Do you think any of the plants know about the greenhouse spells? If they do . . . it's possible they could help me identify which spells Laiken used to create the greenhouses . . ." She shouldn't even be considering this. After all, today's spell hadn't performed the way she'd expected. She'd failed to realize how widespread a spell's effects could be.

On the other hand, she *had* woken them, so it was, technically, a success.

She blurted out the words: "If I knew which spells he used, maybe I could figure out how to fix the greenhouses that failed."

He gawked at her. "Do you think that's possible?"

"I don't know," she said honestly. "But I could try."

"That would be . . ." He swallowed hard, as if he wanted to say so much more but the words had tangled in his throat. He shook his head. "You've done so much already. I can't ask it of you."

"You didn't ask," Terlu said. "I volunteered."

"I know it's been hard . . . After what was done to you . . . If you want to stop here, I'll understand. You've fulfilled your promise. You don't need to do more."

"But there's more to do." Besides, it wasn't as if the situation had changed that much—it was still just her, Yarrow, and the plants on the island. There was no one who'd report her. And if they did . . . *Well, it's too late. I've already cast a spell and broken the law.* "Yarrow, I want to try."

His smile blossomed.

Seeing it, she was even more certain that she needed to try. "No promises this time, though. I don't know if it will be possible." She had no idea how complex the spell would be or if Laiken kept detailed enough notes to replicate his work. She could end up sinking the island into the ocean or accidentally creating a carnivorous forest.

Or perhaps I could restore what Yarrow has lost.

Still looking as if she'd offered him the moon, he nodded. "I understand. No expectations. But I'd start with the philodendron, Dendy. He seems the most sensible. He might have some insight into what the sorcerer did."

"Good idea."

"And Terlu . . . thank you."

Terlu felt a warmth flutter into her rib cage.

Yarrow served the soup into the bowls, and they both sat at the table. She wanted to ask him what it was like here, when the plants were awake and it was full of people. He'd said that it had almost become a village. Had it been a happy place? Had he had a good childhood? And if he had, why was he okay with being so alone here for so long? *Maybe someday I'll be able to ask him whatever pops into my mind.* It still felt so fragile between them, though, like he'd walk away again if she asked too much or pushed too hard.

After they finished the soup, Terlu washed the dishes while Yarrow used the washroom, then he put away the soup while she took her turn. They both finished at about the same time and climbed into the right-next-to-each-other beds.

To her surprise, he was the one who spoke first. "I wish I understood why he did it. He was supposed to protect them. They trusted him. They loved him."

"He was afraid to lose them."

"Then he was responsible for making his own fear come true."

"People aren't necessarily logical. Especially if they're in pain."

Yarrow was quiet. Outside, the snow was falling, a soft *shush* on the roof and the world. The fire crackled and popped, shedding dancing shadows across the cottage. She listened to Yarrow breathe.

"It makes no sense," he said in the darkness.

"I think . . . he wasn't well." She said it carefully, but it wasn't a guess. It was the best explanation she had for why he'd sent Yarrow's family away even though they were desperately needed, why he'd put his sentient plants to sleep, why he'd encoded his spells and his notes, and why he'd made no plans for the future of his greenhouses after his death.

Yarrow didn't answer, but she sensed he was thinking about it. It was a kinder explanation than saying the sorcerer had suddenly turned cruel for no reason. Laiken had needed someone to care for him and intervene when fear began to consume him, but perhaps there had been no one close enough to him to see. Or no one who could help if they did see.

Into the darkness, Terlu said, "When I was a kid, I had a friend a couple of years older than me who excelled at getting me in trouble. She'd insist that of course she asked permission to climb into the volcano crater. Of course it was fine to take the canoe out to the reef. Of course no one would mind if we put a manta ray in my family bathtub—it would be my pet, and every kid deserves a pet. I fell for it every time because I trusted her, and I thought she loved me just as much as I loved and admired her. She was pretty and sparkly, and I wanted to be just like her. One time, we'd swum out to one of the harbor bells. I'd worried about the clouds, but she said they were fine . . ." She trailed off, remembering how Odile would coax her into their next adventure, call her partner and best friend and say she was brave. Next to Odile, Terlu had felt brave and, yes, sparkly, as if those attributes could rub off on her.

"They weren't fine," Yarrow said softly.

"No, they weren't." A storm had sprung up, she remembered. A fierce one. "When waves rose around us . . . It turned out she was hoping her parents would rescue her. They were always busy—her mother was the village healer, and her father was on the council. Helping other people . . . that's what they loved to do, but they never seemed to have time for Odile. And so she was constantly trying to capture their attention."

"What happened?"

"My sister saved us. She noticed I was missing and rallied my aunt, who was the best sailor in the village—she went out in the storm and brought us home. Odile had swallowed a lot of water. She almost didn't make it. And her parents didn't know until the next day. They were both out in a neighbor's field, helping bring in a pregnant cow. After that, my parents forbade me from going anywhere with Odile again, at least not without very direct supervision." She remembered what hurt the most: how Odile didn't seem to miss her. Odile had latched on to another kid to rope into her schemes, and eventually her parents *did* notice, when she broke into the head councilmember's house and stole one of the village relics—a headdress that she wore brazenly to the Spring Equinox Festival. She'd been jailed for that stunt, and her parents had been forced to confront her behavior. "I've forgotten why I started telling you all this."

"Sometimes people disappoint you," Yarrow said.

"Yes. Wait, no. Sometimes people are going through things that you can't see because you're too busy looking up to them. I think

Laiken wasn't who you needed him to be, and he wasn't who you thought he was. His decisions weren't always right."

Yarrow was silent.

"Like putting the plants to sleep."

He grunted in agreement.

"And like sending your family away."

No response.

"You could invite them back, if you wanted," Terlu said tentatively. She didn't want to push, but . . . *He misses them. I miss mine.* She'd write to hers, if she weren't afraid it would endanger them—and even more afraid of how they'd react.

He sighed heavily in the darkness. "They have their own lives now."

How did he know they didn't want to come back? Maybe they were just waiting for an invitation. Maybe they missed the greenhouses. Maybe they missed him. "But—"

He cut her off. "We should sleep. Dawn will come soon, and there's work to do."

Terlu fell silent. She wished she hadn't said anything. He didn't need her theories on a man that she'd never met, especially one who'd loomed so large in his life. *He's probably regretting not sleeping with the plants.*

At last, Yarrow said, "Thank you for today."

"It didn't go exactly the way I thought it would. I'm sorry." All the chaos was her fault. If she'd woken them one at a time, as she'd planned, it wouldn't have been nearly so traumatic for the plants—or for Lotti and Yarrow.

"You woke them, as you promised." He rolled over onto his side, facing her. Firelight flickered in his eyes, and she found herself staring into them. His eyes were as green as the pine trees outside, and when the flames danced in them, they glowed with flecks of gold, like the sheen of his skin. She wondered what he'd do if she reached out and touched him. *He could draw away.* She kept her hands firmly tucked beneath her blanket.

"Tomorrow I'll work on translating more spells," Terlu said. "If

Dendy can help, that'll make it go faster. Maybe the rest can help you with the gardening in all the other greenhouses? You shouldn't have to do it all yourself."

"They just woke," Yarrow objected. "I can't ask them to work."

"It might help them, if they feel they have a purpose," Terlu said. "You could just ask, with no expectations. Make it clear they can say no. They might surprise you."

Softly, he said, "They've already surprised me."

She supposed that was true.

"So have you."

For an instant, she thought he might be the one to reach out, cross the uncrossable space that lay between them, but he didn't do it, and she didn't dare.

CHAPTER FIFTEEN

At dawn, Yarrow made apple-and-cinnamon muffins. She had no idea how he got them mixed and baked so quickly, but by the time Terlu's eyes opened, the cottage was filled with the smell of early autumn, even while the snow fell again outside.

She stretched. "You are a wonder."

"Huh? *Me?*"

It occurred to her that it was possible no one had ever admired this man, ever seen him as more than a son, brother, cousin, nephew . . . the one who stayed behind. She wondered if he had any inkling of how special he was, to devote his life to the care of living things who—with the possible exception of the sentient plants, who had been asleep—could never really care for him in return. She hoped the sentient plants, now that they were awake, were properly nice to him. If they weren't . . . well, she'd never yelled at anyone before and wasn't sure she could, but she could certainly tell them she was disappointed in them and that she expected better from them. That approach definitely worked on her when her parents had used it. *Hopefully I won't have to.* None of them seemed to have any grudge against Yarrow, though she couldn't say the same about their views on the resurrection rose. "I hope they were kind to Lotti."

"She'll be all right even if they weren't."

"I think she's sensitive, even if she hides it," Terlu said. It must have been hard to be blamed for decisions you didn't remember making—or never made. Laiken could have lied to Lotti as well. She might not have known what he'd intended to do when he entered the greenhouse with the sleep spell. Or maybe she had known, but she hadn't thought to question the man who had created her. She'd trusted him. And now to be the target of so much vitriol while the little rose was still mourning the loss of her father figure . . . *Poor Lotti.*

"I think she's tougher than she looks," Yarrow said. "Like you."

Terlu barked a laugh. "I'm the least tough person I know. I was so unable to handle being a little bit lonely that I broke imperial law."

He shrugged as he pried the muffins out of the tin and arranged them on a plate. He wrapped a few in cloth napkins, embroidered with vines. "People were cruel to you, and it didn't make you bitter. What else would you call that?"

"Naïve? Needy? Pathetic?"

"Strong," he insisted.

Yet again, Terlu felt speechless in front of him.

Yarrow handed her a wrapped muffin and her red coat. "I'm heading into the greenhouse. Do you want to come?"

"Ah . . . Yes. Sure. Of course."

Wow, he was being *friendly.* And kind.

Outside, fresh snow blanketed the forest, covering their footprints from last night. The sky was a soft dove gray, and a lone bluebird sat on a branch and sang.

"Why don't the birds leave for the winter?" Terlu asked. "Why not go someplace warmer?" Her island always had an influx of birds every winter. She loved when they arrived, filling the skies and covering the roofs.

He shrugged.

"You feed them."

"I like to bake; they like to eat."

"You take care of every plant and every bird, every living thing on this island," Terlu said. "Who takes care of you?"

Another shrug. *Him and his shrugs,* she thought. She never knew shoulders could talk so much. "I don't need taking care of," Yarrow said. "In case you didn't notice, I'm grown."

"That has nothing to do with it." As they reached the door to the greenhouse, Emeral flew from the treetops into Terlu's arms. He nestled against her, instantly purring.

"Who did you have looking after you?" Yarrow challenged.

"No one," Terlu said.

He held the door open, and she and Emeral went inside.

"But if I had," she added, "maybe I wouldn't have ended up as a statue."

They walked through the greenhouses, with Yarrow pausing to check on various plants. He pulled a few weeds from a flower bed, pinched dead blossoms from a petunia, and examined the leaves of a bush that was covered in white berries.

After he stopped to fuss with a perfectly healthy-looking clump of daisies, Terlu asked, "Shouldn't we check on Lotti and the others?"

"Yes, we will."

He straightened, and they continued to the next room, where he paused to re-pot a plant, shifting it from a smaller clay pot into a larger one, where it had space to expand. Its leaves flopped over the sides of the pot. As he watered it, he seemed to feel that Terlu was watching him, and he glanced up at her.

Gently, she asked, "Are you delaying?"

"No."

She waited.

"I don't know what we're going to find," Yarrow admitted.

"Come on. Lotti will be waiting for us." She led the way, with Emeral curled, as usual, around her neck like a furry and feathery scarf. She ignored her own imagination, as it helpfully supplied her with all the ways it could have gone wrong after they left last night, starting with the others being cruel to Lotti and including all of them reverting to catatonic states as her spell failed for some unknown reason that she couldn't fathom but could still be possible.

She took a deep breath as she opened the door, and then the

chatter from within hit her like a wave. Grinning back at Yarrow, Terlu stepped inside the sentient plants' greenhouse.

All the plants were clustered on the walkway, their pots abandoned. The ivy was in a coil like a snake, and the thistle was laughing, its leaves quivering and its burrs bobbing back and forth. Bits of soil fell off its soil ball, wrapped in roots.

"*This* is how humans dance!" the daisy cried, and it bounced in a circle with its petals flapping as it waved its leaves up and down.

The fireweed cackled, nearly falling over.

"No, it's more like—" The thistle trotted on its roots, while shaking its purple flower back and forth as if it were a head bobbing to a drum beat.

Lotti laughed and clapped her leaves together. "Yes, that's it!"

"How about this?" the ivy offered. It spiraled up into a column and then swooped down and began undulating around the other plants while they laughed and cheered.

"Guess they survived the night," Terlu said, her hands on her hips as she surveyed the dancing plants. *Survived and thrived.*

"Terlu!" Lotti screeched. "Yarrow!" She hopped toward them, and the other plants hurried to circle excitedly around the two humans.

The winged cat let out an affronted hiss at the chattering and laughing plants before he launched himself off Terlu's shoulders toward the rafters. Perched above them, he began to lick his feathers, while glaring disapprovingly down at the mobile flora.

Lotti bounced around Terlu's ankles. "You missed Viria telling us about the time Laiken almost mixed up wild carrot and hemlock."

Terlu wondered which one was Viria. Except for Lotti and Dendy, they hadn't shared their names. She opened her mouth to ask.

"Both have clusters of white flowers," Yarrow said, "but the stem of a wild carrot is covered in little hairs, while the stem of hemlock is smooth. Also, hemlock is poisonous."

"It's ooonly funny becaaause nooo one was huuurt," Dendy said.

"Nah, it's objectively hilarious," Lotti said.

"The look on his face!" The calla lily, whom she guessed was

Viria, tossed their white flower back and laughed, their yellow spadix quivering. "After that, he insisted his gardeners label every single plant—hundreds of thousands of signs meticulously written out and placed in each and every pot."

Dendy said in his deep, slow voice, "He remoooved them laaater."

The laughter faded.

"I liked having a sign with my name," the prickly pear said in a squeaky voice. "A gardener drew a picture of me on it. I looked pretty."

Several of the closest plants hastened to reassure the prickly pear it was still very pretty, and the cactus told them they were pretty too—and the compliments flew back and forth, escalating until they'd all fully established that each of them was as pretty as sunshine in the springtime, after which an argument broke out between the ivy and the flytrap about whether the sun was lovelier in springtime when it was sprouting season or summer when they could bask in its heat.

Terlu interrupted them. "Since you don't have signs anymore, can you tell us your names and whether you prefer we refer to you as she, he, or they? We'd love to get to know all of you."

Behind her, Yarrow murmured, "Would we? All of them?"

She knelt on the walkway, and the plants bunched around her, each of them calling out their name: the philodendron was Dendy (he), the ivy was Risa (they), the orchid Amina (she), the calla lily Viria (she), the thistle Tirna (they), the fireweed Nif (he), the wax myrtle Ree (he), the prickly pear Hosha (they), the flytrap Sut (he), the morning glory Zyndia (she), the fern Mirr (they) . . . She committed as many names as possible to memory. "And how are all of you feeling? Are you all right?"

Yarrow added, "Do you need anything?"

The wax myrtle bush, Ree, launched into a sea shanty: *"All I need is the wind at my back, the deck at my feet, and the seeeeeeeeeea before me!"* He shook his leaves as he sang.

"Hush," Lotti told him. "Yarrow is serious. He's nice, and he wants to help."

And that prompted an outpouring from all the plants: they were fine, they were a little dry, one requested a new pot, one thought the soil could taste better, one wanted more humidity, one said the ivy (Risa) snored, another said the calla lily's (Viria's) laugh was too loud, the chrysanthemum wanted to know when her favorite gardener was coming back, and the fern (Mirr) wondered why they hadn't been mixed up with the other non-talking plants. They all wanted to know what they'd missed while they were asleep. Crowding around Yarrow, they asked him about gardener after gardener, by name, until Terlu thought he was going to bolt through the door and keep running until he reached the dock. He inched backward, shifting behind Terlu, as the plants crowded closer.

Lotti shooed them backward. "Give him space. I told you: he's the only gardener here, and he and Terlu are the only two humans. Plus the various beasties and bugs that Laiken created. There's also the cat, Emeral, but he's a terrifying monster."

"Not a monster," Terlu interjected.

"But that makes no sense," the ivy, Risa, said to Lotti. "There are hundreds of greenhouses that require care. It takes a team of gardeners, working day and night, to keep them weed-free, pest-free, properly pruned and cared for."

Terlu jumped in. "And that's why we need your help."

She paused, waiting for Yarrow to ask for their assistance with his daily tasks, but instead he said, "Since Laiken's death, many of the greenhouses have failed—the magic has failed, shattering the glass and causing the temperature spells to go haywire."

A few of the plants gasped.

"Terlu has been translating his journals," Yarrow said. "That's how she found the spell to wake you. Now she's going to find the spell to restore the dead greenhouses and save Belde."

I am?

Well, that seemed like a lot of pressure. She hadn't said she could, just that she wanted to see if it was possible. What if she couldn't? *I don't want to disappoint anyone.* "I'm going to try," Terlu said quickly. "I'm not a sorcerer, so I can't make any promises."

"She understands the language of sorcerers and has broken Laiken's secret code."

It felt like all the plants were staring at her, eyeless, which made her want to step behind a pillar and disappear. She'd never had anyone depend on her before. Usually it was well-known that everyone was going to find her vaguely disappointing. *Nice and friendly, but not so impressive—that's me.* "Yes, but there's a lot of work between being able to read and being able to cast the correct spell . . ."

Yarrow looked at her with puppy-dog eyes, so full of hope. "But you are still willing to try?"

"Yes, of course, I'll try. I just . . ." She sighed. Of course she was going to try! She just didn't want to promise a miracle if she couldn't deliver it. Terlu faced the plants, with their eager, perky leaves and their soil cradled in their roots. "If any of you remember what kind of spells Laiken used to keep the greenhouses stable, that would be very helpful."

"He was private with his magic," the orchid, Amina, said.

"Admit it: he was paranoid," Risa said. They slithered around the orchid. "Even early on. But Dendy was with him for some of it. He might recognize a spell or two."

"I can tryyy," Dendy said. "Thaaat's all I promise."

"Same," Terlu said fervently.

"That's all I ask," Yarrow said, his eyes on Terlu.

Shivering, Dendy curled his leaves as he wormed his way over the snow outside the greenhouse. He left a trail like a snake. He kept his root ball up off the ground, held by a mass of vine-like leaves.

"You look cold," Terlu said. "Do you want me to carry you inside my coat?"

He lifted his tendrils like a toddler asking to be carried. "Yes, please. Plaaants aren't made for extreme temperature chaaanges. Alsooo, I lack feet."

She scooped up his root ball, and he tucked his tendrils around her within her coat.

"Thank youuu," he said. "Laaaiken used to transport us in a wheelbaaarrow. At least until he wearied of our companyyy."

"I can find you a wheelbarrow."

"This is fine, if you dooon't mind."

"You aren't heavy, and you don't wiggle." He was roughly the same size as her first plant friend, but Caz hadn't liked to be picked up—he'd preferred to use his tendrils to swing between the library shelves. She wondered what it was like to suddenly realize you could move on your own and weren't bound to a pot or flower bed. "Did you leave the greenhouse often? You know, before?"

"In the beginning, I went with Laiken everyyywhere, like Lottiiii. Later . . . he didn't like thaaat I had opinions. It's been a looong time since I've seeeen his tower. He performed maaany spells withoout meee. I dooon't know how much help I'll beee, but I'll tryyy."

Reaching the tower, Terlu opened the door and carried Dendy inside. He unwound from her torso and hopped himself in, propelling his root ball forward with his leafy tendrils.

"It's cleaner now than it was," Terlu said.

Since she'd arrived, Yarrow had dusted and scrubbed every surface, and Terlu and Lotti had sorted all the papers and organized the books and notebooks, but there was still a sad, abandoned feel to it. *It's the smell,* she decided. Even after all the intensive cleaning, the workroom still smelled like decayed plants and dusty books, mixed with the smoke of the fire in the stove. *It doesn't smell like life.* No one had cooked soup or baked bread here. The only freshness was the citrusy tang of the soap that Yarrow had used to clean the jars and pots.

Maybe she could fix it. Add a few flowers in jars. Hang herbs to dry from the rafters. Add some curtains. There had been curtains in several of the other cottages. If she was going to keep spending time here . . . *I'd rather stay in Yarrow's cottage than make this home.* She especially couldn't imagine ever using the upstairs room. She hadn't even set foot up there since the first day, when she'd taken the only book in the room, Laiken's final notebook. It was, well, creepy at best. At worst . . . *It feels haunted.* She wouldn't be at all surprised if it was, at least by the residue of despair. Sadness clung to the upstairs room, as if the walls themselves remembered a lonely, paranoid man had lived and died there. She couldn't see herself voluntarily spending any time up there.

At least downstairs had none of that same miasma.

And thanks to Yarrow, it wasn't even dusty anymore.

Hoisting himself up with his leaves, Dendy climbed onto the worktable. He tucked his root ball under his tendrils, as if he were sitting. "Hooow can I help?"

Terlu waved at the papers and the books that filled the shelves, the desk, and the worktable. "I've worked out his code, using the codebook he left with the dragons in the maze, but there are over a hundred notebooks, as well as countless papers. It'll take a lifetime to go through it all, especially since I don't really know what I'm looking for. I'm hoping you can narrow that down."

"I caaan look through them. Seeee if I recognize anyyy."

"Perfect!" Terlu carried over a stack of them and piled them in front of the philodendron. "You're the oldest of them, aren't you? After Lotti?"

"Whaaat gave it awayyy? Am I wilting?" He twisted his viny stems, as if examining himself from various angles.

She didn't know why she'd guessed that. Perhaps because he was so much calmer than the others, or perhaps because Lotti had chosen him to wake first. Maybe it was the way he talked about Laiken, as if he had known him for decades. "What was it like here? Before Laiken sent everyone away. Did you know Yarrow when he was younger?"

"I expected yoooou to ask about the sorcerer, not the gaaardener."

She shrugged, exactly like Yarrow always did. She didn't think it was *that* unexpected. "I'm never going to meet the sorcerer. But

Yarrow is here." *And he's a much kinder person than it sounds like Laiken was.*

"Huh."

"What?" It was natural to be curious about the only other human on the island. She refused to be embarrassed. It wasn't as if she was asking him to gossip. Just . . . to share his opinion, as well as any revealing anecdotes. Extra bonus if they featured an adorable young Yarrow, learning to garden for the first time. She could picture him, caring for plants even though he was barely old enough to lift a watering can.

"I haaave seen curious humans beeefore," Dendy said as he waddled across the worktable. "They typicallyyy end up married."

Okay, *now* Terlu found herself blushing. "He isn't like what I thought he was at first."

Dendy began to look through the notebooks, using his leaves as if they were hands to grasp, pick up, and examine each volume. "Whaaat did you think he waaas like at first?"

"Unfriendly."

"And nowww?"

"I think he has a great heart," Terlu said. "He just doesn't know how to show it to anyone who isn't full of chlorophyll. Lack of practice, I think. Or maybe it's caution?"

"If your gaaardener was here with Laiken at the end, caaan you blame him? Heeee had to learn to guard his heart." He held up a faded green notebook with a frayed spine. "Tryyy this one. Laiken spent a lot of time with this noteboook, I belieeeeve."

Sitting on a stool, Terlu took the notebook, opened the codebook next to it, and began to read as she translated. She barely needed to consult the codebook anymore. She'd internalized much of how Laiken manipulated the language, and besides which, he slipped into standard for about half the jotted notes. It was only the spells themselves that he was careful to obscure. "Do you know what happened to the sorcerer? What made him turn away from everyone?"

"Aaah. Thaaat. Yes, I waaas there when it begaaan." He pulled out a second volume, a thick red notebook with a ribbon. "Hmm, I believe I remember seeing him with thisss one, though I think he used it to traaack supplies that aaarrived from other islands."

Terlu flipped through it. It was lists, and it wasn't in code, with the exception of one half page near the end. She read through the final half page. "There's one bit of a spell—I think it's incomplete. Did he experiment with spells?"

"All the time. He alwayyys wrote his own, or tweaked existing ones tooo his needs."

Wow, the librarians in Alyssium would have loved to have access to this treasure trove. So few sorcerers created their own spells, and here were hundreds. The trick was going to be identifying which spells actually worked and which were failed experiments, and that had to happen *after* she figured out their intended purposes.

She felt the weight of what she'd taken on, hovering over her like a boulder about to fall. It was an enormous undertaking, the work of multiple scholars over lifetimes. Terlu took a deep breath and tried to ignore the butterflies somersaulting in her stomach—Yarrow had looked at her with such hope. *I only said I'd try.* Perhaps if she understood the sorcerer better, it would be a less impossible task? "Why did Laiken create the Greenhouse of Belde?"

"I wasn't there thaaat earlyyy."

She supposed he wouldn't have been. Creating sentient plants was a rare advanced magic. Laiken wouldn't have begun his work with that spell. *Unlike me, who skipped over all the basics.*

"But I doooo know the answer," Dendy said. "He haaad a daughter, Ria. Sweeeet girl. Liked flowers. Got sooo sad when they wilted. Heee built the first greenhouse as a present to her, I waaas told. When I waaas created, she must have been aaabout sixteen, but even beforrre that, she waaas looking beyond the island—she waaanted to see other places, experience other things. Ria's dream waaas to see everyyy flower in the world. We were maaade in part to be her companions. Distraaactions, really."

"He didn't want her to leave," Terlu guessed.

"Heee had good reason. She waaas sick."

"Oh." She could picture it: a lonely little girl with big dreams and a worried father. When you were young, the world seemed gloriously huge and life infinite, and you were unaware of your own limitations and the barriers the world could erect in front of you. Terlu remembered she'd looked beyond the horizon and dreamed of what life would be like *out there.* So many possibilities! She hadn't understood that you couldn't have everything, and every door you walked through meant other doors you closed. There was a cost to leaving, and she'd paid without a second's thought, with no guarantee of what she'd find out in the world beyond. She'd thought it would be easy to find her place.

"He maaade the greenhouse for her," Dendy said. "In the beginning there waaas only a single structure, but he aaadded more and more greenhouses, collecting seeds and plaaant samples from all over. A steady supply of boats would bring them, and she seemed happyyy. He didn't know that Ria had been taaalking to the sailors, and he didn't know she bribed them toooo let her on one of their ships, when sheee felt readyyy."

So far, not a single notebook had mentioned a daughter, but then they didn't dwell on people at all. It was all about the plants and the structures. Terlu wondered if Ria had loved the greenhouses and if she'd ever intended to come back, or had she planned to fly free? *Like me, when I left home.*

"I waaas there the day she left. So waaas Lotti. It waaas the first time Laiken left Lotti without water—he blaaamed her for not telling him about his daughter's plaaans. He blaaamed the gardeners for not stopping her. He blaaamed the sailors for taking her."

"Let me guess: he never blamed himself for keeping her here when she didn't want to stay." She'd met people like that, always convinced everything was the fault of someone else. They never looked at their own choices.

"Heee kept building more, expaaanding the greenhouse, thinking if he could make it graaander and graaander then Ria would waaant to return. The dayyy that the supply ship brought news thaaat she'd died . . . The news broke him."

"That's so sad."

"Saddest waaas he kept thinking she'd return, and he haad to keep this island safe for her. He becaaame afraid that others would destroy the greenhouses. He didn't see that others loooved them too. Or that others had loooved her too."

"You miss her."

"Alwayyyys."

"And Yarrow? Does he miss her?"

"Heeeee was not yet born, when sheeeee died. This happened looong aaaago. Laaaaiken never forgaaave and never forgot. We plaants remember aaand forgiiive."

They fell quiet, and Terlu examined two more notebooks that Dendy had selected. One was focused on fruits and vegetables— spells to make healthier potatoes, spells to keep pests away from peach trees, spells for making pumpkin seeds taste spicy—but the other one looked to focus more on maintenance of the greenhouses themselves. From what she'd translated so far, there were multiple techniques he'd tried to ensure the right humidity levels and maintain the temperature . . .

As she read, carefully jotting down her own notes, Dendy began to sing. He had a soft, furry kind of voice, and he swayed his leaves with the melody. It was an old island folk song about a mermaid and a merman who befriended a child. She half listened as she read.

It was pleasant and peaceful. There was nothing better, in her mind, than reading with company. She didn't need constant chatter, but the companionship . . . *that* she craved. She turned another page—

The door to the tower flew open. Both of them startled. Yarrow stomped inside. He shook himself to shed the stray snow that had fallen on him.

Terlu jumped up. "Is everything okay?" Was Lotti all right? Were the other plants—

"Can I stay here for a bit?"

"Of course, but what—"

"They talk." He sank into Laiken's desk chair. "They don't stop. I just . . . need a few minutes." He put his face in his hands.

She tried to suppress a smile as she returned to her reading. He may have fled the talkative plants, but she noticed he didn't go to his own empty cottage—he'd come here to be alone, with her. He wasn't the loner he pretended to be. He was just . . . shy.

That was a nice discovery.

The day wore on.

Dendy reviewed more books on the shelf, choosing a few while discarding the rest, while Terlu continued her research. Yarrow puttered around them, hauling in firewood from outside and rebuilding the fire. Pulling two potatoes out of his pocket, he put them on the stove to bake.

Outside, there was a rising chatter of voices—frantic. She turned as something thudded against the door. Another thud, and Yarrow hurried to open it. Terlu joined him.

"You found me," he said with a heavy sigh.

Behind him, Terlu asked, "Is everything okay?"

All the plants began speaking at once, their voices overlapping in a cacophony that made it impossible to distinguish individual words. Lotti pushed to the front of the swarm of greenery and shouted over them all, "You have to come! A greenhouse is dying!"

CHAPTER SIXTEEN

The plants led the way—running, hopping, tumbling over one another. It would have been comical if Terlu hadn't seen the look on Yarrow's face. With Dendy galloping beside her, she kept pace with Yarrow, and they raced into the greenhouses.

Through the roses.

Through the ferns.

And into the greenhouse that Terlu had walked through on her first day awake, the one that should have been dripping with humidity. It was overflowing with greenery, every inch filled with fat leaves and tangled vines, but the air felt chill. Above, Terlu instantly saw what had gone wrong:

The sun had died.

She remembered this greenhouse had had a false sun at the peak, so intense that she'd had to squint to look at it. Now its cupola was a smoky gray, like a hearth soot-stained after years of fires.

The dragonflies, the ones who had danced around the sun with their diamond bodies and golden wings, had all already fled. She didn't see a single one left in the dying greenhouse.

Snap.

A crack spread up a pane of glass, branching as it reached up toward the cupola.

"I have to save the plants," Yarrow said.

"Tell us what to do," Terlu said.

"Us?"

Terlu looked at Lotti, Dendy, Risa, and all the other sentient plants. She didn't want to speak for them, but if she was any judge—

"Me," Lotti said.

Dendy said firmly, "Us."

The others shouted their agreement, then fell silent, trembling, frightened but ready. Terlu felt a swell of pride for them. Only a day ago, they'd been caught in an enchanted sleep, and now they were eager to spring into action, to work together to help others.

Yarrow looked at them for a half second as if he wanted to say more, then he nodded. "Last time this happened, the greenhouse temperature plummeted to subzero and then rose to scorchingly hot—the enchantments don't just fail; they go awry. We have to get as many plants as possible out before that happens. Including yourselves. Do you understand? Don't risk yourselves."

Lotti clapped her leaves together. It sounded like fabric slapping against fabric. "You heard him! Let's do this." Pausing, she looked up at Yarrow and Terlu. "What exactly do we do?"

Yarrow was already working. He'd shed his coat on the floor, rolled up his sleeves, and was ramming a shovel into the dirt near a hibiscus bush.

Terlu scanned the greenhouse quickly. Much of the greenery was planted directly into beds on the ground, but the potted plants could be moved first. "You, you, and you"—she pointed to the plants who looked strongest and had the most vines, leaves, and tendrils for grabbing and hauling—"begin with the pots. Drag them into the next room. Yarrow, shovels and trowels? Small enough for the plants to use?"

"Go east two greenhouses, then left at the roses. There's a storage bin in the corner of the citrus room," Yarrow said without pausing.

"I'll get them," Terlu said. "Dendy, as soon as Yarrow gets that bush uprooted, you and your friends should haul it into the next room. It can be replanted after everything is saved."

"Yes, ma'aaam," Dendy said.

She sprinted through the greenhouses, took a left at the roses, and charged onward until she reached a greenhouse filled with lemon, lime, and grapefruit trees. The distinctive scent of citrus curled around her, and she breathed it in as she panted. It flooded her senses. She looked for her favorite orange trees—*Focus, Terlu. Sightsee later.*

Which corner had the tools? She wished she'd asked. Every second she wasted could mean the loss of another plant. Huffing, she jogged to the closest corner. It held a lemon tree, with brilliant yellow fruit nestled between the leaves.

Next corner—

Yes!

Terlu loaded every trowel into a wheelbarrow, plus two shovels—there were more, but trowels would be easier for the sentient plants to grasp and lift with their leaves and tendrils—and she rushed back through the greenhouses. Sweat dampened her armpits, and she puffed as she ran with the wheelbarrow wobbling side to side. She nearly spilled it twice, but she made it back.

All the sentient plants were working, hauling pots across the dying greenhouse and into the safety of the next room.

Cradling the tools, Terlu halted and puffed. She hadn't run in . . . She couldn't remember when. She wasn't built for it. Her lungs burned as she gasped in air. But she forced herself to move again and begin distributing the tools.

"Give me a shovel," Risa demanded.

Terlu handed one of the shovels to Risa, who wrapped their vines around the handle. With one end, Risa secured themself around a pillar and used that as support to dig into the soil. Dirt flew into the air, landing on their leaves, the ground, and the walkway. They didn't slow.

As the others presented themselves, Terlu handled out trowels. Most were large enough to grasp them with their leaves or vines or, in one instance, roots. All the plants except Lotti.

"I want to help!" Lotti cried, her petals quivering. "Terlu! Terlu, I don't know how to help. Please help me help." She was dwarfed by the massive jungle plants in this greenhouse, too small to drag any pots and too small to hold a shovel or even the tiniest trowel. "Terlu, please. I can't just watch. Never again. I won't be just decorative."

Terlu considered the tiny rose. "Can you climb?"

"Yes. Why—"

There was no way to know how quickly the spells would fail or when they'd run out of time. They had to move as many plants as possible before the greenhouse became uninhabitable, which meant starting with the easiest to remove. "We need someone who can see the full picture to tell us where to dig and which plants to rescue first. You're in charge of triage. Identify which flora is fastest to save and shout to whoever is nearest and able."

"Yes! I can do that!" She scampered up the nearest pillar like a flowery squirrel. From the rafters above, she began barking orders. "Dendy, three rows to the left, there's an alocasia that hasn't spread—yes, there! Nif, help Hosha with the potted fern in the third bed on the left. Ree, the grasses! Yes, those! Zyndia, help Ree!"

Claiming a shovel for herself, Terlu began to dig around the base of a small palm tree. She hoped the edge of the shovel wasn't cutting through too many of the roots. The tropical trees and bushes had been growing for many years, and they'd spread their roots deep and wide into the soil. She didn't know if they'd survive transport, but she knew they wouldn't survive staying where they were.

The talking plants worked as hard and fast as they could, for their size and strength. As soon as one chunk of flora was unearthed, a slew of sentient plants clustered around it to haul it to safety. Lotti perched above it all, directing them to the next rescue, calling out whenever one of the sentient plants or Yarrow or Terlu needed assistance. Shouts would go up whenever a tree, bush, or plant was ready to be moved, and everyone would swarm.

Terlu's arms ached, and she felt blisters forming on her palms from the shovel handle. Her shoulders ached too, and she was drenched in sweat. Freeing the palm tree, she dragged it into the other room and then returned. She picked the next tree to uproot.

A few yards away, Yarrow was focused on digging, digging, digging—his shovel didn't stop. Dirt flew, covering him and filling the walkway behind him. He barely paused to wipe the sweat and dirt out of his eyes.

A moment later, he tossed the shovel on the ground. Dropping to his knees, he began pawing at the dirt to free the roots. Terlu joined him, working her fingers between the roots to loosen them without breaking them. After they'd worked around the base, Yarrow jumped up and began pulling at the trunk. He freed it from the soil, and they carried the tree through the door into the next greenhouse. Its outer branches snapped as they yanked it through the doorframe, but there was no help for it. They hauled it to an empty stretch of walkway.

He didn't speak as he rushed back into the dying room to dig up the next tree.

She helped the prickly pear, Hosha, and the orchid, Amina, maneuver another bush out the door. The morning glory hauled another pot out, while the delphinium and the fireweed worked together to unearth several clumps of lurid red flowers. In the adjacent greenhouse, the greenery was beginning to pile up. It was going to need to be replanted, and she wasn't certain it would all survive the shock of being extracted from the earth. The rescuers were all being careful, but was that enough? Also, she didn't know how they'd replicate the heat and humidity conditions of their original greenhouse.

But that was a worry for later, after they'd saved as much as they could. Taking a deep breath and rolling her shoulders, Terlu dove back in. With Lotti directing her, she cleared a bed, using the wheelbarrow to transport the smaller plants to safety.

Pausing to catch her breath, she scanned the greenhouse—it was still overflowing with green. If they were merely trying to hack it down, that alone would have taken hours, but to remove the plants carefully with roots intact . . . This was a project that could take days. *I don't think we have days.* "Any guesses how much time we have?"

"Not enough," Yarrow said grimly.

Terlu picked up her shovel again. If there were more gardeners on the island, maybe they'd have a chance of moving it all, but even with every single sentient plant helping . . . *It's not enough.* They couldn't work fast enough or hard enough. She pushed the shovel into the dirt again.

And she shivered.

She shouldn't be *cold.* She was sweating so much, but the sweat chilled on her skin. She felt cold sink into her bones. Looking up, she saw frost lacing the cracked glass. "Yarrow!"

He raised his head, and his breath fogged in front of him. "Everyone, out!"

"Lotti, get down from there!" Terlu called. She scooped up her coat and pulled it on. The ivy was in the middle of hauling a banana tree. With stiffening hands, Terlu helped her load it into the wheelbarrow. She rolled it out of the greenhouse and then went back in.

Dendy was shoving his trowel beneath a plant with elephant-ear leaves and shiny yellow flowers that looked like trumpets. Its leaves were flopped over him, and the whole plant shook as his trowel hit against its roots.

"Temperature's falling," Terlu told him. "Your leaves will freeze."

"Just a few more minutes."

She joined him with her own trowel. It grew colder and colder, seeping through her coat. Her breath fogged in front of her. She saw frost begin to form on the tips of the philodendron's leaves, and he began to shiver. "Okay, that's it."

Dendy wrapped his tendrils around the roots of the bush as its shiny yellow blossoms drooped and shriveled into brown husks. "I can't leave them—"

"Yarrow!" Terlu called. She looked up and saw Lotti was clinging to one of the rafters. The little rose still hadn't left yet either. "Lotti, you have to come down *now*!"

Yarrow ran to them.

As Dendy insisted that he wasn't leaving until the plant was extracted, Yarrow began digging at the roots to the flowering elephant-ear-leaf bush. Lifting his trowel with his leaves again, Dendy dug too. Soil flew into the air as the temperature plummeted.

Shivering hard, Terlu hurried to beneath the rafter where Lotti was perched. "You need to come down! Lotti, please! You'll freeze!"

"I can't!" Lotti wailed. "It's all iced up! I'll fall! I'll splat!"

The cold was beginning to hurt. It burned her throat as she breathed in. The temperature had to have plummeted far beneath freezing, beyond what any plant could survive. If Lotti stayed, she'd die. *If I stay* . . . She'd have frostbite if she lingered any longer. These weren't normal winter temperatures. It was deeply, deadly cold.

"You can catch me!" Lotti said.

"No, don't—" Terlu wasn't good at catching. When she was a kid, a favorite beach game was tossing a cloth ball to your teammates, keeping it away from the other team, but she was routinely the last to be picked to play, due to the fact that she tended to close her eyes whenever anything flew at her.

But Lotti was already pushing herself off the edge. "Wheeeee!"

Terlu felt as if everything faded around her, the world narrowing to just her and the falling rose. She reached her arms up, and she felt as if she were moving slowly, so slowly, too slowly. Her hands felt too small—*I'll miss, and she'll fall and splat, and it will be my fault* . . . She scooted to the left. *No, right. No, left*—

Lotti landed in her palms.

Terlu breathed again.

She cradled the little plant to her and jogged out of the greenhouse. She burst into the next room, into the warmth, and fell onto her knees. Heat pressed into her, and her fingers and toes felt as if they were burning. "Yarrow?"

No answer.

He hadn't joined them.

"Dendy?"

The philodendron wasn't here either. Both had stayed in the deadly cold greenhouse. The windows were iced in flowerlike patterns that rendered them opaque.

She set Lotti on the ground, and the ivy, Risa, circled her, coiling snakelike, tight around the rose. "I'll warm you," Risa told Lotti.

The little rose shivered. "Thank you."

Terlu forced herself to stand. She had *not* prepared properly for an emergency like this—a lifetime of studying languages and then a stint as a statue did not make one as physically fit as a full-time gardener, which was normally fine.

She plunged back into the frigid greenhouse.

Both Yarrow and Dendy were attempting to pull the flowering bush toward the door. She joined them, but as she grabbed for one of the branches, it snapped off. "It's frozen," she said gently. "Dendy, it's over. We have to go."

The philodendron was stiffening.

"Yarrow, you have to leave it." She scooped Dendy's root ball and leaves into her arms. "Come on. It's subzero. You can't stay in here."

"Take him," Yarrow said.

She hesitated.

"Go!"

Scooping up Dendy, she ran to the safety and warmth of the next greenhouse. The plant felt brittle in her arms. "Almost there," she whispered. "Hang in there. You'll be okay."

She reached the doorway and half fell through it.

Joining the others, Terlu dropped to the ground. "Dendy, say something. Please."

He was silent. And still.

"What do I do? He's so cold." She touched one of his leaves and then cried out as it broke off in her fingers. She felt tears well up in her eyes. Every bit of her hurt. She'd tried so hard. All of them had. And it wasn't enough. "Dendy . . . Please, wake up."

She felt hands on her shoulders.

"He needs warm water," Yarrow said behind her. "Bring him by the stove."

She got to her feet and carried the philodendron, his tendrils of frostbitten leaves trailing behind them. He felt so thin and brittle in her arms. His root ball barely had any soil, as if his roots were no longer able to hold dirt together. Some of his leaves had blackened.

"I'll find a pot," Yarrow said.

He met her by the stove with a pot that was already three-quarters full of warm, soft soil. Gently, she placed Dendy in it. He should have burrowed his roots into the fresh soil by himself, but he didn't, and so she cupped dirt in her hands and buried his roots in the soil.

Yarrow began to snip off the dead leaves. "He'll grow back. Philodendrons are hardy."

"The flowering bush?"

He shook his head.

"And the rest of the plants?"

"I need to replant the ones we rescued as quickly as possible," he said, not answering her question—which was its own answer. His golden skin was speckled with sweat and dirt, and his eyes looked haunted. "Stay with Dendy. He . . . shouldn't be alone when he wakes."

She nodded, and he stood and walked away.

Cradling Dendy's pot closer to her, she soaked in the warmth from the stove. She told herself she'd help Yarrow as soon as Dendy woke. She felt a pressure on her shoe and looked down. Lotti had climbed onto her foot and was attempting to crawl up her sock. Reaching down, Terlu scooped up the little rose and set her on her lap.

"I tried to help," Lotti said.

"Me too."

"It wasn't enough."

There wasn't anything that Terlu could say to that. She cuddled both the resurrection rose and the silent philodendron closer to her. After a bit, the winged cat flew to settle next to the stove. He curled up beside her, and with her free hand, she petted him as well. Nearby, the diamond dragonflies perched on branches and flowers and vines. They no longer danced.

Through the doorway, in the failing greenhouse, the tropical plants froze and then burned as the enchantments flared and then died.

She cried silently for the loss of all those innocent plants, for Yarrow, for feeling helpless, and for Dendy, who still had not spoken or moved, despite the warmth of the stove, the fresh soil, and the pruning.

At last, the tears stopped.

She took a breath.

She felt as if she could move again. "I should help Yarrow."

"I'll help toooo," Dendy said and stretched out his remaining leaves.

CHAPTER SEVENTEEN

By nightfall, Yarrow had found buckets and pots for most of the plants, with the help of Terlu and the sentient plants. They'd need to find permanent homes for them inside the greenhouses with the most appropriate temperature and humidity levels. It wouldn't be ideal, especially since so many of the still-surviving greenhouses were overcrowded already, but the vast majority of the ones they'd rescued would live, he said.

He insisted on walking through the newly dead greenhouse, once the temperature had stabilized. It was still cold, but only as cold as the outside wintery forest. Not the kind of cold that chilled flesh in seconds, like before. The vast majority of the plants they'd had to leave behind hadn't survived the extreme fluctuation, but he returned with a few that he thought might be hardy enough to coax back to life.

"I'll search for seeds tomorrow, when it's light," he said. "Maybe the species can be saved, even though the plants themselves are gone."

"I can help you," Terlu offered.

Lotti piped up. "We all can—and will."

The other plants agreed with her.

"We will staaay with the refugees tonight," Dendy said, "aaand monitor their health."

A floral chorus, the nearest plants agreed as well—they'd care for the relocated plants, tend to their roots, ensure they had water and nutrients. The orchid offered to sing to them, and the myrtle offered to teach them a sea shanty. The thistle said they'd dance to cheer them up and proceeded to bob their globular flower back and forth.

"Thank you," Yarrow said. He rubbed his face with his hands, and she noticed how tired he looked—as tired as she felt. "I can't . . . It's not enough. We couldn't save them all. This is why I needed a sorcerer, to keep this from happening."

Ouch. She knew it wasn't her fault that she'd been sent instead, but the words still stung. "I'm sorry."

He lowered his hands. "I didn't mean . . ." He trailed off, and she knew he *did* mean it, though she didn't think he blamed her. *He simply wishes someone else was here.* It wasn't personal, even if it felt very, very personal.

"For what it's worth, I don't think you need another sorcerer," Lotti said.

Risa added, "We don't *want* another sorcerer. They might force us to sleep again."

"What we neeeed," Dendy said to Yarrow, "are more of *youuu.* More gaaardeners." He waved his leaves expansively.

Yarrow shook his head. "There's only me."

Across the walkway, the fireweed, Nif, was sparking faintly, and the other plants were clustered around him. The morning glory cuddled against him, shivering so hard that her petals fell. The daisy was quietly sobbing, water sliding down their stem.

Terlu knew the obvious answer. She didn't even have to think about it. "You could ask your family for help. Just until I find the right spells to strengthen the greenhouses. You said they never visit. Maybe it's time. If even one of them came, it would double what you can do alone." She didn't have the expertise to be of much use—she had no illusions about that, though she'd done her best—and the sentient plants didn't have the size or strength. "Extra bonus: you'd have the chance to make sure they're all okay."

His eyes slid to the dead greenhouse, and she could tell he was considering it. The pain of the most recent loss was written in the lines around his eyes. He shook his head, though. "I wouldn't know what to say. I don't . . . I'm not good with words."

That wasn't a no. *It's a good idea.* She'd thought from the beginning that this was all too much work for one gardener, and she'd thought he shouldn't be without his family. "I could help."

He looked so vulnerable as he stared at the windows.

"I could write it for you," she offered.

"I . . ." He halted. "Yes. Yes, please."

Sitting at Yarrow's desk, Terlu wrote the letter on pale yellow paper. And then she rewrote it. And then she glared at it for a while. And then she went for a walk in the woods.

The air was as crisp as a ginger cookie. She shoved her hands deep in the pockets of her coat as she trudged beneath a sky that was vibrantly blue. Snow, lacing the trees and coating the ground, shimmered. It crunched beneath her feet as she walked between the trees. She didn't have a destination in mind and didn't think she was going anywhere in particular until she walked into a section of the woods that felt familiar.

Frowning at the trees, she tried to figure out *why* it was familiar. She hadn't spent much time outside the greenhouse, with the exception of the walk between Yarrow's cottage and Laiken's workroom. She hadn't even been back to the blue cottage, the one that she'd picked out as hers. Since then, there had been a string of more important things to do, such as finishing that letter, helping Yarrow search for seeds, or helping replant the rescued plants—all of which she should be doing right now. Really, she didn't have time for a stroll in the woods, but she'd felt the need to clear her head. She didn't know why it was so hard to write a simple letter.

Walking slowly between the trees, Terlu realized why she knew this spot: it was where she'd awakened, where she'd been given a second chance. She wished she knew the date—it could be her re-birthday, celebrated each year with honey cakes. Of course, that was assuming she got to have re-birthdays and that she wasn't turned back into a statue after anyone official discovered that she not only cast another spell but was planning to cast many more.

That was why this letter was so hard to write, she admitted to herself.

When she'd suggested it to Yarrow, she'd been thinking of him and the plants and the greenhouse. She hadn't been thinking about herself. If anyone answered the letter and came back to the greenhouse, Terlu would be vulnerable. They could choose to report her, and she would, once again, be guilty. Worse, she'd be a repeat offender.

The wind blew, and snow flew off the branches of nearby pine trees. It swirled around her, sparkling in the sun like flecks of diamonds. She turned to face the greenhouse, barely visible through the forest.

She didn't regret what she'd done. Waking the plants was the right thing to do, and saving the greenhouses would be too, if she could figure out how to do it, but the law was the law, as overreaching and draconic as it was. For as long as the Crescent Islands Empire stood, one did *not* defy imperial law, as she really should have learned by now.

Such a shame the lesson didn't stick, the other librarians would say.

Her family . . . How would they feel if they knew she'd been condemned, saved, and then lost again, all because of her own reckless choices? She watched a bird—a cardinal, with brilliant red feathers bright against the snow—fly between the pines, and she wondered if Rijes had really meant for Terlu to return to a life of crime so quickly. What if she'd misinterpreted the head librarian's letter?

I didn't misread anything.

The thought was as sudden as it was definite.

This was exactly why she'd been sent here. But she was also certain that others weren't likely to be as open-minded as Rijes. The head librarian was a rare person: highly intelligent, highly educated, and highly empathetic. How did Terlu know anyone else would be as willing to forgive the blatant defiance of imperial law?

She trusted Yarrow—he cared more about his plants than legalities codified by some faraway emperor—but could she trust his family?

On the other hand, do I have a choice?

The Greenhouse of Belde was too much for a single gardener to maintain, even with the assistance of a former librarian and a somewhat excessive number of talking plants. Yarrow needed expert help, and he was finally willing to admit it. She couldn't let her own fear stand in the way. *If I'm turned into a statue again, at least I'll know I did the right thing.*

Why wasn't that more comforting?

A hint of movement caught her eye, and she glanced over to see a cat-size gryphon swoop beneath a branch. It held a fish in its beak, and its lion tail swished behind. A lone feather fell from its wings as it brushed against the needles of a pine tree. Iridescent black, it drifted down onto the snow. She crossed over to it and picked it up.

She was going to have to trust that whoever answered the letter cared about the plants and about Yarrow and that would be enough to override whatever devotion they felt to imperial law, or whatever moral qualms they had about aiding and abetting a criminal.

It was that or continue to let Yarrow try to save the world on his own.

I said I'd try to help, and I'm going to.

Feeling more resolved if not exactly better, Terlu walked back to Yarrow's cottage. As she knocked the snow off her shoes, the winged cat stretched sleepily in her bed. She tossed the gryphon feather to the cat. With a delighted "Murp!" Emeral wrapped his paws around it and lazily chewed on the tip. He purred as he munched and kicked his hind paws.

"Once I send this letter, we could have a new visitor. Are you ready for that?" she asked him. "Do you think Yarrow's ready?"

Granted, it was possible that none of Yarrow's relatives would come, and it was even more possible that, if one did, it would be weeks from now. It was unlikely that anyone would just abandon their life in Alyssium and rush to the remote island of Belde. If anyone came, it would be at their convenience, when they had a gap in their responsibilities. More likely, there would be a few letters exchanged, with a visit planned for the spring or summer. Given the magnitude of what they were asking—for one of Yarrow's gardener relatives to return to their distant home for an unspecified amount of time—this wasn't going to be an immediate solution, so she should finish up the letter as quickly as possible and then return to scouring the sorcerer's notebooks for answers.

Sitting back down at Yarrow's desk, Terlu picked up the pen. She dipped it into the inkwell and wrote without stopping. It was the best way to do it, keeping the quill tip to the paper—it kept her second thoughts and third thoughts from interfering with the sentences. When she finished, she blew on the ink until it dried, then folded the letter and tied a ribbon around it. Yarrow had already prepared a tag with the name and address of his aunt and uncle in Alyssium, the florists. She fixed it in place with a bit of resin that she melted over the fire. He'd said he didn't want to read the letter when she finished it—she had offered, but he'd insisted that she send it as soon as she was done, before he changed his mind. He'd left her a pouch with payment to give to the supply runner to deliver the letter.

She wasn't going to tell him she had doubts too. This was the best course of action for the sake of the plants, regardless of their personal concerns. Yarrow couldn't do it alone. *Or even alone with a former librarian and multiple sentient plants.*

Maybe especially then.

"I'll be back as soon as it's sent," she told the cat.

At least *he* didn't seem concerned.

After banking the fire, Terlu put her coat back on and this time walked in the opposite direction: toward the dock. Yarrow had said to bring it there to send it and leave it with the payment, which should be half the pouch he'd given her. She didn't stroll this time;

she strode. She didn't want those pesky second and third thoughts to turn her around. Once the letter was off . . . well, then it would be done, and it would be up to others to choose whether to be kind or not.

Terlu heard the sea before she saw it, rhythmic bursts like steady drums as the waves crashed into the rocks. Salty sea air mixed with the crisp pine of the forest, and she smiled as she stepped out from between the trees to view the expanse of dancing blue.

The waves seemed to say: *Don't worry.* She felt the tension in her shoulders loosen. In the distance, the silver sails of a boat reflected the sunlight.

"It's beautiful, isn't it?" a voice said. "The sea."

She jumped and noticed the two-foot-tall shrub that wasn't rooted in the ground. Squatting on a rock, he held his root ball beneath a wad of leaves. *Ree the wax myrtle,* she remembered. "It is," she agreed.

"Yarrow said you're writing a letter to his family," Ree said. "I told him I'll deliver it myself." He fluffed his leaves, and she had the impression he was puffing up his chest. His voice sounded young. She wondered how old he was.

"You will?" She tried to figure out how to politely ask *how.* "It needs to reach Alyssium, which is . . ." She wasn't certain exactly where Alyssium was in relation to Belde. ". . . far."

"Don't worry about me," Ree said. "I'm a halophyte."

"Ah, congratulations?"

"I'm salt-tolerant," he translated. "Also, I'm brave."

"Ah." That was all very nice, but it didn't explain how he was going to deliver a letter across the sea. He couldn't be planning to swim, could he? Could a shrub swim? She tried to imagine it and had to press her lips together hard so she wouldn't laugh out loud.

"There's a flag in the box at the end of the dock," Ree said. "If you raise it, a supply-runner ship will know to come by. When it does, I'll go with it."

Suddenly, she didn't feel like laughing. "You want to leave Belde?"

"Oh yes," he said, the longing clear in his voice. "I've always wanted to see the world, to sail the sea, to feel the salt on my leaves and the wind on my bark. Laiken never understood. But Yarrow . . . He said if it's what I want, then it's what I should do."

Terlu thought of Laiken's daughter and wondered if Ree had known her and her dream. He must have heard the story—and heard how the daughter had never returned.

"I have to find my place," the shrubbery said. "My purpose."

She understood that completely. "Raise the flag, you said?"

"Yes, and a ship will come."

Walking out to the flagpole, she noticed a box affixed to the dock beside it. She opened it and took out a flag—the fabric was white, and it had been embroidered with silver thread in the shape of a lily. She touched the design lightly and wondered who had created such a beautiful piece. Did Yarrow have yet another skill? Or was this made by one of his relatives? She wondered what his family was like. Did they miss him? Did they worry about him? What would they do when they got the letter? She hadn't specified which relative should come, and she'd asked for the letter to be shared. Any gardener would do. Presumably they'd pick whomever could be spared. If she were lucky, maybe two or three would visit for long enough to make a difference.

Terlu clipped it to the line on the flagpole and raised it. A breeze made it dance, and she shielded her eyes from the sun to watch the silver flash as the flag flapped.

She wondered how long it would take for a ship to come this way. Yarrow hadn't said how often they came by, only that they watched for the flag. If Belde was on a popular shipping line, it could be soon. But she didn't think Laiken would have built his enchanted greenhouse anywhere well-traveled.

Terlu watched the ship with silver sails on the horizon and waited to see if they changed direction, but she didn't see any noticeable shift. *It could be days.* She couldn't just stand here and wait. She could, however, watch from within the sorcerer's workroom, if she repositioned the desk a bit. She liked that idea.

She kept the letter and the pouch with the sailor's payment with her for now, though Yarrow had said she could simply leave it in the box. "I'm going to watch from the workroom," she said to Ree. "Do you want to join me?"

"I'd rather wait here. Feel the sea breeze in my leaves. Don't you think the crash of waves is the most beautiful sound in the world?"

She smiled. "I'll come back outside when a boat docks."

As she headed toward the tower, she heard a sound behind her, like a trumpet. Ree gasped, and Terlu turned back toward the sea.

Beyond the dock, between the island and the sailboat, a sea serpent breached the water. She gasped, transfixed. She'd never seen one outside of illustrations in the older library books. Its scales were mother-of-pearl, and its featherlike fins were spread to catch the wind. It was singing like a trumpet as it arched through the air. It dove into the waves with a flick of its broad feathery tail.

It felt like a sign: she was doing the right thing.

Comforted and awed, Terlu went inside.

She was halfway through translating a spell that *might* be for window glass, or could possibly be for cleaning used jars, when she heard Ree shrieking, "A sailboat! It's coming!"

Looking out the window, she saw a boat with silver sails sailing toward the dock. Closing the notebook, Terlu darted for the door and grabbed her coat. She was outside before she had it pulled halfway on.

Waving to the sailboat, she skipped down the steps to the dock. The wind had picked up since she was last outside, and she hugged her coat closer as she stood on the dock, barely keeping herself from hopping from foot to foot. Ree was already at the end of the dock, quivering with excitement. Terlu didn't pause to consider why she was so excited too until she could see the face of the sailor:

Another person!

More than that, it was a person from beyond the island of Belde. It was easy to believe that the rest of the world was only a distant memory, not a thing that currently existed, while you were surrounded by impossible greenhouses.

The sailor was a woman with silvery skin, the same tone as her sails. Her white-and-black striped hair was tied back with a silver ribbon, and she wore all blue with black boots up to her knees. She grinned at Terlu as the boat slid beside the dock. "Tie it off, would you?"

She tossed a line to Terlu, and Terlu (to her relief) caught it. She knelt to tie it to one of the clamps on the dock—she'd tied off canoes often enough on Eano that her fingers remembered how to shape the correct knot, despite her years in the library.

"You the one who raised the flag?" the sailor asked. "What do you have for me?"

"Hi," Terlu said. "Thank you for coming. It's really nice to . . . Well, lovely to meet you." She pulled the letter out of her coat pocket.

"I'm Ree," the shrub said. "And you . . . wow. Hi. You're a *sailor.*"

The sailor laughed, not unkindly, and said, "Hello, Ree. Yes, I am." To Terlu, she said, "You could've just left the note in the box. That's what the gardener does. You the new gardener? What happened to the other one? He okay?"

"He's fine. I'm . . ." She had no idea how to describe who she was or why she was here. She held out the letter, as if it was a viable answer. "I'm a friend. I'm helping with the greenhouse."

"Huh. Good for him." The sailor grinned. She had a friendly smile, broad and open. She glanced at the letter before tucking it into a pouch at her side. "Not a supply list? He usually leaves a list of what he needs—flour and wax and yeast and such."

"It's a letter to his family in Alyssium. Do you know how long it'll take to reach them?" She wasn't certain how to say she didn't know where she was without it sounding too odd. She knew Belde was far from Alyssium, but was it north, south, east, or west? How many miles? She didn't think Belde was one of the outer islands, given the lack of storms—the outer islands were known for wilder weather, at least according to the stray bits of news she'd heard in the library—but did she really know? "Not to pressure you, but if I could give him an idea of when to expect a response . . ."

Ree blurted out, "I love the sea."

"Me too, my new friend," the sailor said. "Me too."

Terlu grinned at the little shrub, who seemed awed by the sailor. "Ree would like to accompany the letter, to make sure it reaches its destination. If you don't mind the company."

"This won't be a short or easy jaunt. I don't know that the open ocean is any place for an inexperienced, um . . ." She trailed off, clearly not certain what Ree was.

"I'm a wax myrtle," Ree said. "I'm a halophyte. You're a *real sailor*."

"He wants the ocean," Terlu explained.

Ree jumped in. "I won't be any trouble! I'll clean the deck. All the time. So much cleaning. And I'll climb the mast. Oh, can I climb the mast? Please? I can climb the mast and shout, 'Land, ho!'"

"I'm sure you'd be spectacularly helpful, but I don't need a deckhand. I'm a solo sailor. Besides, Alyssium isn't the best place to sail these days. It's a mess, with the revolution and all. It'll be a while before the city settles down."

Wait—revolution? *What did I miss?* "What's happening in Alyssium?" She tried to sound casual, as if this wasn't significant news that could alter the course of history and potentially affect her life and her future and her safety, as well as the life and safety of everyone she knew both in the capital city and beyond. "A revolution, you said?"

"You haven't heard?"

"The seagulls don't gossip much, and we don't get many other visitors."

The sailor laughed again. "Fair enough. The short version is the revolutionaries finally overthrew the emperor—like, literally, they threw him out a window—and the empire has pretty much fallen. It's been brewing for some time. You must have at least known that?"

She'd been a statue for six years. So, no, she didn't know. "I've been busy."

"Well, the long and short of it is that Alyssium is in chaos, and there's no more Crescent Islands Empire. It's just the Crescent Islands now. You're sure the gardener is okay? He hasn't ever sent a letter to anyone before."

"He's well, but it's important his family receives it quickly, if it's at all possible to sail there." How chaotic was it? Was Yarrow's family in danger? What about the library? And Rijes Velk? *Don't be silly. Revolutionaries wouldn't touch the library. It's full of treasures.* She was certain that it and the head librarian were fine.

The sailor shrugged. "If it's important, I can manage it."

"I can help," Ree pleaded. "I eat danger for breakfast."

"You eat breakfast?" the sailor asked.

"I only eat danger."

"That's hilarious and adorable, but the answer is still no." To Terlu, she said, "I'll deliver the letter as quickly and safely as I can. You've got my payment?"

Terlu gave her Yarrow's pouch. He'd said to offer half—the other half was for if she decided to send her own letter as well to another destination. But she offered the full amount. "Will this cover taking a letter to Alyssium, as well as taking on and training a new crew-mate?" She nodded at the shrub.

With leaves quivering, Ree whimpered, "Please?"

The sailor peeked into the pouch and whistled through her teeth. "Okay, I take it back. I'll sail wherever with whomever for this. Label says these are summer squash from Rivoc. My ma has been wanting to plant them for seasons, but you can't get them anywhere anymore. You tell Yarrow thanks from both of us and that I'll bring an extra bag of flour when I come back around for the monthly delivery." She grinned at Ree. "When *we* come back around."

"Gah," Ree said, so excited that he'd been rendered speechless.

"Thank you," Terlu said.

Shedding leaves, Ree cried, "My captain!"

"Call me Marin. It's short for Mariner, but I always thought that was a bit too on the nose. Also, risky of my parents—what if I hadn't liked to sail?"

"Who wouldn't like to sail?" Ree asked.

"My feelings exactly."

"Thanks, Marin. I'm Terlu." Belatedly, she wondered if she should have given a false name. She had no idea if she was a fugitive in Alyssium or not, especially given the news from the capital. Swiftly, she changed the subject. "Have you known Yarrow a long time?" The sailor seemed to care about Yarrow. How well did she know him? Had she known his family?

"Yarrow. Didn't even know his name." She shook her head. "Only talked with him a couple times—first time to ask when he'd need supplies, second time to ask about payment. Quiet guy. Polite. Didn't try to haggle, which was refreshing. Some people see a supply runner coming, and they assume we want to cheat you so they try to cheat me first. It's a game to some of them." She nodded toward the forest. "Your guy never played games. I respect that."

My guy. Terlu felt herself blush and changed the subject again. "Did you see the serpent earlier? It was singing like a trumpet. I've never seen one in person before. I always imagined the trumpet description was just people being poetic, but it really did sound like music."

"That was Perri. He's my buddy."

She had a sea serpent for a friend? Wow! "I have so many questions."

Tucking the pouch of seeds alongside the letter, Marin grinned. "I'll tell you someday. Or maybe not. Maybe I'll make up a few fabulous stories, and you can decide which one is true. Everyone always expects sailors to have incredible adventures to faraway lands . . . And yes. Yes, we do."

Terlu opened her mouth to ask more.

Marin held up a finger. "Another time. I've only so much daylight to ride the wind and a lot of islands in my path. I'll deliver your gardener's letter. And then someday I want to hear about *that* story, how you befriended the Reclusive Gardener of Belde. I will be disappointed if there isn't at least one passionate kiss involved."

Terlu sputtered.

Laughing, Marin untied the sailboat from the dock. "Come on, new deckhand. The waves wait for no man, woman, or shrubbery."

Ree scurried onto the boat. "Tell the others I'll be back with stories too!"

Still laughing, Marin shoved off the dock with her foot. She pulled on a line until the sail caught the wind. Crossing to the mast, Ree wrapped his branches around it and climbed.

"Happy sailing! And thank you!" Terlu called after them.

Marin waved and then she tilted her head back and sang a cascade of notes. Out toward the open sea, an iridescent serpent leaped out of the waves, trumpeting the notes back to her.

On the dock, Terlu watched until the sailor, the shrub, and the serpent disappeared from view.

CHAPTER EIGHTEEN

After two weeks of research, with the frequent assistance of Dendy, Terlu had amassed a stack of spells that she didn't think would cause anyone or anything to blow up or transform unpleasantly. She was sorting through them when Yarrow poked his head into the sorcerer's workroom. "Lunch?" he offered.

He was carrying a plate covered with a tea towel. She smelled the herbs as soon as he stepped inside. "That smells amazing," she said. "What it is?"

"Carrot and zucchini bread. My own recipe." He looked sheepish as he said it, as if it were of lower quality because he'd invented it. "It tastes better than it sounds. Inspired by my aunt Rin's carrot muffin recipe."

"It sounds wonderful." She wondered if Aunt Rin was one of his relatives in Alyssium. After she'd told him Marin's news about the revolution, his face had squinched up in a worried kind of way, but he, of course, hadn't wanted to talk about it. He had, though, started baking more recipes that he said were theirs, so she knew he was thinking about them.

She cleared a spot on the worktable, and he set down the plate. The aroma of baked bread wafted up. It smelled like a fall harvest. Or like a farmer's market when the sun has been shining and the rain's been falling and everything has grown so tremendously well that no one will be hungry all winter. "When did you have time to bake this?" He, with Lotti and the other sentient plants, had been working to replant the rescued plants from the dead tropical greenhouse. They had managed to save more than Yarrow would have been able to transplant on his own, but it was still only a fraction of what the sun-drenched room had held.

Yarrow shrugged. "Finished with the emergencies. Now it's up to the plants themselves to root. There's nothing I can do to help them do that." Removing the tea towel, he revealed the loaf: golden-brown, with a beautiful split through the length of the top crust. He sliced the loaf with a knife he'd brought and passed her a wedge on a napkin.

"Thank you." Inside, the bread was flecked with herbs, as well as curls of carrot and zucchini. It was as moist as a cake and smelled of cinnamon, nutmeg, and hints of sweet spiciness. She wondered whether it would be rude or flattering if she shoved the entire slice in her mouth.

"Wait." He withdrew a small pot from one of his pockets, as well as a spoon. "It tastes better with honey butter."

She smeared on a pat of honey butter and took a bite. It tasted light, sweet, and full of herbs that she couldn't name but knew she'd want to eat again and again. Closing her eyes, she savored the next bite. When she opened them again, she saw Yarrow was watching her. He looked away quickly and cut another slice. "If you ever want a second career," Terlu said, "you'd make an incredible chef."

He shrugged. "It's just bread. Glad you like it."

It wasn't just bread. It was the fact that he'd thought of her while he baked it, had carried it through the snow with a pot of honey butter in his pocket, and worried about whether she'd like it. If she hadn't, she was certain he'd have disappeared and returned with another even more delicious concoction that he'd describe as "just bread" or "just a snack" or "just breakfast" when it was a perfectly laminated almond croissant served inside a squash carved to look like a swan, or something equally exquisite—she wondered if a squash *could* be carved to look like a swan. Maybe a duck?

She spent a bit of time imagining what kind of animals could be created out of a squash before she turned back to her notes. "I think I found a few spells that could work."

He quit chewing. "Why didn't you say that when I first came in?"

"You brought bread."

"This is more important than bread."

"How could anything be more important than bread, especially with honey butter?"

"Terlu."

"Sorry. It's just that the key phrase is 'could work.' You see, Laiken liked to experiment, and while he kept meticulous notes about the ingredients he used in each experiment, he was less meticulous about recording the results. Most of the time I've been drawing conclusions based on what he tweaked for his next iteration. Anyway, I *think* I found the final version of his spell for the greenhouses—it's a complex, multistage spell with interwoven effects that simultaneously fortifies the glass and insulates it to allow for the stabilization of the temperature and humidity within the structure, though"—she spread out the papers—"I question his use of *rwyr-ent* in line three . . . Anyway, the point is: to proceed any further, I need to experiment."

He picked up the nearest spell and looked at it.

She did *not* tell him he was holding it upside down.

"You want to experiment?"

"Yes, preferably in a dead greenhouse. If you can pick one that's far away from any other living greenhouse . . ." Just in case she was wrong about the effects of the spell.

Yarrow nodded and put down the spell. "Do you know what ingredients you need?"

She presented him with a list.

"Are the spells dangerous?"

Every spell could be dangerous, if you made a mistake. There was a reason that the emperor had outlawed unauthorized magic. He may have taken his edict too far, but the initial caution was rational, which was why there hadn't been more than a handful of protests from scholars and other like-minded people when the laws were passed. Well, that and the fact that the imperial guard had cracked down on all protests with overwhelming force. Terlu shuddered as she remembered the fate of some early protesters: turned to ice in the summer. They'd melted into the canals in the heat of the afternoon. "Yes. Possibly."

Yarrow grunted. "I'll ask Lotti to keep the other plants away." He pulled on his coat. "Meet me by the roses. I'll have the ingredients with me."

She put on her coat too. "Can I keep the leftover honey butter?"

"Sure."

"Do you care if you don't get the pot back?"

Yarrow shrugged. "Do whatever you want with it."

"Thanks." She covered it and stuffed it in her pocket.

He stared for a moment, and she had the sense that he was struggling between his curiosity and his desire not to make extra conversation. "Is it a spell ingredient?"

That would be a lovely coincidence. "No. I just thought the dragons would like it."

"You don't need to feed them," Yarrow said. "They have everything they need in the sunflower maze. Laiken ensured they were self-sufficient."

"I know, but it might make them happy."

He smiled. "Okay."

"What?"

"Nothing."

She tried to read what he was thinking, but she couldn't guess.

"Let me know whenever you want more honey butter," he said.

A few minutes later, Terlu solved the chrysanthemum puzzle on the door and let herself into the sunflower maze. "Hello?" she called. The pine trees at the start of the maze were already parted. As soon as she stepped forward, the sunflowers flopped their heads toward her.

Approaching the first intersection of the maze, she opened the pot of honey butter. "Hello, dragons? I thought you might like this, since you liked the honeycomb."

She held it up on the palm of her hand.

A silver-scaled little dragon soared in a spiral above her. It cried in a caw, and it was joined by three others.

She didn't move, keeping her hand upraised.

The silver dragon landed hawklike on her forearm, its talons digging into her coat, and she was grateful for the thick wool of the sleeve. A falconer's glove would be a good investment, she thought. She wondered if she could request one the next time the supply runner returned to Belde. The dragon dipped its snout into the pot of butter and licked with a silver tongue.

It let out a metallic catlike purr.

Lifting off, it flew into the air, and a second dragon, with green-and-blue scales, landed on her arm and licked the butter. "You can take it all," Terlu offered. With her free hand, she scooted the pot closer to the dragon.

Another dragon flew down beside it, and together the two dragons lifted the little pot of honey butter into the air. They flew up toward the rafters, where they were met by a small flock. She heard them coo at each other, like the chatter of children but with no distinguishable words, and she wondered if it were possible to learn to speak dragon. *A task for another time,* she thought.

Terlu turned to leave, and she heard a chirp behind her. Turning, she saw the little silver dragon was holding a red rock in its talons. She held out her hands, and the dragon dropped the rock into it. "Thank you."

Looking closer, she saw it wasn't just a rock. It was a ruby, uncut but still a deep brilliant red that looked as if it had swallowed the sunset. A treasure from its hoard. "You don't need to—" She held it out to return it.

The dragon squawked at her as if offended.

"All right, all right. I'll take good care of it," she promised. "Thank you."

Tucking the gem into her pocket, Terlu exited the maze and returned through various rooms to the one overflowing with roses, where Lotti was in a heated discussion with Dendy about the proper way to trim a rosebush.

"Everyone okay?" Terlu asked.

Lotti broke off midsentence. "This *nonflowering plant* thinks that you're supposed to cut all but three to five canes and leave only two or three buds." She waved her leaves in the air to emphasize her outrage. "Can you believe this?"

Stretching out his leaves as if he were waking from a pleasant nap, Dendy said in his low and slow voice, "The caaanes will grooow stronger if—"

"Not if you mistake new shoots for suckers," Lotti said with a dramatic huff. "You can't just prune willy-nilly."

Dendy sniffed. "I never dooo aaanything 'willy-nillyyy.'"

Terlu knew absolutely nothing about how to prune roses. She held up her hand. "I'm going to experiment with a spell. Can you two help Yarrow keep the other plants far away? I don't want to risk any accidents."

Behind her, Yarrow said firmly to Lotti and Dendy, "You'll need to corral the others on your own. I'll be helping Terlu with the spells."

Intending to tell him that wasn't necessary (and could be risky), she turned to face him. Yarrow was carrying two baskets, both overflowing with branches, leaves, berries, and fruit, each so overladen that she could see the curve of his arm muscles through the sleeves of his shirt. Eyes widening, she gawked at both his arms and the baskets. "Oh my, that's a lot. I didn't think the list was that long."

Shifting one basket on his forearm, he looked a bit embarrassed. "Some species have multiple varieties. I brought them all to be on the safe side."

He's amazing. She'd known scholars, supposedly detail-oriented people, who weren't as thorough or as dedicated. "You don't need to come with me," Terlu said, belatedly—she wondered if he'd noticed she'd been gawking at him. "I can't guarantee the results. It would be better if I'm the only one at risk. You could be hurt."

He shrugged. "Or you could be hurt. If I'm there, I can pull you out."

"And if we're both hurt?"

Another shrug. "Then we save each other."

She smiled. "Well, that's okay then."

Lotti curled her purple petals. "Ugh, I feel like I have sugar on my leaves. Quit it with the oversweetness, you two."

"It is a biiiit much," Dendy agreed.

Feeling herself blush, Terlu looked everywhere but at Yarrow. "You two will keep the others at a safe distance?" she asked Lotti and Dendy.

"Yes, yes," Lotti said. "Shoo. Go drool over each other somewhere else."

Still blushing, Terlu followed Yarrow through greenhouses overflowing with flowers, bushes, vines, trees, and vegetables—as well as one with hundreds of tomato plants, each row guarded by marigolds with lionlike faces in the center of their blossoms. She remembered Yarrow telling her about the tomato greenhouse, but he hadn't mentioned it also had leonine marigolds who growled as they walked by. She wanted to ask about them, but he was walking with purpose. *There will be time later,* she thought, *for questions and exploring and all of it, after I perfect the spells.*

After we *perfect the spells?* Could she say "we"?

After the tomatoes, they crossed into dead room after dead room, until at last he stopped. He didn't say anything at first. He just turned in a slow circle. She looked too: at the cracks in the glass, the brittle dead plants, the cobwebs in the cupola, and the heavy layer of dust that lay over it all like a gauzy shroud.

"This was the first room we lost," Yarrow said as he set down the two baskets of ingredients. "My father and I. We only found it after it was too late. We thought if we'd been faster . . ." He trailed off. "There was never enough time."

Standing beside him, Terlu took his hand. She felt the calluses on his palm from years of gardening, but his hand was still warm and soft.

He didn't pull away.

A minute later, he took a deep breath. "Where do we start?"

Reluctantly, she removed her hand from his so she could spread her notes on the ground. She wanted to ask more about his father and the rest of his family, if he was worried about them, if she could help, but she'd promised to work on the spells. *This is how I can help.* "Near as I can tell from the notes, this is the primary spell Laiken cast on each greenhouse. It's highly advanced and very convoluted, but as far as I can understand, it simultaneously strengthens the windows *and* fortifies the perimeter so that the structure can maintain whatever conditions are established inside."

Yarrow grunted.

"It seals the glass."

"Ahh."

"Maybe," she amended.

He raised both his eyebrows.

Terlu showed him the spell. "See, the word *terilis* has multiple meanings, depending on context, and I don't exactly know the effect of pairing it with *rwyr,* which is essentially an activation word, with connotations that the spell will influence the natural world—an important word when dealing with plants because the suffix *-yr* is often linked with chlorophyll, except in cases where it's paired with *vi,* which this is not, which is why I believe—"

He took her hand back in his, and she cut off, staring at her lavender hand engulfed in his golden one. *He's never touched me before.* She'd touched him plenty of times—point of fact: she'd taken his hand just a few minutes ago—but he'd never reached out to her. A tiny difference that felt immense.

"I trust you," he said.

Still staring at their hands, she gave a little laugh. "I'm not a trained sorcerer."

"I know."

"If it goes wrong—"

"It will be fine."

It might not be fine. All of a sudden, the seriousness of what she was doing hit her. There was a valid reason that the judge had wanted to make an example of her. She couldn't guarantee that the spell wouldn't do more harm than good. *Maybe this is a mistake.*

"I'll be here, whatever happens," Yarrow said. "You aren't doing this alone."

Terlu felt her insides melt.

Yes, the spell might fail, but that was why she'd asked for a greenhouse that was already dead. How much more harm could she do? "All right. We try it. For this one, we need the sand, the elderberries, the seeds from an iffinal bush, a fern frond, the bud of a primrose, and the fruit of a sweetbriar tree."

Kneeling by the baskets, he extracted each item.

"Close the lids when you're done," Terlu said. She'd learned from when she'd accidentally woken all the sentient plants at once—don't leave extra ingredients out in the open air.

He obeyed.

"Pile those together so they're touching, please. And then . . . I don't know . . . hope really hard that this works?" Taking a deep breath, Terlu began, pronouncing each word that she'd translated painstakingly into First Language from the sorcerer's code. She was careful to speak clearly, emphasizing the correct syllables, breathing only at the ends of phrases.

When she finished, she fell silent. Yarrow waited beside her, patient, trusting.

Above them, the glass darkened to a smoky gray. It blocked the sun, and the greenhouse plunged into shadows. One by one, stars began to appear on the glass. They spread, thickening into clouds of stars that swept across the false sky.

"Beautiful," Yarrow said.

It was, but . . . "Not at all what I thought it would do." She craned her neck, trying to see all the stars. It was a replica of the summer night sky: she recognized a few of the constellations. She'd had an aunt who loved to take all the children onto the roof and point out every constellation she could name and tell stories about them, old myths from Eano and the nearby islands: the dolphin who greeted the dawn, the mermaid who was searching for the ocean, the cat who flew twice around the sun and became a part of the sky. She pointed toward a collection of eastern stars. "That one is the Sun Cat."

"Why are there stars?"

She frowned at the spell. It wasn't the words; there were no words that hinted at night or stars. "Are there any ingredients that have a connection to the night?"

"Primrose," he said promptly. "We used an evening primrose, blossoms after sundown." He knelt by the baskets. "There are several hundred varieties of primrose. I brought six of the most common." Opening the first basket, he held up a cluster of yellow flowers. "Cowslip primrose." Another, purple flowers on long stems. "Candelabra primrose. Common primrose. Rose primrose. Oxlip . . ."

"Which one blooms in sunshine?"

He handed her a bud with wool-soft leaves. "Common primrose. Usually blooms pale yellow. Prefers light shade and moist, loose soil, but can thrive in full sun."

She traded out the evening primrose bud. "Try again?"

He gazed up at the stars for a moment and then nodded.

Terlu cleared her throat and recited the spell a second time, with the new ingredients in her hands. Above, the deep blue cleared, and the stars faded. Lemon yellow spread across the glass, and at first she couldn't tell if it was from the inside or the outside, but it continued to brighten into an amber so glaring that she had to squint.

"Not primrose vulgaris then." Yarrow began to sort through the other primrose buds.

The third try toned down the yellow. Ordinary sunlight streamed through the glass, and Terlu made notes as to what they'd done differently, noting the exact species of primrose. "The key is: Did it seal the glass?"

This was essential to restoring the greenhouses, perhaps the most important step. If the structure could be fixed and fortified, with the cracks mended, the glass sealed and reinforced, and the entire edifice fully insulated with a barrier that both protected the walls from damage and stabilized the temperature within, then she could focus on figuring out the spells to control the heat, water, and humidity so that species from different climates could exist within, regardless of the external weather. But first the structure itself had to be mended.

He crossed to one of the windowpanes. She followed him, watching as he laid his hand on the glass—and the glass melted under his hand into water. It poured over his fingers and down the other panes. And then:

Whoosh.

Pane after pane dissolved. They waterfalled down the walls—

"The spells!" Terlu cried.

She ran toward the center of the room, where she'd left her papers with all her notes and spells on the ground. Gathering them up as quickly as she could, she hugged them to her chest.

A second later, the ceiling dissolved. Terlu shrieked, curling around the spells, as water crashed down, soaking them. Yarrow opened his coat and swooped at her, shielding her with his coat and his body. She leaned against him, the spells crushed between them, as water, along with the snow that had collected on the roof, slammed down on both of them.

A minute later, it was over. Only the steady *drip, drip, drip* remained. She peeked out from around his coat. "Well," she said, her voice trembling, "that didn't work exactly right."

His chest began to shake.

She realized he was laughing.

Terlu checked the spells. They were rumpled but dry. As to the ingredients . . . they floated in the half inch of water that covered the greenhouse floor. "I don't have the training for this. You deserve a real sorcerer, not a librarian who thinks she can study her way to any solution. I'm sorry."

He pulled her closer. "Don't talk like that."

"What? But I flooded the place."

"You tried. No one else would have tried. And you'll try again, right?"

"Yes, of course I will." Freezing water had splashed into her boots and soaked her socks, but she felt his arms warm around her. Tilting her head, she looked up at him. He was smiling down at her, the same look he'd given her when she'd first arrived, before he knew who she was, except now he knew all she was and all she'd done. "Wait, you *want* me to try again? After this?"

"I still trust you."

Terlu gawked at him, at the hope in his deep green eyes. She was aware she was pressed against him, his arms around her. He was drenched, his hair dripping onto his coat, his coat dripping onto the floor, but his chest was warm and dry. She'd never wanted to kiss someone so badly. He was smiling at her, and she stared up at his lips. Wet, his lips looked like molten gold. She wondered if they'd taste golden. "That's not really logical, given how badly I just failed."

He shrugged, and she felt his whole body move. "You made magic." He stepped back and began gathering up the damp ingredients. Suddenly, she felt cold, and she wished he hadn't moved away. "Tomorrow, try again in a different greenhouse? With dry clothes?"

"Sure."

She wished she'd dared kiss him instead of talking more, but she helped rescue the remaining waterlogged ingredients, and then they splashed through the greenhouse and out the door.

CHAPTER NINETEEN

Terlu was chilled to the bone by the time they reached Yarrow's cottage. Within her wet socks, her feet felt like blocks of ice. Coming inside, she shed her coat.

"You can lay your wet clothes by the fire," Yarrow said. He added more logs to build up the flames. The fire sizzled where he dripped on it. Immediately, he stepped back and stripped off his wet shirt.

Before, whenever he changed, she'd politely looked away or she'd been in the washroom, but this time, he'd acted so fast that she was looking straight at him. He was . . . wow. So many muscles. Broad shoulders, yes, she'd noticed *that* with his clothes on, but she hadn't seen his bare chest or bare arms. She stared at the way his arm muscles flexed as he shook out his shirt and draped it on a chair near the stove.

She hadn't realized she'd made a sound—a chirp-like *peep*—until he looked over at her. Blushing hard, she pivoted to face the bed and pet the winged cat. "Nice kitty."

Curled in the blankets, Emeral purred. Terlu felt her face flush all the way down her neck. *Nice kitty?* Ugh, why couldn't she just—

She felt his hand on her shoulder. Warm. Solid.

Terlu turned and looked into his eyes. He had flecks of gold in his irises, swimming in emerald green. Her breath caught in her throat. He had the kind of eyes you could sink into.

"You're dripping on the cat," he said.

"Oh!" She jumped away from the bed. Scurrying over to the fire, she shed her clothes and pulled on a dry tunic that he handed to her. It was made of the softest wool, and it hugged her body. *Act normal.* "Should we heat up soup?"

"I'll bake rolls," he offered. "The dough should have risen by now."

"When did you have time to make dough?"

He shrugged. "It relaxes me."

"Oh. Oh! I didn't mean to imply that you shouldn't be taking the time to make dough." She wished she dared say that she could think of another way to relax . . . She also wished she could command her cheeks to stop blushing.

He divided the dough and began rolling each chunk into a ball. He paused halfway through and frowned. "Honey butter," he muttered as he turned toward the sink to wash his hands.

"I'll get it," Terlu offered.

She went to the icebox and found a full pot of honey butter. Carrying it over to him, she noticed he was staring at her—*Probably because he thinks I'm odd, not because he thinks . . . anything else.* She was certain he didn't dislike her anymore, but that wasn't the same as wanting to kiss her. She tried to not fixate on his lips and instead she plastered a smile on her face as she held out the butter.

"A spoonful on each roll," he said.

He didn't move away as she scooted closer to spoon a heap of honey butter on each unbaked roll. Without looking at him, she was conscious of his nearness—her skin was as aware of him as it was of the warmth of the fire. She listened to him breathe as she spread the butter. Her hand shook slightly, and she hoped he didn't notice.

Stop being ridiculous. He barely tolerates me, and that's only because I can read spells. She stepped away when she finished, and he slid the tray of rolls into the brick oven.

"What's your favorite memory?" she asked him.

Yarrow began to shrug for the millionth time.

"You don't have to answer." She wasn't sure why she'd asked, except she wanted to know more about him, to know what he was thinking and what he was feeling. Maybe if she could understand him . . . if he could understand her . . . the awkwardness would melt away. "My favorite memory is of an orange."

"An orange?"

"I grew up on Eano," Terlu said. "Lots of sandy beaches. Lots of guava and sweet-berry juice. No snow ever. My grandmother had an orange tree, a very special orange tree that had lived three hundred years, at least according to family stories. Not sure if that's true; it easily could have been like my cousin's pet koi that my uncle kept swapping out for a new fish every time it died. Anyway, not the point. My grandmother's tree bore fruit very sparingly—three oranges a year, if it felt like it—but they tasted like sunshine. Sunshine at dawn on a perfect day. Everyone would compete to be worthy of one of these sunrise oranges, and she'd dole them out as a reward for special achievements. Like one year, a kid down the street saved his sister from drowning in a riptide. He got an orange. My aunt gave birth to twins. She got an orange. Anyway, my parents wanted me to spend the summer working in their store, learning what it was like to earn a wage, but instead of stocking shelves like I was supposed to, I read—I'd come across this old book in my grandmother's house, and it was written in an old Eanoan dialect that no one these days speaks. People knew a few words here and there, but no one was taught to read it anymore. So I taught myself." It was the first language she'd ever taught herself, the first time she'd realized she had a knack for it. Her parents had thought it was a waste of time. A near-forgotten language. What was the point? "On my grandmother's birthday, I surprised her by reading stories from the book. It was an old book of tales that her parents used to read to her. She didn't know how to read the language, even though she could speak it—she hadn't heard those tales read out loud since her father had died." Even though Terlu's parents hadn't understood, had in fact punished her by not paying her for the time in the store (which she'd admitted was fair since she hadn't done the work she was supposed to), it had been every bit worth it. "Grandma gave me an orange that day."

"And it tasted like sunshine?"

"Like sunshine at dawn." Terlu smiled as she remembered it. Some tastes you never forgot—they were too packed with memories. "It was the first time I realized I could be good at something. Before that . . . well, it was a memorable moment. Okay, your turn."

"Um . . ." Yarrow shifted.

"You don't have to." She didn't want to force him to share if it made him uncomfortable. She just thought . . . "It's fine. I think the soup's ready."

He checked on the rolls. "A few more minutes."

"Okay." She busied herself with pouring water and setting out bowls and spoons. Over on the bed, Emeral stretched, spreading his wings out and then folding them onto his back.

Yarrow spoke into the silence. "When I was six or seven, I was given a plant to care for. After a few weeks, its leaves turned yellow, it developed spots on the stem, and the roots began to rot. I thought it had developed some kind of disease." He paused. "Wait, you said a favorite memory. I don't know if this one qualifies."

He was talking. That was all she wanted. "It's fine. Go on."

"It was a nice memory, I guess, in the end. I went to my father, and he told me I'd overwatered it. I hadn't known that was possible. All I knew was that plants needed water, so I thought I was doing the right thing." He paused and took the rolls out of the brick oven. The cottage filled with the scent of fresh bread.

Terlu ladled soup into the bowls, and she scooped some grouse into a bowl for Emeral. Hearing the sound of the food plopping into the bowl, Emeral perked up. He launched himself into the air and flew across the cottage, while Terlu and Yarrow sat at the table.

She'd missed this, at the library: having a meal with someone.

I'm not going to jeopardize it by throwing myself at him. She didn't need love. She just needed soup and fresh bread and someone to talk with. And he was, miraculously, talking.

"I was crying, and it was my tears that convinced my father I was ready, that I cared enough to want to learn. He started lessons that day on how to care for plants." He continued the story while they ate. "We went through an entire greenhouse, and he identified each plant and told me how to prune it, re-pot it, and water it. The next day, he asked me to lead him through and parrot back what he taught me. When I failed, he started over."

Hot, the rolls tasted like honey-drenched clouds, and the soup was even richer than it had been the day before, now that the herbs had seeped into the broth. She split her attention between his words and the broth.

"Once I mastered one greenhouse, we moved on to the next."

"You learned plant by plant," Terlu said. "All of them?"

He shrugged. "Eventually. Took a bunch of years. But it only took a month until that plant—the one I'd overwatered—was healthy enough to bloom."

"Your father must have been proud of you," Terlu said.

"It was a good day. I wish . . ." He trailed off.

"What?" she prodded.

"I just hope he's all right. That all of them are okay."

"You said they're florists, right?"

He nodded.

"Then there's no reason to worry. A florist shop wouldn't be anywhere near the palace or any place revolutionaries would strike." She said it with as much conviction as she could. "I'm sure your family is fine, and we'll get a reply from them any day now."

Yarrow exhaled and a rare smile crossed his lips. "Thank you."

She felt herself blush.

After they finished the soup and the bread, they cleaned up together, and Terlu, for once, didn't feel the need to fill the silence with words. It was a nice silence, side by side. *It would be nicer if we were kissing.* But no, she wasn't going to allow those thoughts to ruin a lovely moment. *He opened up about an emotion. And he told me about himself.* That was a huge victory.

It wasn't a trivial detail either. This was formative. Plant by plant, he'd learned to care for this place . . . *Maybe that's the way to fix it.* She'd been trying to recreate Laiken's spells, but he'd been a master sorcerer. "Maybe . . . I need to think smaller."

Yarrow raised his eyebrows, listening, waiting for her to say more.

Pulling out the spells, Terlu spread them over the bed and studied them. She could identify a few of the disparate parts. What if she extracted a few lines of spell at a time and focused on fixing just a small facet of the greenhouse, instead of trying to tackle the entire structure? If it were a smaller bit of magic she was attempting to work, then maybe the results wouldn't be so . . . wet. "The spell's too large, at least for me. It's like you trying to care for a plant without knowing how. I just don't know enough to understand how much of what to do when, at least not in the way a sorcerer with massive amounts of training would, and there's too much that can go wrong. If I break it down into pieces . . . Like here." She pointed to a section of the text. "This line is for fortifying an individual pane of glass. In the context of the full spell, Laiken did it all at once, to seal the full greenhouse in one spectacular effort, but . . . I think I could adapt it to focus on healing a crack in a single windowpane, which might be a much more reasonable goal, at least at first." She shook her head. "But what if another greenhouse fails while I'm taking it slow?"

He shrugged. "Slow is better than not at all."

Terlu frowned at the spells, trying to rearrange the lines in her head. "Do you have any writing charcoal here?" She'd left the set she'd been using in Laiken's workroom.

Opening a drawer at his desk, he withdrew a writing set. She sat cross-legged on her bed and began to work. Outside, the moon rose higher, spilling pale blue light across the snowy forest. Inside, the winged cat curled up by the hearth.

"You should sleep," Terlu told Yarrow.

"*You* should sleep," he replied. "Especially if you're going to work magic."

She waved that off. She was close to an idea. "As soon as I finish this . . ."

Terlu fell asleep with her face smushed against her notes. Waking, she blinked at the moonlight streaming through the window. She hadn't used the privy before falling asleep and now she desperately needed to. She dumped her notes on the table as she padded past it.

She used the toilet, swished some toothpaste in her mouth, and then stumbled out. Her limbs felt heavy, and her eyes were only half-open. She climbed back into bed, grumbling a bit at how much space the winged cat was taking up, and fell immediately asleep.

Hours later, when sunlight streamed through the window, Terlu realized that she'd crawled into the wrong bed. It took a moment for the facts to penetrate her foggy-with-morning brain: she was nearer to the window than usual, the winged cat was sprawled across the other bed, and Yarrow's arm was flopped across her.

It was nice.

Very nice.

And she should definitely not be in his bed, uninvited.

But if she moved, would that wake him? What was she going to say? What was he going to think? Did he know she was here already? Was he going to think she'd climbed into bed with him on purpose? *And would that be a bad thing?*

Yes, yes, it would. If she was ever going to move beyond friends— were they even friends yet?—with Yarrow, then she wasn't going to do it by being sneaky. He deserved to have a choice.

Yarrow shifted in his sleep, curling around her. His breath warmed the back of her neck. She felt like she fit within his arms, like a book properly shelved.

She dithered so long about whether to stay or move that Yarrow woke up.

"Um, hi?" he said.

"Hi."

"You're in my bed."

"Yes, I am." She winced at herself. "I got up in the middle of the night and . . . uh, missed my bed."

"Ahh," he said.

He didn't move his arm from around her.

Terlu searched for what to say. "Did you sleep well?"

"Yes, very well," he said gravely. "You?"

"Very well." Her voice squeaked a bit.

"Good."

"I'm glad you slept well too," Terlu babbled. "It was . . . warmer this way, even if it was a mistake. Because of the cold outside. There must be a draft from the window, but I couldn't feel it. Because it's warmer with two." *Oh, for the love of the sea, stop talking!*

"It is warmer," he agreed. Then: "It was a mistake?"

"Yes," she said.

Should I have said no?

He began to withdraw his arm.

"No," she said. Then winced. "I mean, yes, it was a mistake, but it was a nice mistake."

"A warm mistake?"

"Yes," Terlu said.

Yarrow slid his arm back around her, and she wondered what it meant. And then she wondered if she was being an idiot—and then she decided that even if she *was* being an idiot, that didn't mean she had to continue being one.

Terlu twisted until she was facing him, within his arms, her breasts pressed against his chest. His eyes were wide, the flecks of gold brighter than she remembered. "I'd like to kiss you," Terlu told him, "if that would be okay with—"

He kissed her.

CHAPTER TWENTY

She had kissed and been kissed before, but never like this, like she was the most precious jewel in all the Crescent Islands. His lips were warm and soft and tasted like honey—how did anyone taste like honey when they first woke? His hands were on her back, pulling her so close that she could feel his heart beat through the fabric of their shirts, and she wanted to be closer, to be enveloped by him—

A thud thumped on the door. "Yarrow! Terlu!" Lotti called from outside.

They broke apart.

Yarrow disentangled himself and threw himself out of bed. Terlu felt as if a bucket of snow had been dumped on her head. He yanked open the door and demanded, "What's wrong? Is another greenhouse failing? Which one?"

"No. Not that." Lotti hopped inside and then shook her petals and leaves. Bits of snow flew around her. "Eeks! Cat!"

Half falling out of bed, Terlu launched herself forward and grabbed Emeral before he could fly at the little rose. She cuddled him as she carried him to the icebox, where she offered him some grouse. Forgetting the talking plant, he dedicated himself to nibbling on the unexpected breakfast.

"Tell me what's wrong," Yarrow said. He was shedding his night-clothes and pulling on work clothes, heavy pants with many pockets and a warm shirt, and Terlu tried not to remember how it had felt to be pressed against him—that moment had passed, and she had no idea if another mistake like that would happen again, or if he wanted it to.

Lotti sighed dramatically. "It's the other plants."

"Are they hurt?" Yarrow demanded.

"No."

"Are they asleep again?"

"No."

Terlu tried not to glance over at Yarrow as he buttoned his shirt over his chest. His chest hair was golden, tapering in between his muscles. Clearing her throat, she asked, "Are they being unkind to you? I can talk to them."

"It's not that," Lotti said. "They're . . . *singing.*"

Slowing as he secured his belt around his waist, Yarrow scowled at the little rose. "They're supposed to sing. Laiken spelled them to sing."

"No, no, not the enchanted musical ones. They're great. It's the others, the ones like me. They're trying to sing with them, and they're *terrible.* Well, not Dendy, he's fine, but the others!"

Yarrow grunted. "That's hardly an emergency."

Lotti flopped dramatically onto the wood floor. "It is to me. My ears!"

"Do you have ears?" Terlu asked, curiously. She hadn't inspected Lotti's petals up close to see if she was formed different from other non-talking plants. As far as Terlu could tell, Lotti didn't have ears or eyes or a nose or a mouth. Her petals moved when she spoke, but not because they were lips. Perhaps because of the vibration in the air? Terlu very deliberately didn't look at Yarrow again, even though he was fully dressed now.

Lotti waved her leaves in the air dramatically. "Obviously not, but I *do* have perfect pitch, which the vast majority of my fellow sentient plants do *not* have."

Frowning, Terlu tried to remember the exact words of the spell that created Caz. It could have been all wrapped up in the word "ansara," which had the root word for "life," but it wasn't life as in breathing and existing—that was linked with *rwyr*—it was connected with experiencing life . . . If the magic translated that as experiencing the five senses . . .

"What do you want me to do about it?" Yarrow asked mildly.

"Take me with you today," Lotti begged. "I told the others that you need my help with the magic. Please, Terlu, let me help you with the spells. I'll do anything. Sort ingredients. Prop up your notes. Sit quietly in the corner and pretend to be invisible. Whatever you need."

Terlu glanced at Yarrow to see what he thought, but he looked to be waiting for her to decide, as if her opinion mattered more than his. *He cares what I think. Values it.* She couldn't think of anyone else who had ever—

"Ooh, wait—am I interrupting something?" Lotti asked. She hopped forward and plopped herself down in front of them both. She folded her leaves as if they were multiple hands clasped in front of her bud. "What did I miss? Come on, details."

Terlu felt herself blush furiously. "Not at all, and nothing." *Focus, Terlu Perna.* She'd wanted no plants with them in case anything went wrong, but today she was planning on experimenting with a much smaller, more focused kind of spellwork. Maybe it was okay? It wasn't as if she needed to be alone with Yarrow for any reason . . . "I thought you'd want to spend time with the other sentient plants, at least the ones who aren't singing. Why do you really want to come with us?"

Lotti's petals drooped. "They . . . They don't understand that I miss Laiken. For them . . . it's different for them. He was different with them. And I . . . just need a little break."

Terlu wanted to give her a hug. No matter what kind of man Laiken had been, what problems and flaws he had, he'd still been important to Lotti. Of course she'd miss him. "If you promise to be silent when I'm casting the spell . . ."

"I can be silent! Silent as a mouse, which is an odd expression since mice squeak and chitter and have those scratching paws when they—"

"Let me just get dressed, and then we can go." Terlu stepped into the bathroom to wash and change into a sturdy wool skirt and blouse. She took an extra minute to take a deep breath and convince her cheeks to quit blushing such a vibrant pink. *It was just a kiss,* she told herself firmly. *It probably won't even happen again.*

When she came out, Lotti was still talking, describing the melodies of her fellow plants in tones of horror. Apparently, some were trying to add lyrics to the singing plants' music, and the rhymes were unbearable.

Terlu pulled on her shoes and coat. She took the spell she'd worked on the night before. It was short—only three lines long—and it was entirely possible that it wouldn't work at all, now that it had been excised from the context of the larger enchanted-greenhouse-creation spell, in which case, Lotti would be in no danger at all.

"Carry me," Lotti ordered, and Terlu picked her up.

"Can we also bring a mortar and pestle?" Terlu asked Yarrow. "I think we should mash the ingredients into a paste this time. If I'm doing smaller magic, it will need to be directed." Or at least that was her current theory, which seemed to match her recent experience.

He took a mortar and pestle from his kitchen supplies and added it to the basket of spell ingredients. He then handed her one of the leftover rolls from dinner the night before. "Breakfast?"

"Thank you." Their fingers brushed as she took the roll, and she stared at their hands for a moment—his golden and hers lavender—and wondered if he felt what she felt, but by the time she looked up at his face, he'd turned away and was opening the door.

Outside, the morning air was crisp and smelled like the sea.

"Did you want to, um, talk? About earlier?" Yarrow asked.

In front of Lotti? "Later? Maybe?" Or not at all. If he was going to talk about how it was a mistake, then she'd rather the silence, at least for now, at least until the feeling of his mouth on hers faded from her lips.

"Good," Yarrow said.

They kept walking.

"I could handle the singing until the rhyming started," Lotti continued to complain. "Do you have any idea how many words rhyme with 'blue'? So many. So very many."

Yarrow led them to another dead greenhouse, far from the rest.

While Yarrow blended the ingredients into a paste, Terlu studied the words of the spell. Lotti hopped from one dead flower bed to another. "Were these unique species?" the rose asked.

"Unique to the Greenhouse of Belde, yes," Yarrow said. "Thankfully, as far as I know, none of these species are extinct in the Crescent Islands. It was a tragedy but it could have been worse."

"Can you send for more seeds and regrow them?" she asked.

"If the greenhouse can be fixed, yes."

"Good," Lotti said. "Laiken saw this as both a sanctuary and a fail-safe. If the rest of the world destroys their plants, at least all won't be lost."

"He didn't have a high opinion of people," Terlu observed.

"He loved plants," Lotti said.

Terlu didn't remind her how Laiken had let her fall dormant, or how he'd enchanted the others to sleep. His love wasn't the kind of love that Terlu ever wanted. *Do not look at Yarrow,* she told herself firmly.

Yarrow glanced over at Terlu. "Are you ready?"

No. "Yes."

Standing, she took the paste from Yarrow and walked to the closest wall of windows. Cracks ran through the glass. She chose one, dipped her fingers in the paste, and smeared it over the first crack.

"Careful," Yarrow said behind her. "Don't cut yourself."

She was being careful. It was cracked but not shattered, and it wasn't sharp. *He cares.* That had to mean something. He hadn't just kissed her because she was there, had he? She didn't think so, but it wasn't a question she was ready to ask. Terlu finished coating the crack as far as she could reach, until she was out of paste.

Now, the words.

It was a simple spell: a noun with descriptors to identify the target, a verb ("strengthen," with the connotation of healing), and then the invitation to the magic of the world to flow via the verb to the noun. That was what magic was: coaxing the ineffable spirit of the world's magical energy into a chosen path. She hadn't actually read much about magic theory—those were dry texts, usually geared to echo lectures, and since she wasn't in school for sorcery, she'd skimmed past them. She was far more interested in how language was used. There was beauty in the precision of its poetry.

"Terlu?" Yarrow asked.

"Sorry." She took a breath and then spoke the words:

Svaniga vi rayna,
Ami pri nessava,
Biana te biana me vi pri rinaka.

She finished.

Silence.

"That's it?" Lotti asked.

Yarrow hushed her.

"That's it," Terlu said. "It may not be enough, without Laiken's full—"

The glass crackled. She watched as the paste began to glow a warm, sunny amber. It bubbled as it liquefied and then dissolved into the glass, spreading as a yellow haze.

The crack in the glass knit itself together as the yellow spread and dissolved. In minutes, the glass was smooth and clear. Terlu laid her hand on it. It tingled beneath her palm.

It was only a single pane. *But it worked.*

She grinned and turned around. "I know it's not flashy or exciting, and it's just a single crack out of thousands, tens of thousands, and at this rate, it will take weeks of work, many weeks, given the number of dead greenhouses, but—"

"It's amazing," Yarrow said firmly.

Terlu felt herself start to blush.

He added, "You're amazing."

She blushed harder. "If we make more paste—"

Yarrow nodded and began portioning out more ingredients into the mortar and pestle. Terlu tilted her head back and scanned the greenhouse—there were a countless number of cracks that ran through every pane up to the ceiling. "Lotti, how do you feel about climbing?"

"I'm an excellent climber."

"Could you reach the cracks in the ceiling?"

"Just watch me."

They set to work: Yarrow creating the paste, Lotti scampering up the walls of the greenhouse to smear it on the cracks, and Terlu reciting the spell for each one.

It's working!

She started in on the next spell and tripped over a syllable, pronouncing "nessava" as "nessavara." Instead of sealing the crack, it expanded it—the crack spread like the veins of a leaf. Lotti, hanging upside down from a rafter, turned her petals toward her. If the rose had had eyes, it would have been a glare.

Concentrating harder, Terlu repeated the spell.

She didn't make any more mistakes.

After three nonstop hours of spellcasting, Terlu felt as if she'd been swallowing sand. Unfortunately, each itineration of the spell only healed a bit of broken glass at a time and so she'd had to recite the spell again and again. "Tea?" she croaked.

From the rafters, Lotti called, "I could use a break too, and a soak."

Yarrow looked up, and she could tell he was counting the remaining cracks. They'd barely done a sixth of one greenhouse. At this pace . . . *It's not fast enough.* She knew he was thinking it too, but he didn't say it. "We're nearly out of ingredients," he said instead. "It's a good time to take a break."

They trooped back through the dead greenhouses until they reached the warmth of the rose room. The sweet scent curled around them. While Terlu plopped down onto the edge of a flower bed framed by pink roses, Yarrow filled a bucket of water and carried it back to Lotti.

The resurrection rose lowered herself into the bucket with a sigh, holding on to the edge with her leaves and dunking her roots into the water. "Ah, that's nice."

"How much of the ingredients do we have left?" Terlu's voice broke on the word "ingredients." She swallowed to ease it.

"Rest your voice," Yarrow said. He crossed to the enchanted stove in the center of the greenhouse and pulled out a kettle to boil. "Rose tea?"

She nodded but didn't speak.

She sat in silence while Yarrow bustled around the greenhouse, pruning random rosebushes as he waited for the kettle to boil. Lotti soaked in silence as well, dipped in the bucket. From a nearby greenhouse, Terlu heard the faint sound of off-pitch singing.

When the kettle whistled, Yarrow prepared the tea, using rose hips and petals. He carried a mug over to her, and Terlu opened her mouth to thank him.

He put his fingers to her lips. "Rest."

She was tempted to kiss his fingers, but he removed them too fast, and she wasn't sure how he'd react if she did anyway. Holding the mug under her nose, Terlu breathed in the steam. It smelled heavily of roses, and perhaps another spice? She didn't know what he'd added to it, and it wasn't worth using her vocal cords to ask. She sipped the tea and then winced as a faraway singer hit a note that was more screech than song.

"Ugh, can't someone stop them?" Lotti asked.

As another plant shrieked in dubious harmony, Terlu took another sip of tea and felt it scald the back of her throat, soothing it as it stung. A few more sips later, and she began to feel better. She wasn't sure, though, how many hours she could do this for, if her voice felt so tired after just a quarter of one greenhouse. "We need help," she said. It came out scratchy. She swallowed and tried again. "We can't do it with just the three of us."

"You sent the letter," Yarrow said. "No one replied. Either they didn't want to return or they couldn't. The fact is no one's coming."

"You don't know that. It could just be a long journey." Or he could be right. Marin could have failed to find Yarrow's relatives. The chaos could have spread as far as wherever their florist shop was. She didn't say that out loud. It was equally likely the boat was just slow. She was sticking with that explanation until proven otherwise. "The fact is we don't know if anyone's coming or not."

He snorted.

"I was thinking of asking the plants."

A grunt, but it was less skeptical. He was thinking about it.

Of course, enlisting all the sentient plants to help with casting illegal spells would absolutely be frowned upon. But then, Terlu had already broken the law spectacularly by waking them, and then she'd compounded that by learning and casting a new spell multiple times. How much worse would it be if she turned a dozen or so beings to a life of crime with her? Yarrow and Lotti were already her accomplices, after all.

If an imperial investigator discovers what I've done here . . .

Hopefully, they were all too busy with the revolution to worry about one lowly ex-librarian on a distant, mostly abandoned island. If she were lucky, they'd been disbanded when the empire fell, though that seemed too much to hope for.

Regardless, she wasn't going to stop helping now. Perhaps there was a way, though, to keep the other plants innocent. What if they merely gathered the ingredients and didn't cast the actual spell . . . ? Of course that still left her repeating the spell a thousand times, which didn't really solve the problem. *I should just ask them. Put the choice in their hands. Or leaves.* So long as she was clear about the risks . . .

"If it's their choice . . ." Yarrow said, echoing her thoughts.

"I'll talk to them," Terlu decided.

"You might want to bring earplugs," Lotti said.

Carrying her mug of rose tea, she opened the door between greenhouses and entered the room with the singing plants and trees. She was swamped with a wave of sound—the lovely harmonies of the enchanted flowers, but above it a caterwauling that sounded like raccoons arguing over a tree. As for the sentient plants—

The ivy, Risa, was dangling from one of the rafters. They cradled the daisy in a loop of their vines and was swinging her like a child on the world's most dangerous playground, while the daisy shrieked, "Higher!"

The fireweed, Nif, was spurting sparks into the air like he was attempting to emulate a fireworks display, while the flytrap, Sut, tried to catch the sparks between the lobes of his trap. The calla lily cheered them on.

In the center of the greenhouse, Dendy had his leaves raised, swaying them from side to side as he sang in his soothing, pleasant voice:

"In the morning, the skyyy is bluuue,
And the birds all caaall, 'Coo-coo-coo,'
They flyyy so that they get a viewww
Of the ocean that's alsooo bluuue . . ."

Sure, it was all a little circus-like, Terlu thought, but it wasn't so terrible. Dendy had a nice voice, a deep baritone, while the enchanted plants crooned a chorus of—

Three of the other sentient plants chimed in, each of them off pitch in a different way. *"Blue so blue!"* The thistle joined in with a shrill arpeggio that did not match any note producible by any known instrument. Nearby, the delphinium warbled discordantly.

Terlu winced. *I take it back. That's terrible.* "Um, Dendy?"

He kept singing while the polyfloral chorus harmonized (or more accurately failed to harmonize) with his melody:

"The fish beeelow swim in the stewww
Of the ocean that's alsooo bluuue . . ."

She raised her voice. "Dendy?"

"Hmm?" He stopped singing and swaying. "Oh, heyyy, Terluuu. Wait. That also rhymes! Want me to sing a song about youuu and your eyes so bluuue?"

"They're purple, and I'm sorry to interrupt your creative pursuits, but we could use your help, and the help of the other plants, if they're willing."

Nif shot a three-inch flame into the air, and the flytrap doused it.

"Ignore them," Risa said. "Go on."

She explained about the spell—how it repaired the cracks, but it was a painstakingly slow process. They'd experimented with smearing more paste over cracks, but regardless of the amount of ingredients used, each utterance of the spell only seemed to work until it hit a fork in the crack, which meant that for a badly splintered pane, it needed to be repeated multiple times before it was smooth. "It's the first step to fixing the greenhouses. If we can make the glass sound, then we can focus on how to insulate the greenhouse and then how to regulate the temperature, provide the water, and handle all the other necessities." She couldn't, though, spend her time researching other essential spells if all she was doing for hours on end was sealing cracks in glass. "It needs to be your choice, though," Terlu continued. "According to imperial law, only trained sorcerers are permitted to work magic. What I'm asking—well, I shouldn't be asking at all. It's illegal, and if you're caught, the consequences could be serious. You absolutely should say no if you feel at all uncomfortable."

Breaking off their cacophony, the sentient plants began to whisper to one another. The enchanted trees and flowers that belonged to the room continued to croon, softly and sweetly. Risa lowered the daisy onto the floor, and the fireweed stomped out the last of his sparks.

"Think about it," Terlu said, backing away. She did not want to pressure them into this decision. She could keep healing the cracks herself, if she had to. "You don't have to decide right now—"

"I caaannot speak for the others," Dendy said. "But it is a yes for meee."

She cautioned, "There is a substantial risk—"

"Weee all saaaw the greenhouse die," Dendy said. "If I caaan help, then of course I waaant to help." The other plants crowded forward, all of them chiming in that they agreed with the philodendron.

The morning glory, Zyndia, rose up on her vine and proclaimed, "For light and life!"

The others cheered.

"For glory and love!" she cried.

More cheers.

Terlu smiled. She hadn't expected *this* much enthusiasm. She'd thought maybe a handful . . . but all of them seemed adamant.

"For—" Zyndia began.

"That's enough, dear," the fern, Mirr, said. "But yes, we will help."

"It's not glamorous work," Terlu warned all of them. "And it might take a while—there are a lot of failed greenhouses, and they each have hundreds, if not thousands, of cracks. You'd be risking your freedom, even your lives, for a tedious task."

"A necessary taaask," Dendy said. "Correct?"

"Well, yes, if the glass can't be fixed, the greenhouses can't be used," Terlu said.

The ivy vine coiled around Terlu's feet and wound up her calf to her knee. "Then we will do it," Risa said. "It's nice to be alive, but we also want to matter. Besides," they added as they slithered down and coiled themself in a pile, "I hate singing."

CHAPTER TWENTY-ONE

Risa volunteered to orchestrate gathering the necessary ingredients, once Yarrow showed them which items were needed. They drafted two other plants—the orchid and the daisy—to assist. Hosha, the prickly pear, offered to prepare the ingredients. They could pound them into paste with their needle-crusted pads. The calla lily helped, using the spike-like part of her flower like a mallet, and the flytrap used his lobes. Dendy, along with the fireweed, the thistle, and the chrysanthemum, agreed to learn the syllables to the spell. Terlu taught them the phrases and had them practice over and over until they could recite it perfectly with every intonation precise. Now that the others were no longer caterwauling, Lotti was willing to lead a group of her fellow plants—the morning glory, the delphinium, and the fern—up the walls to slather the paste on the cracks.

Once everyone was trained and ready and eager, they began.

By nightfall, Terlu was so tired that she fell asleep in her own bed and didn't wake once. Yarrow snored lightly nearby. In the morning, they only talked about the day's plan: which greenhouse they'd focus on next, how much of which ingredients they'd need, and how to ensure it all went smoothly and safely.

"I don't know if they really understand what they're risking," Terlu worried as she munched on one of yesterday's muffins. Not only had she been breaking the law by casting spells, but now she was encouraging innocent plants to do so too? This was a terrible idea. She didn't know how the news from Marin about the fall of the empire would affect its laws, and it would be a mistake to assume the plants were safe.

He snorted. "They do. They've slept for decades."

"They could be put back to sleep as punishment," Terlu said. "Or worse." The muffin was still soft and sweet, just the right amount of fruit and sugar. He'd sprinkled cinnamon on top. Finishing, she licked her fingers. It was difficult to maintain a high level of worry while tasting sugary cinnamon, but she felt she *ought* to be worrying, since no one else seemed to be.

"You gave them a choice."

She noticed he was staring at her fingers. "Yes, but—"

He handed her her coat. "*You* know what you're risking. Why are *you* doing it?"

Taking it, Terlu glared at him. "Fine. But if we all get turned into statues, I expect you to plant nice flowers around us." She stalked outside as she wrapped her soft scarf around her neck.

Following her, he said mildly, "I won't be planting anything if I'm a statue too."

She was the one who snorted this time.

They trekked across the snow into the greenhouses. She'd expected to find the sentient plants with the singing plants again, but only the enchanted musical plants were singing in their greenhouse, their sweet cascading harmonies reverberating off the glass in a swell of notes, without a single discordant extra singer. Similarly, the rose room was empty of all but roses.

"Where are they?" Yarrow grumped.

"Maybe they already started?"

"It's barely after dawn."

Crossing into the dead greenhouses, they found the sentient plants. In one corner of the brown-and-gray room, Lotti was slathering the paste over the cracks, while the prickly pear crushed more ingredients with a mortar and pestle. Halfway up a pillar, Dendy recited the spell at the nearest paste-covered crack before moving on to the next one. In another corner, the thistle was preparing more paste by whacking it with their bulbous flower head, while the fern spread it over the cracks with its frond. The chrysanthemum recited the spell crisply and clearly. Nearby, the morning glory dangled from a rafter, all her blue flowers in bloom, as she smeared paste on yet another crack.

The plants had all split into teams, and all around the room, each set of plants was performing the same actions: preparing ingredients, covering the cracks, and casting the spells. The air crackled with magic, so palatable that Terlu felt the hairs on her arm stand up.

"You were right," Yarrow murmured.

"They care," Terlu said softly back.

She didn't dare disturb their concentration. All of them were working in concert, no words except for the spell—efficient and effective. With Yarrow, she marveled at the scene in front of them for several minutes more.

They don't need us.

Yarrow touched her sleeve, and she met his eyes. He nodded toward the door. The two of them retreated out of the greenhouse.

"They're helping," Yarrow marveled. "And the spell is working."

"Lotti must be happy they aren't singing, though technically they could sing the spell, and it should still work, if they emphasize the correct syllables musically . . ."

"Do *not* tell them that where Lotti can hear you."

Terlu grinned.

Yarrow grinned back, and she nearly melted into a puddle at his smile.

He held out his hand, and she took it. "Now that the plants have everything under control with the broken glass, what spell do you want to try next?" he asked.

"I've a few ideas, if you're willing to risk—"

"I am."

Together, they half walked and half ran to an empty dead greenhouse. She didn't want to let go of his hand, but she did when they entered, in order to pull out her notes on spells. She'd been able to split off another potential spell, but it was unclear where exactly to end the phrasing.

"For this one, there are three possible ways to vary the words in the third line"—she held the paper out so he could see it—"but what I don't know is which is going to generate the results we want. Each conveys a slightly different meaning, like this one—"

"Terlu, I trust you. Choose whichever you want, and we'll try it."

"Oh. I—okay." She supposed the last spell had worked like . . . well, like a charm, so that should give her more confidence. But that one had been far simpler to parse out than this one. She pointed to the list of ingredients. "These are the only items we need for the spell, or at least for the first attempt."

"What does this spell do?" Yarrow asked.

"So, the first step to fixing the structural integrity of the greenhouses is to repair the shattered glass, which the plants are working on," Terlu said, "but the second step is to establish a layer of protection, essentially a shield that's fitted right up against the windows. That layer of insulation is what makes it possible to maintain the environment inside. It's the key to Laiken's enchanted greenhouses. It's how he was able to make each one into its own bubble of summer."

"A shield?"

"Yes, like an invisible bubble that sits just within the glass."

"Ah."

She showed him the spell. Her notes were scrawled in the margins, but she'd copied the necessary syllables neatly to prevent any mistakes due to illegibility. "I *think* I isolated the piece of the spell that creates the bubble from the rest of it. Possibly."

"Possibly?" Yarrow raised his eyebrows. He had expressive eyebrows, she'd noticed. "What happens if it fails?"

"That's what I'm not sure about. See, the word for protection . . . There are a couple of different variations, depending on how you align it with the activation word—essentially, the verb. Honestly, it might be best if I cast this one by myself, and you wait outside?"

She was certain he wasn't going to agree to that, and she was correct.

"No."

She expected him to explain why, but that was all he said. "No?"

"No. I stay with you."

"That's nice, but if something goes wrong . . ."

"Then I'll be here with you," Yarrow said. "We talked about this."

"Yes, but this is a different spell. A much less certain spell." Terlu attempted again to show him the words, pointing to the ones that she was unsure about. "See here? It could create an entirely different effect if I stress the end syllable on the third line, as opposed to if I—"

He pushed the paper down and wrapped one arm around her waist to pull her up against him. Then he kissed her, even more thoroughly than he had before. She felt his tongue against her lips, and she opened her mouth. His breath was her breath.

Her thoughts scattered, and the spell slipped from her fingers. It fluttered to the ground, and she didn't care. She wove her fingers through his hair. He cradled her back with one hand and her neck with his other. She tasted the honeyed heat in his kiss.

A few seconds, minutes, an eternity later, he drew back, and she could breathe on her own again. His voice rough, he said, "Cast the spell."

"Okay. Yes. I can do that." Terlu took a step back, out of his arms, and waited for her brain to begin functioning again. She picked the spell up off the ground. "Um, was that just to shut me up, or . . . Never mind. I don't actually want to know. That was . . . nice."

"Good." He was staring at the ceiling, at the glass walls, at the flower beds full of withered, brittle plants, anywhere but at her.

"Right. Okay. You . . . um, the ingredients?"

Yarrow knelt by the basket and removed the items on the list.

"I think they should be . . . combined." Why oh why did the word "combined" conjure up images that were not at all relevant to a greenhouse spell? She swallowed hard. "Yes, um, mix them." *Think boring thoughts. Boring thoughts. Like breakfast.*

She thought of waking up so close to Yarrow, of the taste of honey rolls, of the way the sunlight bathed the naked wood of the cottage . . . *Nope, not boring. How about dirt? Dirt is boring.* Except when it was on Yarrow's hands after a day of gardening, and he washed them off in the sink, meticulously rubbing each golden finger.

How about turtles? There was nothing sexy about turtles, right? She thought about turtles for a while.

By the time he'd finished combining the ingredients into a sandy mixture, she was calm enough to take it from him. She walked the perimeter of the greenhouse, scattering it onto the ground, taking care not to allow more than a few inches of space between the grains.

Terlu felt Yarrow's eyes on her as she walked, but she didn't know what he was thinking about. Their kiss, or turtles? Returning, she handed him the empty bowl. "Do you prefer land turtles or sea turtles?"

"Sorry? Um, sea turtle? We have one, with the ocean plants."

"I've heard some species of sea turtles can live up to five hundred years," Terlu said. "There's an island—aptly named Turtle Island—where the oldest sea turtles come to lay their eggs every year without fail. Its inhabitants have a festival every year to celebrate when the eggs hatch, and they have all these amazing myths about the Great Turtle, Marzipul, who created the Crescent Islands, hatching them from eggs she—"

"Terlu." He looked amused.

"The spell. Yes." She looked down at the paper, then took a deep breath. She tried to think of the syllables and only that. It was easier when she was looking at the words. She'd always taken refuge in words whenever anything was difficult or confusing or too much. They were both her shelter and her shield.

Calmer, Terlu read the words of the spell.

Around them, the air shimmered, wavering like heat over a stove but with colors in it: flecks of amber and emerald. She reached out a hand—it was so vivid that she felt like she could touch it. Yarrow caught her wrist. "You don't know if it's safe," he said.

She withdrew. He continued to hold her wrist, softly, from behind her, his arm wrapped lightly around her waist. All around the greenhouse, the air undulated.

If Laiken were still alive, she would have had a very pointed discussion with him about his incomplete notes. When she'd finished airing her grievances, he could have described what a successful spell looked like versus a failed experiment so she'd know the difference.

The shimmering air began to form spheres. Soon, the greenhouse was filled with iridescent bubbles. They floated past Terlu and Yarrow. One rose to the ceiling and then popped. Others began to pop, a cascade of gentle *pop, pop, pop.*

"Not what I expected," Terlu said.

Yarrow released her and rummaged through the basket for another set of ingredients, while Terlu walked through the array of bubbles. She touched one, and it popped. She smelled strawberries. She popped another and thought it smelled like citrus. "Yarrow, you have to try this."

He paused, stood, and popped a bubble. "It smells like cinnamon."

They strolled around the greenhouse, popping bubbles. "Ooh, this one . . . what's this one?" She didn't recognize it. It vanished nearly as quickly as the bubbles themselves, but Yarrow still leaned forward and sniffed.

"Anise." He popped another. "Vanilla."

"Love vanilla."

"It's a vining orchid," Yarrow said. "Needs a warm climate—cold slows its growth. It takes three years before the plant begins to produce beans."

"You should put your gardening knowledge in a book, preserve it for the next generation," Terlu said. "Preferably not in code."

He shrugged. "Not enough time."

Maybe he would have enough time if she could fix the greenhouses. Or if he had more help. But she'd tried sending the letter, and she wasn't sure what their next move was.

She wasn't about to say it out loud, but she was grateful that none of his relatives had come back. She *did* wish they'd written so that Yarrow would know they were safe. She could tell he worried about them, even though he didn't say the words out loud often. But she didn't wish that they'd come. If a member of his family actually had showed up, she wasn't sure how they'd have reacted to her trying (and failing) to fill the late sorcerer's shoes.

There was no hiding this much magic.

Of course, that meant she'd need to come up with another solution to how to care for the massive Greenhouse of Belde. "Do you think you could train the sentient plants to become full-time gardeners?" They had helped with the dying greenhouse, and they were helping now with sealing the cracks in the glass in the already-failed greenhouses. She thought they'd be willing to do more.

"Only if they want to be trained," Yarrow said. "They didn't ask to be created. It should be their choice what they do with their lives."

"Some of them might choose to help, if they were asked. Look at how eagerly they jumped to fix the glass." Everyone wanted to have purpose, regardless of whether they were flora or fauna. "And for those who don't want to . . . maybe they could be trained to be better singers."

He laughed.

As soon as the ingredients were ready again, Terlu tried the next variant of the spell. She watched as the air shimmered again. This time, it coalesced around them into a large bubble.

"Better," she said.

She walked to the edge and popped it. It dispersed around them into shards of tiny rainbows. A rain of rainbows. Glancing back at Yarrow, she saw the rainbow shards were clinging to him. Smiling, she crossed back to him. "You have a little—" She brushed a wiggle of rainbow off his cheek.

"So do you." He knocked a puff of colorful cloud off her shoulder. It dissipated in the air. He flicked another away from her hair, and she shooed away more colorful wisps of air from his arm.

Laughing, she leaned forward and blew away a puff that lingered near his neck.

A flick of seriousness passed over his face, and she looked into his eyes to realize she was only inches from him again.

"You have another rainbow . . ." He cupped her face in one hand and rubbed his thumb over her cheek. ". . . here."

"Oh?"

"And here." He touched her lips.

"You want to kiss me again," Terlu stated. He withdrew his hand. "It's okay. I want to kiss you too. But is it just because I'm the only one here, or because you actually like me? Because I didn't get the impression you like me very much, and I don't want to be kissing someone who is just kissing me because I have lips."

"I . . ."

"It's okay if you don't like me, if I'm just useful. Admittedly, the bubbles and the rainbows aren't useful, but I have the potential for usefulness, and you need help. But needing me and liking me aren't the same thing either."

He took a step backward. "I don't . . ."

"And I feel like there's a lot I don't know about you," Terlu said. "Have you ever been in love? Do you ever want to be in love? Not that I'm in love." *Yet,* a piece of her whispered. "As I said, there's a lot we don't know about each other, but I'm not good at kissing without caring. You should know that up front. I get all my emotions mixed up together, and if you don't want to feel the same way—potentially, I mean, not right now, but at least being open to it in the future . . . then we shouldn't even start down that path, because it will make it difficult to work together, and there's a lot of work to do if we're going to save the greenhouses."

He looked a bit dazed.

She'd been told by past lovers that she was sometimes too much, and here she was doing it again, being too much. *But if he can't handle too much, then maybe this won't work?*

Or maybe she was overthinking things. In time, they'd get to know one another, and then they'd either like each other or they wouldn't. That didn't mean they couldn't kiss right now. Surely, she possessed enough emotional maturity to separate work from whatever happened or didn't happen between them, especially vital work such as preserving the greenhouses. "Sorry," she said. "I overthink things."

Yarrow shook his head. "I've never known anyone like you."

Terlu wasn't certain if that was a compliment or a criticism or just an observation. She forced herself to smile. "Well, to start with, I'm not a plant."

"You aren't," he said gravely.

She'd meant it as a joke. "Let's . . . try again."

Focusing on her notes, Terlu picked out the next spell to try. It was far easier to study the words than to try to read his face right now. She wished she could try again on the conversation. *I should have just kissed him.* She hadn't meant to complicate everything, but if she grew to care about him (and his honey cakes and honey rolls and honeyed kisses) while he only liked her for her proximity . . . She didn't want that kind of heartbreak. It would be better to stay friends, if that was even what they were.

Quietly, he asked, "Who hurt you?"

She froze and looked at him. "I didn't say . . ." Closing her mouth, she swallowed. She didn't know how to answer that. It wasn't as if she'd had a grand heartbreak. She had no real trauma to explain why she was the way she was. It was more just years' worth of little cracks in her heart, like in the glass panes of the failed greenhouses. Her family loved her, but she never really found her place with them on Eano. And the library . . . She never truly fit there either. She drifted through life, wanting and reaching but never having, always feeling just a little lost and just a little empty and just a little lonely. "I'm just too sensitive."

Yarrow grunted. "I don't know what that means."

"I'm hurt when I shouldn't be."

"If you're hurt, you're hurt. It doesn't matter if anyone else thinks you don't have a good enough reason. Pain doesn't require approval."

She opened and closed her mouth. No one had ever said that to her before. She turned the words over in her head and decided that it was easy to say that, but he hadn't been there when she burst into tears after a library patron had told her that she'd brought him the wrong book. The patron had questioned her credentials, and she'd cared too much what he thought. Or the time she'd worn silk scarves with a brightly colored dress to what she'd thought was a romantic dinner, and her date had only wanted access to a spellbook on the shelves to help her cheat on a university exam. Little nothing moments that she should have been able to forget but instead they lingered with her. "I always want everyone to like me."

"I—"

She wanted him to say "I like you." Or anything reassuring. Perhaps he liked that she didn't snore at night or he liked that she always hung her towel so it would dry or that she had woken the plants or that she didn't whistle in an annoying fashion. But he didn't get the chance to say whatever he was going to say.

Several plants barreled through the door, with Lotti in the lead, bounding ahead on her roots and leaves. "There are *people* on the island!" the rose announced.

CHAPTER TWENTY-TWO

People? Who— Before Terlu could ask out loud, Yarrow charged through the greenhouse. She glanced at the plants. Lotti held up her leaves, toddler-like, and Terlu scooped her up as she hurried after Yarrow.

"Where?" she asked as she huffed. Being a librarian had involved a lot less running than being a gardener/pretend-sorcerer did.

Lotti clung to the fabric of her skirt. "Dock."

"A boat?"

"Yes. You're bouncing a lot."

Glancing back, Terlu saw that the other plants were trailing after them in a ribbon of green on the white snow. She wondered if it was wise to bring the talking plants to meet the new arrivals. Granted, they'd been created years ago by a legitimate sorcerer, and there was no need for anyone to know she'd woken them recently, but that was no guarantee that the newcomers wouldn't leap to conclusions and cause complications that they didn't want or have time for. "Who are the arrivals?" Terlu asked. "What do they want?"

"I don't know," Lotti said. "We came to get you as soon as Dendy spotted all the passengers ready to come off the boat as soon as it docks."

Slowing, Terlu waited for Dendy to catch up. "Want to climb on?"

The philodendron climbed up her leg and wrapped himself around her waist.

"Me too!" Risa demanded.

Terlu stayed stationary while several more plants climbed onto her. A few of the smaller plants stuffed their root balls into her coat pockets. Once they'd all wrapped themselves around her or found other ways to hold on (the orchid clung to her boot laces, the thistle burrowed its prickles into the fabric of her coat sleeve, and the daisy climbed onto Terlu's curls like a living fascinator), Terlu hurried after Yarrow again. She'd lost sight of him through the pine trees, but it didn't matter because she knew where he was headed.

As she trotted down the snow-covered road toward the sea, she heard voices from the dock—multiple voices, male and female, young and old. She tried to squash the temptation to pivot and flee into the forest, taking the plants to safety. How many people had just arrived? And what would they think of the plants, of her, of Yarrow and the greenhouse, of the island of Belde? She felt a tendril of fear wrap around her throat and squeeze.

Why are they here?

Ahead, as the pine trees parted, she saw Yarrow silhouetted against the sea and sky, looking down at the dock, the boat with silver sails, and the cluster of people climbing off it. Puffing, she joined him. The sun glinted off the ocean, and Terlu had to squint to see faces. With the exception of the sailor Marin, she recognized no one, though she supposed that shouldn't have been a surprise, given that there were lots of strangers in the world. Really, the odds that she'd know any of these arrivals were astronomically low. "Who are they?" she asked. And where was Ree, the wax myrtle bush who loved the sea and had left with the sailor?

He glanced at her, then his eyes widened. "Um . . ."

She glanced down at herself, wreathed in greenery.

Dendy waved a leaf at Yarrow. "Heyyy. Hooow's it going?"

Maybe this wasn't the best way to greet the new arrivals, especially before she knew what had happened to Ree, whether these people knew about Belde's sentient plants, and if any of them were going to instantly turn her over to the nearest imperial investigator to be re-statue-ified. "How about you all go to Laiken's tower until we determine if they're friendly?" Terlu suggested. She set the plants down, and they scurried over the snow toward the tower. She watched as Dendy rose up on his root ball to open the door with his leaves before asking Yarrow, "Do you think they're friendly?"

"Oh yes," Yarrow said grimly. "They're friendly."

That sounded like the opposite.

She heard the memory of the courtroom drums, as fast as her heartbeat.

On the dock, the boat with silver sails was disgorging person after person. Marin straddled the dock and boat, helping each person climb out. A second sailor, a man with startlingly purple hair and two crystalline horns that curled in spirals from the top of his head, was hoisting out boxes, bags, and suitcases. At least a half-dozen arrivals stood on the dock already, with crates and suitcases piled around them.

"They're my family," Yarrow said. "My *entire* family."

"Oh! That's . . . great? Isn't that great? They're okay!"

He didn't move. "They're *here*. That's *not* okay."

From below deck, a shrub popped up. He scurried over the deck and climbed nimbly up one of the lines to the mast. *He's fine too!* Terlu grinned. "It looks like Ree delivered the letter."

Granted, she hadn't expected so many to come in response. One maybe, if they were lucky. A spare cousin or an unemployed aunt. Really, she'd expected a letter back with advice—or excuses for why they couldn't just pick up their lives, travel across the sea, and abandon their homes, jobs, and dreams just to save some flora that they'd already given up on, especially in the midst of political upheaval. She watched as Marin unloaded a mirror, a chair, and a hatstand, passing each item to the new arrivals. What did it mean that all of them had come? What exactly had happened in the capital? "It, um, doesn't look like they're here for a visit."

"It looks like an invasion," Yarrow growled.

Clustered on the dock, the group ranged in age from a knee-high toddler to an elderly man with a cane. One woman was helping the man with the cane down the dock. She had gold-and-black hair that was braided and coiled on her head, the same strikingly colored hair as Yarrow. Terlu glanced at him—he was scowling, bearlike, but she could see the family resemblance. She wondered if they had the same sea-deep green eyes.

"My sister," Yarrow said, "and my father."

That should be a good thing, shouldn't it? Why didn't he sound as if it was a good thing? She'd thought he missed them, from his reaction to the cottages and, well, every time he mentioned them, or maybe she'd just been projecting her own feelings onto him? He wasn't particularly easy to read. "I thought you were worried about them."

"I was, but they could have sent a note. That would have been enough."

But wasn't this better? Didn't he want to see them? Talk to them? Tell them how he felt now that he knew they were safe . . . On the other hand, this was Yarrow. "Ahh. Okay. Are you going to . . ."

His face was stiff, and his hands were clenched into fists.

Now he was easy to read.

"Why don't you want to greet them?" Terlu asked quietly. "What don't I know?"

Yarrow shook his head. "You know everything. They left."

"I thought you said the sorcerer Laiken made them leave." Was there more to the story? Had his family not left Yarrow on good terms? Had they not said goodbye? She knew they hadn't reached out after they'd left. *Maybe that's it?* "He took away their jobs, didn't he? They didn't have a choice."

"Everyone has a choice." He pivoted, his back to his family, and he scowled hard at the snow-covered pine forest, at the greenhouse cupolas that rose above the tips of the trees, and at the sky. *He hasn't walked away, but he certainly isn't happy.* She remembered her initial impression of him: a bear, now angry at being woken from his hibernation.

She studied him for a moment more, then looked again at the dock. Wasn't he at least curious why so many had come in response to their letter? Or was he relieved and just didn't know how to handle all that he was feeling? That . . . seemed likely. Gently, she asked, "What if they were just waiting to be invited?"

Yarrow snorted.

She watched them unload several more pieces of furniture: a narrow desk, a folded-up table, a blanket chest . . . She had *not* expected this kind of response. *Temporary help,* she'd written. *Until the crises are averted.* They looked very much as if they expected to stay. "I'm going to greet them. Do you want to come?"

"If I must."

"I'm not your parent. Do whatever you want to do." She was certainly not going to force him. He knew best how he felt and what he could handle, though she wished she understood *why* he was reacting this way. If it were her family and she'd been concerned about their safety . . . Well, it would be awkward, but she'd still be overjoyed to see them. And she'd certainly want to know why they'd all come.

He sighed heavily. "As far as they know, I invited them all."

"I said we needed *a* gardener, singular, if anyone could be spared. This . . . is a surprise. Aren't you at least a little curious why they all came?"

"Guess you're a persuasive writer."

She wasn't so certain of that. This was something more.

"They didn't return for the greenhouses," Yarrow said. "Or for me. If they'd cared about me, they would have replied to the letter first, invaded second."

"You don't know that," she said. "You won't know anything until you *talk to them.*"

Starting down the steps, Terlu pasted a smile on her face and waved. Out in the ocean, the waves were dancing beneath the cloud-streaked sky. She looked for the sea dragon, but she didn't see any hint of its scaly back as she walked toward the dock. Behind her, she heard Yarrow following her, and she was relieved. She wasn't sure how she'd explain it if he'd just fled. Smiling for real now, she called, "Hello! Welcome to Belde!"

Popping up from below deck, the shrub squeaked, "Terlu! Yarrow! Land ho!"

"Hey, Ree!" Terlu waved. "Looks like you had a full boat. Very full. How did everyone fit?" Now that she compared the number of people and the mountain of furniture, suitcases, and crates to the size of the boat . . . it didn't seem logistically feasible. She widened her wave to include all of Yarrow's family. "Welcome, everyone!"

Marin grinned as she helped another of Yarrow's relatives disembark—a middle-aged man with a tuft of white hair in the center of his otherwise bald head. "My boat has a few tricks up her sleeve. Or in her hull, more accurately," she said, with a wink toward Terlu. "Still, it was a squeeze. Some of them are *very* glad to be on land."

"Sorry, Marin, ma'am," the man she'd just helped said. "I'll clean your boat once, you know, everything isn't tilting and rolling so much."

"No, thank you, sir. You just stay on the land. Permanently, please. I didn't think it was possible for a body to expel that much and still have innards." She clapped him on the shoulder. "Maybe don't eat anything for another day or two, hmm?"

"Or a week," he agreed. But he was smiling—a warm and friendly crinkled-eyes and crooked-teeth smile. He shifted his smile toward Yarrow at the end of the dock as he raised his voice and boomed, "Yarrow! Great to see you! You're looking well. Remember me? Your uncle Rorick?"

"Yarrow!" One of the older women rushed forward with tears in her eyes. "Oh, how you've grown! Look at you!" She had tattoos of flowers on her golden cheeks, and the inked petals framed her tears. "You remember me, don't you? Aunt Rin? Ah, little Yarrow, not little anymore! Just look at you!"

And that set off the lot: the arrivals flocked off the dock, crowing his name. Terlu caught a glimpse of panic in his eye, and she lunged in front of him. She pasted a great, false smile on her face and said, "Hi! I'm Terlu. Maybe everyone take a step backward so Yarrow can breathe?" She made shooing motions as if they were chickens crowding around their feed.

Behind her, Yarrow laid his hand on her shoulder. She wasn't sure if it was in warning or in thanks, but she was *not* going to let him be overwhelmed on his own island.

"It's very lovely you all came," Terlu began.

Yarrow murmured in her ear, "Is it?"

"We weren't expecting so many of you. Are you all gardeners?" She glanced at the toddler who was clinging to a woman's hand with one of his and had his other hand shoved into his mouth. With their pale green skin and white hair, they didn't look related to the others. "I'm not sure we have space for everyone to sleep. Marin, do you—"

Marin hefted a final crate onto the dock. "Oh no, can't stay," she called over the crowd. "Got another stop to make before sunset. They're all yours."

Ree sang, *"The sea calls, and we must sail—beyond the horizon, into the bluuuue!"*

The second sailor echoed in harmony, *"Into the bluuuue!"* It was so perfectly pitched that Terlu smiled and thought the other plants could take a few lessons from these two.

One woman with silvery hair and a wide smile patted Terlu's shoulder. She had a bony hand and wore a city-style dress that was embroidered with flowers. She didn't look related to the rest— perhaps she'd married into the family? "Don't you worry about space, my dear. We'll fix up our own homes, and it'll be just fine. This is where we belong, after all."

"Is it?" Yarrow said.

Ignoring him, the man who said his name was Rorick drew a deep breath. "Ah, it smells like home!" He then beamed at Terlu. "Are you Yarrow's wife?"

A woman near the back gave a gasp that was almost a laugh—she was the one who Yarrow had said was his sister, with gold-and-black braided hair. "Whoa, Yarrow married?"

Excitedly, the crowd clustered around Terlu, led by the woman with the wide smile, and she had to explain: no, she wasn't his wife. They were friends. She was helping him with the greenhouses. She'd written the letter, on his behalf—

Yarrow cut through the chatter. "Why are you all here?"

His relatives stilled.

A man's voice said, "You invited us, Yarrow." And the crowd parted so that the speaker was facing both Terlu and Yarrow. *He has Yarrow's eyes.* It felt like looking at a version of Yarrow, aged several decades. He was muscular, though wrinkles lined his arms and face. His back was straight, despite the cane.

Yarrow scowled at Terlu. "What did you say in that damn letter?"

She glared right back at him. This wasn't her fault. "Exactly what I told you I said." Okay, so it was partially her fault since she'd had the idea for the letter, she'd written it, and she'd sent it—*fine, it's* mostly *my fault.*

"I'll ask again then," Yarrow said, no warmth in his voice, "why are you all here?"

Rorick answered, "You haven't heard the news from the capital? There's been a revolution. The emperor was killed, and half of Alyssium burned. The empire has fallen. Until we received your letter . . ."

"We thought that's why you wrote," Yarrow's father said. "To save us."

"We're here," Yarrow's sister said, her arms crossed and her eyes narrowed as if she didn't like the words she was saying, "because we don't have anywhere else to go."

Chattering all at once, Yarrow's relatives described the chaos in Alyssium.

Terlu knew already that there had been a revolution and that the emperor had been defenestrated. What she didn't know was that afterward, in the chaos that followed, the library had burned.

Marin hadn't mentioned that detail.

Not all of it had burned, thankfully, but some of it. Many books were still unaccounted for, and Terlu hoped they'd been stolen rather than destroyed. A stolen book could be recovered, or at least appreciated by whomever owned it, but if all the books had burned or fallen into the canals . . . She was able to extract enough of a description to know that the North Reading Room, as well as a portion of the North Wing, had been lost.

If I'd been in the North Reading Room when the revolution broke out . . .

Terlu shuddered.

And then she realized the truth: *I was* there. That had to have been how she was saved. Rijes Velk must have used the chaos of the revolution to extract Terlu.

The epiphany took her breath away, and as she absorbed it, the voices of Yarrow's relatives faded. Terlu tried to imagine what kind of chaos there had been in the Great Library . . . Somehow in the midst of the bedlam, Rijes Velk had stopped to think of a lowly librarian who'd broken the law and acted to save her. It was an extraordinary gift.

How can I ever repay that?

Suddenly, she knew what she had to do.

Breaking away from Yarrow's relatives and weaving between them with repeated apologies, Terlu ran down the dock, where the two sailors and the shrubbery were preparing to leave. "Marin!"

Marin was untying the line from the dock. "Told you, I can't stay. I've got another stop to make, and this was . . . Let's say there's a reason I'm a supply runner, not a goddamn ferry. But they paid, on top of what your gardener already paid me. And here they are, deal complete." She was still smiling, but it looked strained. For a formerly solo sailor, it had to have been an uncomfortable ride, even with the help of a second sailor and a verdant deckhand.

Knowing she shouldn't ask for more but determined to do it anyway, Terlu dug her hand into her pocket and produced the ruby from the little dragons' hoard. "I can pay. Rijes Velk. She is, or was, the head librarian at the Great Library of Alyssium. I don't know where she'd be now, if the library burned." *Please let her have survived.* She didn't want to think anyone had sacrificed themselves for her. Or that someone so kind and so brilliant and so indomitable as her had suffered.

Behind Marin, the second sailor, the man with the purple hair and diamond horns, said, "We are very sorry, but we aren't returning to Alyssium."

"Plans change, Dax," Marin said as Terlu dropped the ruby into her hands.

"But you said—"

"Ruby, Dax. Really big ruby." Holding the gem up to the light, Marin whistled. "Can't guarantee I'll find her," she said to Terlu.

"Can you guarantee you'll try? If you find her . . ." She felt her throat tighten. How did you find the words to thank the woman who'd given you a second chance? A second life?

"Not going to kill her, if that's what this is for." Marin's tone was light, but the look in her eye was serious.

"What? No! I want you to make sure she's okay. Get her out of the city, if necessary, and take her wherever she wants to go. And . . . thank her for me? Please?" Terlu didn't know if the head librarian had survived the violence, but if she had . . . *She saved me while her world was crumbling around her.* From what Terlu had gleaned from the chatter of Yarrow's relatives, it had been terrifying. During the uprising, the area in the city where Yarrow's relatives had lived had been destroyed. Never mind that many of them had supported the revolutionaries. Fire didn't care. They'd lost their shops, their apartments, their livelihoods, and had been facing lives as refugees on whatever island would take them in when Marin had found them with her letter.

Marin grinned and pocketed the ruby. "You're an odd one, but I like your style. If it's possible, I'll do it. Good luck with this lot." She shoved away from the dock. "And tell your gardener that I'll be back by Winter Feast with his usual supplies, times ten for the new folk, especially if he can get me some zucchini seeds—that's a promise."

"Thank you," Terlu said.

"Ree, hoist the sails," Marin called.

"Yes, Captain!" the plant shouted, and then he scuttled toward a winch, his branches flapping with excitement. The other sailor, Dax, joined him and together they raised the sail.

Terlu watched them for a moment. Ree, it seemed, had found his place. She hoped the three of them could find Rijes Velk and that, when they did, she'd be safe and well. *I've done what I could.*

As they pushed back from the dock, Terlu trudged back up to the cluster of refugees and tried to smile as if they were ordinary visitors and hadn't just delivered news that the world had turned upside down.

Yarrow wasn't even attempting to appear welcoming. He looked as if he wished he could dive into the sea and swim after Marin. Anywhere but where he was right now.

Reaching him, Terlu said, "We should get them all inside where it's warmer." She pitched her voice low so that only he would hear.

"Not my cottage," Yarrow whispered back, a hint of panic in his voice.

"Laiken's tower?" she asked him. "It's closest." Sooner or later, they'd need to meet the sentient plants. Perhaps it would be a reunion for some of them.

"Fine."

Facing the crowd, she murmured to Yarrow, "Who is who?"

Yarrow's sister pushed her way to the front. "I'm Yarrow's sister, Rowan. And this is my wife, Ambrel. My cousin, Vix. My aunt, Rin." She pointed to each person and named them and then continued on through the crowd. Most were relatives, she said, but a few were neighbors and/or close family friends. The toddler, Epu, was the child of their neighbor, a woman named Pipa with zigzag tattoos on her pale green cheeks. Terlu shoved as many names into her head as she could, using a trick she'd developed when she first arrived in Alyssium—she assigned them each a different bird or animal: a squirrel for cousin Finnel (brown hair and a tiny nose), a sparrow for uncle Ubri (feathery hair and quick movements), a duck for cousin Percik (a broad duck-like smile), an emu for aunt Harvena (beady black eyes and long legs) . . .

Stepping closer, the older man with the cane, Yarrow's father, said, "And I am Rowan and Yarrow's father. My name's Birch. Yarrow . . . son . . . It's good to see you again."

She looked at Yarrow, expecting at last here would be the reunion that she was certain he'd been aching for. It had been him and his father for so long, and his father had only left because he'd become too ill to stay. Surely he'd greet him.

Yarrow grunted, and then he turned and walked away, back toward the greenhouse.

"I had hoped he'd forgiven me by now," Birch said.

She hadn't known there was anything that needed forgiving. *Why couldn't he have shared more* before *I wrote that letter?* Forcing herself to smile again, Terlu patted Yarrow's father's arm. "Come inside, all of you. You've had a long journey."

CHAPTER TWENTY-THREE

As Terlu led the way to the late sorcerer's tower, she spotted a mat of greenery clogging one of the windows. The plants were watching their approach. She waved to them, hoping this was the right choice.

Immediately, the window cleared of green.

A few seconds later, the door was thrown open, and the sentient plants poured out.

And the reunion she'd been hoping for between Yarrow and his family happened between the plants and the people. The greenery swarmed around Yarrow's relatives, and there were hugs and laughter and chatter. The philodendron, Dendy, climbed up Yarrow's father, chattering with him, while the calla lily, Viria, laughed uproariously with Yarrow's uncle Rorick. The toddler, Epu, poked his pudgy finger at Risa, who twisted their vines around him like a boa constrictor. Loving it, Epu giggled. Watching it all unfold, Terlu finally felt as if she'd done something right, possibly.

Piling inside, the people and plants quickly filled the workroom to bursting, but it was at least warm. Everyone began to make space: moving the worktable to the side of the room, positioning the stools and desk chair for the older relatives to easily sit, and scooting aside Laiken's equipment. Terlu was glad she'd taken the notes and journals she needed back to the cottage for study. The rest were filed neatly on the bookshelves with only a few piles on the table, and she hoped they'd be left alone.

"We'll start fixing up our own cottages soon," said Harvena, the older woman who had reminded Terlu of an emu because of her tiny black eyes and her long legs. She had a perpetual scowl that made Terlu think of Yarrow—perhaps the scowl was genetic.

"I can't wait to show you my cottage!" Yarrow's sister said to her wife. *Rowan and Ambrel,* Terlu remembered. And Yarrow and Rowan's father was Birch. Others were Vix, Rin, Finnel, Ubri . . . She silently ran through the names, fixing them in her memory, as Rowan said to Ambrel, "If it's still standing, of course, which there's no guarantee."

Some of the relatives stomped upstairs to Laiken's bedroom. Terlu supposed that several could sleep upstairs and a few on the floor here. It would be squashed but not unmanageable, so long as they didn't mind all the creepy shadows. Perhaps the leftover miasma would fade with the addition of so many living people. She hoped the privy could handle the influx. She knew it worked, since she'd used it, and it was fine, as far as no mold or other unpleasantness, but there weren't enough towels or soap—

"We'll make do," Yarrow's father, Birch, said beside her. He was leaning against his cane as he surveyed the late sorcerer's workroom. She wondered if her worry was written on her face and decided it must be, given that he clearly felt he needed to reassure her. "If we'd needed all the amenities ready for us, we would have sent word that we were coming."

"Why didn't you?" She smiled to soften the question. "It's fine that you didn't—you're quite welcome—but we could have prepared food, toiletries, places to sleep." She wasn't sure *when* they would have done that, between waking the sentient plants and rescuing plants from the dying greenhouse, but they could have tried.

"Some of us wanted to reply to Yarrow's letter, but I vetoed that. I didn't want to risk him changing his mind and withdrawing the invitation, which he could have if he knew I was coming."

"Why would he? You're his father. He loves you." Also, Yarrow needed the help.

Birch sighed, and he sounded so exactly like Yarrow that it was clear they were related, even though he had bushy gray hair, rather than Yarrow and Rowan's black and gold. His eyebrows were even bushier, like woolly caterpillars napping above his eyes. He had the same eyes, the kind that looked like they held depths, though his had more amber flecks in the green, and the same golden sheen to his skin. If the two men were at all similar, she wondered how much had been left unsaid between the two of them. "He didn't like that I left," Birch said.

"But you were ill. He said so. You had to leave."

"He didn't like *how* I left. I tried to force him to come with me. I didn't think it was good for him, to stay here on a deserted island by himself."

Terlu agreed with that, but forcing him was no kind of answer. What Yarrow's father should have done was come back, as soon as he was healthy enough for the journey. She didn't say that, though. "He had to take care of the greenhouse."

"He didn't have to, though. It wasn't his responsibility. The sorcerer"—he gestured around the workroom with his cane—"was dead by then, and we'd done all we could, in my opinion. There was no future here."

An edge crept into her voice. She couldn't help it. "If he hadn't stayed, there absolutely wouldn't have been a future. Leaving would have doomed this place."

"Exactly what Yarrow said at the time." Birch beamed at her, and she saw echoes of Yarrow's smile in his. "I see why my son likes you."

She wasn't so certain he liked her very much right now, given that it had been her idea that had resulted in this . . . influx, but she didn't argue it, especially to a man who shared Yarrow's smile. "Without him, the plants wouldn't have survived, much less thrived. He's done amazing work, even with the enchantments failing around him."

"The greenhouses were dying," Birch said. "I knew it was just a matter of time before they all failed. I told him . . ." He sighed again. ". . . I told him to let them die." He said the last in a low voice.

Terlu glanced at the closest plant, the daisy, but she didn't appear to have overheard. She was chattering to one of Yarrow's cousins, while the thistle bobbed his globular flower happily.

"I didn't think . . . I had no idea that the talking plants were just asleep. I thought they were gone, and we were living in a graveyard. I didn't believe there was a future here. Yarrow . . . disagreed. We didn't part with kind words."

"So when you got his letter . . ." She was beginning to understand. Yarrow had wanted help saving the greenhouse, which was why he'd allowed her to send the letter. He hadn't expected or wanted a reunion or a reconciliation; he'd just wanted to save the plants. Nothing more and nothing less. But Birch had seen the letter as more. He'd hoped for more. "The greenhouses are still dying, but we're hoping to reverse that."

"Maybe I gave up too soon," Birch said.

Or maybe you have nowhere else to go and are clinging to any shred of hope you have, Terlu thought, but she didn't say it out loud. She knew what that felt like, and it made her want to throw her arms around all the refugees. "Have you all eaten? I can see what food I can find . . ."

One of Yarrow's aunts, Rin, a woman with faded tattoos of flowers on her cheeks, said, "We've enough for a few days. But don't worry, my dear—we aren't afraid of hard work. We'll have the greenhouses up and producing in no time."

The vegetable greenhouses were already producing fine for Yarrow without any outside intervention. She felt a trickle of unease. He wasn't going to like all these people intruding on his space. On the other hand, he couldn't do it all alone. The loss of the tropical greenhouse proved that. *This will work out.* She hoped.

"Birch, can you help with the fire?" Harvena, the emu-like aunt, called.

He hobbled across the workroom toward her. Rowan was already beside the stove, squatting in front of it with a bundle of tinder in her hand. "I know how," she protested.

"Yes, but you're a disaster," Harvena told her. "Birch?"

Rowan squawked a protest, and her wife, Ambrel, laughed. She began relating an anecdote to Harvena about Rowan failing to boil water for tea—Harvena laughed heartily. Yarrow's uncle Rorick jumped in with another story that involved snails and mussels and a young Rowan who hadn't realized you weren't supposed to eat the shells . . .

"I'll be back," Terlu promised them all, but none of the people nor the plants were listening to her anymore. They were busily and cheerfully hauling in their belongings and setting themselves up for the night. A few had already ventured out, to scout out what needed to be done to the cottages to make them livable again.

She had the very clear sense that she wasn't in charge, and she knew Yarrow wasn't. His relatives had swooped in, and for better or worse, were making themselves at home.

She hoped this wasn't a mistake.

When she reached Yarrow's cottage, the door was locked. Terlu knocked.

"Who is it?" he called.

"It's Terlu."

"Who else?"

"Just me."

She heard a chair scrape on the wood floor. The door opened, and he popped his head out, looked down the snowy road, and then retreated. She scooted inside and hung up her coat while he shut and locked the door behind her.

"I'm sorry," she said. "I didn't imagine that they'd all come."

He snorted. It didn't sound like an I-don't-believe-you snort, more of an I'm-unhappy-with-the-situation, which made her feel a tiny bit hopeful. Maybe it would be better once the arrivals were settled in and had their own cottages fixed up again? She hoped they didn't disturb any of the papers or notebooks in Laiken's workroom. She had the most important ones with her here on Yarrow's desk, but there could be more that she'd need to reference.

If she was even going to be able to work more magic.

There were now a *lot* more eyes. She wasn't certain she'd be able to proceed with their experiments without drawing attention. It was bad enough that the sentient plants were awake and busily casting spells to fix the cracks in the greenhouse glass. *Maybe they'll assume it was Laiken who taught the plants magic?* Or maybe this family of gardeners wouldn't care, so long as the greenhouses were being fixed? She was depending on a lot of "maybes."

"They don't have anywhere else to go," Terlu said. For that reason, they might keep her secret, if (when) they discovered it. It wouldn't be in their best interest to draw imperial investigators to the island . . . if there *were* imperial investigators anymore. According to Marin and the new arrivals, the empire had fallen. What did that mean for its laws and for its law enforcement? Who was in charge now, and how did they feel about unlicensed magic? She added that to the list of questions to ask Yarrow's relatives, subtly. "And at least here you know they're safe."

"They're acting as if they've come home," Yarrow said, crossing to the window and looking out it, as if expecting a relative to pop out from behind a pine tree. "Yet every single one of them abandoned this place and didn't look back."

She'd sailed away from Eano and hadn't returned, but she still thought of it as home. Her childhood home, at least. It would always have a place in her heart, even if her future wasn't there. She thought of Ree, so happy on Marin's boat—he'd found his place. "You don't know how they felt about it or how they feel now. You could try talking to them."

Another snort.

"You don't have to forgive them, but they could help. You've a family full of gardeners eager to make this place somewhere they can live. Use that."

"I just . . . don't want anything to change."

Gently, she said, "I think things will have to change." The sailboat disgorging so many new arrivals, each with their own hopes and dreams and plans, ensured that. "The empire fell. Everything's changed." The only question was *how* it had changed.

"Not for me it hasn't. Everyone else can do what they want, but I want to continue to experiment with the greenhouse spells." He must have seen hesitation in her expression because he added, "Unless you don't want . . . I mean, you can do as you please, of course."

She tried to sort out how to respond: She wanted to keep trying with the spells, but should she? Was it wise, right now? Or would it be smarter to wait? But if she waited, how many more greenhouses would die? What she was doing was important. More than that, it was *right*.

But would all of their new arrivals see it that way?

"It's not just us and the plants anymore," Terlu said.

"We could pretend it is," Yarrow said. "With a bit of effort, I believe we can completely ignore my family and act as if they don't exist."

Terlu laughed.

He didn't laugh with her.

"Oh, wait—you're serious. That's neither healthy nor practical, but even if we did . . . there could still be imperial investigators out there, searching for lawbreakers, maybe even searching specifically for me. We don't know what's changed with the revolution. It could be worse, not better."

Yarrow took her hands. "I wouldn't let them take you."

"You couldn't stop them."

"Then we'd be statues together." He'd moved closer, only inches away. "They'd have to make a double pedestal for both of us, because I won't let go."

Her throat felt thick, and her eyes heated and blurred. That was . . . well, terrible, but also beautiful and sweet and perfect. She blinked hard, trying not to cry.

Spotting something outside, Yarrow suddenly released her hands, crossed to the door, and opened it. Emeral waltzed in, his tail held high and his wings folded on his back.

Terlu wiped her eyes and got herself back under control. "You'll need to communicate with your relatives at some point in some way," she said, sidestepping the issue of spellcasting and statues altogether for the moment, "at least to tell them what needs to be done in the greenhouses." Otherwise they'd invent tasks for themselves, and Yarrow might like that even less. It would be better if he coordinated his efforts with theirs.

"They'll know what to do." Yarrow poured water in a bowl for Emeral and fed him a piece of fish. The winged cat accepted the gifts with a pleased *murp* noise.

"But it's your greenhouse."

"It's Laiken's greenhouse."

"He's gone, and you've been the one caring for them," Terlu said. "I think that makes them yours. By love and by law." She wasn't certain if the law for abandoned property had changed now that there had been a change in government, but she knew that Yarrow's longevity here gave him clear claim to it. He'd put blood, sweat, and tears into this island.

"Not yet. Later, I'll talk to them. Some of them. As needed."

She studied his face, his clenched jaw, the furrows in his forehead. *He's afraid.* "I said 'in some way.' You don't have to talk to them directly, if you don't want to. I can talk to them for you whenever you need me to. If you want to tell them anything about the greenhouses or the cottages or the island, I can be your go-between."

He looked over at her, eyes wide. "You'd do that?"

"Of course." *He said he'll be a statue with me.* "You don't have to face them until you're ready." Did he think she was going to force a reunion, now that he'd made it so clear he didn't want one? Granted, she had been insistent about sending the letter—and really, now that the initial shock had passed, even he had to admit that the letter had been a grand, if unexpectedly complicated, success. So many gardeners! But she wasn't going to push him any more than she already had, not now that she understood at least a tiny bit more how he felt.

"You keep surprising me, Terlu Perna."

She hoped that was a good thing. Brightly, she said, "I think it's going to work out fine." Maybe the laws against magic use had changed. Maybe the gardeners would embrace her use of spells. Maybe all her worries were just a reaction to the trauma she'd experienced and not grounded in the current reality. Maybe the fall of the empire meant the fall of the imperial investigators and the pardoning of all former criminals. Maybe everything would be okay.

Yarrow let out a sound that was almost a laugh.

"What?"

"You don't let anything dim your light," Yarrow said. "You were sentenced to a fate worse than death—don't tell me it wasn't. You lost everything. Unfairly punished. You're terrified it will happen again. And yet you still open your arms to everyone. How?"

"I . . ." She'd never been asked that or ever even considered the question. "What's the alternative?" As she asked the question, she realized he had chosen the alternative. He hadn't gone with his family. He'd chosen to stay behind, by himself, to devote the rest of his life to what everyone else considered a lost cause. "I suppose I choose to think it will all be okay because then at least, even if I can't control what happens, I can control how I feel about it."

"You just choose."

Terlu thought about it. "Yes."

He shook his head. "I'm not made like that."

"That's okay too."

"Huh."

Both of them fell silent. He moved to the kitchen counter and began to slice a squash and then a tomato. She watched him create the precise, thin slices for a moment, and then she turned her attention to building up the fire. When she finished, she located a broom and swept the floor.

"You're not talking," Yarrow said.

"I thought you might need some silence."

"Oh. I . . . Yes." There was so much relief in his voice that she smiled.

In silence, he cooked while she cleaned, and then they ate dinner and prepared for bed, all still in silence. She wondered if his family had settled in for the night, if they were able to sleep, what kind of dreams (or nightmares) they had after leaving the lives they'd built for themselves and then seen torn down.

Only when the lights were out, the fire was low, and Terlu was about to climb into bed did Yarrow speak. "It's warmer together," he said.

"It is," she agreed.

She slid into his bed, and he wrapped the covers around her.

"I won't . . ." he began.

"We'll just sleep," she said.

He was quiet for a moment and then said, "Thank you," before he slid his arm around her waist and drew her close to him.

Outside, it was quiet as well, except for the gentle call of an owl.

CHAPTER TWENTY-FOUR

At dawn, Terlu woke to the smell of honey cake. She blinked open her eyes to see six cakes already cooling on racks on the table, while Yarrow mixed batter for another batch.

"How many?" he asked.

"What?" Sitting up, she patted at her hair, which was poking out at odd angles.

"One for every three people, or one for every two? They'll be hungry."

"You're making them all breakfast?" Of course he was. She thought of how he'd fed her, set up a bed for her, let her live with him, even before he knew her. That was what he did: he claimed not to care and then he did something like this that proved the opposite. She smiled.

"Nine cakes?" he guessed.

That was a *lot* of cake. Each tin made a loaf. "If you can manage that many, they can eat the leftovers for lunch as well."

He nodded. "Will you take them?"

"Of course."

"I can't."

"I know. It's okay. I'd be happy to. Let me just get dressed." She could take messages and deliver honey cakes and whatever as long as he wanted. Sure, maybe it wasn't the healthiest way to handle it, but if he wasn't ready, then he wasn't ready.

Besides, she wasn't in any kind of position to give advice on how to handle one's family, given that she hadn't even told her family she was alive.

"The last batch still have to bake, so take your time," Yarrow said.

"I can help—"

He waved her off and then poured the batter into tins. "I'll make twelve. Ten for them, one for us, and one for the dragons in the maze. They'll like that, won't they?"

"Yes, they'll absolutely like that." Terlu didn't specify which "they" she meant, but it didn't matter since she meant all of them. She slid out of bed and stepped over Emeral, who was lounging by the hearth.

By the time she was clean and dressed in her favorite soft pants and a warm top that cuddled her curves, Yarrow was stirring rose petals and sugar into a pot to make rose tea while the honey cakes baked. Without looking at her, he said, "I cut you a slice."

She spotted a wedge of honey cake on a plate with a dollop of jam beside it. Just one plate and one fork. "Did you eat?"

"Not hungry."

"Did you sleep?"

He shrugged.

"Do you want to talk or not talk?" Terlu asked. Sitting, she dipped a bite of the honey cake in the jam and popped it into her mouth—sweet and airy with a tartness from the lemon-raspberry jam. She almost let out a little moan. It made her feel as if she'd been dipped in sugar. She had sugar for blood and raspberry for breath. Shaking herself, she focused again on Yarrow. He had no idea of the effect of his baking. "I'll listen, whenever you want to talk. But you don't have to."

If what he needed to do was bake, she absolutely had no objections.

Yarrow wrapped the finished cakes in cloth napkins. Finishing, he stared at them and then spoke. "When I was a kid, my uncle Rorick decided I needed to be toughened up. He said I was too dependent on my father, and if I was going to be a contributing citizen of the

Crescent Islands Empire and, more importantly in his mind, the Greenhouse of Belde, then I needed to learn self-reliance."

She studied his face. He was focused on the wrapped cakes as if seeing something else entirely. *This isn't going to be a good story.*

"He said we were playing a game, and if I found my way back home, I'd win," Yarrow said. "He convinced me to put on a blindfold, and he led me for what felt like miles. He told me to count to ten, then remove the blindfold. When I did, I was alone in the dark. Pitch dark. I'd thought he was bringing me to a greenhouse on the opposite side of the island. But instead he brought me into the caves beneath the island. And he left me. Without light, without food, without water except what I could lick from the walls." He fell quiet. The tea began to boil.

"Did you find your way out?" Surely, his uncle had come back for him. Or maybe he hadn't been far from the entrance.

"Three days. Never liked mazes after that. Or caves."

Three days, under the earth, alone in the darkness, with no food and no water. She shivered. "How old were you?"

"Nine."

"Nine years old, and no one came to find you? What about your parents?"

He shook his head. "My mom was years gone by then, and my dad . . . I'm told my grandmother fought with my father and Uncle Rorick to send a search party, but they refused. Up until the very end, I thought they'd come for me. It was supposed to be a game. An afternoon."

She wanted to cross to him and hug him. Or march over to Birch and Rorick and yell at them loudly with very pointed vocabulary.

"When I got back, I asked my father why he didn't come for me." Yarrow poured the rose tea steadily and calmly but still without looking at Terlu. "He said he had work to do."

"I'm so sorry, Yarrow." *I'd come for you,* she wanted to say. She took her cup, the tea warming her hands. She breathed in the sweet steam. "That wasn't right, what he did. You were a child. Even if you hadn't been . . . I'm sorry."

He nodded abruptly. He looked so tense that she thought he'd shatter if he stepped out into the wind. He didn't touch his tea. "If they ask why I didn't bring the cakes myself . . ."

"I'll tell them you have work to do."

He almost smiled.

Alone, Terlu carried the honey cakes and the kettle of tea down the snowy road to the sorcerer's workroom. She listened to the soft whoosh of wind over the snow. Overhead, the sky was a cloudless blue, and the air smelled of pine and sea. In the distance, she heard cheerful voices and the echoing ring of a hammer.

Yarrow's relatives were swarming over the blue cottage.

Terlu called to them, "So you know, that one"—she pointed up the road at the first cottage she'd visited—"has feral gryphons. Also, I brought breakfast."

Grinning, a woman with gold-and-black hair hurried over— Yarrow's sister, Rowan. Terlu recognized her instantly from the prior day. She had the same cheekbones as Yarrow but a wider smile. She was wearing a heavy brown coat over sturdy work clothes. She'd tied back her braids today with a purple ribbon. "You are a gift. And yes, we know about the gryphons. That was our late Aunt Misla's house, and she confessed before she passed that she'd left cake in the cabinets, which was a crime against cake and an invitation for a feral flock—wild gryphons have a sweet tooth. You're Terlu Perna, yes?"

"Yes, and you're Rowan? Welcome home." She remembered Yarrow had said the blue cottage, the one she'd set her sights on before she knew Yarrow would welcome her into his own cottage, was his sister's. It was also the one that would be easiest to make livable, perhaps because it hadn't sat abandoned for as many years. She noted the relatives seemed to have helped themselves to Yarrow's tools and supplies and wondered what he'd thought of that. *Probably fine with it, so long as he didn't have to talk with them.* "Hope you slept all right."

"Oh, yeah, slept like a hibernating bear. The upstairs folk had a restless night, due to the ghost, but we'll get the cottages back into shipshape in no time." Rowan relieved Terlu of the kettle. "Come, let's bring it back to the workroom. Most of the others are there, getting themselves up and ready. Hey, Ambrel! Terlu brought breakfast!"

Ambrel trotted toward them. She was shorter than Rowan and had sky-blue skin and an apple-round face. She wore a puffy blouse with embroidered flowers underneath a blue coat. She'd already collected sawdust all over the coat.

"My wife, Ambrel," Rowan introduced her.

Terlu greeted her. "We met yesterday, but I— Ghost, did you say?"

"The old sorcerer, Laiken," Rowan said. "Not a surprise. He was both magical and unhappy, exactly the type to leave a ghost behind."

"*I* was surprised," Ambrel said.

Rowan shrugged—a move so identical to her brother Yarrow that Terlu felt her eyes bulge as she stared at her. "He's harmless. Mostly just moans."

"He could be singing arias, and I still wouldn't want to live there," Ambrel said.

Laiken's ghost was upstairs from his workroom? She'd thought it felt haunted, but she hadn't made the leap to realize it was *actually* haunted. She remembered how shadowy and creepy it had felt and how she hadn't wanted to go upstairs since the first time she climbed the stairs—she'd even thought to herself that she wouldn't be surprised if his despair had lingered, but she hadn't made the leap to thinking that he himself had. It might have been useful to know his ghost was still in residence. "Can he communicate?" If he could tell her what spells to use and which were purely experimental or, worse, dangerously flawed . . .

"You've never met a ghost before, have you?" Rowan said, with just enough of an air of tiredness that Terlu was certain she had met at least one. As far as Terlu knew, they weren't very common. She wondered what stories lay behind that tone of voice. "They're bundles of leftover emotions. Whatever was strongest while they were alive. No real awareness or thought process."

"Just a whole lot of *sad* leaking all over the place," Ambrel said.

Rowan wrapped her arm around her wife's waist. "Which is why I convinced everyone to fix up my cottage first," she said to Ambrel. "So it can be *our* cottage."

"It's a lovely cottage," Ambrel said. "Ghost-free and gryphon-free."

Terlu didn't mention it was the one she'd picked out for herself. Clearly Yarrow's offer of any cottage she wanted didn't stand anymore, now that the original owners were back. She was surprised how pleased she was at that. She wondered how he felt about having a more-permanent roommate. He hadn't mentioned fixing up the other cottages since that first day, so she liked to think he'd be fine with it. *I should ask instead of just hoping he's okay with it.*

He'd probably just shrug, though.

Or maybe he'd say it was warmer.

She wondered if he knew about Laiken's ghost.

"When did you last see your brother?" Terlu asked. "I mean, before yesterday." And the follow-up question: Why hadn't Rowan stayed on Belde too, with her father and brother? Yarrow had been clear that it was just him and his father at the end.

"Five years ago? Six? My aunt and uncle wanted help in their florist shop, and Dad thought it would be a good opportunity . . . Aunt Rin and Uncle Ubri offered to send me to the university, and I always wanted that."

"As it turned out, she already knew more than most of her class," Ambrel said with a fond smile. "That's how we met. I was assigned to tutor her, to bring her up to speed with the rest of the first years, but she didn't need my help." She caressed her wife's cheek fondly.

"I *did* need your help," Rowan said. "Just not with classes."

Ambrel grinned broader. "Zero sense of fashion."

"I knew how to dress to work in a greenhouse," Rowan said. "But in Alyssium . . ."

Terlu remembered when she'd first arrived in the capital city. It had been overwhelming to view the wide array of what people wore. It only clicked with her when she realized that it was its own kind of language. What clothes people chose communicated what they expected of their day, what they thought of themselves, and how they wished others to react to them. She'd been delighted to discover that librarians wore a standard kind of tunic but had the freedom to adapt it however they'd liked. She took to wearing brightly colored ribbons that reminded her of the bright birds and fruits and people of Eano.

It occurred to her that the clothes Yarrow had provided her probably originally belonged to Rowan or one of his other relatives. She hoped they didn't want them back. She had no interest in wearing her old librarian tunic. That wasn't who she was anymore.

"On our first day off from classes, I took her shopping," Ambrel said.

"You bought me a scarf. Prettiest thing I'd ever seen."

"For the prettiest thing *I'd* ever seen," Ambrel said.

Rowan smiled as if her wife was the sun, the moon, and every star, and Terlu caught herself about to sigh in envy. She wanted to be looked at in that way, with so much trust and faith and joy. "It was decorated with flowers and vines that reminded me of the greenhouses, and Ambrel guessed that—she knew I was homesick and wanted me to have a piece of my past that also fit into my future."

Ambrel smiled back at Rowan with just as much adoration.

"I wore that scarf at our wedding," Rowan said.

"And now we're here," Ambrel said, "back where you came from, and I want to see and experience everything that made you *you,* except the clothes. I do not want pants like that."

Rowan grinned at her own pants. "They're thorn-resistant."

"They're like wearing solid wood." Ambrel turned to Terlu. "Fashion aside, I am thrilled to be here. Rowan has never once stopped talking about all the wonders in the Great Greenhouse of Belde. Like the dream flowers."

"You tell her," Rowan said to Terlu. "The dream flowers are the best."

Terlu shook her head. "I don't know what those are."

"What! Yarrow hasn't shown you . . . ? Well, we need to fix that," Rowan said. She looped one arm through Terlu's and then looped her other through Ambrel's. "Both of you need to see this right away."

"What about breakfast?" Ambrel asked.

Stepping out of Rowan's arm, Terlu delivered the honey cakes to the nearest relatives—Harvena and Finnel, she remembered—to distribute, along with the tea. "From Yarrow," she told them. "He . . . He'll see you all later. Sometime. Maybe. Anyway, enjoy your breakfast!"

Well, that could have been less awkward. At least no one had asked why Yarrow hadn't come himself. She hoped they assumed he was just busy. Or shy. She thought of the story he'd told her and wondered if any of them had known young Yarrow had been abandoned in a cave. Had they known about it, either before, after, or during? Had they tried to intervene or stop it? Had they yelled at Rorick and Yarrow's father afterward, or just accepted it? She wondered what other childhood stories she didn't know and if they were better or worse.

With a smile, they thanked her for the honey cakes and resumed work. Retreating quickly, she joined Rowan and Ambrel as they strolled toward the greenhouse.

Rowan was chattering about how the dream flowers were her favorite—she'd encountered them first when she was a little kid and prone to nightmares. "You know, the usual falling off a cliff while naked and being eaten by flytraps kind of nightmare."

"That is a very specific *you* nightmare," Ambrel told her.

"It's not that unusual," Rowan said as they reached the greenhouse. Each of them shed their coats as they crossed into the bubble of summer. The air smelled of warm, earthy soil and the sweet lure of just-bloomed flowers. "Terlu, what about you? Do you have that kind of nightmare?"

Mine is being unable to move, unable to speak, left alone for years to lose all sense of time, of place, of self... She lied, "Sometimes I have a nightmare about falling."

"It's the flytraps," Ambrel told Rowan. "That's what makes it unusual."

"Have you ever seen a flytrap? They dissolve their prey. An insect will take ten days to be digested." Rowan shuddered. "I'm not saying that they aren't fascinating and precious and whatever Yarrow would say about them—he's never met a plant he didn't like, and I suspect that hasn't changed—but they make my skin itch, thinking about it."

"The one I met was nice," Terlu volunteered.

"I will strive to be polite if I ever meet them," Rowan said. "Now . . . if I remember correctly . . . Ah, yes, this way to the dream flowers!" She tugged them toward the next door, and they walked into a room that was filled with lilacs: deep purple, lavender, and white. The aroma filled the air so thickly that for a moment, none of them spoke; they walked through, breathing in the lilac. Thick, the bushes grew up to the ceiling, their branches weaving together, tangled behind their green leaves. Clusters of lilac flowers cascaded from the green.

"Beautiful," Ambrel breathed.

"Did you know any of the sentient plants?" Terlu asked Rowan. "I mean, from before you left?" She couldn't remember how old Yarrow had said he was when they fell asleep. A child? From the order of Laiken's notes, she knew that he'd already begun to dismiss his gardeners when he'd begun to experiment with the sleep spell. She wondered if any of the gardeners at the time had suspected it wasn't a natural sleep.

"Dendy used to babysit me when I was younger. Keep me from falling into the ocean or ingesting any poisonous berries, that sort of thing. He was great." Rowan opened the door to the next greenhouse, which was filled with row after row of leafy bushes. "And Hosha— they're the prickly pear—they used to offer up their flower, whenever they grew one. I didn't know Lotti. Guess she was already dormant by the time I was old enough to be loose in the greenhouse, or else he kept her in his tower, away from us. Anyway, when their magic failed and they all stopped talking . . . yeah, that wasn't a good day."

She missed them. Had she missed her brother? Had she ever planned to come back? Would she have come back if Alyssium hadn't fallen? Would any of them? "If you don't mind me asking, why didn't anyone come back to Belde before now?"

"Why didn't Yarrow ever come to us?" Rowan countered. An edge crept into her cheerful voice. She marched faster through the greenhouse into the next one and then the next, without pausing to look at the blossoms that overflowed their pots, the towering trees whose leaves kissed the ceiling, the delicate vines that wound up the pillars, or the countless flowers that bloomed around them. "Do you have any idea of how many letters I wrote him that he didn't answer? How many times I begged him to come to Alyssium? Even if it was just to visit? I saved up. After school, I worked in the florist shop, and I saved every little coin that I earned so that it could pay for Yarrow to take a boat to come see us. Enough for a return trip, if he didn't want to stay. I just wanted him to come. Do you know how many times he wrote back to me, to explain why he wasn't coming?"

She could guess, but it was a rhetorical question.

"I needed my brother with me. And my father. When at last Dad came and Yarrow wasn't with him . . . I wrote him a big letter after that, explaining all the reasons he should join us."

After two more lefts through greenhouses that Terlu had never seen (one full of decorative cabbages of various shades of green, white, and purple, and one full of thick greenery that was speckled with caterpillars who resembled tiny stretched-out cats), they reached a door with smoky glass. Or maybe the greenhouse on the other side was dark and hazy? Squinting, Terlu tried to see through—she saw shadows of pillars and trees. It was oddly dark.

Stopping, Rowan stared at the glass door as if not seeing it. "Not once. He didn't write a single letter back to me ever."

Then she pushed through the door and pulled Ambrel in with her.

Terlu lingered behind, thinking about Rowan's words. She'd never asked Yarrow if he'd reached out to his relatives, and he'd never said. Granted, it wasn't her business, but she'd privately dumped all the blame on his father, sister, cousins, aunts, and uncles for leaving him behind. She hadn't thought about the fact that he'd chosen not to go just as much as they'd chosen not to stay. Following them through the door, she asked, "Was the letter I sent the first time he'd ever tried—"

She halted and stared.

False moonlight bathed the greenhouse in a pale blue light. At the peak of the cupola, an imitation moon was cradled in a web of glittering strands. Swirls of sparkling cloud drifted through on a breath of impossible wind. The flowers were a deep blue, black, and gray—the colors of a garden at night. Even their leaves were a dark gray. Starlike sparkles drifted up from the blossoms, as if the flowers were breathing out stardust.

It smelled like jasmine. Terlu inhaled deeply as she walked forward.

"You'll want to sit down for this," Rowan said.

Ambrel dropped to sit cross-legged on the ground, and Terlu sat nearby. Rowan plucked the nearest flower. It looked like a black teacup, with petals that curved in her palms. She knelt and held it out to her wife first.

"Is it safe?" Ambrel asked.

"Would I tell you to do something that wasn't safe?"

"You would if you thought it would be funny," Ambrel said. "Is this going to be make me act like I think I'm a monkey?"

"Embarrassing isn't the same as unsafe," Rowan said, a wide smile on her face. "And you were a cute monkey." She bopped her wife on the nose.

Ambrel bared her teeth at her and made monkey noises. Both of them laughed. "Sorry," Ambrel said to Terlu. "This was several months ago, back in Alyssium, before the revolution, when we all thought everything would be fine and it would be resolved peacefully. Rowan and I went to a party thrown by a minor sorcerer. He'd offered as entertainment spell-candies that were supposed to transform you into an animal for five or ten minutes."

"In reality, the spell was a trick. It only made you *think* you were an animal."

"Rowan believed she was a hedgehog."

"Spent the entire time rooting around the carpets, searching for insects with my nose," Rowan admitted with a grin. "I'm told I made snorting noises."

"But at least *you* didn't try to swing from the chandelier and throw pâté at all the other guests," Ambrel said. Her eyes sparkled with the memory, and Terlu thought their experience of Alyssium had been very different from hers. She hadn't been to any parties, except the Winter Feast at the Great Library. Sorcerers, minor or not, did not consort with Fourth Librarians. *Or at least they never consorted with me.* There had been one once, a lanky green-skinned sorcerer from one of the outer islands, who had acted like he wanted to woo her—it hadn't taken her long to figure out he just wanted access to restricted books. He hadn't been subtle. She'd cried for a few days over him.

"The sorcerer deserved pâté in his hair."

Ambrel grinned. "He really didn't like that. He'd spent a lot of time and magic on his hair. As I recall, it changed color every few minutes."

Rowan snickered. "After the pâté, it alternated between green and gray. Anyway, dream flowers aren't like that. You are the one who guides the dream." She lifted the blossom to her nose and said, *"Dancing on the beach."*

Closing her eyes, she inhaled, then smiled.

A few seconds later, Rowan opened her eyes and exhaled. "Easy," she said languidly. "My beach had warm sand, gentle waves, and a breeze."

"You just . . . ask for whatever you want to dream about?" Terlu asked. She hadn't seen a spell for this in Laiken's notebooks, but there were still many she hadn't translated, much less studied. She wondered what other wonders she hadn't discovered yet.

Ambrel took the blossom from Rowan. "I want to dream about kissing you."

"You can do that any day, any time," Rowan said.

"On the moon," Ambrel clarified. She inhaled the dream flower's scent, closed her eyes, and then opened them again a few seconds later and leaned forward and kissed her wife.

She passed the blossom to Terlu.

Terlu cupped it in her hands and looked down at the sparkles that floated in it. She could ask it to show her any dream she wanted to see. But as she looked at the depths of the flower, she realized she didn't want to be here, at least not right now.

She had wanted friends, people, conversation. She'd wanted it so badly in the library that she'd risked her life for this kind of companionship. And now, these two had welcomed her along, opened up to her, talked to her, included her in their jokes and stories, but instead Terlu just wanted to find Yarrow and share this with him. *I don't want just someone. I want* him. Even though he refused to deal with his feelings about his family. Even though he hadn't shared anything about his anger and his disappointment in them before they'd arrived. Even though she still didn't know how he felt about her.

"I'm sorry, but I have to go," Terlu told Rowan and Ambrel.

Neither of them noticed—they'd plucked another blossom and were holding it together, their fingers laced around the petals.

I want what they have, Terlu thought.

Laying her blossom gently on the ground, she left the lovers and the dream flowers in search of her silent gardener.

CHAPTER TWENTY-FIVE

It took Terlu nearly an hour to locate Yarrow, and she only found him by narrowing in on where he wasn't. He wasn't with his family members who were working on restoring the cottages. He wasn't with the talking plants fixing the cracks in the dead greenhouses. He wasn't visiting the mini-dragons in the sunflower maze. He wasn't helping his father with the roses, his uncle with the orchids, or his cousin with the tomatoes. And he wasn't in Laiken's workroom with additional relatives, family friends, and the late sorcerer's supposed ghost.

She found him in the silence of a greenhouse full of miniature trees. He was bent over a tiny juniper. Focusing on the branches, he didn't so much as twitch as she crossed to him. She watched him snip with tiny silver scissors.

Snip.

Snip.

Snip.

"Are you going to tell me how I should be with my family?" Yarrow asked.

"Do you want to be with your family?"

He snipped again. "No."

Terlu sat cross-legged next to him and watched him continue to prune the juniper. She couldn't tell why he was making each cut, but he was doing it with precision so he must have had a reason. "Your sister showed me and her wife the dream flower greenhouse."

"Ah. Did you like your dreams?"

"I didn't try any," Terlu said.

He paused, looking at her. "Why not? They're harmless."

You weren't there, she wanted to say, but she didn't. She wasn't sure how he'd react to that. So she just shrugged.

"Laiken made them for us, the kids, to entertain us while the adults worked."

"That was nice of him."

Yarrow's lips quirked into a half smile. "He wasn't nice. He thought children were a distraction to his workers and a menace to his plants. It was to keep us busy so we wouldn't be underfoot."

"Maybe he wanted to be nice, but he didn't know how," Terlu said. She thought about what Dendy had told her, about the loss of Laiken's daughter, Ria. She wondered if that had colored his view of children. Not that it was an excuse, but it could be an explanation.

He snorted. Moving on to a miniature pine tree, he examined its branches and then began meticulously pruning its tiny limbs. He swept the debris carefully away from the roots.

"Is Laiken's ghost really upstairs in his tower? Your sister thinks it is."

He paused again. "Huh. I'd forgotten. I suppose, yes, he's there. Just the bitterness, though, not any of his consciousness. I used to yell at him in the beginning, when the greenhouses first started to fail. He just moaned."

"How did you forget you had a ghost?" Terlu said. She thought that should have been something that got mentioned, especially when they started to spend more time in the tower. It should have been on the initial tour. Or at least added as an interesting sidenote.

"It's just his leftover regret. Not him. Doesn't do any good. Doesn't do any harm." He rotated the pot that held the pine tree to study it from another angle. "I should have told you, though. And I should have shown you the dream flowers."

"It's all right. You have responsibilities—"

Standing up abruptly, he tucked the scissors into one of his pockets and then held out his hand toward Terlu. "I can show you . . . I mean, if you want . . . Do you want to see another wonder of the greenhouse?"

She took his hand and stood up. Her smile felt bright, as if it was beaming out of her. "I want to see everything you want to show me."

"Has anyone ever made a map of all the greenhouses?" Terlu asked as Yarrow led her through greenhouse after greenhouse—one with tulips and daffodils, one with rows of grapevines, one with water lilies in ponds on either side of the path and fish-shaped flowers hanging upside down from the rafters above. Minnow-like silvery fish swam between them, as if the air were water. She watched the school of flying fish zigzag, switching directions as one, between the blossoms.

"Never needed one," Yarrow said.

"I should make one." She added it to her to-do list, after she uncovered all the spells that would save the greenhouses. They passed through a greenhouse with a willowlike tree, with drooping branches that held glowing bubble-like orbs. It had a sweet, elusive scent, like a long-ago summer's day that was slipping from memory. She inhaled deeply. A bird circled above, vanished in a puff of smoke, and then reappeared—another of Laiken's experiments or just a random magical bird, drawn to the wealth of enchantments? She wished she had the time to study all the magical creatures here. "Also, a list of species living here. Might be useful to our new arrivals too."

"They aren't staying."

"Oh? Did they tell you that?" She knew for a fact he hadn't spoken to them yet.

He opened the next door and held it for Terlu.

She walked into a room with rows of thick grasses, topped with fistfuls of white flowers. It smelled like— "Garlic?" She smiled at him. He'd remembered she'd said she wanted to see it.

It was vast. Row after row of garlic.

"It smells nice," Terlu said. "I thought it would be overwhelming." She walked between the rows. Each plant was in a neat row, planted with precision—with love.

"It's more pungent when it's cooked."

"Thanks for showing me this." Maybe it was just garlic. No diamond dragonflies, leafy mice, tiny dragons, or multicolored butterflies, but this was a room he clearly loved. A piece of who Yarrow was. It meant something that he'd chosen to share it with her.

"There's more I want to show you." He held out his hand, and she took it. They walked hand in hand between the garlic rows. "My family doesn't have to tell me for me to know they're going to leave," Yarrow said. "I know them. They don't want to be here."

"They won't leave."

Yarrow halted outside a blackened door. "Close your eyes."

She obeyed. "They won't leave because they don't have anywhere else to go. Besides, your sister seemed happy to be back. I think they missed this place. And you."

He snorted.

Terlu laughed. "You know, it's not impossible that some people might find you likable." As soon as the words were out of her mouth, she wished her eyes were open so she could see his expression. He didn't say anything, but he drew her forward by the hand.

She felt the temperature change as she crossed the threshold into the next greenhouse. It was cooler, but not cold. She breathed in and thought the air was heavy with the smell of a sweet, familiar flower. Perhaps lilac? And roses? And . . . She sniffed, and the air teased her with other sweet scents that she couldn't name. "Can I open my eyes?"

"Yes." He was right beside her. She felt his breath warm on her ear, and she shivered. She felt as if her skin was aware of his nearness. Without meaning to, she leaned toward his voice, and she felt the brush of his shirt on her back—he was that close.

Opening her eyes, Terlu saw stars everywhere. She gasped.

A galaxy was spread out before her.

"It's the most spectacular if your eyes have already adjusted," Yarrow said. "That's why I had you close them. So you could see the stars between the stars."

"Are they all"—she reached toward a constellation—"flowers?"

"Bioluminescent flowers," he confirmed. Above, a flower-star streaked across the glass sky. He added, "Enhanced with an enchantment." He took her hand again, and they strolled through the greenhouse. The path curved through the star field, and everywhere she looked, the flowers sparkled and danced. "They don't require much care, so I'm not here often. Except when I want to remember that the universe is vast."

"It's lovely."

In between the lights, she saw the vines that filled the greenhouse. She wondered if they were a map of the stars above the island or whether they were a galaxy that didn't exist.

"Why did he make this? For his daughter?" Terlu asked.

"He created it after she died."

"A tribute? A goodbye? An apology?"

"Does it matter?" Yarrow asked. "It's ours now."

Ours. Wow, did he mean . . . *No, he means him and the plants. Or him and his family.* His father. His sister. His aunts, uncles, and cousins. It of course belonged to all of them, the people who'd been born here and returned. He didn't mean her, a woman with no ties to him or the greenhouse. She wasn't even a gardener. Now that she thought about it, she was embarrassed that she even thought for a second he was talking about her—

"Let me show you the ocean room."

"Ocean room?"

"I think you'll like it," he said. "Maybe even more than the garlic."

"There isn't much better than garlic."

Yarrow smiled, and they kept walking.

He'd mentioned ocean plants once before, she remembered, and she hadn't asked how and where they grew. Perhaps in ponds like the water lilies? She didn't ask—let him surprise her.

He was still holding her hand, and she decided it was her favorite sensation. His hand swallowed hers, and it was like being wrapped in a warm blanket. She could feel the calluses on his palm and fingers from the work, but he held her hand so gently that his felt soft. She wondered if he liked holding her hand as much as she liked holding his. With his hand encompassing hers, Terlu didn't even feel the need to talk. They strolled side by side through a greenhouse with translucent flowers and then another that was full of flowers that, every few seconds, released a puff of petals into the air like a miniature firework. The floor was littered in petals, and the air smelled like overripe plums.

When they reached the next door, she saw blue through the glass, a wavering, pearlescent blue. Could that be water? "When you said 'ocean room,' you didn't mean actual—"

He opened the door.

Inside was a tunnel into the bluest blue.

"Oh. Oh my. Oh, you did."

Still hand in hand with Yarrow, Terlu walked forward. Seawater filled the greenhouse on all sides of the tunnel. Looking up, she saw fish—brilliant blue, silver, and gold—flashing through the water, swimming between several-stories-tall strands of kelp that waved gently back and forth.

Beneath her feet was sand. It was dry within the tunnel, but on just the other side of glass, it teemed with life, both plant and animal: grasses and corals and anemones. She saw a bright blue crab scuttle over a rock and then dip out of sight.

"You see why I couldn't leave Belde?" Yarrow said, his voice hushed, even reverent. "There are wonders through every door."

"I don't see how anyone could leave." She walked deeper in, staring around her in awe. The scale and complexity of the magic to create and sustain such a miracle . . . It was a slice of the sea, encased within the greenhouse. How had Laiken done it? And how long would it last? If the glass in this room failed . . . She had to solve the secret of the spells before that happened. "We *need* to save this place."

He squeezed her hand.

Marveling at the majesty of the kelp, she asked, "How do you garden here?"

"There's a ladder. I'll show you." Yarrow led her through the tunnel to the far wall, where a ladder, also encased in a bubble-like tunnel, led toward the ceiling. Looking up, she saw a walkway above the water. He released her hand and began to climb.

Terlu began to climb after him. *Don't look down,* she ordered herself. The rungs felt sturdy, even though they had flecks of rust on them. Against the glass, she could almost see into the next greenhouse, a smear of deep tropical green with splashes of bright red. Behind her, she could hear the water sloshing within its tank. She was panting by the time she reached the top.

Yarrow was there to help her onto the platform.

"High," she puffed out.

"Look," he said. He nodded to indicate behind her, and she turned.

They had reached the top of the greenhouse, snow-flecked glass above them and the blue-white sky above that. Before them was the surface of the water. Kelp and other seaweed floated on top. And then a sea turtle poked its head above water.

It swam toward the edge, and Yarrow grinned at it. "Good to see you, buddy."

"We have a sea turtle?" Terlu said with a gasp.

Yarrow grinned more broadly. "You said you like sea turtles. He's been with us for decades. My sister tried to release him once—she *did* release him. Three times, actually. And each time he beached himself, then dragged himself, on flippers, back to the greenhouse. I guess he decided we're his family."

Terlu reached her hand into the water, expecting it to be as cold as the winter sea outside. Ooh, it was summery warm. "I'm swimming with him." She immediately began pulling off her tunic before it occurred to her that maybe that wasn't okay with Yarrow. She peeked over the collar before she had it fully over her head. "Is that—"

"Whatever you want." He was looking up at the ceiling and blushing so hard that his golden cheeks practically glowed.

She hesitated for only half a second and then her top was off. Pants followed in a heap next to it. In undergarments only, she climbed over the edge and lowered herself into the water beside the sea turtle.

He swam around her, bumping gently into her.

"You should come in," Terlu called to Yarrow. "The water's perfect." She used to swim with the sea turtles outside Eano. There was one breed in particular that was very fond of humans, perhaps because they associated the people of Eano with treats, but this turtle was the same kind. She laughed as he danced around her.

"You go ahead," Yarrow said. "I'm more of a land mammal."

"You're sure you don't mind?"

"Enjoy yourself. I'll have a towel ready when you're done."

She hadn't thought about a towel, or the fact that it was winter outside. Yes, she'd taken off her outer clothes, but her undergarments were now soaked. She probably should have thought this through. The sea turtle headbutted her again. He seemed eager to have company in the pool. She wondered when the last time was that anyone had swam with him. The turtles of this breed she knew had been friendly creatures, happy for interaction.

She gripped the edge of the sea turtle's shell and took a deep breath.

The turtle plunged down into the water. Terlu hadn't swum like this in years, and she felt every bit of childhood joy flood into her. She was eight years old again, beneath the waves. Fish darted around her, in the bubbles of the turtle's wake. She saw the kelp forest in front of them, and the turtle weaved through it before swimming up to the surface again.

She broke through and took another gulp of air. "Again!"

They circled the greenhouse tank, creating their own current, rising so that she could breathe before plunging down again. At last, she released the turtle's shell and floated on her back on the surface of the seawater.

"Thank you for showing me this place," Terlu said to Yarrow.

"It's nice to see you happy."

"I *am* happy," Terlu said. "You've been kind to me, and this place . . . this entire island is amazing." *And so are you,* she wanted to say but didn't dare. She swam to the edge, and Yarrow helped her out of the water. He wrapped a towel around her—he'd magically produced it from somewhere. Fingers on the edges of the towel, he hesitated before he stepped backward. "I'm thankful to be alive and to be here. Without you, I'd still be a statue, much less able to swim with a sea turtle again and see star flowers and . . . all of it. I don't even know how to begin to express how grateful I am."

"I don't want your gratitude." He turned away.

She dried herself and wrung out her hair with the towel. "I am grateful, though. You saved me."

"I didn't do it for you."

"I know. But . . ." Terlu didn't know how to put into words how she felt. Even though he hadn't known her, hadn't meant to save her, had only meant to help his greenhouse, he had changed her life. He'd given her a second chance.

He turned toward her again while she was still drying her hair. His eyes widened, and she realized she was only in very wet undergarments. Whatever he was going to say was lost.

He wants me.

I think.

"There were sea turtles in the water around the island where I grew up," Terlu said lightly, as if he were a bird she didn't want to scare off. "I used to swim with them all the time. After I moved to Alyssium . . . there weren't any sea turtles in the canals, and you didn't want to swim anywhere near the capital island. The closest water wasn't clean, with that many people living there. I think this sea turtle missed having someone swim with him." She wasn't sure why she was saying all of this. Maybe to avoid saying what she wanted to say, which was, *Do you want me like I want you?*

Yarrow couldn't seem to stop staring at her. "Why didn't you stay with my sister and enjoy the dream flowers? Why seek me out? You didn't know I'd have a sea turtle to show you."

She countered with her own question. "Why did you show me the turtle and the stars and even the garlic? Why not continue your gardening work?" He could have easily kept pruning and weeding instead of bringing her on this tour, and she would have understood. She hadn't gone to him with any expectations.

"I thought you'd like the sea turtle. You said once that you like them."

Terlu took a breath. "I like *you.*"

His eyes widened, and she thought he looked a little panicked. She hadn't meant to frighten him. Quickly, she pulled her tunic back on and secured the buttons.

Trying to sound as if everything was perfectly platonically normal, Terlu said, "I think it would help if I could construct a timeline of when the different greenhouses were built. I can match that against when Laiken recorded spells in his notebooks and narrow in on which sections most likely include the spells that made this ocean room, which made the star flowers, and so forth. It would be terrible if the world lost all of this wonder."

"I missed it, didn't I."

Fully dressed and mostly dry, she paused at the top of the ladder. "Missed what?"

"The moment when I should have kissed you."

Terlu felt a smile blossom from deep within her. "It's not possible to miss that." She walked across the platform—it took only two strides to reach him—and she rose up onto her tiptoes to press her lips on his.

He kissed her back, softly and sweetly, while the sea turtle splashed in the water nearby.

CHAPTER TWENTY-SIX

The kiss ended, gently, and Terlu stared into his eyes, their lips still so close that she was breathing his breath, as sweet as honey. She felt as if she were floating.

"Why?" Yarrow asked.

She stared at his lips and thought the question made zero sense. Because a kiss couldn't last forever, even if she wanted it to? Because you eventually had to take a full breath? She repeated the word, "Why?"

"I am not someone that anyone would choose," Yarrow said, as if it were objective fact.

Oh, by the sea. Did he think she just kissed anyone who wandered by? Terlu rolled her eyes so hard that they nearly hurt. "Stop it. I like you. It's not any more complicated than that."

"I know I'm the one who woke you, and I know you feel sorry that I've been alone—"

"It's not pity. Or gratitude." Stepping back from him, she poked his shoulder, hard. "Is that what you think?" Yes, that was what he thought. She could see it in his face. He was perfectly willing to walk away from . . . whatever this was, if she said she didn't want him. "Maybe just accept that I wanted to kiss you."

He took a deep breath. "Everyone I have ever cared about left."

"And I got turned into a statue," Terlu replied. Ugh, this was absurd. She started to climb down the ladder. "We both have issues," she shot up at him. "It doesn't mean we're doomed to be lonely and unhappy forever. Unless that's what you want."

"Obviously not," Yarrow said, starting down after her.

There was nothing obvious about it. He'd chosen a hermit's life. "Your sister said you never wrote back to her." Perhaps she should take that as a warning. Was that how he handled all his relationships? Just let them wither away? You could only have a relationship of any kind, be it family or friends or lovers, if both people were willing to reach toward each other. It wasn't, as some said, hard work in the sense of being unpleasant or tedious or painful—that was a myth perpetuated by people with a vested interest in telling you to stay in a terrible relationship—but it *did* require effort. You had to try.

"I didn't know what to say."

"You could have said *that*. It's better than silence." She hadn't meant to start an argument, especially after the swim with the sea turtle and the kiss. Halfway down, she twisted to see the aquarium behind her. The turtle drifted by, his flippers propelling him sideways through the water. She continued to climb down.

Above her, Yarrow said, "What about your family? What have you said to them?"

Oh? That was where he wanted to go with this? "That's different," Terlu said.

"Is it?"

Yes, it absolutely was. If she wrote to them, it could endanger them. Or her. Or both . . . though maybe since Alyssium had fallen, no one would care that she'd been de-statued? Okay, fine, perhaps he had a point. She shouldn't be so afraid that they'd be disappointed in her. They loved her. "Maybe I will."

"And maybe I'll talk to my family. When I'm ready."

"Good!" Terlu reached the bottom of the ladder, and she realized they'd just both agreed to do exactly what she wanted—to reach out to their loved ones, to choose to connect—and every bit of annoyance faded away. It wasn't a compromise; it was a victory. "I'll write to them and tell them I'm alive and well." How they felt about that would be up to them.

He reached the bottom of the ladder too.

She studied his face as if it would tell her what he was thinking and feeling. She hadn't meant to harp on his family, especially when she just wanted to talk about her and him. The swim with the sea turtle had been a lovely gift, and the kiss . . . lovelier still. She didn't know how to step back into that moment and the way they'd both felt when she'd climbed out of the water. They both stood in silence, looking at each other awkwardly, with the slice of sea above them.

As a peace offering, Terlu said, "Do you want to try the bubble spell again?"

He softened but said, "Are you sure? You don't need to, if you aren't comfortable. My family . . . I know them well enough to know they won't betray you, not if you're helping the greenhouse, but you don't know them yet . . ."

"There are a few more variations that I'd like to try. And I *do* need to. Greenhouses are still dying."

"You're more important than any greenhouse," Yarrow said.

Terlu forgot how to breathe.

She stared at him for what felt like an extraordinarily long moment before she inhaled again. Wordless, she held out her hand, feeling a bit as if she were trying to coax a deer to come close enough for her to pet. He'd been left behind over and over by the people who were always supposed to stay by his side. Whether he should have gone with them or not, whether he should have tried to stay connected or not . . . it still left scars.

Yarrow took her hand.

While the sea turtle swam through the water above them, they walked together through the tunnel. Neither of them spoke, but the quiet felt like the silence within the water, peaceful and natural. She thought about the turtle and wondered if he was lonely. He'd returned to the greenhouse on his own, Yarrow had said, but did he miss the sea? Other turtles? She resolved to return and swim with him as often as she could.

She'd abandoned the spell ingredients in the greenhouse they'd been practicing in when Yarrow's relatives had descended, and she was pleased to see they were all exactly where she remembered. None of his relatives had found this place, which meant it was unlikely they'd interrupt the spellcasting. *Maybe I can do this without them noticing at all.*

"Let me prepare them," he offered. "You focus on the words."

"Thanks." She picked up the pages of her notes. Now, which variation should she try first? She had theories about the third line . . . It could be that the parameters of the bubble were fixed by a piece of spell that she'd excluded. So if she took the measurements from the prior section, which focused on growing the pillars and support beams . . .

They worked side by side.

After a bit, Yarrow wordlessly handed her a slice of honey cake on an embroidered napkin. She munched on it while she ran through the words of the spell, adjusting them in her mind. The key was to focus the spell on its purpose while also defining its size. As near as she'd been able to tell, the protective bubble lived a hair's distance away from the glass. She didn't know which had failed first in the dead greenhouses—the bubble or the glass—but if the shield ruptured first, it could have caused the cracks in the glass by expanding against it. Of course other spells failing too didn't help, like the sun going out and the temperature regulation spell going haywire . . . She wished she knew what exactly had caused the failure. Regardless, this bit was key to restoring the greenhouses. If she could master this spell, then they could cast it on the greenhouses after the talking plants fixed the cracks. Once that was done, she'd then work to master the other spells that made the environments extraordinary.

Step by step, she thought. *I can do this.*

Yarrow will stand by me. She was certain of that. Whether the spell worked or not, whether she was able to restore the greenhouses or not, she wasn't alone.

Terlu stood up. "All right. I think I'm ready to try."

"Good," Yarrow said.

He'd mashed the ingredients into a paste. She turned in a circle, surveying the dead greenhouse. Sunlight pierced the snow-laden ceiling, and it fell in patches, making the bare soil and withered plants look dappled. "I think we should spread the paste out, to define where we want the bubble."

"You want the full perimeter of the greenhouse?"

"A smaller circle, for the first test." Showing him, she walked in a circle that incorporated a few of the flower beds as well as the central junction of the paths, where they stood, approximately a twelve-foot diameter.

He smeared the paste in a thin line behind her until he completed the ring. "Ready."

Coming to the center of the circle, Terlu spoke the words, careful to pronounce each syllable the way she'd rehearsed in her head. She focused on the ring of ingredients as she rolled through the lines. As she reached the end, she held the last syllable as if it were a final note in a song before she let it die into silence.

For a moment, nothing happened.

She was about to apologize to Yarrow. It might take a lot more trial and error before she made any real progress. After all, Laiken had been a master sorcerer with extensive training and decades of experience, while she was trying to eke out bits of spells from left-behind notes and—

The bubble rose from the circle, a shimmering veil. It spread up, curving to connect above them, sealing into a dome. Like a soap bubble, it shimmered with colors as the sunlight through the greenhouse glass hit it.

"It worked," Yarrow said, awe in his voice.

"Wow." She hadn't expected it to just . . . work. Like that. She'd thought she'd have to try out several more variations of the spell before it resulted in a dome this perfect. Walking toward the bubble, Terlu examined it.

No breaks. No seams. Also, it was beautiful. She watched the colors shift and undulate, more colors than she'd ever seen before, in shades that blurred into one another before swirling away, like a living rainbow. "If we form it against the perimeter of the greenhouse, we'll be able to control the temperature and humidity inside the dead greenhouses. You'll be able to have summer in the middle of winter again." Terlu paused. "Assuming this holds heat."

"We can test it. I can light a fire. I have a starter with me."

"Good idea." She loved that he came so prepared.

He crossed the walkway to retrieve dried grasses from the pots of dead plants. After collecting a few handfuls from within the bubble, he reached for a wad of grass just beyond—and his hand stopped with a thump. "Huh. It's solid."

He laid his palm flat on the bubble and pushed, and it didn't pass through.

She hurried to his side. They'd walked through greenhouse after greenhouse, passing through the invisible barrier in the doorways, and it had never been a problem. This bubble spell was modeled after that. It was supposed to act as insulation, not as a wall.

Terlu knocked with her fist on the bubble. It rippled but didn't dissipate. "Okay, maybe it's not perfect yet. We'll have to try again." She told herself she shouldn't be disappointed. Of course it hadn't worked right away. She wondered which line she needed to tweak to make it passable without being permeable—

He pushed harder at the bubble. It bowed out but didn't break. "Huh."

Terlu leaned against it with her shoulder, expecting to pop out the other side—but instead she bounced back. A wiggle of worry wormed itself into her throat. It was just a bubble. They couldn't be *trapped*. Could they?

He drew out his clippers and tried to slice into it. The bubble bent around the blade. "I think we're trapped," Yarrow said grimly.

"That's . . . not good." *Don't panic. It's just a bubble. It'll pop.*

While Yarrow bashed his clippers against the bubble, Terlu hurried back to the spell. She read through the words. It didn't say— *Oh.* She saw the line that specified the durability of the bubble. It was required to ensure that the bubble was capable of keeping in the levels of heat and humidity, but it didn't include a line to allow everything else to pass through. Perhaps it was supposed to call back to a line in a different part of the original spell?

At the perimeter of the bubble, Yarrow was now ramming his shoulder into the bubble, putting all of his strength and weight into it. He was beginning to utter oaths under his breath. Each hit reverberated with a *thud* that was then swallowed by the bubble, rippling like an innocent rainbow around them.

What if he couldn't break it? What if they were truly stuck?

"Someone will find us," Terlu said in the most soothing-librarian voice she could manage. She told herself that she had to focus on solving the problem, not on the *what-if*s.

"Unlikely," Yarrow said.

"Eventually, Lotti will wonder where we are."

"And what will anyone do when they come? It's impenetrable."

"Working together . . ." If enough force were placed on it from the outside, that could break it, couldn't it? Granted, the spells on the greenhouses had lasted for decades, perhaps centuries, despite all the wind, snow, and rain that the sky could throw at them. They only burst when the magic decayed enough to fail. What if she'd created a spell that was *that* solid? "Okay, maybe we need a better plan than wait for rescue."

"What's its weakness?" Yarrow asked.

"I'm not sure," Terlu said, studying the spell. Concerned about the fragility of the bubbles in her prior attempts, she'd been more focused on its strength. *Did I take it too far? What have I done?* She couldn't have just trapped them here for decades, without food, without water, without . . . "Oh. Oh no."

"What?"

"I didn't want it to rupture, shatter the glass, and kill all the plants. So, I made it as strong as I could." She'd dialed up that section of the text, using a word that would amplify its abilities. It had made sense at the time. "It's holding in air."

"And us."

"But *air,* Yarrow. It's not letting air in or out."

Yarrow stopped shoving at the bubble. "You mean to say that if we don't break out, we are going to run out of air?"

Terlu nodded. She felt tears prick her eyes. She knew she shouldn't have messed with magic. These spells . . . It had just been ego to think she could understand them, and now . . .

"Don't," Yarrow said.

She gulped back the tears that were about to spill out. "I'm sorry."

"Look at your notes and figure out how to break it," Yarrow said, calm and confident and just as soothing as her librarian voice. He didn't sound angry or fearful. *He should, though,* she thought. *He should be angry at me.* But he wasn't. "You can do this."

Terlu shook her head. "I shouldn't have—"

"Later, you can do the should-have, shouldn't-have. Right now . . ." Crossing to her, he knelt next to her. "Terlu Perna, look at me. It's not your fault."

She almost smiled. "It's absolutely my fault."

"Well, yes, but you're trying to pull off a miracle. You weren't really expecting it to work right away, were you?" Gone was the Yarrow who had been throwing himself at the iridescent wall like a furious bear. Now his voice was soft, his eyes understanding, and his hands on her shoulders gentle.

"I wasn't expecting it to be deadly right away! It's a bubble. Not . . ." She shook her head. Wallowing in guilt wasn't going to help. "Okay, how to break a spell. You broke the spell on me. I broke the sleep spell on the plants." In both cases, though, they'd used an additional spell to reverse the effects of the initial one. She didn't have a counterspell on hand that she could cast on the bubble that would break it. Maybe there was one, but she didn't know it. If she had access to the full library of Laiken's notebooks . . . But all she had were the spells she'd brought with her, the ones that she thought were relevant. Perhaps the clue was in them somewhere. Spreading her notes out in front of her, she studied them.

"You read," Yarrow said. "I'll keep trying to break through." He hefted up a pot and hurled it at the barrier. The bubble bowed out, absorbing the impact, and the pot was flung back into the circle. It crashed to the ground and shattered.

The words swam in front of her. She balled her fists and tried to focus. Her throat felt dry. Swallowing hard, she said, "What if we dig under it . . . ?"

He pulled out a trowel and, kneeling, began to dig. As he dug through the soil by the edge of the bubble, she tried to read. *What if it didn't work, what if the air ran out, what if no one found them . . .* Her thoughts chased one another, tossing up horrible scenarios.

A few minutes later, he reported, "It goes into the earth."

Of course it did. It had formed a sphere.

Do not *panic,* she ordered herself. *You can think your way through this.*

He rested his hands on his knees. "Can you . . . I don't know . . . reverse the words?"

"It doesn't work that way. Every spell requires the correct words to activate certain ingredients . . ." An idea came to her. A spell was words plus items. What if you took away the items? Getting excited, she suggested, "What if we destroy the ingredients?"

The protective shield was an active spell, continually maintained. Laiken's notes had been clear about that. In fact, her primary theory about why the greenhouses were failing was that the ingredients had degraded. She'd even thought about trying to refresh the ingredients rather than recasting the spell, but since she didn't know where Laiken had positioned the original ingredients for each greenhouse . . . Regardless, that wasn't the case here, and the bubble had thankfully formed *beyond* the ingredients, trapping them inside with Terlu and Yarrow.

Yarrow began to stomp on the paste, smearing it into the dirt.

"That won't destroy it."

"Fire?" he asked.

"Maybe?" Except, didn't fire use oxygen? "Wait, what if the fire eats all the air?"

"Do you have another idea?" Yarrow asked.

Wordless, she shook her head.

He withdrew a fire-starter from his pocket. Looking around, Terlu spotted more dried and withered plant material within the bubble. She broke as much of it off as she could to serve as kindling. Carrying it to Yarrow, she handed it to him. He wound it into a kind of makeshift torch and then lit the end.

A spark caught. The flames spread along the dried plant matter. He blew on it, and she wondered how much air they'd used already and how much more the fire would eat. If this didn't work . . .

Squatting, he held it to the paste. It charred at the lick of flame. Meticulously, he crawled around the perimeter of the circle, burning the ingredients.

She held her breath.

How much air was left?

What would it feel like when the air was gone? Would it hurt? Or would they just fall asleep? She pushed those thoughts from her mind. It had only been a few minutes since she'd cast the spell and sealed them in. There were plenty more ideas to try before their lives were in danger. Except that she didn't have any more ideas. She knew very little about how to break spells without access to a specific counterspell. *Perhaps that's something I should have studied before trying to cast any.*

As each wad of grasses burned to ash, Terlu fed him new kindling. He added it to his makeshift torch, trying to keep the flames from touching his hands. She saw him wince as a spark landed on his fingers. She opened her mouth to tell him to be careful and then shut it again. He knew to be careful; he had to be thorough.

Finally, he reached the last bit, grinding the flame into it.

And the bubble dissipated like a cloud dissolving in the air.

Yarrow swatted the air. "It worked."

Clutching the pages of her notes, Terlu darted outside the circle and sagged against a pillar. She was never going to try that again. It was too much of a risk. The laws were right—magic should be left to trained sorcerers, and amateurs shouldn't experiment with spells, no matter how convinced they were that they understood the First Language. A real sorcerer wouldn't have endangered their own life and the life of the person they loved.

Loved?

She liked him. She wanted him.

Love?

He crossed to her and wrapped his arms around her. She leaned against him and breathed in his solid strength, as well as the smell of smoke. "Are you burned?" she asked.

"I'm fine. You?"

"Fine. I'm sorry."

"Don't be. Accidents happen. Next time, we know how to break it faster."

She shook her head against his chest. "There can't be a next time. It's too dangerous." It had been foolish to try, even egotistical. She was playing with forces she didn't fully comprehend, and she had no one trained in spellcraft who she could ask. She was winging it, and she'd nearly gotten them both killed.

He tightened his arms around her. "*Next time,* I'll be there with you again. *Next time,* we'll know more. *Next time,* I'll have the fire ready."

She almost laughed, but she was afraid if she let the laugh escape, it would turn into a sob. "You trust me to try again? After that? We could have died. If we'd run out of air . . . If that hadn't worked . . ."

"It worked," Yarrow said, "and I know we can do this."

He sounded so confident. So calm. Leaning her cheek against his chest, Terlu breathed in and out, trying to calm her racing heart.

We, he'd said.

He believes in me. In us.

"All right," Terlu said. "We try again. But only after I figure out what went wrong and am absolutely one hundred percent certain I won't accidentally murder us again, at least not in the same way."

"Agreed."

She kept her cheek against his chest, breathing steadily, until she felt her heart rate slow from a gallop and the panic subsided to a soft hum. Above, she heard snow falling softly on the glass ceiling. Far in the distance, a plant was singing.

CHAPTER TWENTY-SEVEN

At dawn, Terlu helped Yarrow make another batch of honey cakes. Together, they slid them into the oven and then washed the bowls and mixing spoons side by side while the cakes baked. Outside, the snow was crisp white in the morning sun. A cardinal was perched on a branch of a nearby pine tree, a brilliant red against the white and the green. Inside, the only sounds were the swish of water, the crackle of the fire, and the purr of the winged cat. It was perfectly peaceful, and Terlu had never felt more at home anywhere.

As she put away the flour, Terlu said, "After I deliver the cakes, I want to stop by Laiken's workroom, and, if no one's around to see, check the other notebooks for more clues as to the shield spell."

He nodded. "Are you bringing Dendy?"

"He's working with the other plants to seal more cracks." She wanted to ask Yarrow to come with her, but she had no rational reason. She just wanted his company.

"Need my help?"

Yes. "Only if you want to come."

"I . . ."

"You don't need to. Up to you."

He smiled at her in thanks.

It's worth going alone for that smile. It warmed his eyes, and it made her knees feel gooey. She leaned against the kitchen counter for support.

"Let me know when you're ready to try the spell again," Yarrow said. "I'll be in the vegetable rooms. The lettuce is nearly ready to harvest, plus I need to weed the carrot beds." He pulled the cakes out of the oven, picked up one, and thumped its golden bottom. The cottage smelled of honey and cinnamon and warm bread. "They're done."

She wrapped the fresh cakes in cloth napkins and tucked them into a basket. "Emeral, how about you? Do you want to come? Someone might have fresh fish."

Emeral stretched in her bed, which was now the cat's bed exclusively. He licked his paw and then leisurely stood, stretched his wings, and flew up to Terlu's shoulders.

She laughed. "Guess he knows the word 'fish.'"

"Smart cat."

He curled around her neck and settled his wings.

Yarrow murmured, "Lucky cat."

She met his eye, and Yarrow gazed back at her. For a moment, Terlu wondered if she dared kiss him goodbye. But she had a cat around her neck and a basket full of honey cakes in her hands, and before she could make a decision, he turned back to the sink to wash out the still-hot baking tins. "Yarrow . . ."

"Hmm?" He turned to look at her.

She didn't know what she wanted to say. "Nothing."

"I'll see you soon?"

"Soon," she promised.

She just . . . She'd come so close to ruining everything, and he'd forgiven her without any kind of hesitation. It was so very different from anyone she'd ever known. At home, whenever she made a mistake—well, they just didn't let her forget it. Terlu remembered the first time she'd tried to cook dinner for her family, and she hadn't opened the flue in the chimney. She'd filled the house with smoke, and her family had forbidden her to cook anything for months. Every time she'd entered the kitchen, she'd been treated like she was going to make a disaster. And she'd been teased about it for years—never cruelly, but still, it had stung. When she'd tried to explain once to her sister how it felt to never be trusted, Cerri had told her that she'd nearly burned down the house so what did she expect?

He didn't blame me.

In fact, it was the opposite. He hadn't turned on her when things went wrong. It hadn't become *you* did this or *you* failed to do that. It was *we*, even though it had been entirely her fault. Maybe especially because it had been her fault? He hadn't wanted her to feel the weight of that blame. He hadn't wanted her to stop believing she was capable.

Buttoning her coat, Terlu walked out into the winter morning with the cat warm around her neck and a basket of honey cakes on her arm. She wondered what her family would think of Yarrow. He was quieter than any of them were. She'd grown up in a family where the loudest person was heard and so you learned to bellow if you wanted any attention for yourself. None of them thought she could ever be a librarian, knowing how much she liked to both talk and be heard. She'd tried to explain there was a role for librarians who weren't quiet—an important role, to connect the knowledge with the people who needed the knowledge—but they just thought of librarians as quiet hermits who looked down on anyone who wasn't quietly reading. Rijes Velk had understood when Terlu had interviewed for the position, as had the librarian in charge of the second floor. She'd been promised a patron-focused role. It wasn't anyone's fault that the laws changed . . .

Which laws have changed now?

She wished she knew what was going on in Alyssium. What had happened to the library? What happened to Rijes Velk? Was she okay? Was she safe? Had the books survived? So much knowledge, so much history, so many life stories.

At least Yarrow's family was safe. And he'd talk with them. Eventually.

Until then, the honey cakes are his words.

As she approached the blue cottage, she saw that Yarrow's relatives had already made significant progress. One of the cousins, Percik, was up on the roof, repairing the shingles. Another relative, Finnel, was working on a window, while an aunt, Harvena, and an uncle, Ubri, cleaned inside. Greeting them all, Terlu handed out the honey cakes. This time, it was far less awkward than the first morning—there was no expectation that Yarrow would be with her. They chatted amiably about the cakes, the weather, and the work, before she left to continue on.

She made her way toward the sorcerer's tower. Ahead, she heard the waves crashing against the rocks. The sky was streaked with clouds, but the sun peeked out between them. Birds were circling over the dock, and she saw one of the cousins . . . Vix maybe? . . . was fishing off the end of it. She'd have to ask his name again to be sure. Emeral launched himself off her neck to soar toward the dock. She had no doubt that if Vix had any luck, the winged cat would have an excellent breakfast. His meows were irresistible.

She took a deep breath of the sea air. She loved the salty sharpness of the breeze mixed with the scent of pine. In the distance, the seabirds were calling to one another, and she heard the steady crash of waves on the rocks.

She hadn't known it was possible to fall in love with a place so quickly.

Terlu walked up the steps, now clear of snow due to the number of people who'd come and gone in the past few days. Hearing voices from within the workroom, she hesitated for a moment. She wouldn't be able to look at the notebooks without being asked why, which made this a wasted trip. On the other hand, she could still deliver honey cakes.

She knocked on the door. It was opened a second later by Ambrel. "Ah, good morning, Terlu! Ooh, you brought Yarrow's honey cakes? Please tell him thank you and I'm looking forward to meeting him. I know technically we met when we all arrived—but that was such chaos that I don't think it counts."

Behind her, Rowan piped up. "You will meet him, and he will be friendly and welcoming. I'm going to insist. He can't keep avoiding us forever."

Well, he could if he tried. He *had* taken the first step by agreeing to talk to them, but that didn't mean he was ready to actually do it yet. "I don't think forcing it—" Terlu began.

Rowan reached beyond Ambrel to pull Terlu inside. "Come eat breakfast with us, and we can gossip all about my antisocial brother." She was halfway through dressing, with a loose sleep dress on top and work pants underneath. Her black-and-gold braids were unpinned and curled around her face like vines before they wrap around a trellis. Ambrel was already fully dressed, in a wide skirt with many pockets beneath a heavy leather apron. Her hair was pinned up under a scarf. A curl had unfurled next to her cheek. As Rowan passed by, she lovingly tucked Ambrel's curl back under the scarf before asking Terlu, "Are you sleeping with him? Is that why you're so willing to overlook my brother's faults?"

Terlu felt herself flush bright red. She was *not* going to answer any questions about her relationship with Yarrow.

Ambrel swatted Rowan's arm. "Be nice. It's completely inappropriate for you to badger her about Yarrow. She can't control whether he wants to talk with us or not."

Rowan protested. "I'm just making conversation."

"She misses the florist shop," Ambrel said to Terlu. "That's why she's being difficult."

"I'm sorry you had to leave it," Terlu said.

"It burned. There wasn't anything left to leave." Rowan sighed heavily. "Sorry. You've been kind to welcome us. And sorry about"— she waved her hand vaguely—"harping on Yarrow. He is the way he is."

"It's your home," Terlu said. "Of course you're welcome here." In truth, *she* was the new arrival. She didn't think she had any kind of say over whether they came back to their home or not.

Rowan shook her head. "It *was* our home, and I think it can be again. But you . . . You belong here, I can tell. You love it here."

Terlu wondered if she'd seen her outside, thinking that very thought as she looked out across the sea. *It's so true that even a woman I just met can see it.* She wondered if it was as obvious how she felt about Yarrow. She'd never been good at hiding her emotions; she felt them across every inch of her skin. Blushing, she set the basket with the remaining honey cakes on the worktable and turned to view the workroom.

In the wake of Yarrow's relatives' arrival, the workroom had been transformed—drying laundry hung on strings that crisscrossed the room. The table was covered in stacks of recently cleaned dishes, as well as a pile of lettuce heads. She thought of Yarrow, going to check on the lettuce harvest. It looked as if one of his relatives had already been there. She wondered how he was going to feel about that. A mound of mushrooms was in a basket in the sink, waiting to be washed. Blankets and quilts and pillows were everywhere—every inch of the workroom had been used for sleeping.

Seeing her observing all of this, Rowan said, "Mmm, we kind of invaded. Sorry about that."

"We'll be moving into the cottages soon," Ambrel said. "I'm about to head out to work on the chimneys."

"Ambrel used to do metalwork in the city," Rowan said. "She knows a lot about chimneys and forges. Everyone agrees Ambrel is useful. And smart. And beautiful." She nuzzled her wife's shoulder.

"Most of my work in Alyssium was ornamental," Ambrel said to Terlu, "but I can fix hinges and nails and other practical work. In fact, it's often the most satisfying kind of work. I will eventually get a forge set up for all of that, but first step is to fix the chimneys."

"Sounds like you're planning to make this home," Terlu said.

"I'd been looking to leave Alyssium even before the violence began, so this isn't a hardship for me," Ambrel said. "Coming here was more difficult for some of the others who were more attached to city life, but we'll all adjust. And if we can make this a viable place to live . . ."

Rowan hushed her. "That's a later idea."

"What's a later idea?" Terlu asked as she scooted aside a stack of folded laundry in order to surreptitiously study the spines of the journals stacked nearby. If they didn't leave, she'd try to take a few back to Yarrow's cottage to examine.

Ambrel shot her wife a look and answered, "We weren't the only ones to lose homes. If this place works out, there are some friends we'd want to invite to come start lives here."

"Only if the island can support it," Rowan said quickly, both to Ambrel and to Terlu, "and it's not guaranteed that it can, especially with the greenhouses dying. We won't ask too much of Belde." She shed her sleep dress and pulled on a tunic-like top. "Contrary to what my ornery brother thinks, we *do* care about this place."

Terlu wondered how Yarrow would feel about more people coming to live on the island. It would be good if it became a true community. Wouldn't it? There was still the issue of her illegal spellcasting. Fixing the greenhouses was going to require a lot more magic. And the more strangers who came, the less safe she'd be. She didn't know what to hope for.

Lightly, she said, "Guess we'll have to see what happens."

"Do you want us to distribute the rest of the honey cakes?" Ambrel offered.

"That would be wonderful. Thanks." Her eyes slid to the notebooks. If they left, maybe she'd have a chance to peek at a few . . .

Rowan wrapped a ribbon around her braids. "If you're looking for something fun to read, that's not it." She nodded at the journals.

"Oh, I'm just . . . Yarrow wanted me to pick up a few things, while I was here. Notes. His notes. On the plants. He . . . forgot them." Terlu tried not to wince at how unconvincing she sounded. She wasn't used to lying about books. Or lying about anything, really.

Ambrel tugged on Rowan's arm. "Let the woman be. She has things to do, and so do we."

Do they know? Terlu wondered. *About my spellcasting?* It was possible they'd guessed after seeing the sentient plants. Still, no one had said anything to her yet.

"You're welcome to join us for dinner," Ambrel said. "Vix is fishing so we should hopefully have an actual meal to offer."

She'd been right that that was Vix.

"Bring Yarrow if he wants," Ambrel said.

"Or bring him even if he doesn't want," Rowan said. "He can't keep avoiding us. Or maybe he can. He's good at that."

"Rowan," Ambrel scolded.

"Sorry, but I thought I'd get at least a reunion if not an apology."

Terlu bristled. He was trying his best! And he'd made honey cakes. Never mind that she'd also expected a reunion. *It's not up to me or Rowan or anyone to decide what he's ready for.* "He was the one left behind," she pointed out.

"By choice," Rowan said. She then held up her hand. "I know, I know, he could say it was my choice to leave. I can forgive if he can. But he has to *talk* to us."

"Give him time," Terlu pleaded.

"Humph," Rowan said.

Ambrel tugged her out of the door. "Come on."

Following them to the door, Terlu asked, "Out of curiosity, what does Laiken's ghost think about this—about all of you, coming back?" It felt odd to talk about a ghost, especially the ghost of a sorcerer of immense power, as if it were a commonplace fact.

Wrapping her scarf around her, Rowan shrugged. "Don't know and don't care. He's caused enough problems. I don't think he gets a say anymore." She waved as she headed outside with Ambrel and the rest of the honey cakes.

Emeral waltzed in through the door as they departed. He was carrying a fish in his mouth. Depositing it on the hearth, he purred as he tucked in to nibbling at its side.

"Good for you," Terlu told the winged cat.

Relieved to be alone at last—which was, she thought, a novel feeling, given how much she used to hate solitude—she pulled another one of the books off the shelves and began to skim through it. She wasn't sure what she expected to find—a treatise on exactly the information she needed? How had Laiken solved the problem of making the bubble permeable to humans and air but keeping the temperature in? He had to have done it, because it was repeated in greenhouse after greenhouse. She wished she could ask him.

She eyed the stairs and wondered if she could. She'd never met a ghost before. How much did they remember of who they were and what they'd once known? And how much could they communicate with the living?

I could find out simply by going upstairs.

If she *could* communicate with him and if he wanted to be cooperative, it could cut her research time down significantly. Perhaps it could even be the key to saving the greenhouse. Or maybe she was just hoping for a miracle.

Leaving the notebook open on the desk, Terlu walked up the twisty, narrow stairs. She felt colder as she walked up and wasn't sure if it was a ghostly cold or just because she was farther from the stove. Wasn't heat supposed to rise? It should be warmer upstairs, but instead it felt dark and drab. Like it should have a ghost. She shivered and hugged her arms as she looked around.

Yarrow's relatives had sprawled their belongings over the upstairs too—heaps of clothes on the bed, a hairbrush on the dresser, a tiny statue of a gryphon on the bedside table—but somehow it still felt gray and unwelcoming. She noticed that no one seemed to have slept in the bed, which was odd. It wasn't as if Laiken needed it anymore, and it had been years since he'd died. She would have thought practicality would have won over sentiment.

Crossing to the bed, she asked softly, "Sorcerer Laiken? Are you here?"

She didn't hear an answer or feel anything other than the chill of the room.

"My name's Terlu Perna, and I'm trying to figure out the spells to save your greenhouse. The magic is failing, and your plants are dying. If you help me . . ."

She heard a sigh like the wind in the trees.

"Sorcerer Laiken?" She turned toward the window. Had it been the ghost, or had it been the wind? "Just point me to where I can find the answers. Can you do that?"

Silence.

She began to feel ridiculous. Either he didn't understand or he didn't care. *Or he isn't here.* She'd never seen a ghost, and she'd certainly never heard of one contributing to anyone's scholarly studies. Of course if she *could* find a way to communicate . . .

Perhaps if she brought a few of the books up here . . .

"One second. I'll be back." It might be a waste of time, but she was certain she'd sensed some kind of presence in his bedroom. If he retained any of his old self, he'd want to save his greenhouse, wouldn't he?

Terlu trotted downstairs. If he could indicate which book she should focus on—

Before she could select more than a handful of volumes, the door to the workshop slammed open and Dendy lurched through the doorway, his leaves sprawling across the floor. "Terluuu! Aaanyone else here?"

She rushed to him. "Just me and Emeral. What's wrong? Are you okay?"

"Another greenhouse is faaailing! Caaalling everyone tooo come help." He darted back outside, swinging himself out by his tendrils.

Terlu dropped the notebooks on the table and followed, grabbing her coat as she passed by it. "Which greenhouse?" she yelled after him. "Where do I go?"

"The siiiinging one," he called as he hurried toward the dock.

CHAPTER TWENTY-EIGHT

The enchanted plants were still singing as their world crashed down around them. Terlu passed by one of Yarrow's cousins as he carted out a pot with a flowering bush that was belting out a wordless melody in a high soprano. Scanning the greenhouse, Terlu spotted Yarrow in the center, digging at the roots of one of the tulip trees, with his father beside him. Neither were talking, both focused on the task at hand. The tulip tree crooned, a baritone.

Lotti was in the rafters shouting directions to the gardeners and sentient plants who swarmed beneath her. Everyone was moving at top speed, working together to get the singing trees out of the soil and to haul the pots with flowers into a safe greenhouse before the temperature went haywire. At least half the pots had already been transported, which was remarkable.

Terlu called up to her, "Lotti, can you see where it started?"

"What?"

Louder, she asked, "Where did the failure start?" She knew she should help with the digging and hauling, but if she could pinpoint the cause . . . She couldn't stop *this* greenhouse from dying, but perhaps knowing the source could help her predict which greenhouse would be next to fall. If she could guess that with any degree of accuracy, they could move the plants to safety preemptively. It was worth sparing a few precious seconds now.

"Firrrst cracks were on the east waaall," Dendy said as he passed her, propelling his root ball forward with his leaves. He spared one tendril to point eastward.

She hurried to the east wall of windows, where the cracks were continuing to spread. Each new crack sounded like a slap. Swarming over the glass, multiple talking plants—the ivy, the orchid, and the fireweed—were casting the crack-healing spell as quickly as they could.

That won't help if the temperature fluctuates like it did in the last one.

But she let them try.

"What doesn't make sense is why all the spells fail at once," Terlu said, mostly to herself. It had to be that one failure triggered the next, not that they all coincidentally failed simultaneously every time. All the greenhouse-creation spells were linked to one another, as she'd discovered when she tried to pry them apart, which meant it had to be a cascading failure, didn't it? So if she were able to stop the first malfunction . . .

Kneeling, she traced the cracks from the floor upward. What caused the failure? She'd thought it was simply the age of the ingredients. If that were the case, though, then the greenhouses should be failing in the order in which they were created, and they weren't. She knew for a fact that this greenhouse was a later one. According to the dates in the notebooks, Laiken had only experimented with the singing plants well after he'd collected seedlings from around the Crescent Islands. The earlier greenhouses were all straightforward recreations of environments on the other islands. In fact, the very earliest ones held vegetables, and the majority of those had shown no sign of failure yet.

So why this greenhouse? And why now?

Was it just random, or was there a reason? She thought of Laiken's ghost and wondered if it had any idea as to what was causing this. *I have to find a way to ask.* This couldn't be allowed to continue to happen. It didn't matter how much of his code she cracked or how many spells she puzzled out if it was all going to be destroyed in one catastrophic moment.

Around her, the chaos swirled as the people and plants worked and shouted, but she blocked it all out. Working alone, she followed the cracks, tracing them to their source. All of them started from the foundation and spread upward. *Why? What does that mean?* Could the failure come from the earth somehow? Had Laiken buried the ingredients? She knew from his notebooks that he hadn't. He'd kept them open to the air, for a wider area of influence—he'd specifically noted how he'd discovered that was necessary. So why did all the cracks begin at the ground? Why not the cupola, which had to suffer the bombardment of wind, rain, and snow? Why not the seams between the windows, which had to be the weakest points?

One of the sentient plants shrieked for help.

Questions can wait; there are plants to rescue.

Leaving the mystery, Terlu hurried back to the others. Yarrow passed her a trowel, and she began to dig at the roots of a flowering bush, moving the soil away from the soft naked strands beneath the plant. The flowers crooned in a minor key, punctuated by wail-like arpeggios.

Up in the rafters, Lotti began to howl, "Cold coming!"

Terlu looked up to see frost spreading across the cracked glass. It blossomed in flowerlike patterns, as the pillars and rafters became coated in ice. The leaves of the bush in front of her shriveled, and the flowers collapsed into shriveled, brown knots. Its song quieted into a whisper, then fell silent. *Oh no, it's happening.* She'd hoped they'd have more time—

"Grab what you can," Yarrow called, "and get out *now!*"

The sentient plants, who had been through this before, sprinted for the doorway. The humans were slower, but Yarrow abandoned the roots of the singing tree he was working on and instead herded his relatives out the door.

His father continued to struggle with the roots of his tulip tree.

"Leave it," Terlu said. "The temperature will fall too fast. You'll die too."

"Help me," Birch cried.

She dug into the roots with her trowel, hacking at them—*better a wounded plant than no plant at all*. The tree sang louder, a kind of wailing keen, as its petals shriveled into brown husks. The faint floral smell deepened into a medicinal kind of odor, the stench of decay.

Yarrow returned and the three of them unearthed the tree. They dragged it by the branches to the doorway and through. Yarrow slammed the door. He turned on his father who, without his cane, was sagging against a pillar. "What were you thinking?" Yarrow exploded. "I said to get out!"

"I couldn't leave it," Birch said. One of the cousins handed him his cane, and he clutched it. "I left before. I'm not going to do it again."

"Your heart—"

"—is fine."

One of the others gasped, and they broke off their argument to look to the door. Frost spread over the glass, and then a second later, it melted away. Terlu sank to the ground and panted.

"Nasty spellwork," Birch said.

"What do you mean?" Terlu asked, looking up.

He waved his hand at the door. "That's not natural."

Well, obviously it wasn't. None of the greenhouses on Belde were natural. "I think it's a cascading failure," Terlu said, "stemming from a single weak point in—"

"There's no evidence of any enemy at work," Yarrow said to his father, over her. He was scowling at Birch, and his hands were clenched at his sides. "I've been here longer than you, and since you left, there hasn't been a single soul to step foot on Belde in—"

Terlu got to her feet. "Wait, what enemy? What are you talking about?"

"It's one of the many things we disagreed on," Birch said. He leaned heavily on his cane, and she noticed that his muscles were shaking. He'd pushed himself too hard, too fast. She glanced around, looking for a chair to shoo him into, but he wasn't budging. Continuing to shake, he scowled at his son. "I believe that the failures aren't natural. They're caused by a spell, cast by a rival sorcerer."

"And I say there's no rival sorcerer," Yarrow snapped. "How could there be? Laiken spoke to no one, and there's no one but us on the island. It's simply the old spells decaying. That's all. Entropy, a natural occurrence. If we can revitalize the spells—"

"They'll still fail." Birch stabbed the ground with his cane for emphasis. "I am telling you, there's something rotten at the core of this island. Say you're right, and there's no rival sorcerer. Only Laiken. Still doesn't mean it's natural. It could be his fault—he could have sabotaged his creation. He didn't want the greenhouses outlasting him and so he ensured they'd die."

"You're wrong," Yarrow said. "He wanted them to last forever. In fact, it was his major concern." He turned to Terlu. "You've studied the spells. Tell my father it's just time and decay."

Terlu froze. She hadn't told any of Yarrow's relatives that she'd studied Laiken's spells. What if Birch asked *why* she'd studied them? What if he connected the plants' activities to her? What would he say when he realized she broke the law?

But Birch didn't even glance at her. He was too busy glowering at Yarrow, his bushy eyebrows so low that they nearly swallowed his eyes.

Maybe he doesn't care that I've cast spells?

Or maybe he was too distracted to care now, but he would later when he'd had a chance to think about it.

"The island's cursed," Birch insisted. "We should have never come back, and you should have left with us."

"There's no curse," Yarrow said.

Mulling it over, Terlu frowned at the door to the dying greenhouse. *Actually,* she thought, *it would explain a few things—the suddenness and randomness of the failures, for example.* What if there was a spell intended to cause the failures? If there was, then no matter how many greenhouses they fixed, they'd still continue to fail.

"And no rival sorcerer," Yarrow said stubbornly.

She'd seen no evidence of any spellwork that didn't originate with Laiken. But she couldn't let go of the idea that the failures were deliberate. She didn't know why anyone would want this, but it was possible. There was, of course, one person who would know for certain. Or, more accurately, who *knew*.

"I say it's—" Birch began.

Stepping between Birch and Yarrow, she said, "I need to talk to the ghost."

Yarrow stopped glaring at his father to blink at her. "What?"

"To do that, I need your help, both of you," Terlu said. "Laiken doesn't know me. I know neither of you want anything to do with him, but he might have answers, and he's more likely to listen to one of his gardeners than to me."

Yarrow shook his head. "He didn't have any interest in his gardeners."

His father agreed with him. "He wasn't good with people."

Nudging Terlu's foot with her leaf, Lotti piped up, "Take me! If Laiken is there, even a piece of him . . . I want to talk to him. He'll listen to me. I think."

She might be right. Lotti held up her leaves, and Terlu bent down and lifted her up. Closing her petals tighter, the rose curled her leaves around her root ball.

"Come with us," Terlu pleaded with the two men.

She expected an argument or even excuses, but instead Yarrow merely nodded. Sighing, Birch nodded as well.

While the other gardeners and sentient plants reorganized the singing plants and took stock of what survived—nearly all the plants this time, thankfully—Terlu headed out of the greenhouse with the resurrection rose, Yarrow, and his father.

———

Back in the sorcerer's tower, Terlu, with Lotti, climbed the stairs first, followed by Yarrow and Birch. They'd quit arguing and dropped into an angry silence, which she didn't think was an improvement, but at least they'd both come.

She lowered Lotti onto the bedside table. "Can you sense him?"

Lotti waved her petals and leaves in the air. "Laiken? Are you here? Papa?"

Terlu wondered if she should leave the rose alone with him. But no, she had important questions to ask. Or try to ask. There was no guarantee that a ghost could understand anything the living said—it depended how much of him remained.

She shivered.

Was that him, the chill in the air, the shadows on the wall?

"If you're here, your plants need you," Terlu said.

"Why did you— No, that's not what we're here to ask," Lotti corrected herself. She folded her petals as if she were petitioning a judge. "We need your help. Your children need you. We're awake, you see, but the greenhouses are failing. Can you help us stop it?"

The windows rattled.

"Wind or ghost?" Terlu whispered.

"Wind," Birch said, arms crossed. He was scowling hard, more bearlike than Yarrow had ever been. "He doesn't care."

Another whoosh, and the sheets on the bed shifted.

Lifting his voice, Birch said, "Isn't that right, Laiken? You don't care about anyone or anything. You don't care about the gardens— you just made them because of how powerful they made you feel. You didn't care about your daughter—you just wanted to control her."

He knew the daughter, Terlu guessed. Dendy had said she'd died before Yarrow was born, but Birch and the other older gardeners may have known her personally. They'd watched the tragedy unfold, and they'd seen Laiken become more and more paranoid and been unable to stop any of it. They'd been there when he forced the plants to sleep—and then when he forced all of his dedicated gardeners to leave their jobs and their homes.

"Quiet," Yarrow growled at him. "You'll anger him."

Birch snorted. "What does that matter? He turned his back on us. All of us. We devoted our lives to this place, to the vision of what it could be. We believed it was important, that it was bigger than ourselves. But to him . . . it was a toy. A toy he discarded."

"I'm more than a toy," Lotti said.

"Absolutely you are," Terlu said firmly. "You're more than what anyone made you to be." She wished she could propel those words right into the little rose's heart, so she'd believe them. She deserved so much more than he'd been capable of giving her.

"He made me out of love," Lotti insisted. "He loved me. He loved all of us. He just . . . got so scared he'd lose us that he went too far." She turned in a circle to face her bloom toward all of the room. "But we're alive. We're awake. Dendy. Risa. Amina. Tirna. Nif. Zyndia. We're all alive and well, and we want to stay that way. Won't you help us?"

A breeze blew through the room, and the curtains rustled.

There was no open window, no source for the wind.

"I think that was a yes?" Lotti said.

"Ask him if there's an enemy causing the failures," Birch said.

Yarrow shook his head but said nothing.

Lotti repeated the question and lifted her petals higher. "No," she said.

"See?" Yarrow whispered to his father. "I told you."

Terlu wanted to ask her how Lotti could be so sure of his answer, but she didn't want to break whatever tenuous connection the ghost and plant had established. She tried the next question, "Are the greenhouses failing because the spells are old?" That was her and Yarrow's original theory. It was logical, and if so, then the cure was to fix the failures, ideally before they happened. Replace the spells.

The wind blew through the bedroom, counterclockwise.

"No," Lotti said.

No?

She tried being more specific: "Are they failing because the spell ingredients have decayed or been damaged?"

"No."

Terlu wanted to go back to the idea of an enemy, but he'd already said no to that. "Is it a specific spell causing the failures?"

"Yes."

Yes? But what kind of spell . . . Why? And who had cast it? What was the point of such a spell? And if it wasn't cast by an enemy, then who was responsible? She shook her head. This didn't make sense. "Is the spell supposed to destroy the greenhouses?"

All of them held their breath.

"No," Lotti said.

A malfunctioning spell. Ah, now *that* she understood. "But what . . ." No, that was too complex a question. "Is it your spell?"

Silence.

Then: "Yes," Lotti said.

"An old spell or a new spell?" Terlu asked. And then she realized he couldn't answer that. "An old spell?" No. *Huh, so it isn't one of the creation spells gone awry.* "A new spell?" Yes. "From after you died?" No. *Of course no, dumb question,* she scolded herself. "A spell you cast before you died?" Yes. "A new spell you were experimenting with when you died?" Yes, again.

She remembered the notebook she'd found on his bedside table. "Did you keep notes in the journal that was by your bed?" She hadn't read that one. It was too recent, and she'd been looking for the spells from the initial creation of the greenhouse, so she could recreate those. But if he'd cast a malfunctioning spell and then died before he had a chance to fix it . . .

"Yes," Lotti said.

Terlu exhaled. *Yes.* She had the book that held the answers. "Thank you, Lotti," she said fervently. "Thank you, Laiken." She knew where to begin now. She flew down the stairs. Dimly, she heard Yarrow and Birch behind her.

"Why does this matter? So now we know, but what are we supposed to do with this?" Birch asked Yarrow. "Your girl . . . She's not a sorcerer, is she?"

She paused on the steps, listening to how Yarrow would answer.

"She's amazing," Yarrow said.

"Ahh," Birch said. He asked no other questions.

Her head buzzing with hope, Terlu continued down the stairs and across the workroom. She picked up her coat and pulled it on. She knew exactly where the notebook was: back in Yarrow's cottage, on the desk with the book about the care of orchids.

Yarrow reached her. He was still wearing his own coat.

"How can I help?" he asked.

She loved when he asked that. "I don't know yet."

"Good luck," he said. And he kissed her, in front of his father, Lotti, and possibly Laiken's ghost. When he released her, she felt as if she could climb mountains, swim oceans, and definitely and absolutely save the Greenhouse of Belde.

CHAPTER TWENTY-NINE

On the bed by the window in Yarrow's cottage, Terlu curled up with the notebook, a stack of paper for her to take notes, and a charcoal pencil, wrapped tightly in a strip of rag to keep her fingers clean. Yarrow had returned to the greenhouse to help rehome the singing flora, while she puzzled through the pages. By the final notebook, Laiken's code was even more complex. He not only used his codebook, but he wrote backward as well. It was going to be a slog to translate.

She dug in.

Outside, sunset stained the sky rose and amber above the pine trees. Wind whistled softly through the branches, swirling clouds of stray snow. The fire crackled in the fireplace. She heard a scratching at the door. *"Rrr-eow!"*

Leaving the notes on Yarrow's desk, she opened the door. Emeral trotted in. "Hello, sir," Terlu said to him. "Welcome home from your latest adventures." She filled his water dish.

Curling around her ankles, he meowed for dinner, despite the enormous fish she knew he'd eaten earlier, and she caved and gave him a slice of cooked grouse from the icebox. While he ate, she returned to the bed and continued to work.

After devouring the grouse, he flew to the bed, kneaded the blanket, and settled down beside her. She showed him the page she was reading. "In this instance, what do you think *isador* means? Is it acting as a verb on its own or . . . No, wait, it's modified. Look here, this word . . . Yes, it normally means growth but it has a strong connotation of finite time." She'd only seen this combination once before, in a poem in which the writer bid goodbye to their dead lover. It was often interpreted as a metaphor for aging, mourning the loss of one's youth. "But I think the literal translation is more apt because of the fact that the sorcerer died. Not that he knew he was going to die—it was an accident—but I think he was feeling his own mortality."

"*Rr-eow?*" Emeral said.

"He knew he could die someday. Frankly, I think he was overly preoccupied with his own death, given that he wasn't sick or injured."

If she was interpreting this correctly, he had been working on a spell that would take effect after his death. *Well, that had happened.* So what was it he'd wanted to be his legacy?

The door opened, and Yarrow came inside, stomping the snow off his boots and hanging his coat and scarf on a hook. "Temperature's dropping outside. Going to be a cold one."

"Mmm."

"Did you eat?"

"Nnmmm."

"I'll cook."

Terlu glanced up. "He was working on a spell that would be triggered by his death. Did anything unusual happen on the island or in the greenhouses when he died?"

Yarrow added more wood to the fire, and the flames crackled gratefully. "Not that I know of. In fact, that's one of the things I remember about it—that it was all so ordinary. This great man who created miracle after miracle, who shaped all these lives, who created his own world . . . he died in such an ordinary, random, pointless way."

"When did the first greenhouse fail? How soon after his death?"

He considered it for a moment. "A couple months?"

She frowned at the notebook. Okay, maybe his final spell *wasn't* connected to the failures. He might not have had a chance to finish and activate the spell, whatever it was.

"But the first failure could have happened sooner," Yarrow said. "That's just when we discovered it."

"Hmm." Terlu continued to translate the pages, scratching out options on her notepaper and then writing the translation into the margins of the notebook when she was certain she had it correct. She was careful not to leave any marks on any of Laiken's text, in case a later reading caused her to change her mind.

While she worked, Yarrow cooked. He had two fillets of a fish that he laid on a skillet over the fire. He sprinkled on herbs, salt, and pepper, then added cranberries. She could smell them as the scent permeated the cottage and the butter popped around the fish. He hummed softly to himself, which made a soothing background as she read.

When the fish was finished, he carried a fillet over to her on a plate.

"Oh, I can come to the table." She brought the notebook with her. He laid the plate in front of her on the table, and sat in the opposite chair with his own fillet. Ignoring the fish, she didn't stop reading. "I think he added nonsense in the middle of this page just to throw off anyone who was trying to translate. Or there's some extra code . . . But I think it's actually just gibberish."

"Sounds like something he'd do."

"Who did he think was going to steal his work?"

"Everyone," Yarrow said. "By the end, he trusted no one. Dad suspected he was on the verge of sending us away, leaving zero gardeners on Belde. If he hadn't died . . ."

Terlu looked up from the notebook. "Would you have gone then?"

He took a drink of water before he answered. "I don't know if I would've had a choice, if that had happened. This was Laiken's greenhouse."

"It's yours now." She wondered if he'd ever stop thinking of it as the sorcerer's. Laiken's ghost haunted more than just his tower, metaphorically at least. Literally, it did seem to be confined, which she was grateful for.

He shrugged. "Suppose so. Yes. He left no heir, unless you can find a record of it. By law, it falls to whoever inhabits and cares for it, which would be me. And the plants." A hint of a smile crossed his lips. "Laiken would have hated that a gardener inherited. He viewed us the same way he viewed a shovel or a bee, a tool to keep his gardens alive. In one of her letters, my sister asked if I had stayed merely to spite him . . . Maybe in part I did."

He's right. Laiken didn't want anyone to have this place. The sorcerer had dismissed all but two of the inhabitants of the island, and he'd put the sentient plants to sleep—he'd intended to leave the island fully uninhabited. "I think he wanted to seal his greenhouse away from the world." She showed him a passage on the eighth page of the journal. "He was experimenting here with variations of the word that means protect, which is also found in the bubble spell."

"Eat your fish before it gets cold."

Emeral sauntered over to the table and wove between Terlu and Yarrow's legs.

"Or before the cat eats it."

She put down the notebook, a safe distance from the food, and took a bite of the fish. Closing her eyes, she savored how light and fresh it was. Not fishy at all. It tasted of salt and sweet, with a hint of bite from the cranberries. She opened her eyes and realized he was watching her. "Perfect."

He smiled.

Together, they ate.

He slipped a chunk to Emeral beneath the table. She raised both her eyebrows at the cat. "How do you still have an appetite?"

Smug, the cat returned to the hearth and curled up next to the fire. He began to wash his fur and his feathers.

It was nice to eat together, knowing they were each wrapped in their own thoughts and knowing those thoughts overlapped. She wasn't wondering what he was thinking of her or what he wanted from her. As soon as she finished, she moved to clean her dish, but he intercepted her. "Read," he said. "I'll clean."

"Thanks." She returned to curl in the blankets with the notebook.

When he finished, he sat beside her with his book on orchids. He brought a lantern closer, positioning it so that the light fell onto her lap. "Let me know how I can help."

"You are helping," she said.

He smiled again and opened his book to the sixth chapter, where he'd left a bookmark.

They read side by side as night nestled over the forest and the greenhouse. In the distance, she heard voices rise, then fall. An owl hooted.

Her fingers began to cramp, and she shook out her hand.

Yarrow covered her fingers with his and massaged her palm. She let him caress the base of each finger, the back of her hand, and her wrist. "Better?"

"Yes."

She kept reading until her eyes felt like they hurt when she blinked. She bit back a yawn. "I'm close," she said. "I should . . ."

"You can sleep. No one would blame you."

"But we don't know when the next greenhouse will fail."

"For the first time, we were able to save nearly every plant before the temperature plummeted," Yarrow said. "We'll do it again if we need to. You have time. You can sleep."

Perhaps he was right.

She put the notebook and her stack of notes on the desk near the beds. He lifted the quilt, and she burrowed in, curling up against him. He wrapped his arm around her.

The winged cat flew from the hearth onto the bed, curling up in the dip between their bodies. Pressed together, all three of them slept.

Terlu had never had such a peaceful and deep sleep.

At dawn, she woke.

She launched herself out of bed so fast that Yarrow sat up abruptly and Emeral sprang into the air with a yelp. Yarrow asked, "Are you okay?"

Terlu flipped to near the end of the book. She stabbed her finger at a line. "He cast it, I'm sure of it. He cast it to test it"—*Just like I've been doing, casting bits of spells and learning from them*—"to make sure the spell would stay viable after his death. He was checking the longevity of the spell, not the functionality, so it was an incomplete spell. He meant to disable it as soon as the test was done and recast it when it was complete, but then he died. Maybe he was distracted and rushing because he'd realized the spell had a fatal flaw, and that's why he fell. Or maybe it was just an unlucky coincidence. But regardless, he never stopped the spell. It lurched on, incomplete and flawed, but here's the key: the spell was built with a delay. An intentional delay. So that after his death, there would be a couple months during which any remaining residents could leave the island. Do you see? He intentionally left time in the spell for his funeral and for you to leave."

"But I didn't leave."

"Right, but he didn't expect that. And the spell wasn't complete anyway. The delay worked, yes, but when it kicked in . . . He hadn't finished perfecting it, so when the spell was triggered, it didn't do what it was supposed to do."

Yarrow frowned at the coded spell and at her scribbles in the margins. "What was it supposed to do?"

"It was supposed to isolate the entire greenhouse from the rest of the world. He thought it was the only way his creations could be safe—if they were severed from everyone else. Alone."

Yarrow snorted.

"I know, right? Exact opposite of what he should have done. But fear consumed reason. Anyway, he hadn't completed the spell, and so instead of isolating the greenhouses and making them self-sufficient, the spell destabilizes the existing enchantments."

"And destroys the very thing he wanted to protect," Yarrow said.

"Yes, ironic, I know, but I believe his half-finished spell is still active, and every few months—that delay he was testing, you see—it triggers again and destroys another greenhouse."

His eyes widened. "That . . . makes sense."

"So the question is how do we stop the spell?" She paced around the cottage, certain this was the answer. They'd stumbled on it by accident, while experimenting just like Laiken had. "We discovered the answer the other day when we, you know, nearly died. If we can destroy the ingredients, it'll break the spell."

Yarrow crossed to her, cupped her face in his hands, and kissed her.

The ghost was not helpful.

Terlu nibbled on the leftover honey cake as she glared at the grimy mirror in the late sorcerer's bedroom. "I know you can hear us. Ask again, Lotti."

Perched on the bedside table, the little rose implored, "Please, dear Laiken, sorcerer supreme, if you could grant us an answer to one teensy-weensy question—"

Yarrow leaned closer and murmured in Terlu's ear, "Teensy-weensy?"

"Shh," Terlu whispered back. "Let her do it her way. She knew him best."

Spreading her leaves dramatically, Lotti said, "We would be so enormously grateful and in awe of your brilliance and benevolence. You'd be the Hero of Belde, saving all your wonderful creations. All you have to do is tell us where to find the ingredients. Are they here in the workroom?"

They waited, but there was no sign that the ghost was even listening.

"Are they in the greenhouse?" Lotti tried.

No response.

"Are they on the island?"

The bedroom stayed silent and still. No breeze. No shiver of cold.

Terlu wondered briefly if asking the question had caused the ghost to move on. She'd heard stories about that—once whatever emotion was holding the remnants of them was satisfied, they'd dissipate. Perhaps he'd only stayed until he'd finished being irritating. "Ask him if he wants us to save the greenhouses."

Lotti raised her voice. "Do you want us to save the greenhouses?"

A wind raced through the bedroom, stirring the sheets and blankets on the bed and knocking Lotti a few inches to the side. Yarrow helped her right herself.

"That was a yes," Lotti said.

"Are you sure?" Yarrow said. "It only seemed emphatic."

"A yes smells like a rose. A no is skunk cabbage."

"How . . ." Terlu began. She stopped herself and shook her head. She wasn't here to study ghost behavior. All they needed right now were answers. "Never mind. Ask him: Does he know where the ingredients are?"

A sad breeze ruffled the curtain and did, in fact, stink faintly of skunk cabbage, now that she was aware of it.

Yarrow snorted. "How can he not know?"

"It isn't all of him," Terlu said. "Just the remnant of a regret. A feeling." Maybe love. He'd loved these greenhouses, even if that love had later been warped by fear. "Tell him we'll do our best."

Lotti repeated that and then said to Terlu, "I'd like to stay here with him, if that's okay."

"Of course," Terlu said. If she could have given the rose a hug, she would have. This had to be immensely difficult for Lotti. The rose's petals were spread open, her leaves unfurled, as if she were reaching out to the one who'd made her, loved her, and, in the end, failed her. Swallowing, Terlu turned to Yarrow. "Should we start searching?"

He nodded. "Can you narrow down at least what we're looking for, or do we have to play yes/no questions with an errant breeze again?"

The breeze raced through the room, blowing the curtains, the sheets, and their hair.

Luckily, she knew the answer to that from her translation work.

She patted her curls back down. "Shells. All kinds of shells: the shell of a hickory nut, a clamshell, a conch shell, a robin's egg shell, the exoskeleton of a cricket, the shell of a box turtle . . . And it'll be a large quantity. I vote we start the search here where he did his work."

Together, Terlu and Yarrow searched the upstairs. It didn't take long. A few chests of dusty clothes. A drawer of ointments, primarily medical. Laiken had had very little in his bedroom. Downstairs, in the workroom, they'd already been through everything looking for spells, but they double-checked each drawer and examined every pot and beaker.

"It's most likely in the greenhouse," Terlu admitted.

She'd hoped it would be simpler, but the greenhouse was a far more logical place than the workroom, closer to what the spell needed to affect. How, though, were they going to search all of the greenhouse? It was a mammoth task. She hadn't even visited all the rooms!

We can't do it alone.

She didn't voice that out loud. He wasn't going to like what she wanted to suggest.

Both of them pulled on their coats.

Yarrow opened the door and paused. Outside, his sister, Rowan, was strolling away from the dock with her wife. Ambrel was holding a fishing pole over one shoulder, and Rowan had a bucket that presumably held fish.

He sighed heavily. "The search will be faster with help."

Terlu blinked at him. "Yes, but . . . You're the one suggesting it?"

"I know, I know."

"Want me to do the talking?" Terlu offered.

"Yes!" he said in a relieved exhale. "But . . . I'll come with you."

She took his hand and led him out of the workroom. Jogging toward Rowan and Ambrel, Terlu called to them, "Hey, wait up, please! I—*we*—need your help!"

CHAPTER THIRTY

Towing Yarrow behind her, Terlu caught up with Rowan and Ambrel beneath the snow-crusted pine trees. She panted, catching her breath. Outside, the sky was a washed-out white, and the wind slapped against the pine trees. The waves were crashing harder on the rocks, and the sea's surface looked as if it had been shaken.

"Is everything okay?" Ambrel asked.

Rowan raised both her eyebrows at Yarrow in such a deliberate way that Terlu couldn't help but think, *This is a mistake.* "Oh, look, you've decided to grace us with your presence. I guess we should drop everything and celebrate."

Yarrow opened his mouth and closed it.

"Still have nothing to say to me?" Rowan asked.

"Hush," Ambrel told her. "Terlu, what's wrong?"

Yarrow had shifted partially behind Terlu, as if she could shield him from his sister. She wished she was close enough to take his hand—he should know he wasn't on his own, facing a hostile force. "Short version: I believe the greenhouses are dying because of a malfunctioning spell," she said briskly. "We need to find and destroy the ingredients, or the spell will keep destroying greenhouse after greenhouse. The problem is we don't know where the ingredients are. They could be in any of the greenhouses."

"Or anywhere on the island," Yarrow added.

Terlu nodded. "It's a lot to search." She wished Laiken had kept notes about where he'd cast the spell. He'd left meticulous notes about *what* the ingredients were, but not *where*.

Rowan stuck her hands on her hips. At the same moment, a wave crashed so hard on the rocks that the spray spattered on the snow. "So, you're coming to us for help." She aimed that at Yarrow, as if Terlu weren't even there.

"We need everyone's help," Yarrow clarified.

"But my help, specifically. Me, your sister." The edge in her voice was so sharp that it made Terlu wince. "You remember that, right? That I'm your sister?"

Terlu met Ambrel's eyes. She could tell Rowan's wife felt the same way she did: yes, they should talk; no, it shouldn't be now. She was certain Yarrow was on the verge of bolting and only the fact that they were close to being able to save the greenhouse prevented him.

Ambrel laid a hand on her wife's shoulder and whispered in her ear, but Rowan shifted her glare to her. "I have a lot of unsaid words that need to be said, and I'm going to say them."

Sighing, Ambrel lowered her hand.

Wind whistled through the pine trees, knocking snow from the branches. It thumped down, startling a bird into the sky. *We don't have time for this. And he's not ready.* Terlu stepped forward. "Now isn't—"

Yarrow spoke, "I missed you, Rowan."

Rowan faltered before her rant even began. "Well." She stopped and started again. "It's unfair to jump right to that." She poked his shoulder, her finger sinking deep into his coat. "You never showed it."

"I know," he said. "And I'm sorry."

Again, she was speechless.

Terlu wondered if she should step away. This felt like an important moment, and it wasn't one that she belonged in, but she'd promised Yarrow she'd speak for him—did he still want her to? Standing behind her wife, Ambrel looked almost amused, and Terlu wondered if she'd seen Rowan speechless often. *Probably not.*

Rowan gaped at him. "That's it? You're not going to make excuses?"

He didn't. Not a word.

"Not going to twist it to blame me? Or Dad? Or Laiken?"

"I should have written you back," he said.

She looked unbalanced, like she'd wanted to flap her arms, shout, and stomp, but now . . . "Huh. Yes, you should have. I was not much more than a child. It wasn't my choice to leave, or if it was, I didn't understand that I had a choice. Besides, I thought you'd come too, as soon as you could. I didn't understand it was goodbye."

Yarrow said, "I'm glad you came back."

Rowan narrowed her eyes as she studied him. "You're lying."

"A little," he said. "It was quieter before."

"But you missed me?" Rowan said.

"Yes."

"Well." She stopped again and puffed out air. Her breath hung in a cloud before it dissipated. Over the sea, a gull cawed. "That's something, I guess. Now, what's this about spell ingredients? Since when are you a sorcerer? Wait, the old fool didn't take you on as his apprentice, did he?"

Yarrow shook his head. "He rarely spoke to me. Or anyone."

"And we aren't going to cast a spell," Terlu jumped in. "We're going to break one."

Rowan raised her eyebrows.

Gravely, Yarrow said, "We might be able to stop any more greenhouses from dying."

His sister let out a whistle. "Okay, I'm listening."

Terlu showed them the list of shells. "We need to find where Laiken put the ingredients for his final spell. He would have put them somewhere they wouldn't be disturbed, but there had to be enough of a quantity to affect all of the greenhouses. So, we're looking for a significant number of shells."

"Could he have buried them?" Ambrel asked.

Terlu had worried about that at first, but she didn't think it was likely. "You bury ingredients if you want to limit the effects to a particular target." If he'd buried them, the spell wouldn't have been able to affect so many greenhouses, especially ones that were far apart. "He'd have wanted them as effective as possible, which means keeping them open to the air. So I think they'll be visible. Hidden, but visible." After all her experiments, she could say that with some degree of confidence.

"Ooh, I know: the sunflower maze," Rowan said. "He could have put them in—"

Yarrow shook his head. "We solved it. No shells there."

"You did?" Rowan said. "Wow, I can't tell you how many afternoons I spent in there, before Dad hauled me out to do chores. What did you do about the dragons?"

Ambrel's eyes widened. "Dragons?"

"They like honey," Yarrow said.

"You have to show me how you—" Rowan said eagerly.

Ambrel squeezed her arm. "Focus, Rowan."

"Sorry. Later."

Gravely, Yarrow said, "I'd be happy to show you later."

"All right then," Rowan said.

Terlu had a sudden image of her as a child, so excited to set out on a new adventure in Alyssium. She knew how that felt.

Rowan studied her brother for a moment. "You need help, badly enough to actually face me, which means it's serious." She seemed to reach a decision. "Let's rally everyone."

Without waiting for a response, she trotted down the road.

Ambrel flashed them a smile and joined her wife.

Yarrow squeezed Terlu's hand for either strength or comfort, but he followed his sister toward the rest of his family and every awkward conversation he'd been so studiously avoiding. Terlu held his hand as firmly as she could without squeezing, so he'd know she wasn't leaving his side. He wasn't facing them alone.

True to her word, Rowan gathered everyone—aunts, uncles, cousins, even the two family friends who had been brought to Belde for their safety. With Dendy's help, she also corralled all the sentient plants. She insisted that the plants would want to help, and both Yarrow and Terlu had agreed with her. Everyone, people and plants, assembled in the rose greenhouse.

The roses swayed in the breeze from the overhead fans. Above, the snow had begun to fall softly on the glass cupola, but inside it smelled like summer. The aroma of roses filled every breath, and Terlu felt the knots in her shoulders ease as she breathed it in.

They all came, she thought. *Maybe they'll all help.*

Yarrow distributed slices of honey cake—when had he made more? He had to be just continuously baking. Only other explanation was that the cat had learned how. All the people were sitting on the edges of flower beds, on upside-down pots, and on chairs that had been brought in from the cottages, while the talking plants were distributed throughout the greenhouse. Dendy was up in the rafters with Lotti. Risa, the ivy, had wound themself around one of the pillars, while Amina, the orchid, lurked beneath the branches of a purple rosebush, and Cyna, the daisy, perched on top of a trellis of white climbing roses.

Standing on an upside-down pot, Rowan whistled for attention.

The people and plants quieted.

The fireweed let out a spark. It fizzled in the air.

"Okay, everyone," Rowan said. "Hi. This is Terlu. You've all met her. She has a request to make—a way we can save the Greenhouse of Belde and stop any more greenhouses from failing. Yarrow might talk too, but probably not. Anyway, listen up. This is important."

"Uh, thanks," Terlu said.

Rowan vacated the upside-down pot, and Terlu stepped up onto it, with Yarrow reaching out a hand to steady her. She surveyed the room. Somehow she'd gone from thinking she was alone on the island to addressing a crowd. *We're stronger together. Or we can be.* Like a rope, made of threads woven together. Everyone in this room— human and plant—wanted the greenhouses to survive. She believed that to the core of her heart. Clearing her throat, she began.

She described her theory on why the greenhouses were failing (a malfunctioning spell), what they needed to find (lots of shells collected together), and what they had to do with them (destroy them). It took less than a minute and a half.

And then she stepped down from the pot. She prepared herself for the questions that would follow—how she knew what to do, how she'd cracked the sorcerer's code, how she'd translated his notebooks and studied his spells.

One of Yarrow's younger cousins, Percik, asked, "Are you a sorcerer?"

She *hadn't* prepared for that one, but she could handle it.

"No, I was a librarian." He hadn't flat-out accused her of breaking imperial law, so she could nicely sidestep the issue. She launched into an explanation of how her experience and training with languages, especially extinct languages, had enabled her to—

From the rafters, Lotti shouted stoutly, "She's as good as a sorcerer!"

Oh, by the sea. Terlu felt her breath lodge in her throat.

The orchid, Amina, chimed in. "She woke all of us."

"Yes, we are grateful to her," the ivy, Risa, said.

"Sheee taught us to heal the glaaass," Dendy said. "And sheee has been working tooo understand the spells thaaat created the greeeenhouses, in ooorder to save them. You can truuust her word. If sheee says this is necessary, then it's what must beee done."

What am I going to do? What am I going to say? Panic spiraled up into her throat, and she felt herself begin to shake. She sucked in air. *I should have told the talking plants* not *to talk so much.* When she'd had the idea to ask for help, she hadn't considered that her friends would leak her secret to everyone all at once. How could she know if she could trust all of Yarrow's relatives? One of them could be just like the patron who'd reported her.

I can't go back to being a statue. She wouldn't. Not now, and not ever.

If she had to leave Belde, she'd do it. She'd summon Marin. She'd flee as far as she needed to, even if it meant leaving this place that she'd grown to love.

Yarrow wrapped his arm around Terlu's shoulder. "If anyone has an issue with this—"

"Oh, hush," Rowan said to him. "You think we really didn't know that one of you two has been working magic? We've all seen the plants fixing the glass—Laiken never taught them spells. It had to be one of you."

"Nice job with that," Uncle Rorick said.

Others nodded.

Terlu looked at the faces around her. None of them looked alarmed or appalled. "But . . . it's illegal . . . You don't . . . I mean . . ." It was the opposite of how people had recoiled from her after she'd created Caz. Why weren't they ready to condemn her? "I don't understand."

Rowan asked, "Have you ever used magic to hurt anyone?"

"Well, no."

"To hurt any plants?"

Intentions hadn't mattered in her trial in Alyssium . . . She blinked, suddenly feeling like crying. "Absolutely not. I've just been trying to help."

Dendy said, "She saaaved us."

"So you're righting a wrong," Rowan said, hands on her hips. "Fixing a mistake made by someone else. I think that's admirable." She glared at her relatives, as if daring them to disagree.

Coming up beside her wife, Ambrel agreed. "We aren't in Alyssium anymore. The emperor's gone, and his laws don't reach here anyway. You're not going to be punished for what you did out of kindness."

Terlu had thought that way once before. She'd felt safe in the library, and she'd been convinced that no one would punish her for creating Caz—he was so very obviously a good thing. Adding life to the world couldn't be bad, she'd told herself at the time. She'd thought she would be forgiven, once it was understood that her intentions were harmless and innocent and even kind.

I was selfish, though, she thought. Unlike here, she hadn't woken Caz for his own sake; she'd done it for herself, because she was lonely.

Perhaps what she'd done here was different enough? She was trying to save life that already existed. And she wasn't doing it for herself. *Or at least not just for myself.* She couldn't believe anyone would have wanted her to leave Lotti or Dendy or any of the sentient plants asleep. And how could she turn her back on the failing greenhouses and the dying plants when there was a potential way to stop it?

"You've nothing to fear from any of us," Rowan said firmly. "Right?" Hands on her hips, she glared at the rest of her family. She had, Terlu noticed, just as bearlike a glare as her brother and father.

Yarrow's father, Birch, spoke up. "You're looking after the greenhouses. That makes you a gardener. Like all of us. None of us want the greenhouses to fail." He looked at Yarrow as he added, "We all want what's best for our plant friends. For our family."

She was certain that Yarrow's father's words weren't directed at her at all. But that was fine. At least, for now, she had a reprieve. She didn't know if they were right about Alyssium and the reach of imperial law, but for now, it didn't look like anyone was going to stop her from doing what she could to save this place. She felt her chest loosen, and she blinked hard to keep tears from welling up.

I can trust them.

His family hadn't rejected her, even after learning the truth.

Maybe mine won't either.

From the rafters, Lotti called out, "All right. Enough mushiness, everyone. We're going to be orderly about this. Plants will take the eastern greenhouses. You and you—head west. You lot, start in the north. As you finish, put a mark on the door so we don't repeat efforts. Use charcoal to make an X. No time to waste. Move, everyone!"

Yarrow knew every inch of the greenhouses that required daily care. For those rooms, it was quick work to skirt the perimeter, peek into any toolsheds or supply boxes, and investigate the interior of the enchanted stove, if there was one. Terlu searched with him, careful to watch for any corners that Yarrow might dismiss due to familiarity. The plants checked all the rafters.

A few of Yarrow's relatives had picked the same direction to search, but they branched off when the paths did, until it was only Yarrow's father, Birch, who stuck with the two of them as they entered a greenhouse that overflowed with vines that danced like ribbons in the breeze.

"Never liked this room," Birch said. "Reminds me of snakes."

Yarrow snorted. "They're beautiful in their own way. So are snakes."

"But why enchant them at all?" Birch ducked under a writhing mass of leaves. Above him, several vines braided themselves, knot after knot. Leafy green mice scurried over the braids. "Why not just let them be ordinary plants?"

"I think they're pretty," Terlu offered. Standing, she brushed a vine off her shoulder. It snuck back, trying to wind around her wrist. A mouse chittered at her, as if scolding her for resisting, or perhaps requesting cheese.

Yarrow unpeeled the vine from his thigh and said to his father, "You could search one of the other rooms, if you don't like this one." He reached into one of his pockets and scattered crumbs onto the walkway. Several leaf-covered mice chirped and raced down the braided vines to feast on the bits of bread. One mouse had a single bright orange leaf in the middle of green leaves. It shook itself, and the orange leaf fell to the ground, a bit of fall foliage.

She smiled. *Of course he feeds the mice.*

"Faster if we stick together," Birch said.

"Everyone else split up," Yarrow pointed out.

"All right, yes. I want to spend time with you. I know you have responsibilities and have become accustomed to shouldering them on your own, but I, like Rowan, believe you have been deliberately avoiding me."

"I have."

Terlu almost laughed—that was such a Yarrow response. She checked behind the box of tools before reporting to Yarrow and Birch. "I think this room's clear."

After marking the door with an X in charcoal, per Lotti's idea, so the others would know it had been searched already, they moved on to the next greenhouse, which was filled with cacti and other succulents. Several were orbs covered in needles. Some had thick arms that reached toward the sky. A twisted tree with spikes dominated the center of the room, slicing the view of the sky. Above, a false sun dried the air, and she felt it sink into her skin, sucking out the moisture within her, making her feel as baked as a honey cake. The air tasted of sand, gritty on her tongue. She zigzagged through the greenhouse, sidestepping the spiky tree's needle-coated branches, while Yarrow circled the perimeter. She finished her check and joined Yarrow by the door.

"I've been through all these rooms countless times," Yarrow said. "I would have noticed a pile of shells."

He was right. Still, it had to be here somewhere . . . unless she was wrong about the spell entirely? The ghost had implied she was correct. "You weren't looking for it," Terlu said. "Maybe that's why you didn't see it."

Birch planted himself in front of Yarrow, effectively blocking the door. He thumped his cane on the ground. "She's right. Sometimes we don't see what's right in front of us. Yarrow, I owe you an apology."

"You want me to talk to you? Then help, don't hinder. Keep searching." He marched past his father. He added a charcoal X to the door, threw it open, and stomped through into the next greenhouse.

Mumbling an "excuse me," Terlu slipped past Birch to join Yarrow.

Birch followed them. "You don't have to accept my apology, but I want you to know that I am sorry. When I left . . . There's a lot I wish I could unsay."

Turning stiffly to Terlu, Yarrow said, "I'll check the supply boxes. You walk the perimeter. Maybe you'll see what I missed." Ignoring his father, he stalked toward the corner with the boxes. She heard the lids slam open and then shut.

Birch trailed after him.

Terlu didn't know if she admired Yarrow's father for not giving up or wanted to yell at him for pushing too hard, too soon. She circled the edge of the greenhouse. This one had flowers that she didn't recognize, bell-like blossoms that rang like wind chimes as she walked past them. One larger flower was shaped like a cymbal. She touched it, and it echoed with a brass-like note.

She heard Birch say from across the greenhouse, "You know I didn't want to leave you behind. I thought with time, you'd come to your senses and join us in Alyssium."

"I see how well that worked out for you."

"At least in Alyssium, we were together! You could have been with us, with your family, instead of becoming a hermit here on this dying island—"

"Stop."

Birch sighed heavily. "I am doing a terrible job of apologizing."

"Yes, you are. I told you—I don't need you to say any of this. I don't blame you for leaving. You were sick. You couldn't stay."

"You blame me for not coming back."

"I don't blame you for that." Yarrow slammed the supply box shut. "I blame you for everything *before* that." He stalked out of the greenhouse without a backward look.

Birch slowed when he reached Terlu. "I don't know how to fix this."

She didn't know what to tell him. Maybe Yarrow needed time? Or maybe he needed space? Or maybe he needed the opposite. She tried to think of something helpful to say. It sounded as if Birch wanted to make things right but had no idea how to do so. She knew that feeling. Gently, she asked, "Are you apologizing for his sake or your own?"

"I just want things back the way they were."

"Maybe they weren't great the way they were?" Terlu said. She was aware this wasn't her conversation to have, and she didn't want to accidentally make anything worse. On the other hand, there wasn't much worse she could make it. Yarrow had already left. "He hasn't told me much about his childhood, but there was one story, about his uncle Rorick and a 'game' where he was abandoned in the caves?"

Birch blinked. "That? He was fine."

"He was a kid, and he was scared."

He dismissed it. "It was a long time ago. He can't still be angry about that."

Terlu tilted her head and stared at him. Yarrow wasn't still angry about the cave specifically, but he clearly saw it as representative of how he'd been treated. Abandoned, over and over.

"I can apologize for *that,* but I think he's overreacting," Birch said. "He was always overdramatic. In fact, that's exactly what we were trying to fix. We wanted to teach him to be more self-reliant."

Yarrow? Overdramatic? It wasn't the word she would have ever applied to someone who communicated primarily through grunts and shrugs. "You taught him he can't trust the people who are supposed to love him," Terlu said, continuing to keep her voice as gentle as she could when what she really wanted to do was shake his shoulders until he understood he'd caused pain.

Birch looked shocked. "It was a rite of passage. We celebrated when he made it out."

She shrugged, Yarrow-like. "Not everyone sees the same event the same way. Laiken thought he was doing the right thing for those he loved too."

Birch scowled. "I'm nothing like Laiken."

She didn't want to be arguing with Yarrow's father, especially without knowing all of what Yarrow felt, and she'd never even met Laiken, besides the remnant that was his ghost and the words he'd left in his notebooks. "You could *ask* Yarrow what he wants."

"Ask him? Just . . . ask him?"

She shrugged again.

"Huh."

After marking the door of the finished room, they followed Yarrow into the next greenhouse, where he was scowling at both of them.

"Yarrow . . ." Birch began.

Ignoring him, Yarrow leveled a finger at Terlu. "I am *not* a broken spell. You need to stop trying to fix this," he growled at her before he pivoted and stomped toward the next greenhouse door.

Okay, maybe he is a little overdramatic.

He had his family back. He had a chance to be with them and make up for lost time. On the other hand, they'd hurt him, especially his father, and she had yet to hear a real apology from Birch. He hadn't shown any sign of trying to understand how Yarrow felt, nor had he made any real attempt to change. It wasn't just about what happened in the cave beneath the island—

Terlu halted as an idea occurred to her. "Yarrow? Stop!"

"I don't want to talk." But he halted at the door and listened.

"The caves, the ones you were left in, the ones like a maze," Terlu said, "they run beneath the greenhouses, don't they?" She remembered what she'd noticed about the cracks in the last dying greenhouse: they started at the point where the glass met the earth. Whatever mangled spell broke the glass and ripped through the enchantments . . . it came from *below*.

Birch answered her. "They do. The whole island is riddled with them."

Yarrow turned back toward her. "You think—"

"Yes," Terlu said. "I do."

Only a few minutes later, the three of them bundled in coats and trudged out into the snow. It fell in tiny, dry flakes, like a mist in the sky. Flakes landed on her eyelashes. Yarrow was speckled in flecks within seconds.

"I should be the one to go," Birch said.

Yarrow snorted. "No."

"As your girlfriend has very recently pointed out, I owe it to you."

"You owe it to me to tell the others if we don't come back," Yarrow said. "Send someone in after us if we don't return by sunset. Do what I need, not what you think I need, for once." He headed for their cottage, saying to Terlu, "We aren't going without supplies. Water. Food."

He did not, Terlu noticed, comment on the word "girlfriend." It was, she decided, not the time to discuss it, but she held the word tight. "How about we bring string? So we can unspool it and find our way out?" She'd read a story once about a child who used a string to find his way home through a dark and twisty forest, filled with shadowy monsters. Now that she thought about it, it was an old Ginian folktale that she'd read when she first learned the language. It made sense they'd have stories about navigating mazes.

To his father, Yarrow said, "Can you find us a spool of string?"

"I can do that," Birch said, clearly relieved to have been given a task.

As he trotted away, barely using his cane, Terlu and Yarrow let themselves into the cottage. Warmth and the lingering smell of baked honey cakes curled around them. Both of them unbuttoned their coats, and then he bustled to the kitchen counter.

"You don't need to be the one to do this," she said. "He's right about that. It's not like you know the caves better than other people. We could send your uncle Rorick. It would be appropriate."

His lips quirked. "Tempting. But I need to see this through. As you said, these are my greenhouses." Searching through a cabinet, he located a water bottle.

"Have you been in the caves since then?" Terlu asked. "Has anyone? Is there a map?" She hadn't seen one in Laiken's notes, but that could have been because he was paranoid enough to not want anyone to follow him to where he cast the spell. He most likely had known every inch of this island without needing any notes. *If we do this . . . if it works . . . if I somehow have the time . . . I am making maps of every inch of this island.* And she'd make notes about all of it too. Proper notes, not in code.

"No map. And I only returned once. I didn't stay." Yarrow filled the bottle with water and tucked it into a bag. "You don't need to come with me."

"Obviously I am. You keep thinking you need to do things alone, and you don't. Anyway, I had an idea." She crossed to the cabinets and the icebox and added several jars of honey and a pot of honey butter to Yarrow's bag. "I think we should bring some dragons."

He laughed. "What? Why?"

"They know mazes, and they know treasure."

"You think they'd understand what we wanted?"

"I think they'd be happy to exchange treasure for honey, and I think they'd see shells hidden in a cave as treasure. I don't know if they'll want to leave their sunflowers, but we could ask." You never knew who was willing to help if you didn't ask.

"You always surprise me," Yarrow said.

Basking in the praise, she grinned at him.

He grinned back.

"All right, it's a plan," Terlu said. "We'll bring snacks, water, lanterns, string, and dragons. And we won't stop until we've saved Belde."

CHAPTER THIRTY-ONE

Yarrow didn't stride off to the caves on his own to prove that he needed no one but himself, which was a pleasant surprise. Instead, after accepting the spool of thread from his father with a grunt that resembled a thank-you, he followed Terlu to the sunflower maze.

He unlocked the puzzle door with ease. "After you."

Stepping inside, Terlu held up the pot of honey butter. "Hello, little dragons?" she called.

Overhead, the false aurora rippled over the glass, while the tiny dragons flew like honeybees between the sunflowers. A shining red dragon chirped a greeting or an alert—she wasn't sure which, but it sounded friendly enough.

Lifting the pot higher, she asked, "Want to come help us find a treasure?"

Yarrow began, "I don't know that they can understand—"

Three dragons—the red one, a gold-and-black one, and an iridescent emerald one—darted toward her. Flapping their butterfly-like wings, they settled on her: one on each shoulder and the red one on her head, curled in her hair. "See?" Terlu said. "They want to come."

With a touch of exasperation, Yarrow asked, "Does *everyone* like you?"

She laughed. "I can give you a list of people who don't."

"Then it's a list of fools."

She grinned at him again.

Together, they walked out of the greenhouse toward the dock. Overhead, the snow had stopped, and the sky was now a cloudless blue that made the fresh-fallen snow sparkle like diamonds. As they walked, she explained to the dragons where they were going and why, as well as what they hoped to find. She couldn't be certain they understood her, but they didn't disappear into the woods in search of all the sparkles they could find, so perhaps they did understand. Or maybe they just liked the ride.

A half mile from the greenhouse, after the last cottage but before the sorcerer's tower, Yarrow veered off the road in between the pine trees. The snow had iced into a crust. Yarrow broke through it with each step, and Terlu followed behind, stretching her stride to fit into his footsteps. It was colder than the day before, and everything was coated in ice that sparkled piercingly bright in the sunlight. Unaffected by the cold, the dragons chirped happily from her shoulders and the top of her head. Birds called back at them, a medley of songs that sounded like an unpracticed orchestra.

Yarrow led them to the shore. "Careful." He held out his hand so she could steady herself as she followed him down onto the beach.

The emerald dragon cooed in her ears.

The waves crashed onto the sand in foamy kisses, and she followed Yarrow along the shore to the entrance to the caves. It looked like a doorway into shadows, which she supposed that's exactly what it was. There was no reason for the caves to be lit. She didn't know why that should make them frightening. After all, she didn't have any traumatic event from her childhood here, unlike Yarrow.

It's just darkness, she told herself. *And I'm not going into it alone. Neither is he.* In case he needed to hear it out loud, she said, "You aren't alone this time."

"I'm not afraid."

"I am. It's all dark and cave-like."

He grinned. "Do you want to hold hands?"

"Always, but that's unrelated." She took his hand, and they walked into the shadows. He released her to light the lantern as the daylight diminished around them, and then he reached for her hand again, holding the lantern in his other hand. The dragons chirped as the lantern light spilled into the shadows. The red dragon flew from her head and circled the lantern.

"These caves are a maze," Yarrow told the circling dragon, "and we're looking for treasure in them. Do you want to help us? You can have all the honey you want."

"We're looking for shells." Terlu picked up a stray shell from the bit of sand that had flowed into the cave. She'd explained this to them on the walk, but she repeated it now, hoping they understood. "Like this, but a lot of them and all different kinds. Bird shells, turtle shells, nutshells, and seashells." She held out the honey butter again.

The red dragon grasped the pot in its tiny talons and then, with a squawk, flew into the darkness.

"Do we follow?" Yarrow asked.

She didn't speak dragon. "I don't know. Yes?"

He unwound the string and tied one end to a rock. "All right. Let's do this." They walked into the darkness. A few steps in, Terlu felt the dragon on her right shoulder lift off. It flew forward, its scales sparkling in the lantern light, and soon it disappeared.

They turned with the cave, and then the third dragon flew into the shadows.

Terlu missed the weight of them on her shoulders. She knew this was what she'd asked, but still . . . She squeezed Yarrow's hand tighter. "You okay?"

"It's different this time. Yes."

"Good. I've never been in a cave before. And it seems that I'm not a fan of the dark, which isn't something I realized until, well, *now*. After I was turned into a statue . . ." She stopped, swallowed, and then continued. "They put me in a closet for a while. Just left me there, while they made the pedestal in the North Reading Room. I was in with other storage items. Just a thing to be stored and forgotten. I thought I'd been forgotten. I think . . . I think I forgot my-self for a while." She hadn't thought the cave would dredge up those memories. She'd prefer they stayed relegated to the back of her mind.

"I'm sorry you went through that." His voice felt like an embrace.

She kept going. "When they brought me back out into the light, I woke up a little. I remember when they installed me in the North Reading Room. I remember . . ." Her voice shook. "I thanked them. *Thanked* them. In my head. I couldn't talk, of course. But I was grate-ful because of that little bit of kindness, because of the sunlight, be-cause I wasn't alone. I could watch people as they came to stare at me. I could listen as they told my story. Mangled it of course. Until I stopped listening. And eventually, they lost interest in me. I became a familiar decoration. They stopped seeing me as someone who had once been someone. I think . . . I think I can't blame them, because I *was* a familiar decoration. For years." Six years.

"Can I at least hate them for you? The ones who did it to you."

"I did it to myself. I broke the law and was caught."

"Your punishment exceeded the crime."

"The judge didn't think so."

"I won't let that happen to you again," Yarrow said. The cave twisted, and they followed it, unspooling the thread behind them. She wondered where the dragons had flown. She couldn't hear the flap of their wings or anything but the crunch of pebbles beneath her and Yarrow's shoes.

"You might not be able to stop them."

"If my family is right, 'they' might not exist anymore. While you and I were . . . distracted, things changed in the outside world. But you aren't in the outside world anymore. You're on Belde. Every-thing's different here."

Maybe he was right. She wasn't in Alyssium, and the empire had fallen. Maybe that meant she was safe. Still, though, she couldn't ask anyone to put themselves at risk for her. She'd been the one to learn the spells; she'd take the blame if an imperial investigator came. If she had to, she'd claim she forced the plants to cooperate.

"Besides, the plants won't allow you to be taken away from them," Yarrow said, as if he could hear what she was thinking. He squeezed her hand. "You aren't alone anymore either."

The words felt like a jolt. She'd been saying them over and over to Yarrow—he wasn't alone, he didn't need to be alone, it was better that he wasn't alone—but she had stopped thinking about how they applied to herself, even though he'd said it before too. This time, she allowed the words to sink in. He'd been trying to show her that with every honey cake he'd baked, every greenhouse he'd shared with her, every afternoon he'd spent with her experimenting with spells.

I'm not alone.

She'd found a place for herself. She'd found companionship. Not just with Yarrow, but with Emeral and the plants and the dragons, and now with his family.

Somehow this deserted island had become so very full.

Yarrow halted as the tunnel opened into a cave as massive as a concert hall. "I remember this." He held the lantern before them, but there was already light, a sliver of sun from high above, piercing the darkness, illuminating the vastness with a whisper of day. Stalactites and stalagmites reached toward one another in pillars of dripped stone. The rare hint of daylight danced off the watery sheen, catching the delicate colors of the stone.

She gawked beside him. "It's beautiful."

On one side, water dripped down a wall of ivory stone. It stained the rock green and copper. She hadn't guessed so much beauty lay under the island.

"Come," he said.

He led her between domes of limestone. She looked up at a ceiling of stone icicles, arrested mid-drip, and wondered if anyone else knew what magnificence was hidden beneath the greenhouses. Had Laiken been here? What had he thought and felt when he saw this? Had he been awed by its beauty or was he too consumed by his misguided purpose?

Ducking through an opening, Terlu followed Yarrow into an alcove, untouched by the sole beam of sun from the crack above the cavern. He lifted his lantern. Here, the stone had formed delicate lacelike curtains. "I did come back here," Yarrow said. "Once, years later. I wanted to prove to myself . . . Well, it doesn't matter because it didn't work. I lasted an hour and then I ran out, but I remember this room."

"I love it."

He smiled.

She didn't know that stone could form like this. It looked as if it were made by magic, not by water and time. Or maybe water and time was its own kind of magic.

"I wanted to see this again with you," Yarrow said. "To see if you being here would change it. And it did. You change everything."

"Wow," she said. She winced at herself. *That* was her response? The man she loved just said the most romantic, the most— *Loved?* This was the second time that the word had popped into her head, as naturally as if it belonged. *Do I love him?* She'd known him for a handful of weeks. Not even a full season. But she already felt entwined with him and his life. He felt as much a part of her as breathing.

She heard a flapping sound.

"I think that's . . ."

"Either bats or dragons."

"Bats are quieter." Terlu followed the sound back into the great hall. Up by the stalactites, the red dragon was flying in figure eights. It had something clutched in its talons.

She waited with Yarrow for the dragon to spot them and fly toward them, toward the lantern that Yarrow held aloft.

The dragon dropped the object into Terlu's palms.

It was a seashell.

Her heart beat faster. Yarrow gripped her shoulder, squeezing. "Is that—"

"Show us where you found it?" Terlu asked the little dragon.

The dragon led the way, back into the darkness. Yarrow kept

the lantern steady, and they continued to unspool the thread. After about an hour of walking, Terlu noticed they were running low on the thread. Maybe they could mark the walls? That should work.

When the thread ran out, she used her charcoal pencil to make arrow marks on the cave walls. "How deep does it go?"

"Endless," Yarrow said.

"That's unlikely."

"I don't know. Beneath every part of the island?"

"Much more likely. Are you okay?" she asked.

He paused before he said, "The charcoal is a good idea."

"It won't last forever."

"We stop when it does," Yarrow said. He lifted the lantern higher, and the light danced on the limestone. Shadows writhed at their feet. She noticed she could no longer smell the sea, only a damp, coppery sourness. "We're not becoming lost down here. It's not worth it."

"But she found a shell."

"Not worth it," Yarrow repeated.

"If we don't destroy the ingredients . . ."

He stopped walking. She noticed his hand was sticky with sweat, and he was squeezing her fingers tighter. "Then so be it. We let the enchanted greenhouse die, and we build our own, saving as many plants as we can. I'm not going to risk you for the dream of a dead sorcerer."

"But you love the greenhouse."

"I love you more," he said.

"Oh." Her voice was a squeak.

Yarrow's eyes widened as he looked beyond her. "I don't think we'll have to do that, though. Look." He gestured with the lantern, and she turned to see what he was seeing: in the center of the next cave, the three dragons circling what looked like an altar of stone.

At the center was a tortoise shell, filled with hundreds of other shells.

CHAPTER THIRTY-TWO

In exchange for all the jars of honey, the three little dragons relinquished their new hoard. It was arranged beautifully: each shell lined like shingles, overlapping one another, in a spiral within the upturned sea turtle shell. As Yarrow held the lantern over it, Terlu saw the mother-of-pearl insides of the shells sparkle. After all this time, the spell ingredients were perfectly intact and displayed.

No wonder the spell hadn't ended.

If it weren't stopped, it would keep destroying greenhouse after greenhouse until every flower, every tree, every vine was dead.

He laid the lantern down and pulled a batch of dried grasses from one of his pockets. "From one of the failed greenhouses," he said. "Seemed appropriate." He laid the kindling between the shells.

"I feel as if we should say something profound," Terlu said.

Yarrow grunted, and then he took out his fire-starter and lit the kindling on fire. He continued to feed the flames as smoke rose to the top of the cave.

The dragons chirped, and they all retreated to the doorway. Yarrow carried the lantern with him. The shells within the turtle shell continued to flame and smoke. Every time they dimmed, Yarrow would step back into the room and add more fuel to the fire.

At last, the flames dwindled low, and he didn't add more.

Breathing through her sleeve to avoid the worst of the smoke,

Terlu checked the turtle shell. Within, the nutshells were gone, and the seashells had crumbled into ash.

He picked up the turtle shell as it smoldered. "I think it's destroyed."

"We can throw the ashes into the sea," Terlu said. "Let the tides take them away."

They followed the charcoal markings on the wall back to the start of the string. Terlu picked up the end of the string and began winding it as they walked. The three dragons settled again onto her shoulders and head. One of them munched on honeycomb next to her ear with sweet slurping sounds.

"Do you think the greenhouse is truly safe now?" Yarrow asked.

"I don't know," Terlu said. "But I think so?" It occurred to her that this was the same as her own situation. Now that she knew the empire had fallen, she *thought* she was safe, but would she ever truly know? She supposed it was close enough. To the best of her knowledge, the plants were safe. And to the best of her knowledge, she was safe too. Maybe that was all anyone ever got, a hope and a belief. *Maybe that's enough.*

As she wound the string into a ball, she heard voices ahead. In response, the dragon on her head flapped its wings and crowed. The voices grew louder and more excited.

Light bounced off the walls, and Terlu heard her name being called:

"Terlu? Yarrow? Are you okay?"

"We're here!" she called back.

They rounded the corner. Up ahead, she saw a crowd—Birch and Rowan in the lead, with Lotti riding on Rowan's shoulder. Dendy was hopping beside them. She spotted Yarrow's uncle Rodrick, as well as Rowan's wife, Ambrel, behind them with the other plants. She heard Yarrow's intake of breath, and she knew until that moment that he hadn't believed they'd come to find him, even though years had passed since he was that little boy alone in the cave, even though everyone knew why they were here and what was at stake.

Rowan grinned when she saw them. "Hey, you're not lost or dead! Yay!"

"Glad you're happy about that," Yarrow said.

"Of course I'm—wait, you're happy. I think you're happy. You're actually smiling." She twisted to look back at her wife. "Ambrel, is that a smile on my brother's face?"

"I *am* capable of it," Yarrow said.

"I wasn't sure."

Birch peered at the turtle shell with the ashes. "You found it?"

"And burned it," Yarrow confirmed. "We're going to throw the rest into the ocean."

Birch exhaled heavily. "I was so willing to give up, and all along, the answer was under our feet. I'm sorry. I thought . . . I thought a lot of things that were wrong, but I should never have given up on our home—or on you."

That was a real apology.

Looking at Yarrow, Terlu could tell that he heard it too. Unlike Birch's earlier attempts, this one sounded like it came from the heart—that he both wanted to fix things and understood why they'd broken.

Rowan rolled her eyes. "You seriously can't blame yourself for that. I don't think any of us would have ever have guessed . . . Hey, are those dragons? From the maze?"

Perched on Terlu, the three dragons chirped at Rowan.

She cooed at them. The dragon on Terlu's left shoulder flew onto Rowan's shoulder and immediately curled its talons in her braids, like a cat kneading a blanket. She laughed. "Ahh, that tickles!"

The other two dragons stayed on Terlu. One of them wrapped its tail around her neck, like a necklace of warm jewels. The other curled on the top of her head.

Following the string, they trooped out of the cave together. Hopping between their feet, Dendy reported on the progress that the plants had made with sealing the cracks and how they were preparing more ingredients in order to teach whichever humans wanted to learn.

Lotti talked about how she'd visited Laiken's ghost again and told him how they were searching for the ingredients. She thought he seemed happy about it, though it was admittedly difficult to tell, given how little of him there was left. The ghost's breeze, the rose reported, smelled more like lavender, which was nicer than skunk cabbage.

When they emerged from the cave, the tide had inched closer. It licked at the pebbles a few feet from the opening of the cave. "We should dump the ashes off the dock," Yarrow suggested. "It's deeper there."

"Throw," Terlu said.

"Same thing, yes?"

"But it sounds more dramatic," Terlu said. "Words matter." The right words could heal shattered glass. And hearts. And families. And lives.

"That's too bad, since I never find the right ones," Yarrow said.

"You do, when it matters," Terlu told him, with a smile. She looped her arm through his, and he handed the lantern to his father. He carried the turtle shell cradled in his other arm. They climbed up the slope into the trees and followed the mass of footprints through the snow to the road, and then their little parade continued to the dock.

Yarrow and Terlu walked alone to the end, while the others waited behind them.

"Do you want to do it?" Yarrow offered.

"It should be you. You're the one the spell hurt the most."

"But you're the one who fixed it," Yarrow said.

"Together?" Terlu said.

"Together," he agreed.

They threw the ashes into the waves. A moment later, they threw the turtle shell. It floated for a moment and then gradually, as the waves hit it, it filled with water and began to sink.

"It'll probably wash onto shore," Yarrow said.

"It's okay. This was kind of symbolic at this point. The fire was thorough."

"Good."

They both watched the turtle shell as it disappeared beneath the waves.

Rejoining the others, they walked back through the snow.

As they reached the sorcerer's tower, Lotti asked Rowan to help her inside. She wanted to let Laiken know what they'd done and that his plants were safe, but she couldn't work Laiken's door handle. After transferring the little dragon from Rowan's shoulder back to Terlu's, Rowan and Ambrel peeled away to let the little rose into the sorcerer's home.

The two remaining humans, Birch and Rorick, excused themselves when they reached the cottages to join the work on the roofs, windows, and chimneys. The blue cottage was livable now, as was the one in sunrise colors. They were working on a third now. A lot remained to be done, but at least the family wasn't sleeping all piled together in the workroom anymore.

The other plants stayed with Terlu, Yarrow, and the dragons until they reached the greenhouse, and then they said goodbye and left to continue their work fixing the cracks. Terlu and Yarrow brought the dragons back to the sunflower maze together.

Once the chrysanthemum puzzle door was opened, the three little dragons took to the air and flew back inside with happy trills and coos. They were greeted with calls from the other dragons. Above, the aurora rippled in green-and-yellow ribbons.

"Thank you for your help," Yarrow called after them.

Terlu placed the jars inside the door, where the dragons could easily reach them. "We'll leave the door open from now on." She glanced at Yarrow to make sure he agreed, and he nodded. Just because Laiken had treated the inhabitants of Belde a certain way didn't mean they had to do the same. Like Lotti and the other sentient plants, the dragons had proven they were more than what they'd been allowed to be. *It's time for things to change.* "Let us know when you want more honey."

All three dragons flew back into the maze. She watched them for a moment as they cavorted above the flowers. She wondered if they were telling their story to the other dragons and decided that yes, they were.

"Do you think they'll leave the maze, if we leave the door open?" Yarrow worried.

"Yes," Terlu said. "But then they'll come back. Their family and friends are all here."

"Mmm. Also, their treasure hoard."

"Sure, that too."

Side by side, they watched the dragons fly for another few minutes before Yarrow said, "I wonder if they'd like honey cakes. I could bake smaller portions so they could lift them . . ."

"I think they'd love that."

Leaving the dragons, they strolled back through the greenhouses. She expected him to hurry off to weed or prune or re-pot, but perhaps he didn't need to, now that it wasn't just him caring for the hundreds of thousands of plants. She wondered how he was feeling about the fact that his father had come into the caves for him. Granted, he wasn't a child anymore, and he hadn't been lost, but maybe it would at least be the beginning of something? She wasn't going to ask, though. That was up to Yarrow to work through.

"So, I guess we just wait?" Yarrow said. "See if any other greenhouses fail?"

"I think so." Only time would show if they'd succeeded. But she was certain they'd done it. She trusted her translation of Laiken's final notebook.

"Hmm."

As they strolled through the rose room, beneath the many shades of pink and red and white, Yarrow asked, "Now that you've saved everything·I've ever cared about, what do you want to do for an encore?" He wrapped his arm around her waist and shortened his strides to match hers. Leaning against him, she breathed in his scent—honey and sea and sweat and sweetness—with the roses.

She thought about what came next. "I think . . . I want to write a letter."

"Huh. Okay."

The more she considered it, the more certain she was.

"That was not the answer I was expecting," he admitted.

"I want my family to know I'm alive," Terlu said. "And happy." She was ready, at last, to reach out. She wasn't the same as she'd been when she'd woken cold and alone in the woods, the island wasn't the same as it had been when she first walked through its wonders, and the world beyond . . . it wasn't the same either. *It's time.*

"Ahh," Yarrow said. "Yes. I'll make us lunch while you write. There's a quiche recipe I've been wanting to try . . ." He continued to tell her about the quiche with the same adorable enthusiasm as when he talked about planting garlic.

Snow began to fall again, lightly, on the trees and the cottage and the greenhouse. The winged cat met them by the door of the cottage, and the three of them went inside.

While Yarrow broke several eggs and began whisking them, Terlu sat at his desk and pulled out a clean sheet of paper. She dipped the quill tip into the inkwell.

Dear—

She paused.

Should she write separate letters to her parents and her sister? What about her cousins? Aunts, uncles, grandparents?

Dear Family, she wrote.

She paused again.

"Tell them you're well," Yarrow advised.

She wrote that. And then once those first words were there, she kept writing. She told them about when she first came to Alyssium, full of hope and fear. She told them about the library, how proud she'd been to get the job and how disappointed when it turned out to not be what she'd imagined it would be. She told them about how much she missed home, how much she missed them, and why she hadn't returned—because she wanted to find a place where she belonged and had purpose, and she knew it wasn't Eano, as much as she loved them. But it wasn't Alyssium either. As it turned out, it was Belde.

This place. With this man.

She smiled as she wrote about Yarrow and her life here. *I found a place I want to be and a future I want to have. I'm happy, and I hope you are too. Please write back.*

I miss you.

Love,

Your Terlu

CHAPTER THIRTY-THREE

After a few weeks, the final crack was sealed.

Terlu had been expecting it—she knew the talking plants were working on their final dead greenhouse. In fact, this morning, she'd shortened her daily swim with the sea turtle, in hopes that she wouldn't miss the moment. So when she heard the cheers in the distance, she knew exactly what it meant. When it happened, she was working on spell variations in what she'd dubbed her practice greenhouse, the one where she and Yarrow had nearly suffocated inside one of her earlier attempts.

Lotti burst in with the news. "We did it!" she caroled. "All the glass is fixed!"

"That's wonderful!" Terlu said, celebrating with her. The little rose danced around her with her petals shaking in the air, and Terlu spun to watch. It was indeed a tremendous achievement. After thousands, even hundreds of thousands, of cracks, the glass was at last whole. Every greenhouse could host life again.

"We need a new spell to do."

Terlu laughed.

"I'm serious." The little rose widened her petals, as if she was trying to look more earnest. "It's spectacular that the glass is fixed, but there's much more to be done."

"I don't have a new spell yet." Terlu waved at the pages she was struggling with. She'd written out reams of notes and tried countless variations, but no success so far.

Lotti hopped closer to the pages. "What's this one do?"

"Ideally, if it's working right, it forms a protective shield just within the glass—it's what makes it possible for some rooms to be hot and humid enough for tropical plants and others to grow vegetables so close to the winter solstice."

"But it's not working yet?"

So far, she'd managed a bubble that was permeable enough to allow people to walk through and sturdy enough not to burst—she'd cast it each time from *outside* the ring of ingredients, to be safe. However, it also didn't hold in heat, which was the point. She was confident that if she tweaked the spell enough, she'd get it eventually. She was closer to understanding how the phrases interacted. But the key word was "eventually." "Not yet. How about you get Birch and the others to teach you how to plant seedlings?"

Lotti let out a gasp. "Ooh, do you think I could do that?"

"Absolutely. I think you could do anything you want to do." Or at least anything that was physically feasible for a very small flower with a base of feathery leaves, though really Terlu wouldn't have put any limitations on the rose. "I see no reason why you and the other plants can't be gardeners, now that you've finished proving you can be sorcerers."

"No offense, but I'd rather be a gardener. It's more important."

Terlu grinned. "No offense taken. It *is* more important."

Pleased, Lotti hopped out of the greenhouse.

Terlu jotted a note in her journal about the results of her latest experiment and then collected the ingredients to be set aside for her next attempt. It was a shame that she didn't have anyone she could ask to study the texts with her, because even after she decoded the sorcerer's notes, First Language was notoriously tricky to parse. Ah well, it just meant it would take her more time—which she had, now that Laiken's malfunctioning spell had been disabled.

Not a single greenhouse had died since they destroyed the ingredients, and she was allowing herself to hope that it was over. Additionally, Laiken's ghost had dissipated after Lotti told him the news, which was further proof that they'd done the right thing.

Her theory was that a piece of Laiken had known he'd condemned his beloved plants, which was why his ghost hadn't been able to let go. Now that his mistake was undone, he was at peace, which was nice. At the very least the upstairs bedroom was less windy, even if no one besides Lotti (who slept in a pot on the bedside table) was willing to claim it as their own—there were simply too many memories bound up in it for any of Yarrow's family to move into the tower permanently, and the neighbor with the toddler didn't want a home with either stairs or spells.

After everything was tucked away, Terlu headed out of the practice greenhouse. Reaching the rose room, she strolled through. One of the tiny dragons was busily flitting from rosebush to rosebush—ever since she'd left the door open, they'd chosen to help with pollinating, though they always returned to their sunflower maze by the end of the day.

The dragon, a golden one with sapphire-blue eyes, trilled at her.

"Come by the cottage later," Terlu told her, "and you can have some honey."

Satisfied, the dragon flew to another rose, balancing on the stem as the bloom bobbed beneath her weight. She stuck her snout into the center of the flower.

Continuing on, Terlu found Yarrow outside by the cottage that was formerly home to the feral gryphons—the gryphons, she'd been told, had been relocated to an unused shed on the other side of the island. Luckily, she hadn't been involved at all in that maneuver. Yarrow was working with his father on the roof, fixing the shingles. She noticed that Yarrow was working below Birch, in position to catch him were he to ever lose his grip—she wondered if that was a conscious choice or instinct. *He doesn't even know what a great heart he has.*

"Did you hear?" Terlu called up to him. "All the cracks are fixed!"

"That's fantastic!" Yarrow said.

It would be a while before she'd have enough of a grasp on the magic for the old failed greenhouses to be properly enchanted greenhouses again, but they'd function just fine as they were, subject to the ordinary laws of how greenhouses worked. Some of the destroyed rooms had already been reclaimed, designated for plants that didn't require unnatural heat or for plants that the gardeners wanted to keep in a normal seasonal cycle. Other reclaimed greenhouses wouldn't be used until spring. Yarrow had his eye on one as a future home for herbs from the southern isles—he had seeds squirreled away and had been just waiting for the right space to plant them.

All of the gardeners had plans, and winter was the perfect time for dreaming.

"I thought we could add an extra celebration to the Winter Feast plans?" Terlu suggested. "Something that acknowledges that the glass has all been fixed?" She shielded her eyes from the sun. It reflected off the fresh blanket of snow, glittering so hard that it made her eyes water.

Helping his father first, Yarrow scooted over the roof and climbed down the ladder. A few rungs from the ground, he jumped off and landed near her. "How about a confection made of sugar glass?"

She'd been thinking a toast or some kind of speech, but that was a much better idea. "I don't know what that is, but it sounds wonderful."

He held the ladder while his father climbed carefully down. When Birch reached the bottom, Yarrow helped steady him. Chuckling, Birch said, "I'm probably too old to be climbing on roofs."

"I told you that," Yarrow said mildly.

"It sounds better when I say it myself," Birch said.

Yarrow grunted.

"Will you two be joining us for dinner tonight?" Birch asked as he reclaimed his cane from where it had been leaning against the house. "Rorick caught some stripe fish, and he wants to grill them all while they're fresh."

"You mean he wants to show off how many he caught," Yarrow said.

"Exactly that."

Yarrow glanced at Terlu and lifted his eyebrows.

She shrugged. Whatever he wanted was fine with her.

"Not tonight," Yarrow said. "But if there's leftovers, save some for Emeral." He took Terlu's hand, and they walked back toward their own cottage.

"You have plans for tonight?" Terlu asked.

"Zucchini, squash, and tomato sliced thin, seasoned with thyme, salt, and pepper. I already have dough on the second rise so we can bake a loaf to have on the side."

"If you already prepped all that, why even consider joining the others?" Terlu asked.

He shrugged. "I thought you might want to."

"Not if the dough is already on a second rise." She liked spending lots of time with lots of people, especially ones who enjoyed each other as obviously as Yarrow's family did, but a fresh loaf of Yarrow's bread? And an evening alone with Yarrow? She'd never say no to that. "I attempted another variation of the spell today."

"Oh?"

She told him about what she'd tried and what had happened, as well as her ideas for what to attempt next. He listened as they both went inside and shed their coats. Crossing to the kitchen counter, he began slicing the vegetables and arranging them in a skillet. She built up the fire and put a kettle for tea over the flames.

Seated at the table near Yarrow, she added notes to her notebook— she'd begun her own journal to match Laiken's, though hers wasn't in code. She was aiming for a clear and organized record of everything she'd discovered about the greenhouse spells, which was rather more than her lack of progress with the bubble spell showed.

Terlu had successfully extracted several of his spells: the sunflower maze, for example, as well as the singing plants. She was confident she knew the spell for creating more sentient plants, which she had promised herself she'd use if and only if the other plants asked her to. But the trickiest spell of all remained the convoluted spell that he'd used to create the greenhouses. It was woven from multiple other spells. Granted, she was making strides in understanding how the threads were interconnected, but it could require a lifetime of study before she could recreate what Laiken had done to enchant the greenhouses. At the very least, though, she was going to leave clear notes for whomever continued her work after her. In the meantime, she'd also discovered a spell that would let her swim with the sea turtle without needing quite so much oxygen.

There was so much to learn and so much to do. And so much to eat and feel and think and be! It still left her breathless sometimes to think how close she came to missing all of this, to never even taking a full breath again, much less having a full life.

Yarrow shaped the loaves and loaded them into the brick oven to bake while he cooked the vegetables on the skillet. The scent of herbs and cooked tomatoes filled the cottage, and Terlu breathed it in. "Smells incredible," she said.

"It's an experiment," he said. "See what you think."

"I like your experiments. They're much tastier than mine." Setting the table, Terlu poured water for each of them and added icicles as stirring sticks. She dropped a fresh mint leaf in each glass.

When the vegetables were done, he served them onto two plates. He spooned the rest into a serving dish and placed the skillet in the sink to soak.

"Go on, eat."

She picked up a forkful, blew on it to cool it, and then put it in her mouth. Flavors exploded over her tongue, and every herb filled every bit of her. "It tastes like summer."

"That's what I'd hoped."

While she ate another bite, he checked on the loaves. Taking them out, he thumped the bottom. Satisfied, he set them aside to cool while he returned to dinner.

They alternated between talking and not talking. When a loaf had cooled enough, he sliced it and served it with his dragon-approved honey butter.

"You should make this for the Winter Feast," Terlu said.

"I've been working on another specialty for that."

"Oh?"

"You'll have to wait for dessert. I've been experimenting with that too."

She grinned. "That sounds interesting."

When they finished and cleaned from dinner, he brought out a plate from the icebox. It was underneath a napkin embroidered with pink and purple flowers—a gift from his father who had brought it from Alyssium. Birch had learned to embroider while he was recovering from the illness that had sent him there, a weakness in his heart that only specialist doctors were able to cure. The flowers were lopsided, but it was still pretty.

Yarrow set it in the center of the table and then, with a flourish, he lifted the napkin.

"You do like drama—" she began, and then stopped and stared.

They were chocolate-covered orange slices, each slice perfect and plump as a jewel, with smooth-as-silk chocolate encasing half of them. She felt a lump in her throat. She hadn't known he'd been listening when she talked about oranges weeks ago. He'd barely liked her then. In fact, she was certain he hadn't.

All of a sudden, it felt like her family was here with her, even though they hadn't yet written back to the letter she'd sent—it had been picked up by a passing sailor weeks ago, but no boat had returned with a response. Still, here was a bit of home.

Terlu blinked quickly.

"You don't like them?" he said, concerned. "I know you said you remembered candied oranges from your Winter Feast, but then I thought with your story about the orange tree . . ."

"It's perfect," she said. "You're perfect."

Yarrow snorted.

Standing, she crossed to him. She cupped his face in her hands and kissed him. He wrapped his arms around her waist and pulled her closer. She drank in the warmth of him as her hands moved around his neck to tangle in his hair. He whispered her name as he moved to kiss her neck and her ear.

Much later, they ate the chocolate oranges.

And they were indeed perfect.

CHAPTER THIRTY-FOUR

Snow fell lightly on the sea.

It was five days after the chocolate oranges, and Terlu was in the middle of sorting through Laiken's journals in the sorcerer's tower when she spotted the sea serpent out the window of the workroom. Grinning, she pulled on her coat and hurried down to the dock.

If the sea serpent was back, Marin and Ree wouldn't be far behind.

She waved when they came into view and then watched as Marin steered the ship toward the dock. Ree the myrtle was scurrying up and down the rigging as if he were born to it.

"Welcome back to Belde!" Terlu shouted as Marin tossed a line around one of the dock pilings, then hopped off the boat to secure the knot.

With a wide smile, Marin waved back as Terlu trotted down the dock to greet her.

"Any letters?" she asked.

"As a matter of fact, yes, one," Marin said, as she pulled a letter out of the bag at her side, "though it wounds me that you aren't happy just to see me."

"And me!" Ree shouted.

"Of course I am. It's great to see you both," Terlu said, but her eyes were fixed on the letter. It was tied with a multicolored ribbon—red, yellow, and orange, matching the paint on her family's home. She took it, lifted it to her nose, and inhaled. She could smell it on the paper, the faint odor of citrus and salt water. *Home.* She wanted to tear it open and read it right now. No, she'd wait until she had a moment alone. She'd waited this long; she could wait a little while longer. "Thank you." She clutched it to her chest.

"Not a problem. I was coming here anyway."

"You were?"

"Told you I'd be back in time for Winter Feast, remember?" Marin said. "I keep my promises. Especially when they're paid for with rubies. I've got your gardener's usual supplies, as well as a few special additions." She stepped aside as the ship began to disgorge people: a couple with a child, all of whom had soft tawny fur and tiny antlers poking out of their hair, as well as an elderly woman with silvery scales instead of skin. "Refugees from Alyssium. You've got room here, right?"

"Yes, of course." The words were out of her mouth before she even thought about them, but how could she say no? Especially since they were looking at her with frightened, tired, hopeful eyes. And there were only four of them. Surely, they could fit four more on Belde, couldn't they, especially when one was a child? She greeted the new arrivals and directed them up the road toward where Birch, Rowan, and the others were, and she hoped they didn't mind that she'd just said yes to four more residents. "Third cottage on the right," Terlu said. "You'll find some people who should be able to help you find a place to stay."

The more, the merrier, right?

Unless they were going to cause problems with all the magic use. It wasn't just her anymore. It was all the talking plants, as well as several of Yarrow's cousins and his aunt Rin, who'd helped fix the cracks in the glass.

As the new arrivals left the dock, Terlu lowered her voice so they wouldn't hear. "Only thing is whether they'll be comfortable living

near an enchanted greenhouse. There's a lot of spellwork here . . ."
She trailed off, careful not to say who was casting it.

Marin shook her head. "Can't see that being a problem. Laws
are changing right and left, and no one is going to flinch at a little
spellwork on a sparsely populated island, so long as it doesn't cause
any harm. Causing harm is still illegal. But the law that got you
statue-ified—"

Terlu took a step back. "You know about that? About . . . me?"

"Who do you think brought you here?"

"I . . ." She hadn't known. But if Marin had been the sailor who
transported her as a statue, then of course she must have known
instantly who she was the second she saw a living, breathing person
on the dock who exactly resembled the wooden statue she'd had in
her hull. *She'd chosen not to say anything.* Unsure how she felt about
that, Terlu gawked at the sailor. "You knew all along?"

"Sure." Marin shrugged as if it was a minor detail, not the most
pivotal (and traumatic) event of Terlu's life. "I don't blindly agree to
transport criminals without knowing what they did. I knew, and I
sympathized. Anyway, the law that got you turned into a statue has
been struck. Thought you might like to know."

It . . . *What?*

All her worry. All her fear . . .

And the law had been struck down miles and miles away? If she
hadn't talked to Marin, she might never have known and continued
to live in anxious fear of an imperial investigator swooping down on
her island and ripping her away from everything and everyone she'd
grown to love. "The imperial investigators . . ."

"Disbanded," Marin said.

"And who . . . How . . ."

Marin flapped a hand in the general direction of Alyssium. "Laws
are being rewritten. The provisional government is still figuring out
which foot to put which shoe on, but yeah, the empire fell, which
means a *lot* of changes, for better or worse, but this is one change

for the better that I think will stick. You've heard about the magic storms plaguing the outer islands, haven't you? Or have you? You've been pretty sheltered, first in the library, then on Belde." Marin paused for her to reply, but Terlu was too flabbergasted to do anything but stare at her. "Well, anyway, as it turns out, one of the side effects of the emperor's hoarding magic has been an increase in terrible storms. So everyone's happy to *not* return to the old ways. Less death and mayhem, you know?"

She had no idea there had been death and mayhem while she'd stood frozen on her pedestal, but less . . . Yes, less sounded good. Terlu felt as if her mind was whirling. Marin knew all along that she'd been a statue? And she'd approved of Terlu *not* being a statue, even though there had been a trial, complete with judgment and sentencing? "You were willing to risk . . . ? For me?"

"Yeah, well, what's the point of sailing free, choosing your own horizon, if you won't choose what's right over what's easy?" For an instant, Marin's smile faltered, and she looked out at the horizon.

Terlu opened her mouth and then shut it, unsure what to say.

Ree swung on a line, holding on with his branches, and then released, soaring in an arc off the boat and landing on the dock with a *thump* as his root ball impacted on the boards. "Hey, Marin, did you see that? I did it!"

Marin cheered. "Flawless. Like always." Lowering her voice, she said to Terlu, "First dozen times he tried that, he overshot." She mimed a bush sailing over the dock and splashing into the water.

"Luckily I'm—"

"—a halophyte," Marin finished with him, fondness in her voice. "Yes, we know."

"Welcome back, Ree," Terlu said to him. "Where's the other sailor who was with you?" She didn't remember his name, but he'd had diamond horns. He'd looked at home on her ship; she'd assumed he was a permanent addition.

Marin shrugged. "He's back on land, where he belongs. Not

everyone's made for the sea like Ree here." She smiled affectionately at the shrubbery.

Ree fluttered his leaves like a bird preening.

"Your friends will be happy to see you," Terlu told him. "Glad you made it back for Winter Feast."

"Ooh, speaking of . . ." Marin dug into the bag at her side and pulled out a thin book with a green cloth cover. "I brought you a feast present. Happy solstice!"

A present. Terlu felt as if she'd already been gifted with the greatest present she could have ever imagined: her life, free of fear. And a letter from her family, which she was still clutching to her heart. "I didn't get you anything."

"You gave me a very big ruby, remember?" Rolling her eyes, Marin handed the book to Terlu. "It's a new spellbook that's circulating, written for ordinary people. Supposed to have a lot to do with plants and gardens and such, and since, you know, the whole greenhouse thing . . . I thought it could be useful. Found it in an adorable jam shop, and I couldn't say no."

"The laws have changed that much?" Terlu gawked at the book. It was titled simply *Spells from Caltrey*. She wasn't sure where Caltrey was—it wasn't an island name that she recognized.

"Yep," Marin said.

This was proof, here in her hands. A spellbook for an ordinary person.

"Brand-new world out there. A second chance for a whole lot of people, not just you."

"Oh." It was a lot to absorb. Terlu had spent so much time afraid that she'd be forced to be a statue again, and all it took was the overthrow of a thousand-year-old government. *All it took—hah!* She began smiling. This book in her hands was undeniable proof that what Marin said was true. If the imperial law still stood, it would never have been printed. She hugged it to her chest, along with her family's letter, both so precious. "This is an excellent solstice present."

"My pleasure. Now am I invited to the feast?"

"Absolutely."

From the ship came a voice that Terlu recognized: "Am I invited as well?" And the head librarian of the Great Library of Alyssium, the woman who had fought for Terlu's life and lost but still found a way to save her anyway, stepped out of the hold.

"Rijes Velk!" Terlu chirped. She then bowed. "I . . . oh . . . Oh, wow." She felt tears brimming in her eyes as she turned to Marin. It was all so very much. First the letter, then her freedom, now this? Her knees wobbled. "You found her? How? Wow, this is . . . Wow."

"It was a really large ruby. And it helped that I knew where she was."

Shaking his leaves, Ree said, "Told you she'd be surprised! Whee, we did amazing!"

Terlu hadn't considered the fact that Marin might have known Rijes, but of course she had to, if she was the one who'd brought the statue of Terlu to safety. None of this was a miracle or a coincidence— the two of them already had a connection. Still, it felt like a miracle. "I thought I was asking for the impossible. But here you are. I don't know how to say thank you. I . . . Thank you."

"You look well," Rijes said.

Rijes looked . . . very different. At the trial, the head librarian had been encased in robes made of embroidered silk. Her hair had been braided in a pattern that echoed the latticework on the great door to Kinney Hall, and her face had been painted with symbols that affirmed her oath to honor the history, wisdom, and knowledge of the Crescent Islands. Now, she was in a simple tunic, her onyx face was undecorated and wrinkled, her blue-black eyes red-rimmed and tired, and her thin gray hair unbound. She looked like the older woman that she was at the end of a long voyage and not like the embodiment of her office. "So do you," Terlu said. "You look wonderful."

Her lips curved into a smile. "You always were more kindhearted than the world would allow. I was very pleased to hear that you are thriving here."

Belatedly, she realized they were all still standing on the dock in the chill of the sea breeze. "Come inside," Terlu said. "You must be hungry and tired."

Marin piped up. "I am."

"I'm fine," Ree said.

"Do you have bags? I can carry them." She thought ahead. "The late sorcerer's home is unoccupied. It used to be haunted, but the ghost moved on. You can stay there, if you'd like, for as long as you like." She supposed she should consult with the other residents before welcoming any more people to Belde. She didn't think, though, anyone would mind, especially Yarrow. He knew what Rijes meant to her. And no one would object to Marin and Ree either—the rescuers of the refugees.

Marin ducked into the hull of her ship and emerged with two bags that she tossed onto the dock with a grunt. "I'd rather sleep on my boat, but thanks."

"Same," Ree said.

"How long can you stay?" Terlu asked.

"Only until the wind changes," Marin said.

"Ahh," Terlu said, though she wasn't exactly sure what that meant. A calendar date would have been far more specific, but they were welcome for however long they wanted, though she hoped that Rijes would stay for longer. She picked up one of the bags and staggered. "Books?"

"A few," Rijes admitted.

"Then definitely Laiken's tower. It has bookshelves. Oh, and it also has a talking rose named Lotti. She's in the greenhouse right now, but she lives in the tower. I'm sure she'd love the company. She's very friendly." Terlu waddled with the head librarian's bags, while Marin followed with another pack plus a box of what Terlu assumed was more books. "I've been working through the sorcerer's notebooks . . ." She led them to the workshop and opened the door.

Behind her, Rijes let out a small gasp as she beheld the bookshelves—it was the sound of a woman who didn't expect to find happiness but discovered it anyway. Terlu knew that sound well. "This is perfect," Rijes proclaimed.

It had transformed from abandoned and disheveled to cozy and library-like. "It's much cleaner than it was." She was grateful that Yarrow had scrubbed it so thoroughly. She hadn't expected to be showing it to the head librarian of the most magnificent library in the whole of the Crescent Islands. Terlu lowered the bags of books while Rijes went immediately to the shelves and pulled off a volume.

Flipping through the pages, Rijes frowned at it. "Curious."

"He used a code," Terlu said. "I can show you the translation—"

"Yes, that would be excellent!"

Marin said plaintively, "After food?"

Terlu laughed. "Yes, after food. Why don't you settle in, and I'll be by with some dinner? And the codebook. Ree, I know your friends will be happy to see you're well." If Rijes were interested in the notebooks . . . this could be a truly excellent development. There was no one else on the island with her kind of expertise.

"That would be perfect," Rijes said. As Terlu headed for the door, Rijes said, "Terlu? Sending you here . . . I wish I could have done more, and now I am here to impose on you."

"It's not an imposition," Terlu said. "It's an honor." She meant every word.

"Alyssium was my home for decades. I expected to die, gladly, between the stacks of the Great Library, a servant to the knowledge and wisdom collected by an empire." She sighed heavily. "There isn't a place for me there anymore."

"You have a place here," Terlu said firmly. "For as long as you want. Forever, if you'd like." She meant it. If she could do for Rijes what the head librarian had done for her . . . "This is the perfect place for new beginnings."

Grinning, Marin elbowed Rijes. "Told you so."

"I know," Rijes said, "but it is a lot to ask of anyone."

Terlu couldn't imagine saying no, and she wasn't going to let anyone else on the island say no either, though she doubted they would.

This wasn't just a sanctuary for plants, not anymore. "You saved my life."

"By sending you away from everything and everyone you'd ever known," Rijes said. "It was the best I could do, under the circumstances, but I fear I placed an unfair burden on you, without any hint of what I hoped you would achieve. Are you . . . Are you happy here, my dear?"

That was an easy question to answer. Terlu smiled. "Yes. I am."

"Then I'm glad."

"You risked so much . . . And you barely know me."

"I did what I believed was right," Rijes said. "It's my duty—in fact, I believe it's every person's duty, especially those in power—to reject unjust laws. To choose kindness and empathy, whenever we can."

"I don't know how to even begin to thank you."

"You already have." She indicated the tower and, more sweepingly, the island beyond.

Smiling, Terlu left the head librarian to settle in, with Marin to help, and she headed outside to ask Yarrow if he could bake an extra loaf or two tonight. *She's here!* At best Terlu had hoped that Marin would find Rijes and thank her. This, though . . . She hadn't imagined she'd be able to offer Rijes a second chance in return.

As Terlu approached the cottages, she saw the other new arrivals with Birch and Ambrel. She waved, and they waved back, looking happy. The child, wearing a new hat and mittens, was skipping through the snow. *They must have been told they can stay too.* She was glad for it and also unsurprised—Yarrow's family knew what it felt like to be refugees, forced to hope for kindness from others. She knew they'd welcome Rijes as well. *They'll all be happy here.*

The community on Belde was growing faster than she could have ever expected. It was the seed of a village now, and that was a good thing. This place didn't need to be isolated to be safe—Laiken had had it all backward and mixed up. The only way the island would survive—the only way they'd all thrive—was together.

She liked that thought very much.

Hurrying, she burst into the cottage, where Yarrow was working on his sugar glass. He looked up. She knew she was smiling so broadly that her chilled cheeks almost hurt. "So much to tell you," Terlu said.

"There's tea already warm," Yarrow said.

"I love you," she said.

Those weren't the words she expected to come out of her mouth, but they did.

"I guessed that," he said.

She felt as though she'd stepped into the sun. The words were out there, and they felt right. And he was still here, smiling at her, as if he felt the sun too.

"Tell me everything," he said. "I'm listening."

She launched into a description of the new arrivals: Marin, the refugees, and most importantly Rijes, the woman who'd saved her. "I thought she could live in Laiken's tower?"

"She's welcome to it," Yarrow said. "Everyone will be glad to have it occupied by something other than memories. Do you think she can help you with his spells?"

"She seems interested," Terlu said. "I promised to bring her the codebook."

He studied her for a moment. "There's more."

She grinned. "There's more." Waving the letter in the air, she showed him. "My family wrote back. I'm currently imagining it says all the things I want it to say—that they forgive me, they understand me, maybe they're proud of me?"

"You haven't read it yet?"

"I was hoping you would."

After shedding her coat and boots, she plopped onto the bed with the new spellbook that Marin had gifted her. Curled on the blankets, Emeral made a squawk in protest. "You can keep sleeping."

He stretched his paws out, readjusted his wings, and closed his eyes.

"Ever heard of Caltrey?" Terlu asked Yarrow.

He shook his head. "Is it north?"

"Could be."

"You're sure you want me to read it? Out loud?" He untied the bow around it, and Emeral launched himself forward to pounce on the ribbon. He flew up to the rafters with his prize.

"Silently," Terlu said. "And then tell me if it's going to make me happy or sad."

Yarrow skimmed through the pages. "It's three letters. One from your mother, one from your father, and one from Cerri—that's your sister, right?" She nodded, not trusting herself to speak, while he continued to read silently. He then smiled.

She exhaled like a bubble popping.

"They forgive you, they understand you, and they're proud of you." He handed her the letters. "You should read them."

Kneeling on the bed, she took them and read.

Her mother first—she scolded her for not writing sooner, saying how worried they'd been, saying how happy they were that she was well. Her father—he talked about the tides, how the stars had said she'd find happiness, and how they missed her. "My father says he knew I'd land on my feet. And my sister . . ." She read the letter from Cerri. "Oh! She's having a baby. I'm going to be an aunt. They want me to meet my new niece."

She held the letters to her chest as if she could absorb them straight into her heart. She'd lost six years as a statue, but she wouldn't lose any more. Her family still cared. They weren't angry, and they missed her. Maybe they didn't fully understand, but they *cared*. If they came to visit . . . *When* they came to visit, she corrected herself, she'd try to explain. She'd left Eano to find a place where she had a purpose. It had just taken her longer than she'd thought it would to find it. It would be all right.

I have a niece. And her father knew she'd find happiness.

She reread the letters three times while Yarrow puttered at the counter, kneading dough and then setting it to rise in a covered bowl by the hearth. When at last she'd reassured herself that it was real and her family was fine, Terlu opened her gift, the new spellbook.

She gasped.

On the title page, in curling script, were the authors: Kiela and Caz of Caltrey. Terlu felt her breath catch in her throat. She didn't know who Kiela was, but Caz . . .

It could be a coincidence.

It didn't necessarily have to be *her* Caz, the talking spider plant she'd created all those years ago. It was not a common name, but it wasn't unheard of. Still, it *could* be him. How, though, could he have come to have co-written a spellbook? And where was Caltrey? He'd been in Alyssium, the last she knew. *If it is him, he escaped the burning of the library.* She hoped with all her heart that it was him.

"Terlu?" Yarrow asked, concern in his voice.

She turned the pages. They contained spells, written phonetically, with lists of ingredients. Most were for growing plants and revitalizing trees, but the book also contained a few recipes, one for raspberry jam and another for cinnamon buns, credited to a local baker named Bryn.

But what about Caz? Was it her Caz?

Terlu flipped to the end to find a brief note about the authors: Kiela and Caz were the co-owners of a jam shop on the island of Caltrey. Kiela was formerly a librarian at the Great Library of Alyssium, where Caz, a sentient talking spider plant, had been her librarian assistant. She thanked her husband, Larran, as well as a list of friends. Caz thanked his partner, Meep.

Yarrow wrapped his arm around her shoulders.

She realized she was crying.

"He's okay," Terlu said. "I did the right thing."

CHAPTER THIRTY-FIVE

The day of the Winter Feast, the solstice, dawned bright. Terlu leaped out of bed, and Yarrow joined her. She'd helped him with the dough the night before, and she'd learned enough about baking to know the next step. While she shaped the loaves for the second rise, he ducked into the privy to wash. After he emerged, he began work on the sugar decorations, little roses and vines all made of white frosting. Finishing the loaves, she washed and got herself ready, choosing a jewel-colored dress from Alyssium that Ambrel had loaned her, and then rejoined him by the kitchen counter. He'd dressed up too, in soft wool pants with embroidered vines on the sides and a white shirt that pulled tight across his chest. He'd combed his hair and shaved as well, and she admired him as he set the table for two. Yarrow smiled when he noticed and admired her right back, his eyes lingering on her lips as if he were thinking of a lovely memory.

They ate leftover honey cakes for breakfast, and she fried two eggs. One of the new arrivals had produced a few chickens from deep within the hull of Marin's boat. There was talk of plans to bring more chickens to the island, as well as a goat and perhaps a cow. (Marin flat-out refused to have *that* on her boat, but there were other supply runners who would.) Now that their little population was growing, no one wanted to decimate the local birds with over-hunting them or overharvesting their eggs. More people meant more mouths. *But it also means more ideas and more dreams.* On the whole, she thought it was a definite win.

"Did you talk to Ambrel about the decorations?" Yarrow asked. He'd finished his eggs and had returned to preparing his desserts for the Winter Feast. He'd already piped several trays' worth of decorations, all of them exquisitely elaborate.

"She said Rowan wants to help with them."

Yarrow quit piping the frosting into the shape of a rose. "No."

"Why no? She seemed excited."

He sighed heavily. "She's been crocheting yarn eyes to attach to the plants. She thinks it would be funny."

Terlu grinned. "That would be funny, if the plants are okay with it."

"It was Lotti's idea."

"Then what's the harm?"

He snorted. "It's ridiculous."

"Yes, and . . . ? Winter Feast isn't supposed to be a solemn event. It's a celebration of light in the darkness. Of friends and family. Laughing together at the lonely dark. I think it's very appropriate."

He sighed again, though she suspected his heart wasn't in it. So long as no one asked him to wear crocheted eyes, she doubted he'd object.

"It's going to be fun," Terlu said.

He snorted, but then he smiled and held out the half-finished icing rose. "Taste?"

"You're supposed to be making them for the feast. I can't—"

He popped it in her mouth.

It melted and flavor burst from it. She'd expected pure sugar, but what she tasted was strawberries and vanilla—it was a bite of spring. "Oh! How did you do that?"

"Each color rose is going to have a different flavor."

"You're brilliant."

He blushed. "I'm glad you like it. I'm going to put them all over the sugar glass, to symbolize the cracks that the plants healed."

"Sounds beautiful."

Another snort. "Prettier than crocheted eyes."

Leaning forward, Terlu kissed his cheek. She left traces of sugar on his skin. "You just want something to grumble about. Admit it: you like having your sister home."

"It's fine," he said.

She grinned—that was basically a full admission that she was right. "I'll be back after I check on the others. Rijes is attempting to cook for the first time, and I promised I'd drop by to make sure she didn't accidentally burn down the tower. Apparently, that's a concern?" She couldn't imagine the head librarian wasn't brilliant at everything.

Pulling on her coat, Terlu opened the door.

"Terlu?"

She glanced back.

"For the Summer Feast, we'll invite your family—your parents, your sister, your new niece. And your plant friend as well, if you want."

That was an enormous offer from Yarrow: More people on his island? Especially strangers to him? He even sounded as if he meant it. She accepted it for the gift that it was. "I'd like that."

With a great smile on her face, she headed out into the winter day, wearing her coat, boots, and a bright red scarf. Everyone was awake, despite the early hour, bustling between the cottages and the greenhouse. She waved to everyone she saw, and they waved back.

She made her way down the road, through the snow, to Laiken's tower. Knocking, she waited for the door to open. Marin answered it, and smoke billowed out.

Terlu's eyes watered, and she took a step backward. She didn't see any flames inside, which made her optimistic that this was a past disaster, not a currently in-progress one. "Everyone okay?"

"So, we will not be bringing any food to the feast today," Marin said.

"I have decided," Rijes said from within, "that my contribution to the solstice celebration will be stories. I know many from history that I am certain no one on Belde has heard."

"I think that's an excellent idea," Terlu said. "Everyone loves stories." Squinting her eyes and wrinkling her nose, she came inside and opened the windows to air out the smoke. A pile of charred . . . okay, she wasn't quite sure what they were originally, but it wasn't food anymore. The debris sat shriveled and sad in a skillet, while the workroom reeked of burnt onion. She didn't ask. She supposed even head librarians had limitations. "We'll start at noon, yes?"

"Noon sounds perfect."

Leaving them to their cooking disaster, Terlu headed out. On her way, she stopped by each of the finished (and near-finished) cottages and confirmed that everyone knew the feast would begin at noon. As an added bonus, she got to sample many of the dishes—everyone wanted her to taste-test—and encountered no more charred debris. Yarrow had, apparently, come by his cooking talent naturally. It was all going to be delicious.

Inside the greenhouse, in the lilac room, she met up with Lotti and Dendy, both of them sporting Rowan's crocheted eyes. Dendy wore one on each of his largest leaves, while Lotti had affixed two tiny ones at the center of her petals. "You both look . . ." Terlu trailed off, not sure what adjective they were looking for.

"Amazing?" Lotti suggested.

"Yes, amazing," Terlu said.

Dendy said, "I waaas goiiing for 'absurd.'"

"That too," Terlu agreed.

She strolled with them to the rose room, which was in the process of being transformed into a grand celebration hall. Birch and Rorick were shouting orders to their younger relatives, who were installing tables—newly made tables that they'd constructed from spare planks of wood the week prior. Ubri and Pipa were setting out a variety of chairs, all different sorts, around the tables. One of the new arrivals—Flick, a man with tawny fur and antlers—was arranging napkins, while Yarrow's aunt Rin added bouquets of flowers in vases every few feet. Several of the sentient plants, including the myrtle-turned-sailor Ree, were stringing ribbons from the rafters, draping them in swooping bows, while a flock of miniature dragons perched nearby, nibbling at the ribbons and watching the excitement below.

In one corner, three of the residents who knew how to play instruments, led by Yarrow's aunt Harvena, were setting up. For the meal, a chorus of singing flowers were going to be moved in to provide ambient music, but before and after, anyone who wanted to could take a turn performing. Terlu had volunteered to play as well—Vix, Yarrow's cousin who liked to fish, had a six-string guitar she could borrow. She hadn't practiced since coming to Belde—and had zero practice in her six years as a statue, of course—but no one seemed to care whether the music was good. Just that it didn't stop.

When Terlu had woken alone in the cold snow, she hadn't expected to be a part of a full-out Winter Feast celebration the very same season. She hadn't expected any of what had happened. She supposed that was why today mattered so much to her: it was a day to celebrate the improbable light that now burned in the implacable darkness.

Lotti bounced past her, a ribbon trailing from her petals.

And it's a day to celebrate a whole lot of plants, Terlu thought with a grin.

At noon, it began!

Everyone filled the rose greenhouse, and the voices and laughter reached the rafters where Emeral and the tiny dragons snacked on their favorite treats—the cat and dragons seemed to have agreed to a truce, along with the leafy mice, due to the abundance of food. The two children on the island, the toddler Epu and the son of the newest arrival, had become fast friends and were chasing each other around the greenhouse. Rowan had produced a flute and was playing an upbeat melody while Ambrel danced with Birch.

Yarrow was seated beside Terlu, and he seemed, miraculously, to be enjoying himself, despite the cacophony of the crowd. On the other side of Terlu was Rijes, and she was clapping in rhythm with the music. Butterflies and dragonflies flittered overhead.

Everyone who could cook had cooked:

Carrots that tasted like candy. Asparagus coated in a creamy yellow sauce. Potatoes prepared six different ways—fried, roasted, baked, twice-baked, and cooked with cheese and with cream. Fish flavored with herbs that Terlu couldn't even name but tasted beyond delicious. A few dishes weren't her favorite, like the mussels in butter that Yarrow loved but reminded Terlu too much of slugs, but she loved the dish with squash cut into noodles mixed in a nut-flavored sauce, as well as a sweet carrot bread made by one of the uncles. And Yarrow had prepared her favorite, the layered zucchini, squash, and tomato dish he'd perfected.

They ate, they talked, they laughed, they sang, they told stories, and they danced.

Above the greenhouse, snow fell lightly as the shortest day of the year dipped toward nightfall. When desserts were brought out, everyone oohed and ahhed. Yarrow's sugar glass with flavored roses was proclaimed the star, but there were also berry pies (Terlu contributed a blueberry pie) and cakes and cobblers and an amazing peach tart (Yarrow's grandfather's recipe). And of course, chocolate-covered oranges.

After so much food was eaten that everyone sagged in their chairs and proclaimed over and over that they'd never need to eat again, Terlu tapped Yarrow on the shoulder and whispered in his ear, "What do you think?"

He whispered back, "It's wonderful."

"Are you ready to leave?" she asked.

"I love you," he said.

She smiled. "I guessed that."

Terlu held out her hand, and he took it. They excused themselves from the table, said thank you and happy solstice to everyone. It took them more than a few minutes before they had extricated themselves and were strolling alone, hand in hand, through the greenhouses. She inhaled the delicate sweetness of springtime flowers.

"Were you really okay with today, all those people and plants in your greenhouse?" Terlu asked him, when they were far enough away from festivities that the music and the voices were only a pleasant hum. "Are you okay with all of us living here on Belde?" She hadn't ever really asked him that. It had just sort of happened, and he hadn't had any choice in it. His quiet life had been overturned, and she thought it was a good thing, but did he agree?

"It's fine."

"Really fine, or are you just saying that?"

Stopping beside a lilac, he turned and took both of her hands in his. "Since you came into my life . . ." He swallowed, and she thought for a moment that he wasn't going to find the words, but then he did. Looking into her eyes, he continued. "I thought I was content to spend my life on Belde alone. I had a purpose, and I thought it was enough. You, though . . . You were unexpected."

Terlu bit her lip to keep from asking if "unexpected" was good or not.

"You changed everything."

She swallowed. Yes, she had.

"You changed me."

"I didn't mean to," Terlu said. "I think you're amazing the way you are."

Yarrow shook his head. "What I'm trying to say is you make my world better. Every day, in a million different ways. You brought me to life."

"Then . . . it's good? All of this. Us?"

"Very good," he said. "And you? This isn't the life you planned either. You had no choice about coming here, no choice about being woken in the cold and alone—I am deeply sorry about that day, if I've never said so. I shouldn't have left. After I cast the spell . . . when it didn't work right away, I was certain it wasn't going to work at all."

After all the failed spells she'd tried . . . she absolutely understood. At least he hadn't trapped them inside an impermeable bubble or turned window glass to water. Happily, she hadn't had any disasters lately, and she thought she'd learned enough to at least be more careful in the future. "It's fine."

"Are you happy?" he asked her.

She gave the same answer she'd given Rijes: "Yes. I am."

She'd never imagined any of this—this island, the greenhouses, the purpose she'd found in translating the late sorcerer's spells, the new community they were building, the plants and the dragons, the winged cat, and Yarrow. All of it. She hadn't even known this life was out there to dream about. Now, though, it was the life she wanted.

"I'm home," Terlu told him.

Drawing her closer, he kissed her, and she kissed him back. Above them, the snow fell gently on the greenhouse, while inside and all around them, the flowers bloomed.

ACKNOWLEDGMENTS

I have written thirty books—cozy fantasy, epic fantasy, thrillers, fairy-tale retellings . . . books for adults, for teens, for kids . . . books with lots of talking animals . . . two (so far!) with talking plants. And the one thread that runs through every single story I've ever written is hope.

When I wrote *The Spellshop,* there was one character whom I'd left without hope: Terlu, the librarian who created Caz and was transformed into a statue as punishment. He believed she'd burned when the North Reading Room of the Great Library of Alyssium burned. And I could not stop thinking about her and worrying about her and wondering.

I wrote *The Enchanted Greenhouse* because I believe that everyone deserves hope and love and friendship and second chances and magic in their lives. Also, honey cakes, tiny dragons, and a winged cat.

I wrote it because I believe there is light after darkness, warmth and wonder to be found even in the coldest of winters, and kindness in the world that can heal us. It's my hope that this book can be a bit of light and warmth and a dose of kindness that a reader might need.

In other words, I wrote it for you, whenever you need it.

Thank you to my magnificent agent, Andrea Somberg, and my phenomenal editors, Ali Fisher and Dianna Vega, for believing in me and my greenhouse-covered island! Thank you to incredible artist Lulu Chen and designer Esther S. Kim for the stunningly perfect cover! Thank you to Devi Pillai, Monique Patterson, and Will

Hinton for making my books part of the Bramble adventure! Thank you to my extraordinary publicist Caro Perny and my extraordinary marketer Julia Bergen, as well as Lauren Abesames, Ariana Carpentieri, Greg Collins, Amanda Crimarco, Claire Eddy, Rafal Gibek, Shawna Hampton, Eileen Lawrence, Megan Kiddoo, Katy Miller, Emily Mlynek, Sarah Reidy, Lucille Rettino, Jessica Spracklen, everyone on the fantastic sales team, and all the other incredible people at Bramble, Tor, and Macmillan for bringing this book to life and helping it find its readers! Also, thank you to the amazing audiobook team at Macmillan Audio: Katy Robitzski, Emma Paige West, and Isabella Narvaez—and to my fabulous narrator Caitlin Davies! Thank you to my wonderful Tor UK editor, Gillian Green, as well as Grace Barber, Becky Lushey, Bella Pagan, Olivia-Savannah Roach, Sophie Robinson, Charlotte Williams, and everyone else at Tor UK and Pan Macmillan for bringing my books across the pond! Thank you to Chris Scheina and the sub-rights team, Andy Hahnemann at Fischer Tor, and all the overseas editors, translators, and everyone for sharing my stories around the world! And thank you so much to the booksellers, the librarians, and especially the readers who opened their hearts and embraced my magical islands!

Lastly, thank you with all my heart and every bit of who I am to my husband, my children, my family, and my friends. I love you all forever and always!

And thank you to my cat, Gwen, who dreams of having wings of her own.

ABOUT THE AUTHOR

SARAH BETH DURST is the *New York Times* bestselling author of more than twenty-five books for adults, teens, and kids, including the cozy fantasy *The Spellshop*. She's been awarded an American Library Association Alex Award, as well as a Mythopoeic Fantasy Award. Several of her books have been optioned for film/television, including *Drink Slay Love,* which was made into a TV movie and was a question on *Jeopardy!* She lives in Stony Brook, New York, with her husband, her children, and her ill-mannered cat. Visit her at sarahbethdurst.com.